KAT MARTIN

THE Fire INSIDE

POCKET **STAR** BOOKS

New York   London   Toronto   Sydney   Singapore

An *Original* Publication of POCKET BOOKS

 A Pocket Star Book published by
POCKET BOOKS, a division of Simon & Schuster, Inc.
1230 Avenue of the Americas, New York, NY 10020

ISBN: 0-7434-1915-4

First Pocket Books printing February 2002

10 9 8 7 6 5 4 3 2 1

POCKET STAR BOOKS and colophon are registered trademarks of Simon & Schuster, Inc.

For information regarding special discounts for bulk purchases, please contact Simon & Schuster Special Sales at 1-800-456-6798 or business@simonandschuster.com

Front cover illustration by Tom Hallman; tip-in illustration by John Ennis

Printed in the U.S.A.

"You're a woman. Anything could have happened. Do you know what those men were thinking when they watched you dance?" For once she didn't answer, which only drove him on. "They wanted to tear off your clothes. They wanted to touch your lovely little body. They wanted to drag you down on the ground and drive themselves inside you."

For an instant, her face went pale. Then she squared her shoulders and looked him in the face. "So now you're a mind reader, just like the Gypsies. How could you possibly know what those men wanted to do?"

How could he know? "You little fool," he whispered as he hauled her roughly against him. "I know—because that's what I wanted to do." Then he kissed her. Not a sweet, gentle, tender kiss, but a hot, ravaging, taking kiss, the kind he had wanted from her for as long as he could recall.

For several sweet moments she didn't resist: she just stood there pressed against his chest, her lips parted in surprise, her mouth soft and giving under his. Through the thin silk blouse, he could feel the ripe fullness of her breasts, the slight protrusion of her nipples as they tightened into buds, and his body went rock hard.

With a groan, he deepened the kiss, pulling her more firmly against him, his tongue sweeping in, taking what he wanted, claiming her in some way. At the feel of his heavy arousal, Kitt's spine went as rigid as a stick. She stumbled as she jerked away.

"What . . . what do you think you're doing?" She was breathing hard, swaying a little on her feet, trying to make sense of what had happened.

The edge of his mouth curved up in a smile that really wasn't. "Exactly what those other men wanted to do."

for the ladies of
the Northwest Regional Reading Consortium
(don't you love the name?):
really appreciate your friendship
and the chance to share the joy
of reading wonderful books

1

London, England
1805

"Reckless—that's what she is. The girl is simply too wild and reckless for any respectable young man to marry." Thin gray eyebrows lifted in disapproval, Lady Dempsey peered through her jeweled lorgnette to examine the red-haired girl standing next to the punch bowl. "There was a time, you know, she was the darling of the *ton*. Her father must be terribly disappointed."

"Indeed," Lady Sarah agreed. "Why, the rumors I've heard . . ." She shook her head. "It's a good thing her mother—poor dear woman—isn't alive to see."

Over the top of a potted palm in the Earl of Winston's ornate Mayfair town house, Clayton Harcourt studied the object of the women's scorn. He knew Kassandra Wentworth, had met her four years ago when she was first introduced into the marriage mart. Now, well on her way to one-and-twenty, Kitt had been on the shelf far too long to be fashionable, and her father, the Viscount Stockton, was determined to bring the matter to an end.

Clay watched her as he had a dozen times in the past few months, with frank male interest and a faint, mildly disturbing heaviness in his groin. She was an incredible mix of woman and girl, innocently seductive with her lush breasts, big green eyes, and glorious red hair. When she laughed, there was nothing missish about it. The sound rang with a husky note that spoke of blossoming womanhood and a candor he somehow found refreshing.

Not that he would ever let her know. From the moment they had met, the two of them had been oil and water. As Lady Dempsey said, the girl was far too reckless, too stubbornly independent. What she needed was a man strong enough to take her in hand.

Unfortunately, since he was definitely not in the market for a wife, he wouldn't be that man.

"She is quite something, isn't she?"

Clay recognized the timbre of his father's voice but his eyes remained on the girl. "She's something, all right. Stubborn and willful. Too bloody outspoken for her own good."

"Yes, she is. Perhaps that is the reason I liked her from the first moment I met her."

Clay looked over at the man who had sired him, Alexander Barclay, sixth Duke of Rathmore. The father who had been generous in his financial support, in some ways even his affections, but refused to grant him the legitimacy of his name.

"You've always had an eye for beauty, Your Grace. The girl is certainly that."

"That and more," the duke agreed. He took a drink of brandy from the snifter he cradled in a still-strong hand. "Stockton wishes to see her wed."

"I believe you've mentioned that."

"I suppose I may have done so."

"And seeing as how you and the viscount are in business together, as well as politically aligned in the House of Lords, you would like very much to please him."

"I presume you are referring to the fact I suggested you make an offer for her."

A corner of Clay's mouth curved up. "You may presume that, yes."

"I like the girl, blast it! For the right man, Kassandra Wentworth would make a very fine wife."

"I believe you mentioned that as well."

"Since you are so bloody good at remembering what I mentioned, do you also remember the proposal I made you some months back—the very lucrative proposal—concerning the matter of a marriage between the two of you?"

"How could I forget?" Clay lifted a glass of champagne from a passing silver tray. The servant, in blue and silver livery, disappeared in the crush around them. "You and Stockton are that eager to see her settled?"

"Dammit, just once, is it possible you might believe I simply have your welfare in mind? You need a wife. Kassandra needs a husband. I believe the two of you would suit very well."

Clay scoffed. "You're not serious? We can't be alone in the same room without wanting to kill each other."

The duke's features softened and a look of fond remembrance crept into his eyes. "Your mother and I were that way. We loathed each other on sight—or tried to convince ourselves we did. We battled the attraction, the incredible pull between us. We wouldn't even admit it to ourselves." He sighed and shook his head. "God, I miss that woman. I've missed her every day since the day she died."

Clay studied his father's face, still handsome, though the man was over sixty. The duke rarely spoke of Rachael Harcourt, Clay's mother, the woman who was his mistress for more than twenty years. She had died sixteen years ago, when Clay was just fourteen. The memory of the lonely years that followed still lingered, though he kept them neatly locked away.

His thoughts drifted back to his father and Rachael Harcourt. Was it possible to love a woman that much? If it was, Clay had certainly never experienced the feeling, though he was surely no stranger to lust. He returned his gaze to Kassandra Wentworth and felt the same pull of attraction, the soft tug of desire that she always seemed to stir.

Rathmore's gaze followed his. "She has spirit, that girl. She would give you strong, intelligent sons."

"She's wild and headstrong. Someone needs to take her in hand."

The duke cocked a silver-brown eyebrow. "Are you saying that you, a man of your vast experience with women, aren't up to the challenge?"

Clay laughed. "Oh, I'm up to it. If she weren't an innocent—and your friend Stockton's daughter—she would likely find herself in my bed."

Rathmore chuckled softly. "So you *do* find her attractive." He was nearly as tall as Clay with the same wide shoulders and dark brown hair, though the duke's was now dashed with gray.

"I'm not blind, Your Grace." Clay looked so much like the duke there was no denying his parentage, yet Rathmore had never openly acknowledged him or publicly called him son. As a boy, he'd been resentful.

As a man, he understood. Or at least told himself he did. "With all that curly red hair, and skin like fresh cream, the girl is quite lovely. If she only had a disposition to match."

Rathmore's gaze flicked toward the punch table, where Kassandra stood talking to their host, the stout little Earl of Winston. He laughed at something she said.

"She's full of fire, I'll grant you that."

Kitt smiled, her lush mouth parting, showing a row of small white teeth, and a soft lick of heat curled low in Clay's belly.

"Personally," the duke went on, "I've always rather liked a little fire in a woman."

Clay made no reply. He liked that, too. Perhaps it was the reason he found Kitt so attractive. But dammit, he wasn't willing to marry the girl just to satisfy his itch to have her.

Across the way, Kassandra accepted the arm the earl offered and gave him another of her warm, sunny smiles. Turning, she let him lead her away.

"They're headed for the gaming room," his father said, watching their progress across the crowded floor. "Girl loves to gamble. Your mother did, too. Would have broken a less wealthy man, though she finally learned to play well enough not to lose."

Clay watched Kitt Wentworth disappear down the hall to Winston's gaming room. Unlike his mother, Kitt had a natural aptitude for cards. She was a damned good player; not as good as he was, of course, but better than most of the men he gamed with at the club. He set his glass down on an ornate silver tray.

"If you'll excuse me, Your Grace, I think I feel the urge to play a few hands myself."

This time his father frowned. "May I remind you—
as you, yourself, so cleverly pointed out—the girl is yet
untried. If you have any notion of seducing her, you
had better bear that in mind."

Clay just smiled. He wasn't completely convinced
Kitt was as innocent as his father believed. He remembered the night he had stumbled across her at a boxing match in Covent Garden. At first he hadn't
realized the young lad staring into the ring with such
fascination was a girl. Then he had heard her laughter,
noticed the feminine curves outlined by a pair of snug
men's breeches, looked behind the gold-rimmed spectacles perched on the end of a very small, slightly
freckled nose, and recognized Kassandra Wentworth.

He had hauled her and her young companion, Lady
Glynis Marston, out of there as fast as he could,
though Kitt argued all the way, and ushered them
safely back home.

That was three years ago, but she was still just as
daring, and a woman who took those sorts of
chances—well, who knew what else she might be willing to do. Unfortunately, whether or not she was a vir-
gin, Kitt was the daughter of a viscount and unwed,
which, without marriage, put her well out of his reach.

And yet Clay kept walking, striding across the
noisy salon toward the room down the hall, anticipat-
ing a game of cards that was certain to keep him entertained.

2

A steady hum of tension throbbed in the sumptuous gaming salon of the Earl of Winston's town house. Kitt could feel it in the air, see it in the faces of the men sitting across from her at the green baize table.

They had been playing for several hours, a high stakes game, the richest she had ever taken part in. It was exciting, exhilarating—and exactly the wrong thing for Kassandra Wentworth, a young, unmarried woman, the daughter of a viscount, to do.

As the only woman at the table, Kitt ignored the cold, disapproving stares of the guests who clustered around them.

"Your turn, my lady." Clayton Harcourt's deep, gravel-touched-with-honey voice reached her across the table, and a little ripple of irritation ran down her spine. He had been there almost from the start, with his considerable skill and his dark, unreadable glances.

Kitt had known him for years, knew his reputation with women, and heartily disapproved. In fact, there was little about Clay Harcourt she did approve. Not

his carousing, not his arrogance nor his over-bold
glances. Six months ago, her father had actually proposed him as a suitor. Considering the ridiculously
large dowry that accompanied the bride, that might
have suited Harcourt, but certainly not her.

Which was why she couldn't understand why her
heart speeded up every time he walked into the room.

She glanced his way, saw that he was watching. "I
believe you're right, Mr. Harcourt, it is my turn." She
cast him a triumphant smile as she played the last of
the three cards she had been dealt, trumped his ten of
clubs with a jack, and raked the last third of a very sizable pot over to her side of the table. "I suppose I'll
have to concentrate a bit more on the game."

As if she weren't. As if she hadn't memorized every
card that had fallen.

Harcourt gave her one of his annoying half smiles
and the game started up again. Behind her, she could
hear the women whispering, making snide remarks.

"Such deep play . . ."

"Not respectable . . ."

"Her father will be furious . . ."

". . . ought to be dealt with before it's too late."

Kitt clenched her jaw and simply ignored them.
What did they know, anyway? All they did was sit
around and gossip about other people's business. She
told herself she didn't care what they were saying, that
it didn't bother her in the least. She closed her ears to
their whispered words and tried to concentrate on the
game.

They were playing loo, one of her favorites, though
she loved any sort of gaming and particularly deep
play like this. More to lose meant more to win, but it
was the challenge Kitt sought. The victory of a twenty-

year-old girl over five seasoned men. And for some unfathomable reason, winning against Harcourt always made the prize a little sweeter.

Not that she beat him all that often.

"Your deal, my lady." Robert Prescott, one of the city's most notable barristers, passed her the deck as the men replenished the pot.

Kitt shuffled with ease, dealing the players three cards each, plus three for the "widow." She set the rest of the pack on the table and turned over the top card.

Sir Hubert Tinsley, the portly, gray-haired man on her left, began the play with a five of diamonds, the suit named trump. Thin and stuffy William Plimpton tossed out a ten. The third player, Lord Percival Richards, passed, turning his cards facedown on the table as he had done for the last three hands. Apparently, his funds were running low. Edward Sloan, Earl of Winston, also passed, which brought the game round to Harcourt.

Kitt held her breath, hoping he would pass. She would play her card and the hand would belong to her. Instead, Harcourt exchanged his hand for the "widow," as only one player in each round could do, trumped the ten with a queen, and turned his compelling, golden brown eyes on her.

"My lady?" There it was again, that somehow challenging note that dared her to win.

Kitt's fingers tightened on the cards in her hand. With a triumphant grin, she tossed out the king of diamonds and raked in a third of the chips.

"Well done, my lady," said the earl, though his good friend, Plimpton, didn't look particularly pleased, and Lord Percy, in his godawful bottle-green tailcoat, looked utterly grim.

Two more hands were played. Kitt's stack of chips continued to grow, but so did Harcourt's.

Another hour of play and Plimpton shoved back his chair. "I'm afraid that will have to do for me. I'm completely done in." Wearily, he came to his feet.

"I'm out as well." The earl rose, rubbing his stubby neck. "My wife will be wondering if I've retired upstairs without her."

Kitt smiled. "Then we shall simply make do with—"

"Sorry, my lady." Lord Percy tugged at the wide, white stock at his throat, loosening it a little, a sign he was well and truly finished.

"Time for me, as well," said stately Sir Hubert, who rarely played even this long. "Perhaps you can find yourself another group of players."

But that was highly unlikely, considering the stakes and the way her luck had been running.

Harcourt was the only man left at the table. He lounged back in his chair, his long tanned fingers casually fanning a large stack of chips. "If you're so determined to lose your money, why don't we play one last hand? All or nothing. A single card each. High card wins."

Kitt stared down at the pile of money she had amassed. It had to be somewhere near ten thousand pounds. She didn't want to bet so much on just one hand. She started to decline—and she would have—if she hadn't seen the flicker of amusement on Harcourt's sensuous lips.

He wants to see me back down. He's certain I will—damn his dark eyes to hell!

Kitt set her jaw. The elegant group of watchers had continued to swell, men in perfectly fitted tailcoats, ladies in glittering jewels and high-waisted gowns. Seeing her gaming with a rake like Clayton Harcourt pinched their faces into tight, unflattering lines—which made Kitt's decision crystal clear.

"We'll need someone to shuffle the cards," she said airily, accepting the wager just to watch the women's powdered eyebrows shoot up.

Behind her, a man's bony fingers reached down and plucked up the deck. "Anything to oblige a *lady*."

Kitt ignored William Plimpton's sarcastic tone. It was hardly proper for a young, unmarried woman to cause such a stir, but the lure of victory was simply too sweet to resist. Plimpton cut the deck, shuffled several times, then set the cards back down on the table.

"Ladies first," Clay drawled, goading her in some way, though she wasn't quite sure how.

Her hand trembled. She steeled herself. Reaching down to the table, she cut the pack and turned over her card.

"Queen of hearts," Clay said, his mouth curving faintly. "Very appropriate."

For the first time she allowed herself to look at the card in front of her. The sight of the lovely red queen made her dizzy with relief.

She glanced over at Harcourt, arched a dark red eyebrow, and smiled. "I believe it's the gentleman's turn ... though in your case ..." *I'm not sure you qualify.*

Harcourt didn't miss the unspoken words. He cast her a faintly mocking glance and leaned forward in his chair, drawing his dark brown, velvet-collared tailcoat snug across the considerable width of his shoulders. With his usual confident air, he reached out, cut the deck, and held up his card.

Kitt read it and her stomach contracted at the same

time her mouth flattened out. "King of spades. The only card more appropriate would have been the knave." He laughed as she shoved back her chair. "Congratulations," she said. "It would seem you are the winner."

"Apparently so." His eyes were laughing. He was amusing himself at her expense and it made her want to hit him. "Perhaps your luck will be better the next time we play."

"Assuming there is a next time," she countered with authority.

"Oh, there will be, sweeting. But perhaps the game won't be cards."

Unsure what he meant, she simply ignored him. "If you'll excuse me, I believe it's time I found my companions." He gave her a look that said she never should have left them and stood politely as she rose from her chair. His gaze moved over her one last time, gold flecks shimmering like hot sparks in his eyes.

Ignoring the whispers and smug expressions that seemed to say, *See? You got what you deserve,* she crossed the gaming room toward the French doors leading out to the terrace, desperate for a breath of fresh air. The hem of her high-waisted gold silk gown brushed against her ankles as she stepped out into the night.

Ten thousand pounds, she thought glumly. More than she had ever lost at one time—though most of it belonged to the other players. Even if it had been hers, she could afford it. The money she had inherited from her grandmother amounted to a sizable sum. Still, it rankled her to lose, especially to *him*.

Silently, she wished Clayton Harcourt straight to the devil. Or perhaps he *was* the devil. He was certainly as handsome as sin with his straight, aristocratic nose; hard, carved jaw; and solid, broad-shouldered build. He was also one of the most notorious rakes in London, a man with the single-minded purpose of bedding every woman unfortunate enough to cross his path.

Kitt shook her head, mentally wiping away his too-handsome image. Walking along the terrace, she inhaled the soft spring air, drew the clean night scents into her lungs: daffodils and spongy moss, moist dark earth and new leaves. She rested a gloved hand on the balustrade, her thoughts whirling, beginning to regret her impulsiveness, afraid she would suffer for it later.

It was dark out here, just the faintest shadowy light from the torches along the pathways in the garden. A slight misty dampness hung in the air, and behind her, she could hear the strains of the orchestra through the tall mullioned windows. An occasional burst of laughter escaped from inside.

"You shouldn't be out here, you know."

She turned at the familiar deep voice.

"It isn't good for your reputation," Harcourt said, "not that it has concerned you overly before." More than a foot taller than her barely over five-foot frame, he seemed larger out here, broader in the shoulders, more threatening.

Until this moment, as big as he was, she had never been afraid of him. He was a friend of Ariel's, her dearest friend in the world, and somehow that made her feel safe with him.

But then they had never really been alone.

She straightened, unconsciously stepped farther away, back into a faint circle of light shining down from upstairs. "You're right, of course—it's time I went in. I only came out for a quick breath of air."

She needed to go back where it was safe, back where she could smile and dance and pretend to enjoy herself. But something held her back. He was looking at her the way he did sometimes when he thought she couldn't see, his eyes sultry and darker than they usually were. It frightened her, made her want to run, and at the same time compelled her to stay.

"You played well tonight," he said. "You're becoming a very fine player."

The compliment surprised her. "You think so?" Why his opinion mattered, she couldn't say, she just knew that it did.

"Yes, I do. Of course, you shouldn't have been playing at all . . . not in such serious play . . . not with so much money at stake."

Her chin inched up. Why did he always have to spoil things? "If I hadn't played, your pockets would likely not be bulging with nearly so large a sum. Besides, what I do is none of your damnable business."

He chuckled softly, a rumble in a chest the width of a keg of ale. "Such a little spitfire. Hasn't anyone ever told you it isn't ladylike to swear?"

She hated the way he could goad her with so few words. "I assure you, being a lady isn't all it's cracked up to be. You wouldn't understand that, though, since you're a man. You don't have the same rules, the same constraints. You don't have to worry about what someone will think if you happen to say 'damn.' "

He moved closer, just a little, but it made him seem even larger. "Is that why you like breaking the rules? Because you wish you'd been born a man?"

The look in his eyes made her wary. "Perhaps the

rules I live by are simply different. And I don't wish I'd been born a man. I just wish I could have the same freedom."

He eyed her in that unsettling way of his and a flicker of fear ran through her. What was he thinking? Did he want what most men wanted from a woman? And how far would he go in order to get it? She started to turn, to move toward the light, back to the safety of the house, but Harcourt caught her wrist.

"Since your rules are different, perhaps I can convince you to stay." He drew her toward him. Where his fingers circled her arm a little shiver raced over her skin. He looked massive now, powerful and threatening. Strong enough to drag her off into the darkness, strong enough to hurt her if he wanted. He wasn't that sort, she was sure, yet her mouth went dry and her heart set up a clatter like rain against tin.

Don't be silly. Harcourt can't hurt you. You aren't that far from the house. But the fear remained, an unseen force in the darkness. She hated that about herself, hated the fear inside that could surface without warning, making her feel weak and out of control. It hadn't always been so. As a girl, she had been fearless, ready to take on the world. Now she knew the consequences.

She swallowed past the dryness in her throat, praying he wouldn't notice that she trembled. "I have to go in. Ariel will be waiting."

She had come to the soiree with the Earl and Countess of Greville, two of Harcourt's closest friends. She hoped the subtle reminder would convince him to leave her alone.

"Then go . . . if you are afraid."

Even the challenge couldn't stop her. Not when

every nerve in her body had gone on alert and her pulse thrummed a warning in her ears.

Dragging in a calming breath of air, she summoned a shot of courage, cast him a look she hoped passed for disdain, and started walking—doing her best not to run.

At last, the evening drew to a close. The Earl of Greville's shiny black carriage rolled over the cobblestone street, the whir of iron wheels blending with the jangle of harness and the clatter of hooves, the four matched grays stepping handsomely.

Lulled by the sound and the exhaustion that had begun to set in, Kitt leaned back against the red velvet seat.

"You're awfully quiet." Her best friend, Ariel Ross, Countess of Greville, sat next to her husband on the opposite side of the carriage. "Is something wrong, Kitt? I thought you were having a good time tonight."

Kitt looked up into the faces of her friends. Ariel was blond and fair, the sort of woman who always wore a smile. Justin was a tall man, dark complected, with wavy, coal-black hair. He was far more reserved, a hard-edged, driven man who could send chills down your spine with a single glance. And yet when he looked at his wife, those cool gray eyes always held a trace of warmth.

Kitt summoned a smile. "Nothing is the least bit wrong. I had a very nice time tonight. The evening was extremely . . . pleasant."

Justin studied her with his too-discerning gaze. "I gather it could have been quite profitable."

Quite profitable indeed—if it hadn't been for Harcourt. "I suppose so."

"Your father will likely have my head when he learns the extent of your gaming."

Kitt straightened on the seat. "My father won't say a word, my lord, at least not to you. He considers his business concerns far more important than the misdeeds of his youngest daughter. Besides, the money I lost wasn't his, it was mine."

"Your inheritance, you mean. Yes ... well, I suppose that's true enough. And Harcourt is a very good player."

"Harcourt has the devil's own luck."

Ariel reached over and caught her hand. "Clay shouldn't have pressed you to play that last hand. It was quite ungentlemanly of him."

"I don't believe there's a gentleman's bone in the man's entire body."

The earl chuckled softly and Ariel's mouth quirked up. "He isn't nearly as bad as you make him out."

"Oh, no? When we were out on the terrace, he—" Kitt broke off. What had he done? Nothing but catch hold of her hand.

The earl sat forward, a black scowl on his face. "Out on the terrace, Harcourt did *what,* Kassandra? If the man acted inappropriately, friend or not, I promise you I shall—"

"No, please. It was nothing at all like that. He just ... we simply don't get on well, that's all."

Justin eyed her for a moment more, then relaxed against the seat. "Perhaps in time the two of you will find a way round your differences."

But Kitt didn't think so. Not when every time he looked at her, she wanted to slap his too-handsome face.

And yet, there was something about him. She

thought of him more often than she should and she couldn't forget the odd way her skin had tingled when he'd drawn her toward him on the terrace. At the time she had thought it was fear.

Now she wondered if perhaps he'd meant to kiss her. It was silly, of course. The man was merely baiting her. More likely, he wanted to wring her neck.

"We're here." Ariel sat back in the seat as the carriage rolled to a halt in front of Kitt's town house on Maddox Street.

Moments later, through the mist on the windows in the entry, Kitt watched the conveyance pull away and disappear into the darkness. She wouldn't be seeing her friends for a while. On the morrow, they were returning to Greville Hall, their country estate near Ewhurst. During the Christmas holidays a fire had broken out in the west wing of the house and they were working to make repairs.

Kitt sighed. London always seemed duller when Ariel wasn't in town. They had met four years ago, at Mrs. Penworthy's School of Feminine Deportment, an unlikely pair since Kitt had been raised with money and privilege while Ariel had lived in poverty until she had met the late Earl of Greville, Justin's father, who rescued her and paid for her schooling, though his motives were far from pure. Through the earl, Ariel had met and fallen in love with his son, but that had happened years later. In finishing school both girls had been motherless and unable to fit in with their classmates. Eventually they'd become close friends, sharing their thoughts and keeping the loneliness away. Though she had other acquaintances, Ariel was her only really close friend.

Kitt stared into the darkness outside the window

and wondered what she might find to do to fill the days till Ariel's return.

Naked beneath the sheet riding low on his hips, Clayton Harcourt lounged against the carved wooden headboard. Beside him, statuesque, raven-haired, Gabriella Moreau ran a long slim finger through the curly brown hair on his chest.

"*Tu es magnifique, chérie.* So full of passion—such a stallion, you are. You like Gabriella, *no?*"

Of course he liked her. She was a beautiful, desirable woman. He had been trying to seduce her for the past three weeks. Unfortunately, now that he had succeeded, the entire time he had been making love to her he had been thinking of someone else.

"Of course I like you, sweeting—what man wouldn't?" To prove it, he leaned over and kissed her hard on the mouth, hoping it would revive his lust. When all he felt was a mild, faintly pleasant stirring, he sighed and decided he might as well go on home.

The bed dipped under his weight as he eased to the edge and swung his long legs over the side. Before he could get to his feet, Gabriella slid her arms around his waist. Pale, feminine fingers stroked the muscles across his stomach, making them vibrate and contract.

"Where are you going, *chérie?* Surely you do not leave yet." She pressed a row of soft, nibbling kisses along the muscles in his neck, then across the width of his shoulders. "Stay with me, *chérie.* Make love to me again." Gaby was an actress in Drury Lane. Since he had recently ended a six-month liaison with the promiscuous wife of an aging baronet, Gaby, he'd decided, would do nicely in her stead.

After his encounter tonight with Kassandra, he had

needed a woman badly. He'd been waiting in the wings when the last performance in the Theatre Royale finally ended and Gabriella appeared. Impressed by the expensive sapphire pendant he had sent her, she eagerly accepted his supper invitation, knowing exactly where it would lead. Unfortunately, once they began making love, the needs of his body and those of his mind seemed to be completely at odds.

Clay swore a silent oath, knowing exactly the cause.

He felt Gaby's hands sliding over his chest. A slim finger circled his nipple and his groin tightened.

"You will stay with Gaby, no?"

Perhaps he would. It wasn't like him to leave so soon.

Gabriella smiled, clearly reading his thoughts. She reached down and wrapped her fingers around his shaft, which was hard again and not nearly as reluctant as he'd thought.

"You see? You want Gabriella. You will stay a little while longer."

He might as well. He had nothing better to do and he certainly wasn't going home in this condition. But he didn't really want Gabriella Moreau. The woman he wanted was the little red-haired hellion he'd run into out on the terrace. If he closed his eyes, he could still smell her soft perfume. In the darkness, it had set him on fire.

Unfortunately, unless he married the chit—completely out of the question—she was entirely off limits. The sooner he accepted the fact, the better off he'd be.

He felt Gaby's tongue glide over his nipple and a shudder rippled through him. Gaby was here and he wasn't made of wood—though right now certain parts of his anatomy certainly felt as if they were. She slid her arms around his neck, urging him back down on the bed, and this time he followed, settling himself between her thighs and sliding himself inside her. She was hot and wet, sheathing him nicely and making him harder still.

He caressed a milk-white breast, teased the nipple into a bud, dragged a hand through her shiny black hair, but it wasn't Gabriella he saw in the eye of his mind.

Clay cursed the woman who was becoming the bane of his existence, kissed Gabriella's pretty mouth, drove himself deeper inside her, and began to move.

3

Kitt recognized her father's footsteps pounding furiously down the hall toward where she sat reading in the library. He stopped in front of the door and jerked it open, stormed in, and slammed it closed. The force of his anger seemed to swell at the sight of her, and Kitt sat up a little straighter in her chair.

"Well, I hope you're proud of yourself. You are once again the subject of every wagging tongue in the city."

Kitt set her book, a Gothic novel by Mrs. Radcliffe, down on the marble-topped table. Slowly she came to her feet.

"I'm sorry, Father. I'm afraid I don't know what you mean."

"Is that so? And I suppose you also know nothing about that sordid exhibition you put on with Clayton Harcourt at Winston's soiree last Friday night. Did you actually believe I wouldn't find out?"

Kitt picked at one of the embroidered roses on the bodice of her pink muslin gown. "I didn't do anything wrong. I like to play cards and I'm good at it. I was only having a little fun."

"Fun? That's what you call it? You made a spectacle of yourself in front of half the *ton!* How many other young ladies did you observe playing in a high stakes game of cards that night? How many unmarried young women sat there matching bets with a rogue like Clayton Harcourt. For God's sake, Kassandra—the man is one of the most notorious rakes in London!"

Kitt's chin went up. "Lord Winston was also in that game. So was Sir Hubert Tinsley and Lord Percy Richards. As for Harcourt—six months ago, you suggested I marry the man. He seemed a paragon to you at the time."

"Yes . . . well, bastard born or not, Harcourt is the son of a duke and well favored among the *ton.* Considering how limited your choices have become in the past several years—and the fact his father would be willing to throw his support behind the match—the man would make you a very suitable husband. That does not mean you should be flaunting yourself in front of him—behaving like some high-priced trollop."

Color infused her cheeks. "I was hardly behaving like a trollop. I merely accepted the wager he proposed."

"And lost ten thousand pounds!"

Kitt stared down at the Aubusson carpet. "One of us had to lose."

Brittle laughter echoed in the hall, and Kitt jerked her head toward the door. Her stepmother, Judith Wentworth, silver doorknob in hand, walked in and closed the door. "She'll never understand, Terrance. I swear, humility is beyond her." She was a few inches shorter than Kitt, blond and pretty, with a round face and wide blue eyes.

"Perhaps you're right, my dear." The viscount turned a hard look on Kitt. "I'm beyond tired of hearing your name being whispered every time I walk into a room. You will learn to control your outrageous behavior or you will pack your things and I shall send you off to a convent."

"A convent?" Kitt almost laughed at the image. "You can't be serious."

"Can't I? I'm still your legal guardian. If you don't mend your ways, I swear I shall see it done."

Judith stood there smirking and Kitt wanted to strangle her. She was only four years older than Kitt, far too young for a man her father's age. But the viscount was completely enamored of his youthful bride and he would do anything to please her. Kitt was certain her mother must be spinning in her grave.

Kitt flinched beneath his cold, disapproving stare. Terrance Wentworth was once a handsome man, but nearing sixty, his neck had started to sag, and if he drank a little too much, pouches formed under his eyes. He wasn't a bad father really, just frustrated at her refusal to obey his dictates and determined to do what he believed was in her best interest.

Unfortunately, Kitt did not agree.

"Is that all, Father?"

"No, it is not. For the next two weeks, you will remain locked in your room. You will take your meals there. You will use that time to reflect on your behavior."

Shock rolled through her. Her father had never been harsh with her before, not until he married Judith. But he was a different man these days, remote and unfeeling. Kitt fought to hold back tears, unsure whether they were from anger or pain.

"I'm a grown woman, Father. It isn't right for you to treat me this way."

"A grown woman would be married by now and perhaps have a child of her own."

Kitt said nothing. She never intended to marry. She couldn't stand the thought of the unpleasant duties being a wife entailed, which meant she would never have children. She couldn't help feeling a soft pang of regret for the choice she had made.

"And there is one last thing."

She bit the inside of her cheek to keep her lips from trembling. "Yes?"

"You have two more months in which to choose a husband. After that, I shall choose one for you."

Her shoulders went perfectly rigid. "You can't force me to marry. I have my own money. I can live my own life. I don't need you *or* a husband."

"You forget, my dear, I'm the trustee of your grandmother's estate until you are four-and-twenty. Up until now, I've been generous. After your behavior the other night, that is going to change. You will receive enough money for clothing and incidentals." He glanced at his wife, who nodded. "And in two months' time, if you are not prepared to wed, you will be sent to St. Mary's Sacred Heart Convent, where you will spend the next four years learning to respect your elders."

Her heart seemed to sink inside her chest. Kitt glanced away from her father's furious eyes and her stepmother's triumphant smile, refusing to let them see how much they had hurt her. Judith had been trying to get rid of her since the day she had married the viscount. She wanted her husband's complete, undivided attentions and finally it seemed she would have them.

Silently, Kitt left the library and climbed the stairs. As soon as she walked into her bedchamber, she heard one of the servants coming down the hall, then the click of the door being locked from outside.

Her eyes burned. Tears began to well, but Kitt blinked them away. She had only played cards. Why was that so terrible? If an unmarried man her age had done the same thing, no one would have said a word. It wasn't fair—it simply wasn't!

Kitt's shoulders sagged. *Two weeks!* It seemed like a lifetime. Two days in confinement were as much as she could bear. She could draw, of course. Drawing was her secret passion and she had a considerable knack for it. When inspiration hit her, she could occupy herself for hours on end. But eventually, even that endeavor grew tiresome.

How would she survive being locked up for so many days? And what would she do to solve her problems after that?

Her father expected her to marry. A shudder went through her at the thought. She wasn't about to become some man's chattel. She wasn't about to belong to him, to submit to his every whim as if he were some high and mighty king. She wasn't about to let him touch her, humiliate her in the marriage bed. She was glad that Ariel had found happiness with Justin, but she didn't believe that would ever happen to her.

Kitt sighed into the quiet of the bedchamber. If she could endure the next two weeks, she could surely think of something. She moved closer to the window, felt the warm sun slanting in through the panes. A robin chirped from the branches of a nearby tree, its song a cry of freedom.

Kitt reached out and touched the smooth, warm glass. She wanted to make her father happy. She wanted to find a way to make peace between them.

The real question was, could she stand being locked away for two long, hellish weeks?

4

She lasted just eight days. Standing in the entry of Greville Hall, Kitt shoved back the hood of her damp, rain-soaked cloak, untied it from around her throat, and dragged it off her shoulders. Tossing it to the butler, a thin, long-faced man with a permanently blank expression, she dropped her satchel on the floor and strode past him down the hall.

"My lady, please, if you will just wait—" Racing along behind her, he caught up with her inside the door to the drawing room, his bushy gray eyebrows raising a fraction at her audacity—a wild show of emotion for Perkins. "As you can clearly see, her ladyship is otherwise occupied at the moment. If you will simply—"

"Thank you, Perkins—" Kitt sailed past him farther into the room. "I'll just wait here while her ladyship finishes with the drapers." She dismissed him with a wave of her hand, making his thin face turn red.

Dressed in a pair of buff breeches, knee-high boots, and a brown twill jacket, Kassandra strode toward her best friend, the Countess of Greville.

"Kitt ... what on earth—?"

"I'm sorry, Ariel, I didn't mean to barge in on you like this. I know you have your own set of problems, with rebuilding the house and all. I just . . . I simply had no one else to turn to."

"Don't be silly, you aren't barging in." Ariel walked over and hugged her. "You're my very best friend and I'm always glad to see you." She was tall for a woman, slender and willowy, with the most beautiful silver blond hair Kitt had ever seen. Ariel reached out and took hold of her hand. "Come on. We'll find someplace quiet where we can talk."

They made their way down the hall to a smaller salon that was done in rose and gold. Sitting down on a brocade sofa that looked out over a broad sweep of lawn, Ariel patted the place beside her, motioning for Kitt to join her.

"All right, now, tell me what this is about—and why you are dressed as you are."

Kitt sighed and shook her head, wondering how things always seemed to get so out of hand. "I don't exactly know where to begin. The Winstons' soiree, I guess. My father and I got into a terrible row about it, and he locked me in my room. It was awful, Ariel. He said I had to stay there for two whole weeks. I thought I would go stark raving mad."

"You were never much good at staying indoors for any particular length of time."

"I made it eight whole days."

"Eight whole days," Ariel repeated with amusement.

"Laugh if you want but it seemed like forever, and I simply couldn't stand it an instant more. My only avenue of escape was to climb out the window. Since I couldn't do that in a pink muslin gown, I had no choice but to dress as I am." She glanced down at her rumpled men's clothes. "I borrowed these several years ago from my younger cousin Charlie to wear to the night of the boxing match."

Ariel nodded. "I remember only too clearly."

"As well as getting me out of the house, I thought it would be a safer way to travel."

Ariel's pale brows drew together. "Well, I suppose it was somewhat safer. I take it your father was angry about your gaming."

"Yes, among other things."

"He isn't still pressing you to marry? Surely by now he's given up his matchmaking efforts."

Kitt rose from the sofa, uncomfortable speaking of marriage, uncertain exactly how to explain. Ariel and Justin were happy . . . but for her, it simply could not be. She paced restlessly over to the window. A spring storm had arisen that morning, fat, glossy droplets hitting hard against the panes, slapping against the leaves on the trees. The toes of her boots still glistened with beads of moisture.

"Father hasn't given up. In truth, he is more determined than ever. Before the Season even began, I had half a dozen penniless aristocrats eager to bolster their fortunes banging at my door. You've seen them, Ariel. Not a single one of them wants me for myself. They're only interested in my dowry—which is ridiculously large—and of course, my inheritance. But that doesn't seem to matter to my father. He thinks I should accept one of them and be done with it. He doesn't care which one it is. He simply wants me wed and out of his hair."

"I think he's worried about your future. In the past several years, you've become quite daring, and your reputation has suffered for it. It doesn't seem fair, but that is the way it is."

Kitt glanced down at the clothes she wore and fought down a wave of embarrassment. "So I've dressed as a man once or twice. It doesn't hurt anyone and no one is the wiser."

"It isn't just the clothes and you know it. And as I recall, the last time you dressed as a man, your father was waiting when Harcourt brought you home."

She stiffened. "If the man had let me climb back in through the window the way I wanted, my father would never have known. Besides, Glynis Marston dressed up, too. Glynis just didn't get caught."

Ariel laughed. "And now Glynis is safely wed and already in a family way while you are determined to remain unattached. What did your father say this time?"

Kitt sighed to think of it. "He says if I haven't chosen a husband in two months' time, he shall send me to a convent. A convent—can you imagine? My stepmother was there, gloating with such satisfaction I thought I was going to be sick. I had to get away, Ariel. I tried to obey his dictates, but I simply couldn't stay in that room another day."

Ariel joined her at the window. "You can't always run from your troubles, you know. Sometimes you have to stay and face them."

"I know. But that is easier said than done." Kitt turned toward her friend. "You don't think he'll really try to send me away, do you? I won't go, you know. No matter what he does. I won't be made a prisoner."

"I'll speak to Justin. We'll figure out something. Perhaps you can stay here for a while, give your father's temper a chance to cool. In the meantime, does he have any idea where you are?"

Kitt shook her head. "I left before dawn and traveled by post chaise. He'll be furious when he finds out I'm gone."

"He'll be worried, Kitt. I think you should send word that you're safe."

She glanced back out the window. "I suppose I should."

"And there is one other thing."

Kitt turned toward her. "What is it?"

"Clayton Harcourt is here. He and Justin had some business to discuss this afternoon. I'm afraid he'll be joining us for supper. He won't be returning to London until the morrow."

Kitt groaned. "Perhaps I could simply avoid him. You could have a tray sent up and he won't even know I'm here."

Ariel laughed. "Do you really dislike him so much?"

Kitt made a rude sound in her throat. "You wouldn't believe the gall of that man, Ariel. I saw him at the opera the night you left the city and guess what he said."

"I'm sure I can't imagine."

"He suggested if I really wanted to create a scandal, I should get rid of my companions and leave the ball with him. He said he'd be more than happy to oblige in whatever manner I wished."

"What did you say?"

"I told him to bugger off."

Ariel doubled over in helpless mirth. "Oh, dear God."

"For once in his life, the man was speechless." She tossed her head and a mischievous glint came into her eyes. "Now that I think of it, I don't imagine he'll be interested in giving me much trouble tonight."

"No, I don't imagine he will." Ariel suppressed a smile. "Several of Justin's business acquaintances are also invited. If we can manage to find you something to wear, you may as well join us."

Kitt's spirits brightened. "I brought a few things with me. I tossed my traveling valise out the window before I climbed down. I suppose I could suffer Clayton Harcourt for a single evening."

Ariel hoped so. Clay was a very good friend and she wanted the two of them to like each other. It was a shame they were so much at odds.

She flicked a glance at Kitt and a memory arose of the last time the pair had been together. Clay's eyes had lingered more often than they should have on Kassandra's voluptuous breasts. Kitt had tried to ignore him, but time and again, her bright gaze slid in his direction. Clay was a handsome, virile, extremely attractive man. Deeper and more private than most people knew. And lonely, just like Kitt, though neither of them would admit it.

A thought returned of the last time the two had been together at Greville Hall, sparks flying as they argued over whether or not Kitt should ride one of Justin's temperamental stallions and yet . . . Ariel couldn't help but wonder what a match might be like between such a volatile pair.

Surrounded by dark-paneled wood and row upon row of leather-bound books, Clay leaned back in a comfortable leather chair in Justin's study. "So work on the coal mine is progressing even faster than we imagined."

Justin sat across from him behind his mahogany desk. "Far faster, yes. In the beginning, I wasn't really in favor of investing in this project, but now that we've been able to improve the working conditions so dramatically, I think it's going to turn out very well."

"And very profitably, I might add." Clay and Justin had been friends since their years together at Oxford, both of them bastard sons of aristocrats, young men who knew the shame of being illegitimate, though each, in his own way, had been strong enough to overcome it.

"You might want to have a look at the books," Justin offered. "I can have my man of affairs—"

Clay shook his head. "You've been doing just fine for more than ten years. Better than fine. I'm a rich man, Justin, and I owe it all to you."

Justin Ross was a whiz at finance. Even before he'd inherited the earldom, he had made himself a wealthy man. Early on, Clay had recognized his friend's financial genius. Though dirtying one's hands in commerce was highly frowned upon among members of the *ton*, Justin had been investing the more than generous allowance Clay received from his father, along with the money he earned gaming and whatever else he managed to scrape together, since their early years at school.

It had grown into a sizable fortune.

"Let me know what you think of the shipyard," Clay said. "On the surface, with a little refitting, it looks like it could be a very sound operation. But a couple of other companies are looking at it, as well. If you think we ought to buy it, we'll have to act quickly."

The shipyard was the reason for Clay's visit to the country. He didn't have Justin's knack for management, but he was developing quite a nose for sniffing out good projects in which to invest. And he was coming to enjoy it.

Justin hefted the stack of documents Clay had brought. "Looks like you've been thorough. I'll have an answer for you by morning."

Clay got up from his chair. "Well, then, if we're finished, I think I'll go upstairs and relax for a bit. Maybe do a little reading."

"Good idea. I may do that myself."

Clay cast him a knowing glance. Justin's relaxation would undoubtedly include his lovely blond wife and be far more interesting than the reading he would be doing.

He made his way to the study door. "I'll see you at supper." Clay pulled the door open and stepped out into the hall. At the same instant, the drawing room doors slid open and a small bundle of energy raced into the passage, colliding so hard with Clay's chest the young man nearly went down.

Clay caught the boy's arms to steady him. "Easy, lad. You'd better watch where—" The words died away as he spotted the thick braid of flaming red hair and looked into the pretty face of Kassandra Wentworth. Hardly a boy, he thought, his eyes moving downward, over the lush hills that marked her breasts, down to her shapely bottom, easy enough to see in her form-fitting men's breeches. His groin tightened. No, scarcely a boy at all.

Reluctantly, Clay released his hold. "Lady Kassandra—what an unexpected pleasure." His mouth curved faintly and his gaze ran over her once more. "I don't suppose you would care to enlighten me as to why you are traipsing through the hallways dressed as a boy?"

Kitt's chin hiked up at the same stubborn angle he had seen more than once. "Actually, in a roundabout way, it's your fault I am dressed the way I am."

"My fault!"

"That is correct."

"What the devil could I possibly have to do with the way you are dressed?"

She gave him a too-sweet smile. "If you hadn't goaded me into betting so much money that night at Lord Winston's soiree, my father would not have locked me in my room for two impossible weeks. If he hadn't, I wouldn't have had to dress in breeches in order to climb out the window."

"Ah, so clearly it is my fault you are an incorrigible chit without the least amount of modesty and more audacity than two grown men."

"Exactly so."

Part of him wanted to laugh, but he found himself frowning instead. "Your father locked you in your room for two weeks?" He *had* goaded her into the bet. And he didn't like the notion that he had been responsible for such a harsh punishment. Two weeks would seem a lifetime to a spirited creature like Kitt.

"That's what he intended . . . at least it would have been that long if I hadn't finally escaped."

"How did you get here? Surely you didn't travel dressed the way you are."

Kitt merely shrugged. "I thought it would be safer. There are footpads on the roads, you know."

Something tightened in his chest. She looked young and vulnerable, and incredibly luscious. Any man who saw her would be tempted beyond— He broke off the thought. If she wore a cap to cover her fiery hair, most men wouldn't suspect such a well-dressed lad was actually a woman. He would have, of course, but then he knew Kitt Wentworth, and nothing she could do would surprise him.

"I'll be returning to the city on the morrow," he said. "I'll see that you get back safely."

Kitt shook her head. "I don't think I'll be going home just yet. Ariel said she would ask Justin to speak to my father."

"I'll speak to him. It's my fault you were punished. I'll straighten the matter out and you won't have to run around flaunting your delectable little body in front of half the men in the country."

Color washed back into her cheeks. "No one knew I was a woman. If I'd had my hat on, you wouldn't have known."

Clay just smiled. "I would have known, sweeting. Believe me, I would have known."

Kitt looked truly upset. He had frightened her, he realized, though he hadn't really meant to. Dammit, she ought to be afraid. She needed to realize it was dangerous for her to go traipsing about alone—dressed as a boy or not. Still, when he spoke to her again, his tone was more gentle.

"You need to be careful, love. I know you enjoy your little adventures, but I wouldn't want to see you get hurt."

She eyed him from beneath her thick burnished lashes, wary of his concern. Perhaps it was because they usually sniped at each other.

"I promise to bear that in mind," she said. "Now, if you'll excuse me, I have to go up and change." With a last glance over her shoulder, she started for the stairs.

Clay watched her go, thinking about the risk she had taken. Her father could be a difficult man. In the past few years, he'd paid almost no attention to his youngest daughter. Her older sisters were married and Stockton was enamored of his young blond wife. Clay had heard it said among the *ton* more than once that where Kitt was concerned Stockton listened to Judith's wishes far too often. It wasn't surprising that Kitt rebelled.

"I see you've discovered our unexpected guest." That from Justin, who walked up beside him.

"Yes, we . . . ran into each other a few minutes ago."

Justin's gray eyes followed her assent up the stairs. "I worry about her. She's such a little firebrand. And her father's dictates only make matters worse."

Clay frowned. "I gather he ordered her locked away for all of two weeks."

"Worse. He has told her she has to find a husband in the next two months or he'll ship her off to St. Mary's Convent. He controls her purse strings for another four years. He has the power to see it done."

"She won't have a problem finding a man to wed her. With the dowry he's offered, she's got an army of impoverished noblemen to choose from."

"Yes, and none of them care a lick about her. I can't help feeling sorry for the girl."

Oddly enough, Clay did too, not that it was any of his concern. By rights, he should be glad to see her married. Once she was wed, her status in society would change. Eventually, she'd have the freedom to take a lover. Perhaps he would finally have a chance to entice her into his bed.

But that would be years away. Years when marriage to a man who wanted nothing but her money would surely crush her fiery spirit.

The thought left a bitter taste in his mouth.

5

Kitt tore off the second riding boot, tossed it over to the corner with the first, and fell backward onto the four-poster bed. Harcourt was here. Her face went warm as she recalled their collision in the hallway. He was such a big man and hard as a granite wall.

She could still feel the imprint of his hands on her arms, remember the way her breasts had flattened out against his chest. For some strange reason, the tips still tingled.

She stared down at her borrowed tailcoat, full-sleeved shirt, and breeches. Though she hadn't worn them often, she had always felt safe in her gentleman's clothes. As a lad, people rarely remarked her presence. For a few precious hours, she was simply a member of the elite male gender, with all of the freedoms that entailed.

In those few marvelous hours, she had seen things, discovered things forbidden in the world of young, unmarried women. There was the boxing match she had sneaked off to with Glynis Marston, and the time she had simply prowled the streets of the city, visiting an alehouse, looking in the window of a notorious gaming hell, though she hadn't had the courage to go in. Dressed as a male, she had experienced a side of life she had been sheltered from as a female.

But Harcourt had said he would have known she was a woman. He had recognized her once before. He believed it wasn't safe for her, even in her disguise, and that made her worry.

Damn his black soul, the man had a knack for spoiling things, although, she grudgingly conceded, in this case he might well be right.

Kitt sighed and reached for the book she had borrowed from the library on her way upstairs, Bunyan's *Pilgrim's Progress.* Clay Harcourt was a stone in her craw, a grain of sand that rubbed her raw, appearing when she least expected it, making her think of him when it was the last thing she wanted to do.

Looking at her with what seemed genuine concern, making her wonder if he were different than other men.

Knowing that he wasn't.

He's a man, isn't he? You know what he wants from you. It was there in his eyes whenever he looked at her. He made not the slightest effort to hide it. Still, as much as she resisted, she was drawn to him in a way she couldn't explain.

The thought conjured unwanted memories of another man she had been drawn to, distant memories of an innocent young girl who had foolishly believed in love and happy endings, painful memories she refused to let surface. She buried them as she always did, flipped open the pages of her book, and tried to read, but the pages blurred and her thoughts kept drifting away. Eventually, she simply gave up and set the novel back down on the bedside table.

Unaccountably restless, she climbed down from the bed, went over and fished through her satchel. She dragged out a large pad of drawing paper and several sticks of charcoal and carried them over to the window.

She had always loved to draw. But unlike other young ladies, she wasn't interested in the bland world of watercolor landscapes, or drawing flower bouquets. Kitt drew pictures of life, scenes she had glimpsed in her adventures, pictures that stuck in her head. A fishmonger selling cod on market day. A scruffy black-and-white mongrel, sniffing through the garbage behind a tavern. A ragamuffin child selling small coal in the street. Images that stayed glued like a fixture in her brain until she got them down on paper.

Making herself comfortable on the window seat, she stared through the rain-spotted window out into the garden. But instead of the genteel landscape of colorful blooming flowers that spread out below, Kitt saw the image of a peddler she had seen, shoving his wobbly cart full of fresh-cut flowers along the lane. She had passed him in the village of Godamin as the post chaise rumbled south toward Greville Hall.

He was an old man, she recalled as she moved the charcoal over the page, his thin body hunched over as he crabbed along, his face liver-spotted and wrinkled, his hands gnarled with age. She sketched him with clean, bold strokes, her fingers smudged black with her efforts.

Time slid past as it always did when she was immersed in her drawing. Her fingers began to ache and a cramp dug into her back. When she finally finished the sketch, she checked the time on the ormolu clock on the mantel. The afternoon had slipped away. It was nearly time for supper.

Suddenly, a knock sounded on the door. She set her drawing pad out of sight and went to open it. A maid appeared with the gowns Kitt had brought with her from London, both of them freshly pressed and ready to wear.

"Me name's Millie. Yer bath is on its way, milady." The girl, thin, brown-haired, and passably pretty, did her best not to stare at the wrinkled men's clothes Kitt still wore and the black smudges on her fingers. "When ye've finished, just ring, and I'll come back and help ye dress."

"Thank you, Millie."

The tub arrived and Kitt sank into it gratefully. As her muscles relaxed, her mind slipped back to her embarrassing encounter with Harcourt. She would be dining with him tonight. Properly clothed, she wouldn't be at the same disadvantage she had been earlier, dressed as a boy. She could hold her own with Harcourt or any other man.

She thought of the green silk gown she had brought, cut fashionably low as her stepmother insisted, designed to capture the attention of a potential suitor. Harcourt certainly wasn't that, and the last thing she wanted was to draw his attention to what most men seemed almost obsessed with—the fullness of a woman's breasts.

Womanizing rake that he was, Harcourt was certain to notice. For an instant, she wished she could put on a high-necked gown that covered her from neck to toes. Then she shook her head. She was a woman. There was nothing she could do to change that.

To hell with Harcourt and every other man, she vowed. She didn't need a man to take care of her and she didn't want one.

Still, as she envisioned his tall, rakish good looks and charming, far-too-sensual smile, she couldn't help wondering what the evening might bring.

With Millie's help, Kitt donned the emerald green gown, then sat patiently while the little maid dressed her hair, fashioning it in stylish curls at the crown of her head. She had wanted to cut it short in the current vogue, but her father was vehemently against it and she had angered him enough already.

And in truth, her long, curly hair, a deep vibrant red, was her most feminine feature and she was just vain enough to enjoy the appreciative glances summoned by her unruly locks.

At exactly eight o'clock, she left the bedchamber and made her way downstairs. The group had begun to gather in the Byzantine Salon, a magnificent room done in black and gold with murals of the heavens painted on the ceiling. She spotted Ariel and Justin standing next to Lord and Lady Oxnard, who lived not far away. Harcourt stood conversing with a man she recognized as Bradford Constantine, Marquess of Landen, an acquaintance of her father's.

Ariel spotted her and smiled as Kitt started walking toward her. "Kassandra, you look lovely." Ariel gripped both of her hands and leaned over to whisper in her ear. "Who would suspect you are the same young man who arrived in dusty traveling clothes earlier this morning."

Kitt laughed. "No one, I hope." But of course Harcourt would know. Her glance strayed in his direction and she saw that he watched her. Golden brown eyes moved over her from head to foot and his mouth curved up in a faintly mocking smile. He was thinking of their encounter, she knew, remembering the way she had looked dressed in breeches and boots, and a flicker of irritation rippled through her.

She cast him a look of disdain and turned at Ariel's tug on her arm. "Come with me. I have a surprise for you."

As her friend began to guide her toward the small group gathered around the tall dark Earl of Greville, she saw a strangely familiar blond head she hadn't noticed before. When the woman looked up and smiled, Kitt unleashed an unladylike shriek and raced toward her.

"Anna!" Laughing and smiling, she went into her friend's outstretched arms.

"*Cara,* I am so glad to see you." Anna Falacci, Contessa di Loreto, was eight years Kitt's senior. She was a slender woman; her hair, a thick golden blond, cut fashionably short; her features so fine they were any painter's dream. But it was her warm, caring heart that had made them friends. "I have missed you while I was away."

"God, I've missed you, too." They had met last year in Italy, when Kitt's father had banished her to a several months' visit with her cousin. Emily Wentworth Wilder and Anna were friends, their villas south of Rome not far apart. It was there at the Palazzo di Loreto that Kitt had discovered a kindred spirit—and that Anna was a beautiful person inside as well as out.

"When did you get back?" Kitt asked excitedly. "I thought you were still in Italy. Your great-grandmother—is she . . . ?"

"Sadly, my *nonna*, she died. But she had a wonderful, happy life and her children were there to bid her a final farewell. Now she is with the husband she loved for more than forty years."

Kitt smiled. Anna had a way of always finding the brighter side of life. "I'm so glad you're back from your visit."

"As am I, *cara*." But not everyone would be glad of Anna's return. Among the inner circles of the *ton*, the contessa was considered a notorious woman. Rumor had it she had lived in Italy with both her husband and her lover at the very same time. Both men were now dead, but the rumors persisted. Kitt was among the few who knew the truth.

The dinner bell chimed. "It appears Cook has supper ready," Ariel announced brightly. "I think it's time we went in." Gowned in white silk, with her flaxen hair and blue eyes, she looked like a slender angel. The contrast with Justin's dark good looks made them a striking pair.

The company retired to an intimate dining room off the main salon, which was also done in black and gold. Seated by rank as was the custom, Justin took his place at the head of the table, Ariel at the opposite end. The marquess and contessa followed, then Lord and Lady Oxnard. Kitt was seated last, next to Clay.

Warm, gold-flecked brown eyes came to rest on her face. He smiled as his gaze moved lower, lingering for a moment where her breasts rose above the neckline of her gown. An odd tingling started there. Kitt suppressed a shot of irritation.

Clay seemed not to notice. "I suppose there are some advantages to being born on the wrong side of the blanket," he drawled. He was referring to the fact that he was seated at the bottom of the table next to her. But only the edge of a smile remained on his lips, and Kitt's irritation instantly faded.

Clay rarely mentioned his illegitimacy. Though he pretended not to care, it was hardly a secret that it bothered him a great deal. Hoping for a return of his earlier good humor, Kitt gave him a playful smile.

"Sitting next to me could be dangerous, you know. Since we have rarely had a civil conversation, you may wind up regretting your words."

His mouth softened, curved upward. He could conjure a devastating smile when he wanted to. Apparently, he wanted to tonight. "Is that a threat, my lady?"

"More of a promise. If you don't behave yourself, Mr. Harcourt, you could be in for a great deal of trouble."

Clay chuckled softly. "Ah, but courting trouble in such an exquisite package might be interesting."

Kitt said nothing to that. He was staring at her mouth and funny little curls of heat sank into her stomach. She told herself he was only playing a game. She was Ariel's best friend and still unmarried, which made her off limits to Clay—a very good thing, she was sure, considering the man's reputation.

The meal progressed. An asparagus soup followed by lobster rissoles, canard à la Rouennaise, mutton cutlets, a mayonnaise of chicken, an assortment of vegetables drenched in butter, and for dessert, a compote of cherries and raspberry cream custard.

Clay conversed for a while with Lady Oxnard, who was seated to his right, then returned his attention to Kitt. "Justin tells me you're soon to choose a husband."

Kitt went stone cold, the bite of custard she had taken swelling like a thick paste in her throat.

Clay continued as if he hadn't noticed the stricken look on her face. "Have you decided which of your lucky admirers it's going to be?"

Her hand shook on the stem of her goblet. She swallowed the custard with difficulty and took a sip of wine. "My admirers, as you call them, are nothing but a pack of greedy, impoverished lechers. My father wishes me to marry. I do not intend to do so."

"Why not?" Clay's expression remained bland, yet she caught a hint of something in his voice. "Or perhaps no man of your acquaintance comes up to your ladyship's exacting standards."

Kitt cast him a glance but couldn't read his thoughts. She shook her head. "It's nothing like that. I simply don't want a husband—any husband."

"Why not?"

"I refuse to be owned like a stick of furniture, to submit to some man's will when my own will is equally strong. I refuse to be treated like a vessel for some man's pleasure." There was a time she was naïve enough to view men in a different, more benevolent light, but not anymore.

Clay swirled the wine in his glass. "That is the way you see it? You believe making love is simply an act of submission?"

A rush of heat burned into her cheeks. She knew all about making love. And it was far worse than merely submitting. "I don't believe the subject is suitable dinner conversation."

Clay just scoffed. "Since when have you worried about what is or isn't suitable? Are you not the same young woman who stormed into the house this morning completely decked out in men's clothes?"

Her flush grew brighter. "Yes, and just my luck, I

had to run into you—the most disreputable rake in England, the man who is at present sitting here having a discussion with me about propriety."

He laughed, cranking her temper up a notch. "I'm hardly the most disreputable rake in England. London, perhaps, but certainly not all of—"

Kitt made a low growl in her throat and started to rise from the table. Clay grabbed her wrist and jerked her back into her seat.

"Sit down," he said with deadly softness. "Oxnard and his wife may be friends of the earl's, but they are also notorious gossips, and considering the current state of affairs with your father, the last thing you need is them telling tales about your behavior here tonight."

The fight seeped out of her and she leaned back in her chair. "I don't understand it. How do you always manage to do that to me?"

His mouth quirked. "Do what? Make you lose that magnificent temper of yours? Just lucky, I guess."

"You're incorrigible. You know that, don't you?"

"That is what they say about you."

She couldn't help smiling. "No more talk of husbands or marriage, all right?"

"To be truthful, it isn't my favorite topic, either."

"Don't tell me—let me guess. Either you're as much opposed to marriage as I, or you're afraid some poor, cuckolded husband might wind up shooting you for seducing his wife. Personally, I'd have to choose the latter."

He placed a hand over his heart. "You wound me, my lady."

Kitt grinned. " ' 'Tis not so deep as a well, nor as wide as a church door, but 'tis enough, 'twill serve.' "

Clay laughed. "And the lady quotes Shakespeare as she drives in the knife."

Kitt laughed, too. Perhaps, she thought, she didn't loathe him as much as she thought. Oh, he was irritating. No doubt about that. But he could also be charming.

Then she remembered the way he always looked at her, more boldly than any other man she knew. He wanted her. His desire for her was crystal clear. Kitt shivered as a dark image arose of the two of them together, of Clay's strong arms holding her against him, of him kissing her, forcing her beneath him, pinning her with his big hard body. She closed her eyes, tried to shove the image away, but it only grew stronger, more real.

She jumped at the feel of Anna's gloved hand on her arm, reminding her it was time for the ladies to retire and leave the men to their brandy and cigars.

"*Cara*—are you all right?"

Her face had gone pale. She forced herself to relax, managed to muster a smile. "I'm fine. For a moment, I just . . . I just felt a bit of a chill." It was the truth, in its way.

And at least for the moment, the chilling memories that had shifted unfairly onto Clay had been shoved back into that icy dark place in her past.

Kitt intended that they stay there.

The following day broke sunny and warmer than it had been earlier in the week. Clay concluded his early morning meeting with Justin, who decided they should definitely invest in the shipyard, then wandered out into the garden. Luncheon was almost ready. As soon as he had eaten, he would be leaving for the city.

And his first order of business would be to make a call on the Viscount Stockton.

Stockton was a close friend of his father's. For that reason alone, the man would listen to what Clay had to say and that included the fact that the scene at Winston's soiree was his fault, not Kassandra's. He would apologize, of course. He had enjoyed baiting her that night as he always did, but he had never meant for his actions to cause her harm. He would go to Stockton, assure the man that in future he would be more circumspect where his daughter was concerned, and ask that he rescind his harsh judgment.

Clay had no doubt that he would. The Duke of Rathmore was a powerful man and in some ways that power extended even as far as his illegitimate son.

Clay wandered the gravel pathways, admiring the endless spray of daffodils, purple anemones, crocuses, pansies, and hyacinths that thrust themselves up all around him. He had just turned a bend in the meandering path when he saw her. She was sitting on a wrought-iron bench, surrounded by yellow tulips, her head bent over a sketch pad. He couldn't help noticing how utterly lovely she was.

It was odd, though. He wouldn't have imagined Kitt to be the sort to sit around drawing pictures of the garden. The pastime seemed too bland for her, somehow out of character. He moved closer, until he could peer over her shoulder.

Clay's eyes widened at the black-and-white drawing that rested on her lap. Not a picture of a flower but a tavern maid standing on a table in the middle of a crowded alehouse, surrounded by drunken patrons. The maid had her skirts gathered up above her knees, her petticoats showing as she danced a lively jig.

Clay's mouth twitched. It was strange, but he felt a sense of relief. No wilting flower for his Kitt. Nothing nearly so mundane.

"Either you have a very clever imagination, sweeting, or you have been sneaking out again, doing any sort of naughty things."

Kitt squeaked and stood up so quickly she dropped her sketch pad. Clay reached down and picked it up. She snatched it out of his hand and quickly thrust it behind her, looking for all the world like a thief caught in the act.

"I am merely passing the time before luncheon. And what I draw is none of your concern."

Clay made no reply to that, since it was utterly and completely true. "You needn't hide it. I've already seen the picture and in truth, you are really very good."

She eyed him with a hint of suspicion. "What would you know about sketching?"

He smiled. "Not a bloody thing. But I've been in more alehouses than I care to remember. The image you've captured on paper is exactly true to life."

She tried to appear nonchalant but it was obvious she was pleased.

"So tell me . . . how is it you happen to know what goes on in a place like that?"

Kitt shrugged her shoulders. "I went into one once."

"Dressed as a lad, I assume."

"I've only done it a couple of times, but it was amazing, the things I saw. Enough to fill my sketch pad for weeks."

"I imagine so," he said dryly, not liking the thought of her going into a place like that and especially not by herself. "I hope you don't plan on doing it again."

She sadly shook her head. "I suppose not. You've managed to convince me it isn't really safe."

"Good for me." He stared down at the drawing, appreciating the bold lines and angles, the way she had captured the movement, the action, making the picture come to life. What he'd told her was the truth. She was incredibly talented. It was a shame her drawings would probably never be seen.

"What do you do with them once they are finished?"

She sat back down on the bench and added another ruffle to the dancing maid's petticoat. "Hide them in the attic. We both know what my father would say if he knew the sort of subjects I draw."

"Then why do you do it?"

Her fingers kept moving. She didn't glance up. "I don't exactly know. Sometimes I just feel like I have to. When I'm working on a sketch, nothing else matters. I can forget things, ignore things I'd rather not think about. It's like there's nothing else happening in the world."

There was something plaintive in her words. He wondered what a young woman her age could possibly want to forget.

"My offer still stands. I'll see you back to London if you want."

She only shook her head. "I think I had better stay here—at least for a little while longer."

He looked down at the drawing, at the bold, saucy smile on the tavern maid's face. "I could take you sometime . . . in your boy's clothes, I mean. With me you would be safe." He couldn't believe he had actually spoken the thought aloud. It was insane. He couldn't possibly take her anywhere. And yet he wanted to. He wanted to see her face light up as she drew the world he had shown her.

Kitt eyed him warily. "You're teasing me, aren't you?"

Clay forced a laugh, passing it off as a joke, wondering if he had lost his mind completely. "Of course. You would hardly be safe. The moment I got you alone, I would undoubtedly try to ravish your delectable little body."

Kitt didn't smile. "Well, then, I thank you for the offer, but I believe I'll have to pass."

Clay gazed back toward the house, at the sprawling mansion constructed of pale yellow stone. Rows of mullioned windows filled the rooms with light and air, and great stretches of bright green lawn wrapped around it like a cloak. "Luncheon is probably ready. We ought to be going back in."

"Soon," Kitt agreed. "Just a couple more minutes and I'll be finished." Dipping her head, she started working again, slanting lines this way and that, catching each nuance just right, so immersed in her work she didn't realize he still stood there. A strand of curly red hair fluttered softly against her cheek, glowing in the sunlight like rubies. Clay felt an urge to touch it, to free the heavy mass and slide his fingers through it, to inhale the fragrance, to rub the glossy strands against his skin.

His groin thickened. Cursing, ignoring the faintly disturbing ache that rose there, he turned and walked back to the house.

6

Justin smoothed matters over with her father. Or perhaps it was Clay. Kitt was surprised to discover Harcourt had gone to see the viscount and her stepmother as soon as he returned to London. He had shifted the blame for the entire affair onto his extremely broad shoulders, mollified them both, and garnered her a reprieve from finishing her two-week sentence.

When Justin had asked permission for her to stay at Greville Hall, her parents had reluctantly agreed, sending a trunk of her clothes and her lady's maid, Tibby Moon, to see to her needs.

Kitt grinned. Not only had she escaped her parents' dogged scrutiny, she was able to spend time with Anna—"that notorious creature" as they called her— a woman of whom they strictly disapproved.

Seated now in the Gold Room at Greville Hall, Kitt reached over and took hold of Anna's hand. "You must tell me all about your trip back home. Did you meet anyone interesting? How was Emily? Did you have a chance to see her and the children while you were there?"

"*Sì. Sì.* I saw her and many of my family and friends. For a while it was good to be home. But I missed my children. And the memories of my Antonio, they were still there to haunt me. I am glad to be back in England."

It was the reason Anna had left Italy. For three long years, she had mourned the death of her lover, Antonio Pierucci, the brilliant young artist who had lived in the studio above the carriage house that Anna had built especially for him. Antonio was the father of her children—Tonio, six; and Isobel, four—though in the eyes of society they were the legitimate offspring of her husband, the Count di Loreto, a man forty years her senior.

Their arranged marriage had lasted only three months before the count had fallen victim to a series of strokes. Confined to his bed, the old man had relied on Anna to care for him, and she had done so until the day he died. But she had loved Antonio, and she had never regretted it.

"Now that I am returned," Anna announced, "I am going to have a house party. You must all come and stay with me. We can catch up on the months we have lost."

"Oh, yes. I'd love to do that." And since she was still staying with Justin and Ariel, her father wouldn't be able to forbid her to go. She shuddered to remember his words when he had first learned that she and the contessa were friends.

"Have you gone mad?" he'd asked. "Your reputation hangs by a thread as it is. Befriending a woman like Anna Falacci is bound to set tongues wagging again."

But the truth was she hadn't befriended Anna.

Anna had befriended her. Over the weeks that Kitt remained in Italy, she had told the contessa about her father and stepmother, about how lonely and out of place she always felt, about how she always failed to please them.

In return, Anna had spoken of Antonio, the only man she had ever loved.

"When is the party?" Kitt asked.

"Week after next. Say you will come, *cara.*"

Kitt just grinned. "I wouldn't miss it for the world."

And so two weeks later, along with Justin and Ariel, she was staying in a lovely room at Blair House, three among the fifty-odd guests who had been invited for the week-long festivities. Anna might be whispered about by the gossipmongers, but invitations to her home remained one of the *ton*'s most sought after acquisitions. Some of the most interesting people in London could be found in Anna Falacci's drawing rooms: scholars, politicians, playwrights, physicians, notorious gamblers, displaced French nobles, and even an occasional courtesan.

Social position held little sway. If Anna liked someone, they were simply welcomed into her home.

Sunlight slanted in through the stained-glass windows above the door in the entry as Kitt descended the sweeping marble stairs. She was on her way to join the contessa in a small salon at the rear of the huge Georgian mansion Anna had rented when she had first arrived, and had later purchased.

Blair House stood like a bastion in the countryside. A hundred feet square and constructed of Portland stone, it rose four stories high with rows of mullioned windows and two curving outside staircases that swept up to the wide front doors. The salon Kitt entered was equally magnificent, done in shades of pale blue and peach, with blue-flocked wallpaper and crystal chandeliers.

"*Cara!* Come in! Come in!" Anna hurried toward her, a vision in bright blue silk. She caught Kitt's hand and dragged her over to the sofa in front of the windows, where Anna's tow-headed children, Tonio and Isobel, jumped up excitedly to greet her.

"Lady Kitt! Lady Kitt!" they chimed in their thick Italian accents as she knelt to hug each one.

She drew back to look at them. "My—look how much you've grown. Why, in a few short months, Tonio has become a handsome young man and you, Izzy, have blossomed into a beautiful little girl."

Isobel, the four-year-old, giggled with delight, while Tonio's thin chest puffed out.

"Mama brought us presents from home," he proudly announced. "A castle and knights for me"— he held the beautifully carved wooden pieces up for her inspection—"a doll for Izzy."

The little girl grabbed up the porcelain-faced doll from where she had been playing with it on the floor. She waggled back and forth in front of Kitt, making the doll's curly black hair flop back and forth.

"They're wonderful gifts," Kitt said. "Your mama loves you very much."

Both children grinned.

"Since I love you, too, I have a gift as well."

Tonio's big brown eyes rounded with excitement. "You have a present for us? Where is it? I want to see."

Izzy tugged on her skirt. "Me, too."

Kitt reached for the bag she had set on the floor, dug inside, and pulled out a puppet for Tonio, a black-caped magician, and a little stuffed dog for Izzy.

The children grabbed them up, Tonio sticking his hand inside the puppet, Izzy hugging the little dog against her chest.

"*Grazie,* Lady Kitt," both of them said, almost in unison.

Someone cleared his throat from the doorway. Clayton Harcourt stood in the opening, looking tall and annoyingly virile in buff breeches and a dark brown tailcoat. Kitt felt an odd sort of stirring she firmly ignored. She hadn't known he was among the invited guests, though she probably should have guessed. Anna liked Clay, and of course he was a friend of Lord Greville's.

He cast her a perfunctory glance, then fixed his attention on Anna. "I'm sorry to interrupt, Contessa, but Her Grace, the Duchess of Denonshire, has been looking for you. Since she appeared to be somewhat overset, I thought I ought to come fetch you."

"*Grazie,* Clayton."

"I'll stay with the children," Kitt volunteered.

Anna smiled. "Then I will not worry. And I promise, I will not be gone long."

She watched Anna leave in a whirl of pale blue silk and thought that Clay would surely follow. Men were wildly attracted to Anna, though she paid them little attention. Surely Clay Harcourt, with a penchant for anything in skirts, would be among those vying to seduce her.

Instead he surprised her by strolling on into the drawing room. "I couldn't help overhearing your conversation. I didn't know you liked children." Tonio and Izzy were engrossed in play at her feet, oblivious to Harcourt or anyone else.

"You thought that I did not?"

"You said you didn't plan to marry. I assumed that meant you had no interest in having a family."

Kitt looked down at the two blond heads bent over their toys. "I love children. I always have. It's the husband who comes with the package that I'm unwilling to endure." She reached down, ran her fingers through the little boy's fine, silky blond hair. "Have you met Tonio and Izzy?"

"Yesterday. Already, we're becoming fast friends." He squatted down beside the small boy. "Isn't that right, *mio amico?*"

The little boy looked up and grinned. *"Signore* Harcourt, he take us for a ride in the pony cart."

Kitt stared at him in amazement. As hard as she tried, she couldn't imagine Clay Harcourt riding around in a pony cart with two small children. Then again, perhaps as she had first thought, he was merely trying to ingratiate himself with the children's mother.

The thought was surprisingly unpleasant.

"What do you suppose the duchess wanted?" she asked, pushing her thoughts in a different direction.

"It seems Her Grace discovered that a band of Gypsies are camped on the edge of the estate. She was threatening to have her husband drive them away when I happened along. Since I believe Anna invited them to stay, I thought she would want to know."

Kitt returned the little stuffed dog she and Izzy had been playing with, her interest suddenly piqued. "Gypsies are camped nearby?"

Clay smiled. "More fodder for your sketch pad, my lady?"

"I've read stories about them. I've seen one or two on the street, but it isn't the same. I should love to discover what they're truly like."

Anna floated in just then. "You wish to see the Gypsies? That is good—we will all go and visit the camp."

Kitt grinned—she couldn't help it.

"Well, my lady," Clay drawled, his eyes warm on her face. "It would seem you are about to get your wish."

Rolling through the deep green grass in Anna's carriage, they found the Gypsies camped in a circle: odd-shaped, painted wagons enclosed like moving houses and black mohair tents; horses, chickens, dogs; dark-skinned men and women; and a passel of ragged children.

Color seemed to be everywhere. Scarlet silk shirts, vivid green bandannas, flashing red, yellow, and blue ankle-length skirts, jangling gold bracelets. For the first time, Kitt wished that instead of the black-and-white sketches she drew, she could capture the scene with a palette of vibrant paint.

As the open carriage drew closer, the tribe of Gypsies recognized the contessa's gold crest and started walking toward them. Anna waved in their direction and the conveyance rolled to a halt in thick high grass. Clay helped the women down from the carriage and a tall dark-skinned man who appeared to be the leader came forward.

"It is a pleasure to see you again, contessa." His face was lean and hawkish, his black hair held in place by a yellow bandanna tied round his head.

"It is good to see you as well, Janos. You know my children, Tonio and Izzy. I would like you to meet my friends, Clayton and Kitt." She used first names, the way the Gypsies did. Anna cared little for precedent.

The Gypsy made a slight inclination of his head. "Welcome to our camp." He turned to one of the others, a stout, squat woman with pitch-black eyes and a wary expression. "Bring food and drink for our guests. Tell Lenka to bring the children."

"Please do not trouble yourselves," Anna said politely. "We can only stay a moment. I only wished to welcome you. I am glad that you've returned safely."

Janos smiled, showing the whitest teeth Kitt had ever seen. "Thank you. *Baht*—fortune—was with us."

Anna turned to Kitt and Clay. "Janos and his people travel this way twice a year. I have told them that as long as I reside at Blair House, they are welcome to stay here."

More of the Gypsies clustered around. Two of the young women approached as Kitt stood enthralled with the sights, sounds, and smells of the camp, working to memorize the brightly garbed figures engaged in their various tasks.

"My name is Dina," one of them said with a tentative smile. She was as short as Kitt and about the same age, with long black hair and a full, womanly figure.

"Hello, my name is Kitt."

The other girl eased forward, eyeing the mint green muslin gown Kitt wore, so different from her own peasant-style skirt and blouse. "I am Hanka. I am pleased to meet you." She was equally pretty but more slenderly built. She reached up and touched the tiny false violets on the bonnet Kitt had put on when they left the house. "It is very pretty."

Kitt smiled, pulled the string beneath her chin, and lifted the hat from her head. "Then it's yours."

"Oh, no, I did not mean to—"

"Please. I want you to have it." She turned to the

other girl, pulled off her kidskin gloves and handed them over. "And these are for you."

Both girls beamed with pleasure. Dina stroked the gloves and looked over at her friend, who nodded. "Hanka and I, we wish to give you something in return."

"Oh, but you don't have to do that, I—"

They were gone before she could finish the sentence, darting away like children, one climbing into the back of a wagon painted with big red flowers, the other ducking into a nearby tent.

They returned a few minutes later, swatches of brightly colored silk clutched in their dark brown hands.

"For you," Dina said, handing her a gathered skirt fashioned from a patchwork of multicolored silk. Hanka pressed a matching red silk peasant blouse into her hands.

"Tonight there will be dancing," Hanka said. "You must come and join us. We will teach you to dance like the *Rom.*"

Oh, it was tempting. She fingered the smooth, slick silk draped over her arms. The garments were little more than scraps of cloth. What freedom it would mean to wear such clothes! She looked at the two Gypsy girls. What would it be like to enjoy such a simple existence?

"Thank you for the gifts," she said. "I'll treasure them always. I'll never forget you." In fact, she couldn't wait to get back and start putting their faces on paper. So many images spun through her mind she felt almost dizzy.

"Time to leave, sweeting," Clay said gently.

Kitt glanced up at the endearment, unnerved by the

soft way he had said it. He must have overheard their conversation and realized how much the simple gifts meant. Why was it he always seemed to know what she was thinking? With a hand at her waist, he guided her over to the open carriage and helped her climb in. Tonio and Izzy raced up the iron stairs behind her and plopped down on the seat, still speaking in rapid Italian to the ragged little Gypsy boy with soulful brown eyes they had apparently adopted as a friend.

Clay followed Anna into the carriage and the driver urged the horses into a trot. All the way back to the house, Kitt clutched the soft silk garments the girls had given her, thinking of the Gypsies, wondering what it might be like to watch them dance. She told herself it was impossible, that it would be scandalous—and dangerous—to sneak off by herself to watch such a thing.

She prayed she could convince herself.

The evening settled in, a clear, cloudless sky and a huge full moon that lit the surrounding green hills with a soft, almost iridescent glow. Inside the house, guests enjoyed an elegant supper, followed by a night of music and gaming.

Kitt danced with a notable young playwright named Franklin Brimly Heridan; followed by a deposed French count, Maximilian Dupree, who had barely escaped the country with his head still attached to his shoulders; and Dr. Peter Avery, a young, sandy-haired physician who was endearingly shy and spoke with a mild stutter.

The company was pleasant, yet she found her gaze searching for Harcourt, wondering when he would appear. Eventually, she spotted him at the edge of the dance floor, in conversation with the beautiful black-haired Elizabeth Watkins, Countess of May. They were standing a little too close, speaking as if they were the only people in the room, and Kitt felt a swift, unpleasant tightening in the pit of her stomach.

It was rumored that Clay and the countess had been lovers. From the look of invitation on the lady's lovely face, it was obvious they still were.

When Harcourt leaned down to whisper in her ear, Kitt turned away, determined to ignore them. A dull pain bit into her hand and she realized her fingers had curled so tightly into her palms that her nails had dug through her long white gloves.

Dammit, what did she care what Harcourt did—or with whom? She certainly didn't want him. She didn't want any man and she never would.

But seeing him with Lady May had somehow dimmed the excitement she had felt earlier in the evening. Hoping no one would see her, she slipped out of the drawing room and climbed the sweeping stairs to her bedchamber on the second floor. A lamp had been lit beside the bed and the covers turned back.

Lying at the foot of the feather mattress where she had left them that afternoon were the red silk blouse and colorful patchwork skirt Hanka and Dina had given her earlier that day.

Kitt reached over and touched the soft, slick fabric. She picked up the skirt and held it up in front of her, turned to look at herself in the cheval glass. Dina had been about her same height. The skirt fell at mid-calf, leaving her legs and ankles bare. The blouse would probably be a little bit snug in the bosom, but that would hardly matter.

Still holding the garments, she walked over to the

window and slid it open. In the distance, she could see the red glow of the Gypsy fires, hear the faint, faraway jingle of tambourines. The idea she had been chewing on all afternoon returned like a demon in her head.

The camp wasn't that far away. And Dina and Hanka would be waiting. They had wanted her to come.

If she dressed as a Gypsy, she would hardly be noticed and she wouldn't stay long. Just time enough to watch a little of the dancing and return to the house.

Did she dare?

But how could she not? This afternoon she had glimpsed a different, freer way of life, something she had come to yearn for over the years. She had drawn for hours, but it wasn't enough. She wanted to see more, learn more.

She wanted to watch them dance.

Kitt didn't ring for her maid to undress her. Tibby would be sleeping, certain Kitt was still downstairs enjoying the entertainment, and her little maid was sure to disapprove. Kitt struggled to unfasten her rose silk gown, then tentatively drew on the colorful Gypsy garments. They were light as down, soft and slick, and clinging to her curves. With only a chemise underneath, she felt nearly naked.

And freer than she had ever felt before.

Hurrying over to the mirror, she jerked the pins from her curly red hair and quickly brushed it out, leaving it loose, the way the Gypsy girls wore theirs, letting it fall in a wild, unruly tangle around her shoulders. She glanced toward the window and saw the tree outside, but it was a little too far away and a long way to the ground, even dressed as simply as she was.

Settling on a plan, she tossed her cloak around her

shoulders, lifted the hood over her head, and quietly turned the doorknob. Seeing no one in the hall, she slipped out of the room and hurried along the corridor to the servants' stairs at the back of the house.

At the door to the kitchen, she paused. Damnation, there was bound to be someone working in there. On the other hand, with the hood of her cloak up to cover her hair, no one would know who she was. They would simply assume she was one of the female guests sneaking out for a midnight assignation.

With a deep, steadying breath, careful to keep her face well-hidden in the shadows of the hood, she hurried past the old woman bent over a heavy black pot and out the back door. By the time the woman looked up, Kitt had disappeared into the darkness.

"It's been a long night. I'm afraid I'm beginning to tire." Elizabeth Watkins, Countess of May, looked up at Clay with big, dark, welcoming eyes. "I think I shall retire to my bedchamber."

It's about time, he thought, casting her a faintly satisfied smile. They had played the game long enough. It was time to finish it in the manner both of them wanted.

"I believe I shall end the evening as well. Where is your room?"

Full ruby lips curved into a smile. "At the end of the hall on the right. Just four doors down from yours."

How she knew which room was his he had no idea, but neither did he care. Her proximity was convenient and Liz was an exceptional lover.

"Expect me within the half-hour," he promised, his body tightening as she reached between them and discreetly brushed a slender white hand against the front of his breeches.

"Don't keep me waiting, darling."

He didn't intend to. He'd been randy as a stallion ever since his trip to the Gypsy camp. Kassandra always seemed to have that effect on him, though she didn't seem to notice. He needed a little physical relief and the lovely Liz Watkins, with her smooth, pale skin and raven-dark hair, was just the lady who could give it to him.

He sipped his brandy and checked the clock, gave her another ten minutes, then started up. He had just rounded the corner leading down the hall to her room, when he heard the sound of a door being opened a few feet away. Hoping to preserve Elizabeth's already somewhat tarnished reputation, he eased back into the shadows just in time to see a small, cloaked figure step out into the passage.

Glancing furtively left and right, the lady turned away from the path leading to the main staircase and hurried in the opposite direction, heading for the servants' stairs at the back of the house.

Clay continued on his way, taking only two long strides before realization hit him.

"Bloody hell." A woman that size—it had to be Kitt, and he knew without doubt where she was going. He had heard the Gypsy girls' invitation that afternoon, had seen the wistful look in Kassandra's pretty green eyes. He should have known this would happen. He should have spoken to Ariel, made sure she kept a close eye on her friend. But he hadn't really believed Kitt would be foolish enough to go.

Not into a world so foreign.

Not by herself.

Swearing, calling himself ten kinds of fool, Clay turned away from the comfort he would find in Elizabeth Watkins's bed and followed Kitt down the back stairs. Why he should concern himself, he couldn't exactly say, but in truth, he felt oddly protective of her. Perhaps because he admired her fiery spirit, or because he knew how unhappy she was at home. Perhaps it was simply that Kitt was Ariel's friend and since Ariel was his best friend's wife, that somehow made him feel responsible.

Whatever the reason, he fell in behind her, worried at the trouble she might find. Gypsies were no different from anyone else. There were good men among them and there were bad.

And a woman alone was always easy prey.

He followed her into the darkness, but didn't see her. He wasn't worried. He knew where she was going and he would make sure nothing untoward happened. But what if he hadn't spotted her leaving? His temper began to simmer as he thought of the peril she constantly put herself in. Did she care nothing at all for her own safety? Did she have no idea of the danger?

Clay set his jaw, certain the gravest danger she faced at the moment came from him.

7

Kitt stood in the darkness at the edge of the circle of wagons lit by cooking fires. The smell of burning poplar chips mingled with the scent of garlic and tobacco, and the music of violins drifted toward her on the evening air.

A larger fire blazed in the center of the camp, an assortment of Gypsies clustered around it. They drank from blackened tin cups and their laughter rang into the night. Kitt yearned to join them, but now that she was there, her courage faltered. She felt too different, too removed from the scene, an interloper in a world she knew nothing about. Deciding to simply stay hidden, she peered around the wagon, smiling at the sound of children singing.

She started to move a little closer to the fire, careful to stay out of sight, then gasped as a thick arm slid around her waist, jerking her out of the shadows. The hood of her cloak fell back and she stared into the pitch-dark eyes of a stout Gypsy man.

"So . . . it is the *gadjo* woman who came this afternoon."

He was perhaps in his thirties, not tall but powerfully built. A bare chest layered with muscle gleamed beneath his black leather vest. Kitt tried to pull away, but he held her easily, his hard, stocky body sending a shiver of fear sliding through her.

"Hanka and Dina invited me to come. They said . . . they said I could watch the dancing."

Soft laughter rumbled. "You would like that . . . to see the dancing?" He was attractive, except for a slightly crooked nose and an unpleasant arrogance that exuded from every pore. He released his hold and she took a step away, grateful to be free of him, her heart still thumping with nerves.

"That is the reason I came."

He reached toward her, lifted a strand of her hair, watched it wrap around the end of his finger. "Perhaps there is something else you would like from Demetro."

A second shiver ran through her. She didn't like the way he looked at her, his dark eyes assessing her as if she were one of his horses. From a few feet away, someone called out to him and he turned. It was the tall Gypsy named Janos who was the leader of the tribe.

"It is the little *gadjo*," Demetro called back. "She has come to join the feasting."

Janos smiled at her in welcome. "Come. Hanka and Dina have been watching for you. They were hoping you would come."

Relief filtered through her. The girls were waiting, just as they had promised. She followed Janos into the center of the camp, and Dina and Hanka raced up, their faces flushed, black eyes sparkling with excitement.

"We did not believe you would come," Dina said.

Kitt laughed. "Neither did I."

"Most *gadjo* women would have been afraid."

"I was . . . a little. But to see the dancing is worth the risk."

The girls grinned their approval and Dina shoved a tin cup into her hand. *"Palinka.* We make it ourselves. You must try it."

She took a sip, just to be polite, then coughed as the rough, hot liquid burned its way into her stomach. "You drink . . . this stuff?" she sputtered, and her eyes teared up. She fought not to cough again.

"It is better after another sip or two," Hanka promised.

Kitt didn't think so, but she didn't want to be rude. She took another tentative swallow and surprisingly it wasn't nearly as bad as the first. It almost had a sweet flavor to it.

"Hurry. Soon we dance the *czardas."* Hanka tugged the string holding Kitt's cloak in place and tossed it over an upended log. Taking Kitt's hand, she led her toward the circle of Gypsies gathered around the campfire. "Come, dance with us. We will show you how."

"Oh, no, I couldn't possibly . . ." But Dina took hold of her other hand and they urged her closer to the fire. On the opposite side, two dark-skinned men strummed guitars. Next to them a young man played a violin while another struck a felt-covered hammer against the metal strings of an instrument that looked like a small piano.

"It is Gypsy," Dina said, as she followd the direction of Kitt's curious gaze. "We call it *cymbalom."*

The music quickened, a lively, fast-paced melody

that set Kitt's feet to tapping and the blood rushing through her veins. Hanka laughed and twirled around; Kitt grinned and took a sip of *palinka.* Hands began clapping. The men began dancing, arching their backs and stomping their feet, moving with such power and grace an ache welled up inside her. Shouts and cheers went up. Spoons made a slapping sound against open palms and tambourines jingled like tiny silver bells in the clear night air.

Kitt watched in silent awe, sipping from the cup now and then, feeling the warm glow spread through her. The music grew faster, louder, the shouts more robust. She had never seen such passion, such fierce joy. Yips and shouts filled the air. The beat of the guitars seemed to match the pounding rhythm of her heart.

When Dina took the tin cup from her fingers and pulled her into the circle of dancers, Kitt didn't draw away. She simply closed her eyes and let the hot, sensuous beat of the music sweep over her, urging her to let herself go. The warm *palinka* flowed through her, erasing the last, faint traces of her reserve.

Kitt lifted her skirts and started to dance.

In the thickening darkness, the huge fire blazed into the black, starry sky, a faint shower of sparks floating upward toward the heavens. Clay had come to the camp meaning simply to collect Kassandra, give her a stern, brotherly lecture, and return to the house. But the moment her cloak was stripped away and she stood there in her simple Gypsy garments, he was lost.

From his place in the shadows of a painted wagon, he watched her enter the circle of dancers, as barefoot as the others, looking just as pagan and not the least out of place. She closed her eyes and started swaying to the music, her small feet tapping against the flattened earth, her curly red hair wrapping wildly around her shoulders.

His body quickened, but still he made no move. Like a statue, he stood frozen, a voyeur affixed to the spot. He watched her slim arms lift above her head, watched the way her full breasts quivered beneath her red silk blouse. He watched how gracefully she moved, her legs supple, her hips swaying seductively. His blood thickened and desire burned like fire in his groin.

Above her bright Gypsy skirt, her waist looked no bigger than a handspan. Beneath the hem, her ankles flashed, small and trim, her feet high-arched and well-formed. She let her head fall back and her fiery hair tumbled down, nearly touching her hips.

His shaft grew heavy and began to throb. The beast of lust rode him like a living thing. He wanted to storm into the dancers and drag her away from the circle of men. He wanted to kiss those soft ripe lips, wanted to fill his hands with those high lush breasts. He wanted to tear off her peasant clothes, drag her down on the ground, and thrust his hardness inside her.

It wasn't going to happen.

And the fact that it wasn't made him madder than bloody hell.

He waited for a moment, fighting to bring his body back under control, cursing Kitt Wentworth for making his life a living hell. Stepping out of the shadows, he strode toward her, the throng of Gypsies backing away at the look of fury on his face, parting like the Red Sea in front of him.

The music faded. Guitars no longer strummed. The rattle of tambourines slowly drifted away. For a moment, Kitt didn't notice. Eyes closed, caught up in the music she heard only in her head, she made a last, wild, swirling turn and collided with his chest.

Her eyes popped open and her pretty mouth parted in an *O* of surprise. "C-Clay! What . . . what are you doing here?"

"More to the point, my lady, what are *you* doing here?"

She glanced wildly around, saw the Gypsies watching them with undisguised interest, and her cheeks flushed a soft shade of rose. "I was invited—if it is any business of yours, which it most definitely is not."

"I'm making it my business. Where is your cloak? You can scarcely return to the house dressed half-naked as you are. I doubt even your very indulgent friends would approve."

Kitt glanced down at the low-cut bodice of her peasant blouse, saw the soft cleavage it exposed, and her cheeks flamed brighter still. "What I wear is also none of your concern."

Clay ignored her, gripped her arm, and started hauling her toward the spot where her cloak had been tossed over a log.

"Hold still." She didn't move as he held it up, draped it around her shoulders, then tied the string at the base of her throat. Taking her arm, he started back through the crowd just as Janos, the tall Gypsy leader, stepped in front of them.

"I see you have come for your woman."

"I'm not his—"

"Yes." Clay cast her a look of warning she pretended not to see.

"That is good," Janos said. "Your Kitt—she is a creature of strong passions. She needs the guidance of a strong, virile man."

"I don't need—"

"I couldn't agree with you more."

The Gypsy made a slight nod of his head. "You are both welcome here whenever you wish."

"Thank you." Clay gave her another hard look and they started walking again. They had traveled only a few short paces when Kitt jerked away.

"I have to say good-bye to Hanka and Dina before I leave. It's only polite, since they are the ones who invited me."

"We don't have time for you to be polite. If someone sees us out here, both of us will be ruined."

She smiled a little too sweetly. "Then I suggest you go on without me." Turning, she walked back to bid farewell to her friends. He couldn't hear what the women were saying, but he caught them looking his way and then heard a burst of laughter.

His anger spiraled upward. He waited for her return, gripped her arm, and they started walking again. He was itching for a fight. Thoughts of bedding her were driving him crazy and after tonight it would only get worse. More importantly, the little wench hadn't enough sense to realize the peril she had put herself in. She deserved a dressing down and he meant to give her one.

They hadn't got halfway to the house before he swung her around to face him. "I hope you know what a stupid, dangerous thing that was to do. Do you have any idea what might have happened to you out there?"

Her chin jerked up. "I know what happened—you stuck your nose in where it wasn't wanted as for some unfathomable reason you seem determined to do. And don't you dare presume to lecture me. You don't know what it's like. If you had wanted to go, you simply would have done it. You wouldn't have had to sneak out. You wouldn't have had to worry about what people might say. Well, there are times I get tired of doing what other people tell me. Tonight I did something that *I* wanted to do."

"You're a woman. Anything could have happened. Do you know what those men were thinking when they watched you dance?" For once she didn't answer, which only drove him on. "They wanted to tear off your clothes. They wanted to touch your lovely little body. They wanted to drag you down on the ground and drive themselves inside you."

For an instant, her face went pale. Then she squared her shoulders and looked him in the face. "So now you're a mind reader, just like the Gypsies. How could you possibly know what those men wanted to do?"

How could he know? "You little fool," he whispered as he hauled her roughly against him. "I know— because that's what I wanted to do." Then he kissed her. Not a sweet, gentle, tender kiss, but a hot, ravaging, taking kiss, the kind he had wanted from her for as long as he could recall.

For several sweet moments, she didn't resist, just stood there pressed against his chest, her lips parted in surprise, her mouth soft and giving under his. Through the thin silk blouse, he could feel the ripe fullness of her breasts, the slight protrusion of her nipples as they tightened into buds, and his body went rock hard.

With a groan, he deepened the kiss, pulling her more firmly against him, his tongue sweeping in, taking what he wanted, claiming her in some way. At the feel of his heavy arousal, Kitt's spine went as rigid as a stick. She stumbled as she jerked away.

"What . . . what do you think you're doing?" She was breathing hard, swaying a little on her feet, trying to make sense of what had happened.

The edge of his mouth curved up in a smile that really wasn't. "Exactly what those other men wanted to do."

She stepped even farther away, her eyes big and wary. "It was a lesson—wasn't it? You were trying to prove your point."

He wanted to lie, to say that was all he'd meant to do, but the words wouldn't come. "I wanted you. It's as simple as that."

Kitt looked at him as if he had turned into a demon from hell. Whirling away, her bright skirts flashing for an instant before her cloak fell back into place, she started running back toward the house. She looked shaken and pale, and for an instant he regretted his impulsive behavior.

Bloody hell, it was only a kiss.

But he didn't try to stop her, just followed along in her wake, making certain she got safely back inside. He wasn't completely sure she would go in. He didn't trust the little witch—not one bit.

And the sad truth was, where she was concerned, he no longer trusted himself.

Kitt awakened later than usual the next morning. She felt groggy and out of sorts, her head throbbing faintly from the strong Gypsy *palinka*.

And she hadn't slept well. She had dreamed of the Gypsy camp, dreamed she was dancing again, but this time she danced for Clay. He stood watching from the shadows, his golden eyes following her every move. Seductively she moved her hips, tilted her head back, arched her neck, and his eyes seemed to gleam in the darkness. She knew what he was thinking, but she wasn't afraid. She reveled in the power she held over him, gloried in the desire she read in his face.

Then the dream subtly shifted, turned hazy, and another woman appeared. Elizabeth Watkins strolled up beside him. She whispered something in his ear and Clay laughed. Kitt watched in horror as they slipped away together into the night.

Lying in the deep featherbed, she shoved the dream away and brushed her tangled red hair back from her face, wishing she had taken the time to braid it before she'd gone to bed. Sliding to the edge of the mattress, she tugged the bellpull, summoning her maid, then padded across the Oriental carpet to use the chamber pot behind the painted screen.

By the time she was through, Tibby had arrived to help her prepare for the day. One look at Kitt's disheveled state and she made a familiar clucking sound of disgust.

"Look what you've done to your hair." A woman in her late thirties, Tibby had worked for her father since Kitt was a little girl—and she had never been afraid to express herself. "Looks like a rat's nest. You should have let me braid it before you went to bed."

Kitt kept silent about the pagan dancing that had been responsible for her unruly curls and just let Tibby comb out the tangles, trying not to wince in pain. The maid braided the heavy mass and wound it in a wreath atop Kitt's head, then went to fetch a gown for her to wear.

Dressed in a cream muslin day dress trimmed with Mechlin lace, she descended the stairs to the breakfast room, hoping Clay wouldn't be there. Every time she thought of him, she remembered his fierce kiss and she wasn't yet ready to face him.

Fortunately, she discovered, he and a group of the men had gone hunting and wouldn't be back until late afternoon.

The day passed uneventfully. Kitt, Anna, and Ariel accompanied Justin, the Marquess of Landen, and a handful of others on a picnic in the woods. It wasn't till luncheon was over and the group dispersed to various parts of the meadow that Kitt pulled Anna and Ariel aside to confide her adventures in the Gypsy camp.

"You should have seen them," Kitt said wistfully. "They were so happy, so incredibly free. And the music—dear Lord, it was so full of passion it seemed to consume me. I listened to the rhythm and felt like my blood was on fire."

Anna laughed. "That is what I like about you, *cara*—you've the spirit of a falcon. I only wish that I had gone soaring with you last night."

Sitting beside her, Ariel smiled. "I don't think Justin would have approved, but I admit it would have been fun."

Kitt grinned. "I wonder what Harcourt would have said if he had discovered all three of us dancing."

Anna reached down and plucked a little white wildflower from the grass at her feet. "You like him, no?"

Kitt rolled her eyes. "Are you mad? We don't get along at all." She didn't mention the kiss. Her emotions were still too unsettled on that subject and she was oddly reluctant to cause problems for Clay.

"Perhaps you do not like him, but I think he very much likes you."

Kitt glanced away, kicked a pebble with the toe of

her kidskin slipper. "Clay likes every female under the age of sixty. Currently, he is enamored of Lady May."

Anna just smiled. "Perhaps," was all she said.

The picnic ended and the hunting party returned. Kitt made a point of avoiding Clay that evening, but she refused to go as far as remaining in her room. As it turned out, she didn't have to. His father, the Duke of Rathmore, had appeared with several other late arrivals she hadn't yet seen and Harcourt kept himself otherwise entertained.

Kitt couldn't help but wonder if that entertainment included Lady May, who also seemed conspicuously missing from the evening's festivities. She thought of Clay and remembered once again the way he had kissed her. It was a man's kiss, fierce and frightening, yet on some deep, heretofore hidden womanly level, part of her had liked it.

She wouldn't have expected to. Not now. Not when she knew where such a kiss could lead.

But the truth was, she had enjoyed it.

As the evening wore on, she strolled past Lady Oxnard, who entertained guests on a pianoforte in the Blue Room, and quietly made her way out onto the terrace. It was dark tonight, the moon obscured by a thin layer of flat gray clouds. But the air was cool and sweet with the lingering scent of lilac.

She stood for a while at the balustrade overlooking the garden, enjoying the solitude and the chirp of the crickets, then turned and started back to the house. She had only taken a few steps when a shadow stepped out of the darkness, blocking the path in front of her.

The man was tall and spare, his golden blond hair cut short and stylishly swept back from a face that set hearts aflutter all over London. It was a face she knew only too well, and a wave of revulsion swept over her.

"Westerly," she choked out, barely able to say the name.

"Well, if it isn't the delectable Lady Kassandra." Blue eyes she had once thought beautiful and now thought a shade too pale swept over her from head to foot. When they fixed on the cleavage between her breasts, it seemed as if he had reached out and touched her, and for an instant she thought she might actually faint.

"How long has it been, my dear? Two years, or is it three? Far too long, I think."

Kitt swallowed past the tightness in her throat. "Not nearly long enough." Fighting for composure, she tried to walk past him but Stephen Marlow, Earl of Westerly, continued to block her escape.

"Surely you don't mean to leave so soon. We have so much to catch up on."

"I'm afraid I am suddenly not feeling very well. If you will excuse me—"

"There was a time you weren't so eager to run from me. Do you remember?"

Of course, she remembered. She would never be able to forget. "I was younger then. And I was a fool."

His hand reached out, slender and elegant as it slipped along her jaw. "You've changed, Kassandra. The years have hardened your heart. But you are even more lovely than you were back then."

Kitt jerked away, repulsed by his touch. "Stay away from me, Stephen, I'm warning you. And you had better get out of my way."

He smiled as he took a step backward, moving out of the path in front of her. "Of course, my lady." He let her pass, but his pale eyes followed. Ugly memories of her and Stephen together on her sixteenth birthday filled her thoughts and nausea rolled in her stomach. Skirting the Blue Room, her legs trembling beneath her high-waisted yellow silk gown, she managed to make her way unseen back inside the house, down the hall, and halfway up the stairs.

Unfortunately, Harcourt was just coming down.

He paused on the stair above her. "You look pale. Are you not feeling well?"

Kitt moistened lips that felt too stiff to move. "I-I'm fine. I just . . . I just need a moment to lie down."

"I'll see you up to your bedchamber."

"No! I mean, no thank you." Turning, she raced away from him before he had time to argue. She didn't stop until she reached the safety of her room, went in, and closed the door. Trembling, she leaned against it.

Dear God, Westerly is here. He'd been away on the Continent. She hadn't seen him in years. She had almost forgotten him, forgotten the humiliating things he had done to her. Forgotten the night he had so ruthlessly taken her innocence.

Now he was here, making her remember. Making her loathe herself again.

Tomorrow she would leave, she decided. But she couldn't return to Greville Hall by herself and she refused to spoil the occasion for her friends. She could go back to London, back to her father's house, but that would be nearly as bad as staying here.

Her resolve strengthened. She had put up with Westerly before he'd left England. They had attended the same parties, shared the same friends. In the end, she decided simply to keep her distance.

She didn't think that would be much of a problem.

A man like the earl was interested in only one thing—and he had stolen that from her four years ago.

The day broke clear and warm, a bright spring sun beating down on the hills around Hampstead Heath. Ariel had been enjoying her days with Justin, who, being away from his study at Greville Hall, had actually been able to forget his business interests and simply relax for a change.

It was Kitt she was worried about. Especially after her friend had confided her adventure in the Gypsy camp.

And that Clay had been the one to bring her home.

Ariel spotted him across the salon in conversation with his father and the Earl of Westerly, guests who had arrived late yesterday afternoon. Earlier that morning, she had sent Clay a note and when he saw her enter the room, he excused himself and followed her out onto the terrace. On the lawn across the way, she saw Kitt seated on the grass beneath a tree, playing with the contessa's two children.

"You wished to see me?" Clay asked, drawing her attention back to him. He looked as handsome as sin in his dark green tailcoat and light buff breeches. He smiled but there was something in his eyes, a wariness that somehow added to her fears.

"I wanted to talk to you about Kitt."

His expression remained bland, but a muscle tightened in his cheek. "What about her?"

"She told me what happened the other night. I know she went out to the Gypsy camp. She told me you came after her. She said—"

"It was only a kiss, for chrissake. If she told you it was more—"

"Good Lord, Clay, Kitt never mentioned anything about a kiss. She said that you were upset with her for going to the camp by herself. I was thinking that we should have offered to take her. It was obvious how much she wanted to go. I merely wanted to thank you for looking out for her." She eyed him coolly. "Though now I wonder if perhaps you had a far different motive for your courtly behavior."

A slight flush rose beneath the bones in his cheeks. "I was worried about her, that's all. I had no intentions beyond seeing her safely home. I never meant to kiss her. We were arguing. I just . . . things just got a little out of hand."

"Exactly how far out of hand?"

"As I said—it was only a kiss. And I don't believe the lady was particularly impressed. As a matter of fact, she's been avoiding me as if I had the plague ever since we got back."

Ariel sighed. "I think she's attracted to you, Clay, and she very much doesn't want to be." She cast him a stern warning glance. "Which doesn't mean she's fair game to you."

His mouth curved faintly. "No matter what you may think, I don't make a habit of seducing innocent young women, particularly not one who is your friend."

Ariel gazed off toward the grassy knoll where Kitt played marbles with Tonio and Izzy. "Just be careful, Clay. I know she doesn't show it, but in many ways Kitt is fragile."

Clay followed her gaze, watched Kassandra laughing at something the small boy said. "Strangely enough, that isn't so hard to believe." His dark eyes lingered, studying her a moment more. "She seemed ill last night. From the looks of her today, apparently it wasn't serious."

"I spoke to her earlier and she seems to be fine." Ariel smiled, feeling a little more at ease. "She said you liked her drawings."

He turned back to her, mildly surprised. "She mentioned that?"

Ariel nodded. "I think it pleased her."

"She's extremely talented. I would like to see the renderings she makes of the Gypsy camp."

"Perhaps I'll be able to convince her."

"Perhaps. But I don't think the lady is all that happy with me just now."

Ariel laughed. "Was there ever a time she was?"

Clay laughed, too, but his eyes returned to Kitt, who sat there smiling at the children on the lawn.

8

◦◦◦

It was the last night of the week-long house party and the contessa planned to end the affair with a lavish ball. She had invited the gentry for miles around to join the guests at Blair House and decorated the third-story ballroom to resemble a sixteenth-century Italian villa.

Clay smiled as he entered the high-ceilinged, extravagantly ornamented chamber. Great columns rose past ornate stucco moldings to a pale blue ceiling painted with clouds. A giant bas-relief had been fashioned the length of one entire wall, picturing a scene of Zeus rising over Mount Olympus. Heavy scarlet draperies, brightly feathered stuffed birds in gilded cages, and enormous paintings of Grecian ruins lined the walls. The contessa was a wealthy woman and she had obviously spared no expense.

Clay marveled at the extravagance. The *ton* might not consider Anna Falacci exactly first water, but she was a brilliant hostess and completely unlike anyone Clay had ever known.

Except perhaps for Kassandra, he mentally corrected. Both women were the sort who refused to be forced into any particular mold. Perhaps that was the reason the pair had become such good friends.

Clay strolled farther into the room on his way to join the noisy crowd of guests, his gaze unconsciously searching for the woman who consumed far too many of his thoughts. They hadn't spoken since the night he had run into her on the stairs, and then only briefly. Since the night he had kissed her, she had continued to avoid him.

"I see you finally made it." The familiar voice drew his attention. Carrying a stemmed crystal goblet of champagne, his father walked up beside him. "I thought perhaps you had decided to spend your last night at Blair House in company with your mistress."

Clay cocked a dark brown eyebrow. "If you're speaking of Elizabeth, the two of us are merely friends."

"Very close friends, I gather."

"Actually, our association has come to a rather final end."

This time it was the duke's identically shaped, dark brown, silver-tinged eyebrow that went up. "How is that?"

"It seems Elizabeth has developed some odd notion that I'm interested in another woman. Since I can't abide a jealous female—particularly when her accusations are completely unfounded—I thought it best to end our somewhat dubious affair."

"So who is she?"

Annoyance filtered through him. "Dammit, I just told you—there isn't anyone. Or more appropriately, no one in particular, though I'll admit, with Liz no longer available, I could use a little female companionship."

"You're saying there is no other woman who has caught your fancy?"

"None in particular."

"Not even Kassandra Wentworth?"

A muscle tightened in Clay's jaw. Kitt had definitely caught his fancy. She was all he'd been able to think about since their return from the Gypsy camp. How was it his father always read him so well?

The duke flicked a crumb from the folds of his wide white stock. "I'm not a fool, Clayton. I've seen the way you watch her. You look like a starving man gazing at a banquet. She's been avoiding you, of course, but that only proves how strongly she is attracted to you."

Ariel had said that as well. Clay had wondered before if that might be exactly the truth. "What's your point?"

"My point is this—if you're that enthralled with the chit, why don't you simply marry her? You're in need of a wife. Kitt would make you a very good one."

Clay plucked a brandy off a footman's silver tray, using the time to gather his thoughts. His father had pressed him twice before. For whatever reason, Rathmore wanted this match. He lifted the crystal snifter and inhaled the pungent scent, assessing the gleam in his father's golden eyes.

"How much is it worth to you?" He didn't need his father's money, but the duke didn't know that. He had always seen Clay as his shiftless, rakehell son. Perversely, Clay had continued to let him believe it. He had no intention of telling him the truth now or anytime in the future.

The gleam in his father's eyes grew speculative and even more pronounced. "Name your price."

A month ago, he wouldn't have considered it. He

didn't want a wife and especially not one as troublesome as Kassandra Wentworth. Now he thought, why not? It was past time he married. He wanted sons, and Kitt was obviously good with children. It might be nice to come home to a warm, willing woman instead of an empty house.

He would have to be a bit more circumspect in regard to his mistresses, but aside from that . . .

And the fact was he wanted her. Damn, did he want her. Let his father think the idea was his. The truth was Clay had been considering the notion for some time, perhaps even before he realized it himself. Since the night he had watched her in the Gypsy camp, he couldn't get the thought out of his head.

He swirled the liquor in his glass, enjoying the game he played with the man who had sired him. "You want me to name a price? All right. Fifty thousand pounds."

Rathmore rubbed a hand over his chin, a gesture Clay also favored. "Quite a sum." Though his father had an older, legitimate son, the two of them were nothing at all alike. Perhaps that was the reason it hurt so much that the duke refused to grant Clay his rightful name.

Rathmore studied him closely, trying to read his purposely bland expression. "It won't be easy, you know. She may not accept you."

That was a gross understatement. "You let me worry about that."

"All right, then. If you are successful, on the day you marry Kitt Wentworth, you'll receive a bank draft for fifty thousand pounds."

Clay extended a hand. "Done."

Rathmore smiled with a sense of satisfaction. "A

mere fifty thousand? To see my wayward son wed and happily settled, I would have paid twice that amount."

A corner of Clay's mouth edged up. "I would have done it for half."

Something sparkled in the duke's dark eyes. Over the rim of his glass, Clay caught sight of Kitt Wentworth, walking off the dance floor on the arm of the aging Lord Oxnard. She laughed at something the older man said and the husky sound floated toward him across the ballroom.

Clay thought of the challenge he had just undertaken and anticipation pulsed through him. She would fight him—every step of the way. But sooner or later he would have her.

He set the brandy snifter down on a polished mahogany table. "If you'll excuse me, Your Grace. I believe her ladyship may require a dancing partner. Perhaps it is time I got started on our little business venture."

The duke lifted his glass in mock salute. "As they say, there is no time like the present."

Clay couldn't agree with him more. He loved a challenge. Bringing Kitt Wentworth to heel would be far more than that.

He imagined her delectable little body spread beneath him. He thought of kissing the beautiful breasts that had taunted him from beneath her red silk Gypsy blouse. Clay smiled as he strode toward the dance floor.

Now that his decision was made, his goal crystal clear, he couldn't wait to begin his pursuit.

It was one of the most lavish balls that Kitt had ever attended, and she was enjoying herself. She danced a country dance with Lord Oxnard, then a roundel with the Frenchman, Maxmillian Dupree. A few feet away, Ariel danced with Justin, while Anna partnered Ford Constantine, Marquess of Landen.

Landen was a handsome man, tall and distinguished, his blond hair prematurely edged with a faint trace of silver, though he was no older than his mid-thirties. He was a widower, she knew, with two sons a little older than Tonio and Izzy. The marquess was intelligent and forthright, and determined in his seduction of Anna.

Kitt could have told him it was hopeless. Anna wasn't interested in having an affair. She was still in love with Antonio Pierucci, though he had died of a fever three years past.

"Good evening, my lady."

Kitt glanced up at the familiar voice, a little ripple of heat running over her skin. "Harcourt . . . Good evening."

"I realize your dance card is probably full, but Anna has requested the orchestra play a waltz. Knowing how much you enjoy breaking the rules, I thought you might want to dance it with me."

Her stomach seemed to float up under her ribs. Harcourt wanted to waltz with her. She remembered the way he had held her in the darkness outside the Gypsy camp and couldn't seem to catch her breath.

"You do waltz, don't you? Someone as dedicated to flying in the face of Society as you must surely have learned so scandalous a dance."

He was smiling, enjoying himself. She should have found it annoying, but somehow she didn't. "Actually, I learned to waltz when I was in Italy. Anna taught me. She loves to waltz."

"What about you?"

"I love it, too."

His smile grew wider, brighter. Such a devastating smile. "I had no doubt that you would."

He took her arm before she had actually agreed, laced it through his, and led her out among the small group of people brave enough to participate in a dance that was still regarded as indecent by most of the *ton*.

The orchestra struck up the notes and Clay took her in his arms. She could smell his cologne, feel the texture of his navy blue tailcoat beneath her fingers. Her heart kicked up. She thought of his kiss, a rough, masculine kiss that should have repelled her and hadn't.

They stood there for several moments, waiting for the music to begin, his big hand warm where it wrapped around her fingers. He was tall and well proportioned, thick through the chest and shoulders but narrow in the hips, and as the music started, amazingly graceful. He swept her into the dance and her feet picked up the beat as if they had danced together a thousand times.

"You're very good at this," he said, their feet moving in perfect unison. "But then I knew you would be—I've seen you dance before."

A warm flush rose in her cheeks. He had seen her—dancing half-naked around the Gypsy fire. His eyes said he clearly recalled.

Kitt glanced away, certain what a man like Clayton Harcourt would think of such behavior, suddenly wishing the waltz would end.

"I should very much like to see your drawings."

Her gaze jerked back to his face. "What?"

"The drawings you made of the camp. I would love to see what you've done."

"I thought you didn't approve my going out there."

"I never said that. I didn't approve your going out there *alone.*"

They made a sweeping turn in perfect rhythm. "What was I supposed to do? If I had mentioned it, someone would have stopped me."

"Perhaps. Next time come to me. Now that I've discovered your passion for drawing, perhaps I'll be able to help."

Kitt pondered his words, wondering what there was about him that made her want to trust him. It was foolish beyond measure. The kiss he had taken should have been proof of that. Instead, she thought that at least he had been honest. He wanted her, he had said.

Unfortunately, she didn't want him—or any other man. Not after Westerly. For her, it simply wouldn't work.

She shoved the uncomfortable thoughts away and allowed herself to merely enjoy the dance, closing her eyes as they made another sweeping turn. When she looked at him again, his gaze was fixed on her mouth.

"You were smiling," he said. "You're lovely when you smile."

Something warm slowly blossomed inside her. For the first time she realized that he had drawn her closer. His thigh brushed intimately between her legs, and beneath the bodice of her gold beaded gown her nipples lightly grazed his chest.

A soft ache rose there. Her heart beat too fast and her mouth felt drier than it should have. When the waltz came to an end, she didn't wait for him to lead her off the dance floor, just gave him a nod of thanks and made her way straight to where Ariel stood next to Justin.

"You and Clay dance very well together," Ariel said.

"Thank you," Clay said from over Kitt's shoulder, and her heart took another odd leap. Sweet Jesus, she'd been trying to escape him. Instead, she had neatly trapped herself by joining his two best friends.

"About those sketches . . ." he said to Kitt. "I presume you've finished some of them."

"A few of them, yes."

"As I said, I'd love to see them. What time will you be leaving on the morrow?"

She flicked a glance at Ariel, but it was Justin who answered. "We'll be starting home after luncheon."

"Then how about tomorrow morning . . . say eleven o'clock? I'll wait for you next to the cypress tree in the garden."

Justin arched a thick black brow at Clay while Kitt eyed him with a hint of suspicion.

"I haven't got them finished exactly right. I don't think—"

"You're not ashamed of what you've drawn? I realize the dancing was somewhat erotic, but I never thought you would be afraid to—"

"I'm not ashamed of anything! If you're that determined to see them, I'll bring them down to the garden in the morning as you wish."

Clay's smile held an irritating trace of satisfaction. He made a slight inclination of his head. "I look forward to it, my lady."

One of the men appeared just then, entering the small circle that had felt crowded since the moment of Harcourt's arrival.

"Lady Kassandra?" The physician, Peter Avery, bowed politely over her hand. "I believe this d-dance is ours." His sandy hair gleamed in the candlelight and his smile was warm and bright.

Kitt returned the smile, eager to make her escape. "Yes, I believe it is." She turned to the others. "If you will excuse us . . ." Taking his arm, she flicked a last glance at Clay and saw that he was frowning.

Why that made her smile go wider, Kitt couldn't begin to say.

9

Rising early on the last day of his stay at Blair House, Clay joined Justin in the breakfast room. Over a meal of rich dark coffee, eggs, kidneys, and thin buttered bread, they talked about the ball and the week they had shared with the contessa.

"I found it more enjoyable than I'd imagined," Justin admitted. "And with all the work being done at Greville Hall, it was good for Ariel to get away."

Clay took a sip of his coffee. "You're really happy, aren't you?"

Justin smiled. "More than you'll ever know, and certainly more than I deserve."

That was a load of nonsense. Against all odds, Justin had survived a brutal, loveless childhood to become a hardworking, very successful man, deeply concerned with the welfare of others. He was a devoted husband and a completely loyal friend. He deserved his happiness more than any man Clay had ever known.

"I always thought I would marry," Clay said, "someday in the distant future."

Justin paused in the act of wiping his mouth on a linen napkin. "What is that note I hear in your voice?"

Clay set his gold-rimmed cup back in its saucer. "I didn't mean to broach the subject here, but since we're alone . . ."

"Go on, I'm all ears."

"I believe, in a relatively short period of time, I'm going to be taking the plunge myself."

Justin frowned. "Surely you're not thinking of wedding Elizabeth Watkins? I realize she is beautiful, but there is more to choosing a wife than simply seeking a skillful lover."

Clay laughed softly. "I'll admit I enjoy good bed sport, perhaps more than most, and the lovely young widow is extremely adept, but I'm not a complete and utter fool. No, the lady I have in mind has far more to her credit than just a pretty face."

"Well, don't keep me in suspense. Who is it?"

"Kassandra Wentworth."

Justin nearly choked on the mouthful of coffee he had just taken. "You're not serious."

"Actually, I am. The lady needs a husband. The last time I checked, I remained unattached."

"Kitt doesn't wish to marry. You know her well enough to know that."

"Sometimes what you wish and what is best for you are two very different things. We both know her father's plans, should Kassandra fail to wed. At least with me, she'll be allowed a certain amount of freedom she wouldn't find with someone else."

"Meaning?"

Clay smiled, liking the decision he had come to even more in the fresh light of day. "Kassandra wishes to see things, to learn about life as it really is. I'm willing to show it to her."

"What if she simply refuses your suit?"

"I don't think there's any question that's exactly what she'll do—should I be foolish enough to let her know my plans."

"Let me get this straight. You're going to marry Kitt Wentworth, but you don't intend to ask for her consent. How the devil do you expect—"

"I'm not sure yet. It may require a little help from my friends. Sooner or later, I'll figure it out." Clay stood up from his chair. "Meanwhile, I think it's time I departed." He grinned. "If you recall, I've an appointment with my future betrothed at eleven o'clock in the garden."

Justin didn't smile. He was thinking that his friend must have completely lost his wits. Even if he succeeded in marrying Kassandra, she would probably make his life a living hell.

Or maybe not. Justin watched his friend walk away. It would take a special sort of woman for a smart, virile man like Clay. A simpering little milquetoast would never suit. But a wild, free-spirited creature like Kitt . . .

Perhaps Ariel was right and the two of them would suit very well.

Justin hoped so. Clay deserved to be happy and Kitt did, too. As a boy, Clay had lost his mother too soon and suffered years of loneliness with only a few rare visits from his father. As a man, he had taught himself to be strong and independent, never to count on anyone but himself.

But Justin had discovered the wonder of sharing a life with a woman he loved. He hoped Clay would find that happiness, too.

He wondered what his friend had in mind that could possibly convince Kitt Wentworth to marry him.

Kitt was ready for her meeting with Clay at eleven o'clock, but she waited till eleven-fifteen just to spite him. She hadn't wanted this meeting. She didn't want to show him her work. It was none of his business what she had or hadn't drawn. It galled her the way he was always sticking his nose into her affairs.

Besides, what if he didn't like the sketches? What if he made fun of her as other people had? When she'd been younger, she had foolishly shown them to her cousin Charlie during a visit to his house in the country. She'd been completely humiliated when he burst into laughter.

On another occasion, she'd shown her great-aunt Mildred some sketches she was particularly proud of, drawings of a little beggar boy she had seen near the docks. He was dressed in rags, his face smudged with dirt as he held out a small grubby hand for a coin.

Her aunt had been appalled, of course. "Why, a young lady of quality doesn't notice such things—and she certainly doesn't draw them on paper."

But Clay wasn't her odious old aunt and he had seemed to like her work before. Kitt tucked her portfolio a little tighter beneath her arm, steeling herself for whatever his reaction might be, and continued on into the garden.

She spotted him next to the cypress tree, seated on an ornate wrought-iron bench. He rose at her approach.

"You're late," he said, though he softened it with a smile. "But I suppose it's fashionable for a woman to keep a man waiting."

"I'm scarcely interested in what is or is not in vogue. I didn't want to come at all—as you very well know."

"Then why did you?"

Why had she? She wasn't quite certain herself. "Because I know how annoyingly persistent you can be." She held out the black leather portfolio. "You wanted to see my drawings—here they are."

Clay took the case from her hand. He waited for her to sit down on the bench, then sat down beside her and opened the portfolio on his lap. A picture of the Gypsy leader rested on the top of the stack. Janos, wearing a bandanna around his head, tight black breeches, and a flowing silk shirt, was smiling, making a polite bow of welcome. The next sketch pictured the brown-skinned girls, Dina and Hanka. They were laughing, arms linked together as they raced toward the towering bonfire in the middle of the camp. Another drawing showed the old man who had been playing the odd Gypsy instrument that looked like a small piano.

"Your sketches are wonderful," Clay said, smiling as he studied each one. "I was there, but looking at these, I could imagine exactly what it was like even if I'd never been near the camp."

A feeling of warmth rose inside her. Perhaps this was the real reason she had come. In some deep part of her, she had hoped that Clay would approve. He continued to thumb through the drawings, making comments as he studied each one.

"All that is missing is the color," he said, speaking a thought she'd had more than once. "There were so many vibrant hues—reds, greens, yellows." He glanced up from the drawing he studied. "Why is it you never work in paint?"

Kitt shrugged. "I'm not completely certain. Until I did these, I never really thought about it. I like the force of the black lines against the whiteness of the paper. I like the simplicity and the power."

Clay smiled his approval. "So do I."

"But you're right. In this case I think it would have added an important dimension."

He surveyed a drawing of two laughing children chasing a mongrel dog, flipped to the next sketch and paused, his brows pulling into a frown.

Kitt's gaze followed his and the breath froze in her lungs.

"What's this?" Clay studied the thick black lines slashing violently across the page. Heavy dark clouds roiled on the horizon, gray and leaden with moisture; lightning flashed, the turbulence in the air seemed almost palpable. A torrent of rain brutally sliced toward the earth, where a dense garden grew in wild abandon. Above the scene, a pair of cold, unfeeling eyes stared down with malevolent force.

"Kitt?"

Dear God, she had forgotten the drawing was there, buried among the rest. She wanted to yank it away from him, to tear it into tiny pieces and make it disappear.

"It-it's nothing. Just . . . just something I was playing with." *After I ran into Stephen Marlow on the terrace.*

After Westerly's appearance dredged up all the old painful memories, the awful self-loathing. The drawing had been a cleansing, a means of helping her to forget. The pictures were always very much the same, a tool she had used dozens of times in the past four years.

"I have to say it isn't my favorite," Clay said. "It seems awfully violent, or am I reading it wrong?"

She snatched it away just then, along with the rest of the sketches. "I told you, it was merely a bit of doodling, nothing of any importance." She straightened the drawings in the case, closed the portfolio, and tucked it back under her arm.

"I'm afraid it's time I went in. I-I have some packing to finish upstairs."

That was a lie—Tibby had finished the job hours ago—and she wasn't a very good liar, which Clay seemed to know.

But she didn't like the way he was looking at her, as if she were keeping a secret and he wanted to know what it was.

"All right," he said. "I'll see you back to the house."

Kitt stepped away from him. "There's really no need. I can find—"

"Lady Kassandra?" A red-liveried footman hurried down the gravel path, his shoes crunching noisily, silver bagwig askew. "I'm sorry to bother you, my lady, but a messenger just arrived with a letter for you from London." He handed her a folded piece of foolscap. "He says it's extremely urgent."

Kitt broke the wax seal on the paper. Recognizing her stepmother's thin, blue-inked scrawl, she quickly scanned the letter.

Kassandra,
Your father has taken ill. Please return home in
all haste. Your stepmother, Lady Stockton.

"I hope nothing untoward has happened," Clay said, noting her worried expression.

"It's from Judith. My father is ill. I must return to London at once."

Clay's expression darkened. "I'll see you home. Your maid is with you, I believe. She can act as chaperon."

For once she agreed. She was worried about her father and she needed to reach London quickly. "Thank you. I'll go up and collect my trunks. I'll be down in just a few minutes."

His mouth curved knowingly. "I thought you hadn't finished packing yet."

Kitt lifted her chin. "I'm sure my maid will have finished in my absence." Sweeping past him, she hurried along the pathway to the house. Damn him. He was the most annoying man she had ever known—and she would be stuck with him all the way back to London.

Fortunately, the city was little more than an hour's ride away. Surely she could tolerate Harcourt's company for long enough to reach her father. Her mind ran over Judith's brief message, which said nothing of what illness had befallen him.

Kitt prayed that he would be all right.

10

~~~

The ride back to London seemed interminable. All the way there Harcourt's golden, heavy-lidded gaze swept over her again and again. Kitt spent an equal amount of time trying *not* to look at Clay, accomplishing the task with little success.

Aside from his chiseled good looks and solidly masculine build, there was something about him, a confidence, an air of authority she had witnessed in few other men. That he was the son of a duke was obvious in every word, every movement, every self-assured gesture, yet according to Ariel, Clay had been simply reared in a small country house at the edge of the city, a residence paid for by his father.

His mother had been the duke's mistress, a woman who had loved her son but died when Clay was fourteen. In the years after that, he spent most of his time in boarding school, then on to Oxford, the place where he and Justin had become close friends.

Where his authoritative manner had come from,

she couldn't say. It seemed there was simply no denying his aristocratic blood.

Whatever there was about him, his presence always disturbed her. Her heart beat faster when he touched her. Her breath caught when he smiled. How was it possible? Worse yet, how could it happen with a womanizing rogue like Clay?

"We're arrived," he said, breaking into her thoughts as the carriage rolled to a halt in front of her Maddox Street town house. A footman opened the door and Clay climbed down, reached up, and helped Kitt make the descent.

He escorted her inside, though she would rather he had simply departed. Judith waited for them at the bottom of the stairs in the entry.

"It's about time you got here," she said. "Your father has been asking for you and where have you been? Off galavanting over the countryside on one of your reckless adventures."

Kitt didn't remind her she had only just received the message and returned to the city straightaway. Instead, she simply asked, "What's happened? How sick is he?"

"The physician just left. He's afraid it might be the pneumonia. I thought it best if you were here just in case."

Kitt swallowed back a lump of fear and felt the reassuring pressure of Clay's hand on her shoulder.

"Would you like me to go up with you?"

"No . . . no, I'll be all right. Thank you for bringing me home."

"I'll stop by tomorrow to see how he is."

Kitt just nodded. Turning away, she lifted her skirts and raced up the stairs, worry for her father keeping her from thinking overly of Clay.

The room was dark and stuffy, the windows tightly closed, all of the curtains drawn. Her father lay sleeping in the middle of his big featherbed. She could barely make out his features in the shadowy dimness of the musty room. Kitt sat down in a chair beside the bed, afraid to wake him yet desperate to know how he fared.

She heard him stir, then he sat up in the bed. "What the devil—? Kassandra? Is that you?"

"Yes, Father. I'm right here."

He sighed into the darkness. "I told your stepmother your presence here wasn't needed. I told her to leave you with your friends in the country. I see she has had her way in this, as she seems to be doing more and more."

Kitt didn't know whether to be happy that his illness didn't seem as serious as she had imagined or upset that he hadn't really wanted her to come home.

"I'm sure she was worried about you, Father. She knew I would want to help take care of you."

He sat up straighter in the bed, his stocking cap tilted over his left ear. "Nonsense. The doctor says I'll be up and about in a couple of days. Some sort of ague, nothing to worry about. But now that you're returned, perhaps it's for the best."

Up and about in a couple of days? That wasn't what Judith had said, but perhaps it was good that her stepmother had been so concerned. She sat with her father for a while, convinced him to open the draperies and let in a little fresh air, then returned downstairs to his study to fetch his gold-rimmed spectacles and the book that he had been reading.

"Thank God you are home. I am exhausted from running errands for your father." Judith blew a strand of blond hair out of her eyes and sank down in a nearby chair. "It's time you assumed a little responsibility around here. One would think a girl your age would have better things to do than run around on some silly escapade."

"I've never shirked my duties in this household. And as for my 'escapades'—as you call them—you are the one who drives me away. If you will recall, it was your idea to ship me off to Italy last year. Until my father fell ill, you were equally glad of my recent stay in the country." She eyed her plump blond stepmother with a hint of suspicion. "I think I'm beginning to understand your sudden desire for my return. My father is bedridden and you're tired of taking care of him."

"Your father can be quite difficult at times, as you well know. I'm sick of sitting at his bedside for hours on end, trying to keep him entertained. I needed some help and since you are his daughter, it's your duty to assist me."

Kitt just sighed. Judith might be older, but she was spoiled and pampered in a way Kitt never had been. "I'll be happy to help you, Judith. As you said, he is my father."

Judith made a harrumphing sound, turned, and stalked out of the room. Kitt glanced toward the door with a sinking feeling. Her father was improving, but he was still sick. She couldn't possibly leave him.

Once again, she was back in her cage.

Seated at the desk in the study of his town house, Clay closed the file he had been reading, information on a run-down silk factory at the edge of the city that might be purchased cheaply and refitted to manufacture cotton and wool, a far more profitable business.

It was a large undertaking, but more and more Clay found the business world intriguing. He and Justin worked well together and their endeavors were making them extremely wealthy men. For now, however, he had a more personal matter to attend.

Leaving his study, he strode down the hall and out the front door of his town house. Climbing aboard the smart, high-seat phaeton that awaited him on the street, a snappy little rig he often drove round the city, he headed for Viscount Stockton's town house in Maddox Street, a place he had frequented several times already this week.

What had started as concern for Kitt's ailing father—who, Clay had discovered, was already well on the mend long before Kitt had been summoned from the country—had turned into a means to further his marriage campaign.

As he could have guessed, after a week inside the house, Kitt was chafing at the bit to get out. With her father's help—and he was fairly certain he could elicit the viscount's aid—the chance he had been waiting for just might be at hand.

Sending a note of his visit ahead, he arrived at the house, left the phaeton in the care of a footman, and climbed the front porch stairs. He rapped the shiny brass knocker and immediately the door swung open.

"Good afternoon, sir," the butler said. "His lordship is expecting you. He awaits you in the drawing room."

The drawing room? Clay had expected the old man to milk his infirmity to the very limit. Perhaps this *was* the limit, he thought with a chuckle, recalling the hostility between the man's wife and daughter, the women who were currently taking care of him. "I'm glad to hear he's feeling better."

From the look of the viscount as Clay stepped through the drawing room door, his health was indeed greatly improved. His color had returned and a smile lit his face. Clay's propositon, which would finally see his errant daughter married, seemed to rouse him even more.

An hour after his arrival, Clay had successfully concluded his business. Intending merely to pay his respects, he went in search of Kassandra. As he approached the butler to summon her, he spotted her descending the stairs. Kitt stopped when she saw him, looking as if she wanted to turn and run.

"Your father is doing much better," Clay said casually, surveying her with undisguised interest, liking the way she looked in her simple mint green gown, her fiery hair swept up in pretty curls.

"I'm happy to say that he is." Lovely as she was, he couldn't help noticing the faint purple shadows beneath her eyes and the pallor of her usually robust complexion.

"What about you, my lady? Somehow I get the impression you're not faring nearly as well."

Her chin inched up. "What makes you think there is anything wrong with me?"

"Perhaps the fact that your hands are currently balled into fists and your pretty lips tight as a purse string. Things not going well with your stepmother?"

Kitt sighed. "Things never go well with Judith."

"And I imagine—knowing you as I do—you are feeling a little confined."

"More than a little. Between Judith's haranguing and Father's endless demands, if I don't get out of this house very shortly I swear I'll go out of my mind."

Inwardly he smiled, hearing exactly the words he had hoped for.

"Anna is back in town," he said blandly, beginning to bait the trap he had worked so hard to devise.

"I know. She is staying at the Hotel Clarendon. She stopped by to check on my father when she first arrived in the city." Another wistful sigh. "I should love to visit her, but of course Father would never permit it."

"That's too bad . . . especially considering the guest she's entertaining tonight."

"Guest? Who is it?"

"Not really a who, more of a what. A party of Russian officers have arrived in the city. They brought a bonafide Russian Cossack along with their retinue."

"Yes, I read that in the *Morning Chronicle.* You're saying he is going to be at Anna's?"

"Not the hotel. She's taken a pavilion at Vauxhall Gardens for the affair. It's a shame you won't be able to attend. The man would certainly make an interesting study for some of your drawings."

Something sparked in the green of her eyes, as he had guessed it would. "A Cossack—I should really love to see him. But Father . . . you know how he is about my friendship with Anna. Father claimed he was too ill to receive her even though she had traveled all the way to the city to see him, and Judith was barely civil. There is no way they would allow me to attend."

"That's unfortunate."

"Yes, it is." But he could see her mind already whirling, spinning with ideas Clay could read all too well. Damn, he wasn't sure whether to be elated that his plan might actually work—or turn her over his knee for even thinking of taking such a risk.

For now, it didn't matter. If she sneaked out of the house tonight, he would be waiting. He'd make sure she got to her destination safely. Once they were married, he'd put an end to her dangerous nighttime excursions. If there was someplace she wanted to go, he would take her. The rest of the time, he'd keep her busy in his bed.

His body tightened, began a dull throbbing inside his breeches. Dammit, now that he had made up his mind to marry her, he wanted it over and done.

"The afternoon progresses," he said. "I've a number of things to do before I go home so I had better be on my way. Perhaps I'll stop by on the morrow, tell you about the Cossack."

Kitt just nodded. She wasn't interested in his impressions of the Russian. She wanted to see for herself.

Clay smiled as he turned and walked away.

Kitt waited until the last lamp in the house had been extinguished, then waited a little while longer. Anna's parties lasted well into the night. She wasn't in jeopardy of missing her chance to meet the Cossack.

Dressed once more in her cousin Charlie's borrowed breeches, waistcoat, and coat, her hair piled up beneath a high beaver hat, she quietly shoved open her bedchamber window and climbed over the sill. Ignoring the distance to the ground that always made her dizzy, she took a firm grip on a stout limb of the sycamore that grew next to the house.

She was getting good at this, she thought as she made her way easily down to solid ground, her feet slipping only once in the borrowed shoes. Ducking along the hedgerows of the small informal garden at the rear of the town house, she slipped off into the darkness behind the mews.

She was on her way without a hitch, but she wasn't a fool. She knew it was dangerous to be prowling the city alone this late at night, even disguised as a man. Clay had convinced her of that. Then again, the disguise had kept her safe before and some risks were simply worth taking.

Still, she vowed, *this is the very last time.*

And she meant it. She would indulge herself this one final night, then resign herself to the female costume—and more reserved behavior—for the rest of her days.

But seeing a real live Cossack—"a wild, noble warrior from a glorious, far-distant land," the *Chronicle* had called him—was definitely worth the risk.

Making her way down the alley behind the stable, Kitt went in search of an available hack. It took longer to find one than she'd expected. By the time she saw an empty conveyance parked at the side of the road, she had wandered into an area of shabby, run-down tenant houses, boarded-up buildings, and dirty-windowed alehouses complete with drunken patrons staggering around out in front.

She sighed with relief when she climbed inside the rented hack and asked the driver to take her to Vauxhall. Though she had only been there a couple of times, she remembered the place very well: the meandering walkways through tall, verdant foliage, the paintings and statues, the classical fountains and façades, the orchestra music that softly filled the night air.

Once she reached the gardens, abandoned the carriage, and paid the fee to get in, it was easy to locate Anna's party. A large pavilion on the far side of the gardens overflowed with a crush of guests: members of the nobility, important dignitaries and their wives; even the lord mayor's carriage sat out front.

Banking on the fact the affair was being held outside and she wouldn't have to remove her hat, she approached the entrance to the pavilion. As Kitt had guessed, an attendant carefully checked each arrival against the names on the guest list. Hers wasn't there, of course, but she had no doubt that she could get in.

"Buena sera," she said in Italian to a short, balding fellow wearing wire-rimmed spectacles. "Marco Benvenudo," she continued in thickly accented English, "at your service. I am recently arrived from Rome, a cousin of the contessa. Since she is not expecting me, please be so good as to let her know that I am here."

She hadn't really meant to attend the party dressed as a slightly rumpled young Italian nobleman. She had thought to bring a gown and change into it in one of the ladies' retiring rooms once she reached Vauxhall. But she would surely be recognized and sooner or later, her father would discover she had been there. He would be furious and God only knew what punishment he would devise for her this time.

The more she had thought about it, the idea of simply remaining in what she thought of as her "masculine armor" began to appeal more and more. She spoke enough Italian to get by. And if she kept her accent thick enough, few people would try to talk to her.

She could simply meet the Cossack, enjoy herself a little, and go back to the town house.

The attendant excused himself and returned a few minutes later, followed closely by Anna, who broke out in a peal of laughter when she realized who it was.

"Mìo cugino!" It is so good to see you. It has been far too long, no?"

Kitt bit back a grin. "*Sì, sì,* far too long for certain."

They spoke Italian for a moment, Kitt explaining why she was once more dressed in men's clothes. Aside from Anna's worry that she had traveled the streets alone, she was happy that Kitt had come.

"Well, now that you are here," Anna said, "you might as well meet our guest. You wish to draw him, of course. That is why you have come tonight, no?"

"I thought he would make an interesting subject."

"And you will soon see that you were right." As Anna led her forward, Kitt saw that the Cossack was nothing at all as she had imagined, and no thirdhand description could have given her an accurate portrait of him.

He was tall and spare to the point of thin, with a long black beard, skin like leather, and shrewd black eyes deeply wrinkled at the corners. He wore baggy pants that hung down over rough leather boots, and an odd felt hat with a rolled-up, woolly brim. A wide belt was strapped around his waist and another slashed across his chest like a bandolier.

He stood perfectly rigid, like one of the king's guards, and in one weathered hand he carried a ten-foot lance.

"His name is Zemlanowin," Anna whispered as they approached. "They say he has killed more than thirty Frenchmen with that vicious-looking weapon of his." She turned and smiled at Kitt. "Shall I introduce you?"

Kitt shook her head. It was one thing to pretend to be a man, it was another to fool one who looked as astute as the Cossack. "I think I should rather just draw him. Believe me, I shan't forget what he looks like."

Anna laughed. "No, I do not suppose that you will."

"Good evening, contessa." The deep, rough, honey-coated voice rolled toward her from a few feet away. Kitt paled at the sight of Clayton Harcourt standing like an oak tree in front of her. Though he spoke to Anna, his hard gaze bored into Kitt. "I'm afraid I haven't had the pleasure of meeting your young friend."

Anna's speculating glance slid from one of them to the other, and she worked to suppress a smile. "This is my cousin, Marco Benvenudo—the future Count Firenzo," she threw in just for fun. Kitt fought to hold back a burst of laughter.

"Is it, indeed?" Apparently Harcourt didn't see the humor. There was iron in his voice. It was obvious he knew exactly who she was, surmised she must have traveled to the Gardens alone, and he was furious about it. "For a moment I thought it might be some reckless, hotheaded young woman who hasn't the good sense to know when she is putting herself in danger."

Anna began discreetly backing away. "I believe I will leave the two of you to sort this all out." Ignoring Kitt's silent plea for help, Anna turned and walked back to her guests. Kitt looked up into hard, dark brown eyes.

"What the devil do you think you're doing?" His tone was implacable, his arrogance goading her temper.

"What does it look like I'm doing? I came to see the Cossack. You knew I wanted to come. I told you so this afternoon."

"You also said your father wouldn't allow it."

"Exactly so. Which is why I had to sneak out, why I was forced to dress the way I did."

"And also the reason you traveled through the dark city streets by yourself? I hoped you had learned your lesson, but I see that you have not. You are asking for trouble, my girl, and sooner or later you're going to get it."

A faint tremor went through her. She knew he was telling the truth. "As usual it is none of your business, but since you're so interested, this is the last time I plan to go out dressed as a man."

"Is that so?"

"Yes, that is so. Once I get home—"

"If you think you're going back through the streets by yourself, you're wrong. You have seen your Cossack. Make your farewells to Anna. I'm taking you home before someone besides me figures out who you are."

Kitt started to argue, but Harcourt had a point. Someone might discover who she was. The gossipmongers would have a field day. She couldn't afford to get caught.

But let him take her home? She had hailed a hack to get here but it hadn't been easy. It was later in the evening now, well past midnight and even more risky. Still, she didn't like the notion of being alone with him.

She summoned a too-bright smile. "Thank you for the offer, but I don't need your help. I got here on my own. I'll find my own way back."

"Like hell you will. I'm taking you home—if I have to drag you every step of the way. Now unless you wish to make a scene—which your father will undoubtedly hear about—I'd advise you to head for the exit."

"What about Anna?"

"You had your chance, now get going."

Her jaw clamped. She hesitated for several seconds. With a long-suffering sigh, she turned and started walking toward the gate. Harcourt's heavy footfalls sounded on the gravel path behind her. She didn't doubt for a moment that he would drag her home just as he said and she didn't want any more trouble with her father. Besides, she didn't really look forward to traveling home by herself, and she wasn't actually afraid of him. He was a friend of Ariel's, a friend of her father's. He wouldn't dare do anything to harm her.

At least she hoped he wouldn't as she walked beside him through the darkened pathways of Vauxhall Gardens. When they reached the street, he took hold of her hand and started dragging her away at such a rapid pace her hat flew off. She jerked free, ran back and scooped it up, hurried to catch up to where he waited.

His carriage was parked a short distance from the corner. He whistled and the driver snapped the reins, guiding a pair of beautiful matched bay horses up in front of them. Harcourt opened the door and practically shoved her in.

"Maddox Street," he called up to the coachman from the bottom of the stairs. "Lord Stockton's town house."

Kitt jumped as he slammed the door and took a place opposite her in the carriage. At least he was staying a respectable distance away.

"I hope you're satisfied," she said. "What must Anna be thinking?"

"Anna will know I have taken you home. And as far as being satisfied—" He bit back the rest of the sentence, looking as if it took great restraint. "I won't be *satisfied*," he ground out, "until you are safely returned."

Kitt straightened on the seat. "Need I remind you, I can't just simply stroll back inside through the front door?"

"Fine. I'll have the coachman drive round back. You may break your fool neck climbing the tree outside your window."

"How did you know there was a tree—"

His hard look cut her off. "How else would you have managed to get out?"

She said nothing more as the carriage rolled through the streets, and neither did Harcourt. Just before they reached the town house, he ordered the driver to turn down the alley. A few minutes later the conveyance rolled to a halt behind the stable.

"I remind you of your pledge," he said. "This had better be the last time, my lady. No more running around in the middle of the night. Do it again and I swear I will deal with you myself."

"You have no right to order me about. Just who do you think you are?"

"Someone who cares about you, dammit. I told you before, I don't want to see you get hurt."

Someone who cares about you. Her anger evaporated as if it had been struck by a blast of hot air, replaced by an odd little fluttering in her chest. Kitt said no more as Harcourt opened the door to the carriage, climbed down, and helped her to alight. She thought he would simply leave, but instead he walked her along the pathway through the garden over to the sycamore tree that grew outside her window.

"You'll be lucky if you don't fall on your pretty little backside," he grumbled, lifting her up to catch the bottom branch. She started to climb, knowing by now the best places for her feet to find purchase, but the soles of her shoes were slick. Her foot slipped off the branch, and she heard Clay's soft curse.

"Be careful, dammit! Just take your time and—"

"What the devil's going on out here?"

The sound of her father's voice jolted her so badly she lost her grip on the branch above her head. With a muffled yelp, she started to fall, dislodging leaves and cracking small branches as she fought to catch herself, missed, and plunged toward the earth—straight into Clayton Harcourt's waiting arms.

"I thought I told you to be careful," he said dryly, his dark gaze swinging from her to her father, who stormed toward them from across the yard. He was wearing his nightshirt, and his pointed, tasseled nightcap perched lopsided on his head.

"I should have known," he said. "I should have realized you were sneaking out to meet a man. By God, I should have guessed it would be Harcourt."

Her stomach twisted so hard, Kitt felt suddenly sick. Harcourt? Not until pigs could fly. "I wasn't sneaking out to meet anyone. Put me down," she commanded of Clay, who reluctantly set her back on her feet.

Her father turned his fury on Harcourt, his thin arms flapping like a scarecrow. "By God, if this doesn't beat all. You'll do the right thing, my boy—you hear me? You've compromised the girl. Now you're going to marry her."

Kitt blanched at the words, her stomach heaving over in an ominous roll. "Are you insane? I'm not marrying him. I'm not marrying anyone!"

Her father turned away from Clay and focused his

wrath on her. "You'll do exactly as I say, young lady. You'll marry the man, or I'll ship you off to St. Mary's—just as I said. I'll do it this very night. You won't see the light of day for four long years."

Kitt started to tremble. This couldn't be happening. It simply couldn't!

She fixed a beseeching look on the man standing quietly beside her. "Tell him, Clay. Tell him I didn't sneak off to meet you, that nothing happened between us, that you were only giving me a ride back home. Tell him you don't want to m-marry me."

Judith came out crying and wailing just then. "Oh, my God. She's out here with *him*. The biggest rake in London. Dear God, she'll be the ruin of us yet!"

"Quit your sniveling, Judith." Her father's voice sounded a little calmer, and even more certain. "The girl won't ruin anyone. Kassandra is about to become young Harcourt's bride. Isn't that so, my boy?"

"No!" Kitt flicked a glance at Clay. "He doesn't want to marry me and I don't want to marry him. Tell them, Clay, make them understand we weren't doing anything wrong!" Staring past his shoulder, Kitt noticed two of the lamps in the neighbor's house being lit. Gazing up, she recognized the Baroness of Whitelawn peeking down from an upstairs window. Inwardly she winced.

Clay's voice, when he finally spoke, sounded oddly gentle. "Your father's right, love. You've played the game more than once. Tonight you simply lost. It's time you gracefully accepted the fact. Come. Let's go inside where we may be private."

With a last glance at the baroness, now joined at the window by her husband, Kitt woodenly followed her father back into the house, Clay right behind her. They went into the drawing room and her father closed the door.

"All right now—what say you, Harcourt? When will the deed be done?"

To her amazement and no amount of chagrin, Clay didn't hesitate. "As soon as I can obtain a special license . . . no more than a couple of days."

"No . . ." Kitt stared at him in growing horror. "You can't mean it. You don't want to get married any more than I do."

"Perhaps I've changed my mind. Now that I think on it, it doesn't seem such a terrible notion. And the truth is we don't have any choice. I don't wish to become a social pariah any more than you do."

Tears threatened. Her throat closed up, the words she wanted to say locked tight inside. Clay was right. Even if Judith could be trusted to keep her silence— which was a fairly large *if* in itself—the baron and his wife had also seen them. It was one thing to dally with a widow like Lady May and another altogether to compromise an unwed young girl. If she and Clay didn't marry, both of them would be ostracized from all but a few close friends.

Dear God, she was only twenty years old. She didn't want her life to be over. And she wasn't about to spend the next four years saying prayers in some musty old convent.

She looked at Clayton Harcourt, so handsome he took her breath away. He had seen her drawings, seen her dance in the Gypsy camp, yet he had never condemned her. And he had always been protective of her.

Who do you think you are? she had asked him. *Someone who cares about you.*

Though he didn't completely approve of the things she did, in most ways she trusted him more than any man she had ever known.

And yet she couldn't marry him.

It wouldn't be fair to Clay.

"I need to speak to you," she said, forcing the words past dry, brittle lips. "Alone."

Clay cast a glance at her father, who hesitated, then nodded, caught Judith's hand, and tugged her toward the door.

"We'll be right out here," her father warned him.

"We won't be long," Clay promised.

Not long, Kitt thought. Not long at all—once he knew the truth. The thought made her stomach clench into a painful knot.

11

The heavy sliding doors shut with a solid thud as Clay enclosed the two of them in the drawing room. Standing a few feet away, Kitt looked pale and shaken, and for an instant he regretted his all-too-successful scheme.

Then he thought of her fiery spirit, thought of her married to some impoverished noble who cared not a whit about her, or locked away in some thick-walled convent, and believed he was doing the right thing. He studied her taut features, wishing he knew a way to ease her fears.

"Is this really such a shock?" he finally said. "You knew every time you sneaked out of the house there might be consequences." She moistened her lips and he remembered how soft and sweet they had tasted the night he had kissed her. He wanted to do it again.

"That's true, I suppose, but I never imagined anything remotely like this."

"Do you loathe the idea of marrying me so much?"

She shook her head. "It . . . it isn't you . . . exactly. It's just that I don't want to marry anyone at all."

"We could have children, you know. It's obvious how much you enjoy them. You'd like to be a mother, wouldn't you?"

Her mouth softened for a moment. "You know I would. I'd love to have children, but I . . ." Kitt glanced away. "You don't really want to marry me, Clay. We both know that. And even if you did, you won't any-more—once you learn the truth."

His senses went on alert, though he kept his expression bland. "And exactly what truth is that?"

For a moment she didn't answer. He caught the swift rise of tears, then they were gone.

"The truth is, I am not . . . I am no longer pure."

He should have been shocked but he wasn't. He had known there might be consequences to the reckless life she had led, and he had never placed all that high a value on a woman's virginity.

He paused less than a heartbeat. "And you think I am?" Aside from that, he wanted her. More than any woman he could name. "What's happened in the past is unimportant . . . unless, of course, you are telling me you have slept with half the young bucks in the *ton.*"

Her face went utterly pale. "No . . . no, of course not."

"Then the matter is settled. First thing in the morning, I'll make arrangements—"

"You don't . . . don't understand. There is more to it than that. I know there are women who enjoy . . . a . . . a certain intimacy with their husbands, but I am not one of them. I find the act of submission repulsive."

"I see." Considering the lust he felt for her, they were hardly the words he wished to hear.

"If we were to marry," she continued, "it would have to be a marriage of convenience. I wouldn't agree under any other condition."

A marriage of convenience? That was the last thing he wanted. "Sorry, sweeting. No man worth his salt is going to agree to that—least of all me. It's obvious your first encounters were highly unsatisfactory, but it doesn't have to be that way." He picked up a small Dresden statue and examined it without really seeing it. "Since this has all happened so quickly, after we're married, I'll give you some time. We'll take things slowly, get to know each other better. We won't consummate the marriage until you are ready."

Her mouth pinched stubbornly. "I'll never be ready."

Clay set the statue back down on the table, watching her from beneath lowered lids. Her reluctance to accept her place in the marriage bed was an obstacle he hadn't expected. It was possible she was one of those cold, unfeeling women who abhorred sexual contact and always would. But Clay didn't think so. He had seen her dance with the Gypsies, had glimpsed the fire inside her, burning just beneath the surface.

And he was arrogant enough to believe he could fan that untutored spark into a brilliant flame.

"You know I want you. Can you honestly say you're not attracted to me in the least?"

Color washed into her cheeks. Her lashes fluttered down to cover her pretty green eyes. "There's no denying you're handsome. You're intelligent and when you're not being arrogant and overbearing, you can be extremely charming."

Not exactly high words of praise, but he supposed they would have to do. "What about when I kissed you? Did you find it repulsive?"

She glanced away, the blush growing brighter on her cheeks. "I should have. I thought that I would, but I..."

He closed the distance between them, reached out, and lifted her chin. "Close your eyes." Kitt just stared at him. "Go on, do as I say."

She did so warily, but finally she obeyed. Leaning forward, he very softly settled his mouth over hers. He wasn't prepared for the heat that jolted through him, the fierce rush of desire. Her lips were as smooth and soft as satin. God, she was the sweetest thing he'd ever tasted. His body hardened. He deepened the kiss, but only a little, then he gently ended the contact and took a step away.

"What about now?"

Unconsciously, her fingers came up to her lips. He noticed that they trembled. Her eyes looked big and uncertain, but she had always been unfailingly honest and he was counting on that honesty now.

"Not . . . not repulsive. You have a very nice mouth."

He let the comment pass, though it made him hard all over again. "All right." He turned away, hoping she wouldn't notice the stiff ridge in his breeches. "If you'll agree to marry me, I give you my word I won't do anything to you that you don't want me to do."

She eyed him warily. "I don't believe you. You'll want more from me than a kiss."

"Yes, I will. When the time is right. But I've never lied to you, Kitt. And I'm not a man who breaks his word. I won't do anything that frightens you or that you might find repulsive. All I ask is that you keep an open mind and trust me enough to let me guide you. If I succeed, you'll have the children you want and a certain amount of independence. And I'll have a wife who is a woman in every sense of the word."

Something moved across her features, a wistfulness

that touched him somehow. She wasn't opposed to the idea. In fact, her expression said she wanted very much to succeed at being a wife and mother.

"What if . . . what if I fail? What if I am simply . . . different from other women?"

"Then at least you'll have the freedom you've yearned for so fiercely. A married woman leads a far freer existence than a young unmarried girl."

"And what will you have?"

What indeed? "A very sizable dowry, for one thing," he said wryly. Not that he gave a damn about the money. Marrying her had nothing to do with that. In fact, he wasn't exactly sure why he was so determined to have her. "Think about it, Kitt. What do you have to lose?"

He watched as she weighed the possibilities, recognized the exact moment she decided that the risk was worth taking.

"Are you certain, Clay? Are you sure you're willing to gamble so heavily on your future?"

The edge of his mouth curved up. "We've played for high stakes before, love. I won then. I'm going to win now."

He thought that under different circumstances, she might have smiled. Instead she merely looked resigned. "All right. If you're certain you won't regret it, I'll marry you."

Would he regret it? He wasn't really sure. At the moment all he felt was a strong sense of relief. "As I said, I'll see to the license first thing in the morning. We'll be married as soon as I can manage to get things arranged."

Kitt just nodded. She looked as pale as alabaster, as rigid as a small marble statue.

Clay thought of the challenge he had just undertaken, far greater than the victory that he had just won.

The sooner we're married, the better, he thought, trying not to imagine the wedding night he wasn't going to have, shifting against the uncomfortable heaviness in his groin.

In time it would happen. Clay had no doubt about that. He remembered the feel of her, the way her soft lips had trembled under his. He wanted to taste her again, to feel the fiery passion he was sure he would find locked inside her.

Soon, he told himself. Soon he would have her.

Inwardly he prayed he could crack the marble statue and warm himself with the fire inside.

12

⚜

Today was the day she would wed. Kitt never thought it would happen. At least she hadn't thought so since the day she turned sixteen.

Remembering the eve of her birthday brought a sharp, stinging memory of the party her father had thrown in her honor at Greenlawn, their country estate half day's journey from the city. What had started as the most glorious night of her life had ended in pain and humiliation, in stark disillusionment and endless self-loathing.

It was a memory too painful to recall, and as she had done for the past four years, Kitt ruthlessly shoved it away.

Instead she turned at the sound of a persistent rap and saw the door open. Two familiar female faces peered in through the crack, then Ariel and Anna laughed and rushed into the room.

"We wanted to see you before you went downstairs." Ariel enfolded her in a warm, exuberant hug. "We wanted you to know how happy we are for you."

"*Sì, cara.* You have chosen well. Your Clayton is a very good man. He will make you happy. You will see."

Sudden tears burned behind her eyes. "Oh, Anna. I didn't choose him and he didn't choose me. Clay is making the best of this, but I'm sure he's no happier than I am." Except for the money, of course. Perhaps it would be enough for him. Kitt thought it only fair he receive something in return for the trouble she had caused him.

Anna's smile briefly faltered. "You must not believe that. Your Clayton—he is not a man to be forced to do something he does not wish to do. For months I have seen the way he watches you. He has wanted you for a very long time. Tonight you will see."

Kitt suppressed a shiver. She hadn't told her friends about the bargain she and Clay had made. Though she could talk to them about most anything, the intimacies of the marriage bed were simply too personal. And she was ashamed that she couldn't find pleasure, as she was sure her friends did, in what she saw only as a debasing, humiliating act.

"You look beautiful," Ariel said, surveying the high-waisted cream silk gown she wore, a present from her father. It was trimmed in ivory lace with tiny seed pearls sewn across the bodice. "I used to wonder if perhaps you and Clay might not suit—if the two of you could ever get past your stubbornness. Now I can see I was right."

Kitt tried to smile. "I just wished he hadn't been forced into this."

Ariel gripped her hand. "Anna is right. No one could force Clay to marry you—not if he didn't want to."

Perhaps not. And yet in denying him her body, she

was cheating him out of the thing he wanted most—assuming he kept his word.

Kitt shuddered to think of the night ahead. Her wedding night. Would Clay keep his pledge? Or would he claim his husbandly rights and force her into his bed? Her hands trembled. She pressed them into the folds of her wedding gown.

"Do not be nervous, *cara*. In a short time this will all be over and you and your husband will be off to your new home."

Her new home. The place she would spend the night with Clay. A wave of nausea swept over her, making her forehead bead with perspiration.

"Time to go," Ariel said, taking her hand. "Everyone is waiting for you downstairs."

She walked between her two friends, moving on legs that felt wrapped in lead. At the bottom of the stairs, Clay stood waiting, so handsome that for a moment she simply stood there staring. He was a remarkably imposing man, taller than any of the other guests except Justin, who waited in the drawing room to act as his best man.

The smile he gave her was warm and somehow reassuring. "Come, love. This will all be over soon."

Kitt swallowed and continued down the stairs. Clay took her shaking hand and rested it on the sleeve of his dark brown, velvet-collared tailcoat. She took a firm hold on his arm as he led her to the door of the drawing room and handed her over to her father.

"There's no need to worry," Clay promised. "Everything's going to be all right."

Kitt just nodded. Gripping her father's arm, she watched Clay walk over to the makeshift altar. He turned toward her, waiting for her to join him there.

The drawing room looked lovely. Judith had done a wonderful job of decorating. She had always been good at that, if little else, and she was undoubtedly happy to be rid of her troublesome stepdaughter, as she had dreamed of for so long. Bouquets of white roses had been done up with wide apricot satin bows. Clusters of roses hung at the end of the row of chairs where the few guests in attendance had already taken their seats. In the drawing room across the hall, an elegant buffet would soon be laid out, a lavish wedding feast Kitt would pretend to eat but barely be able to swallow.

Her father walked her to the altar and gave her into Clay's care. A few feet away, the vicar stood waiting, his long white satin robes gleaming in the light of the silver candelabra on the table in front of him.

"Shall we begin?" he asked, looking down at the notes he had placed in the open Wentworth family Bible, his aging hands blue-veined and thin.

The question required no answer and the ceremony started, but after the initial prayer and the "Dearly beloved . . . ," Kitt barely heard the words. It took a nudge from Clay to make the correct responses at the appropriate times, about which he seemed none too pleased. After what might have been seconds or hours, she wasn't quite sure which, the wedding came to an end.

"By the powers vested in me by the holy Church, I pronounce that you, Kassandra, and you, Clayton, are now man and wife. What God has joined together, let no man put asunder." The vicar turned to Clay. "You may kiss your bride."

She trembled when he drew her into his arms, yet his hold was light, nonthreatening, just enough to forestall her urge to run. As he bent his head, he whispered, "Close your eyes," as he had done before.

Embarrassed that she had forgotten, she complied.

It was a gentle kiss, as warm but softer than she recalled, and at the same time possessive. Tender, yet somehow insistent, and just as before, not the least unpleasant. She had thought the kiss would be brief and yet it went on and on, claiming her in some way. She found herself swaying against him, leaning into that rock-hard chest, clinging to his powerful shoulders.

When she looked up at him, his eyes were dark, his smile full of triumph and what she feared was anticipation.

The smile she mustered in return was weak and uncertain, the future she faced more nebulous than any she could have imagined. Turning to their guests, she received congratulations from her father and Judith; Ariel and Justin; Anna, little Tonio and Izzy; and of course there was the duke.

Clay's father stood there beaming, and it brought Kitt the first real ray of sunshine since this whole affair began.

"My dear, it is indeed a pleasure to welcome you into the family. You cannot begin to know how much I've looked forward to the day my son took a bride— and a finer one he could not have chosen."

Kitt flushed at the compliment, wishing it was at least partly true. Clay hadn't chosen her; he had simply conceded to a union he didn't really want. And he certainly could have fared better than to take a wife who didn't want to share his bed.

"Thank you, Your Grace."

It was interesting, the relationship between Clay and his father. It was obvious how much the duke cared for his son, yet Clay didn't carry his name and presumably never would. In public, they addressed each other formally. In intimate gatherings like this, where the duchess was not in attendance, Rathmore often referred to Clay as his son. They looked so much alike there was no denying the kinship, and the affection between them was obvious, yet there was a distance there, too. She knew the situation must weigh on Clay.

The hours passed in a blur. Occasionally, she caught her father's satisfied expression as he glanced at her and her new husband, but she forced herself to ignore it. Her father wanted her wed and he had succeeded. She preferred to believe he was worried about her future, but perhaps, like Judith, he was merely concerned with the threat her behavior posed to the Stockton name.

Though he had spared no expense on the festivities and her dearest friends were there, Kitt couldn't enjoy herself. Not when she had no idea what Clay intended to do that night.

She started at the sound of his voice resonating from beside her.

"You're as jumpy as a cat," he said. "I thought you'd feel better once the wedding was behind you."

"Better? How could I possibly feel better? My life has been utterly turned upside down. I can scarcely credit how calmly you are taking all of this."

He shrugged those incredibly wide shoulders. "I'd always planned to marry, sooner or later. At least with you for a wife my life will never be dull."

It warmed her a little, to think he wasn't all that disappointed in having been forced to wed her. At least he wasn't yet. But what if she could never truly accept her place in his bed? Still, Clay had promised to teach her, not force her, to guide her instead of merely taking what he wanted.

For the hundredth time, she wondered if he would keep his word.

The wretched day finally ended. By the time the sun began to sink below the horizon, Kitt was tired clear to the bone. Her body sagged with exhaustion, yet her nerves were so tightly strung she felt as if she were walking on a razor's edge.

She said little in the carriage on the way to Harcourt's town house—nothing at all once they reached it and he led her inside. As soon as the door was closed, he turned to her and smiled.

"Well, my lady wife, what do you think of your new home?"

Kitt glanced around. What *did* she think of it? It was obvious the town house had been spotlessly cleaned for the occasion, the inlaid parquet floors polished to a burnished glow, the crystal chandeliers newly washed and glittering, not a trace of dust on the marble-topped tables she could see through the door leading into the drawing room.

Though the house appeared to be empty of servants, lamps had been lit throughout, lighting the rooms with a welcoming glow. A huge bouquet of flowers—purple irises, lilacs, snapdragons, and lilies—bloomed from a cut crystal vase on a table beside the front door.

"It's . . . it's lovely, Clay."

"If there's anything you wish to change—draperies, wallpaper, anything at all—you have my consent. A friend helped me with what you see here. I haven't much of a knack for decoration myself."

She doubted that. Clay had impeccable taste and it showed in the olive-striped wallpaper and plush Oriental carpets in the drawing room, the expensive statuary sitting on the tables, the well-chosen paintings on the walls. Still, she couldn't help but wonder at the "friend" he had mentioned—one of his women, no doubt.

The notion brought a sting of jealousy she hadn't expected, raising a thought she had thus far refused to examine. Clay was hardly a man to be satisfied with just one woman. He was certain to keep a mistress, perhaps more than one. Considering her revulsion to intimacy, she had thought such an arrangement would suit her.

Now that they were married, the notion didn't sit nearly so well.

"Shall I show you around the house?"

Her tired muscles screamed in protest and Kitt shook her head, the small movement expanding the pounding behind her eyes. "If you don't mind, I'm terribly tired. For the present, I would prefer to simply retire."

Something darkened for a moment in his eyes, then it was gone. "All right. Let's go upstairs and I'll show you your bedchamber. After a good night's sleep you're bound to feel better."

"Yes, I'm certain I will."

Tibby had been sent ahead to unpack her trunks. Along with the rest of the servants, her maid had been given the evening off to allow them privacy on their wedding night.

Kitt's stomach knotted at the thought, her tension mounting as Clay led her up the curving staircase. The closer she got to the bedchamber, the more she felt as if the walls were closing in. He opened the door to a suite that included a sitting room beautifully appointed with lemon-oiled cherrywood furniture and a small fire blazing in a marble-manteled hearth. The door to the bedchamber stood ajar and through the opening, she spied a massive four-poster bed.

"There are two bedchambers in the suite. You'll find your things in that one. There's a bathing room off to the left. I asked the housekeeper to have a bath prepared before she departed. Hopefully, the water will still be warm."

"Thank you. That was very thoughtful."

"Since your maid has been dismissed for the night, I'll be happy to act in her stead. Turn around so that I may help you undress."

Kitt went completely still. Already it was starting. Once he had removed her clothes, what would he want to do next? Had she actually been foolish enough to believe he wouldn't take what by law was rightfully his?

Anger and fear mixed together. It was anger that won out. "Thank you for the offer, but that won't be necessary. I'm quite capable of doing it myself."

His pupils went dark. His eyebrows drew together like clouds in a storm. "You aren't thinking I mean to break my word? Surely, if nothing else, we are better friends than that."

Her chin inched up. "We're married. Men treat wives differently than they treat their friends."

A muscle ticked in his cheek. "You mean we have no honor where our wives are concerned." He was growing angrier by the moment, yet she couldn't afford to back down.

"You said you wouldn't do anything I didn't want you to do."

The gold in his eyes flared like sparks in a windstorm. "Yes, I did. And I mean to honor that promise. In return I asked that you keep an open mind, that you trust me to guide you." He seemed to be considering his words, coming to some sort of decision. "Since it appears that is something you find nearly impossible to do, I'm going to make it easy for you. I'm simply not giving you a choice."

With that he whirled her around and began to work the buttons at the back of her dark green traveling gown. Before she had time to react, he had finished and stepped away.

"Have a pleasant soak," he said, then turned and walked out of the room.

Clutching her dress in front of her, uncertain exactly what had just occurred, Kitt released a shaky breath. Her dress was unfastened but nothing untoward had happened. Grateful and a little confused, she headed into her bedchamber and firmly closed the door.

Making a careful survey of the room, she found, as Clay had promised, a small copper bathing tub in the middle of a room off to the left, the water still pleasantly steaming. Returning to the bedchamber, she removed the balance of her clothes, turned to toss them onto the bed, and spotted the sheer lavender silk nightgown that Tibby had laid out for her to wear.

She picked up the card that sat on top of it. *For your wedding night with our warmest wishes, your friends Anna and Ariel.*

The garment was little more than a wisp of fabric, so tempting a creation she couldn't resist reaching down to pick it up. Dear Lord, it was so thin you could see right through it! Holding the delicate nightgown up in front of her, she tried to imagine how she might look in such a sensual garment. The image sent a hot blush rushing into her cheeks.

Not that Harcourt would ever see her in it.

At least so far he has kept his word. Yet a niggling doubt still lingered. There was something in his eyes, a glint of determination that warned her to beware.

Kitt wearily finished her bath, dried herself on a white linen towel, returned to the bedchamber, and pulled on a long cotton night rail. Sitting on a tapestry stool in front of the dresser, she plucked the pins from her hair and had started to brush it out when the door swung open and Clay walked in.

He was wearing a dark brown dressing gown edged in gold, looking more handsome than she had ever seen him.

And hard and imposing and more terrifying than she would have believed.

She stood up from her stool so quickly it tumbled over on the carpet. "Wh-what are you doing in here? You said—"

"I know exactly what I said. When we arrived here tonight, I had every intention of sleeping in my own bed while you slept in here. Listening to you, I realize that is exactly the wrong thing to do."

"What are you talking about? You can't just come barging in here and—"

"Listen to me, sweeting," Clay said, his tone a little more gentle. "I have no intention of making love to you. At least not until you are ready. Do you believe that?"

She bit the edge of her bottom lip. "I-I don't know."

"I didn't think so. Which is why I shall now be forced to prove it."

Kitt shook her head and started to back away. Clay reached her in two long strides and swept her up in his arms. "The two of us are married. I intend for my wife to sleep in my bed. That is where you will sleep tonight."

"Let go of me! Put me down!"

But Clay didn't stop, just strode across the sitting room, kicked open the door to the larger bedchamber on the opposite side, and stormed in. He carried her over to his massive tester bed and set her down in the middle of the deep feather mattress.

"I asked for your trust and you promised to give it. If you value your honor as much as I do mine, you owe me at least a chance to win that trust. As much as I desire you, believe me, it will come at a very high price."

She didn't know exactly what he meant, but she had to admit he had a point. She had given him her word, just as he had given her his.

Could she endure another brutal attack like the one she'd survived before? Never. But perhaps, as he had promised, he would truly keep his word.

Her heart was pounding, trying to make its escape from her chest. Her stomach felt tied in a cluster of knots.

"All right," she conceded in little more than a whisper. "Tonight I'll sleep in here."

The smile he flashed was wide and white and utterly disarming. "Good girl." He waited while she climbed beneath the covers, then drew them up over her. Kitt glanced away as he tossed off his robe and climbed in beside her.

"As a concession to your modesty, tonight I am

sleeping in my small clothes. I assure you, it's not my usual nightly attire."

She turned to face him, her eyes wide as they came to rest on his naked, heavily muscled chest. "If you don't wear a night rail or small clothes, what . . . what do you usually wear?"

His grin was utterly wicked. "Not a blessed thing, sweeting. Just the clothes God gave us at birth."

She quickly glanced away, her face a burning crimson. Turning onto her side, she moved as close to the edge of the bed as she dared.

"Good night, love," Clay called from his side of the bed, making no move to come closer.

Still, she couldn't fall asleep, not when she knew he lay just a few feet away, his big hard body all but naked beneath the sheets. She heard the clock chime the hour of one, then two, then three. Still, Clay made no move to touch her.

Her muscles screamed with fatigue. Her eyes felt gritty from lack of sleep, her neck stiff and sore from lying in one position for so long. To appease her battered body and, beginning to believe he actually meant to keep his word, she finally closed her eyes and let exhaustion claim her.

Her sleep went undisturbed, not even plagued by dreams.

Clay lay on his back, staring up at the gold silk canopy above his head. The massive four-poster bed had been a gift from his father, a family heirloom, the duke had said, carved for an ancient Rathmore bride more than five hundred years before, in the days when the Barclays had been powerful and wealthy warlords.

As he fought to ignore the sweetly feminine body

curled beside him and the throbbing hardness that pressed against the sheets, he wished the damnable bed was twice as big.

Clay sighed into the darkness, cursing himself for making this hellish bargain, clenching his jaw at the pressure throbbing in his groin. God's blood, he had known it would be tough having Kitt in his bed.

Now, with her fiery hair trailing over his chest and a small hand curled around his bicep, every muscle in his body screamed for release. His skin felt hot and tight, his blood thick and heavy as it sluggishly pumped through his veins. The dark side of his conscience shouted for him to take her.

He wouldn't, of course. He had given his word and he meant to keep it. One look at Kitt's wild-eyed expression when he had merely offered to unbutton her gown and he had known how important it was. Whoever had initiated her into the pleasures of the flesh had failed miserably at the task. Obviously, he had used her with little regard for what she might be feeling. He meant to rectify that error no matter the cost.

His muscles contracted as she sighed in her sleep, her breath fanning over his skin like a warm caress. He hadn't meant to sleep with her tonight, had meant to give her time as he had promised. But her wariness had changed his mind.

He had to start as he meant to go on, and wasting time trying to talk her into trusting him wasn't going to work. Tonight he had taken the first step in winning that trust. Little by little, he would gentle her, seduce her into giving him what he wanted.

In return, he would teach her to enjoy the pleasure he could bring her.

She cuddled a little closer, one pretty leg sliding

smoothly over his hair-roughened calf. The covers were long gone, the heat of her body more than enough to keep him warm. Her nightgown had bunched with her movements, creeping up mid-thigh. It was all he could do not to reach for her, to run his hands over that smooth warm skin, press his mouth against her soft, tempting breasts.

Instead he closed his eyes, continued to count the gold embroidered stars on the canopy above his head, and pray that the night would end.

13

◦◦◦

Kitt awakened slowly, uncertain for an instant where she was. She was warm, her body surrounded by a solid, unyielding heat, yet the blankets had been kicked off and her night rail had bunched up during her restless night of slumber.

Beneath her hand, short, springy hair teased her fingers. She tested the unfamiliar texture as she opened her eyes, blinked and blinked again. A squeak of outrage erupted from her lips and she shot bolt upright in the huge four-poster bed.

"What are you doing! How dare you—"

"Take it easy, sweeting, I'm not on your side of the bed—you're on mine."

She saw that he was right, that she had shifted toward him in her sleep. Embarrassment lit her face like a red wax candle. She quickly slid away from him, over to the opposite side of the bed.

"I'm sorry. I didn't realize. . . . I didn't mean to . . . to . . ."

"I'm sure you didn't," he said dryly, reaching over

to grab up his robe. This time she didn't bother to look away, couldn't have if she had wanted to. Until last night, she had never seen a man's naked torso. She hadn't known a pair of shoulders could be so wide, or banded with so much muscle, that a stomach could be so flat and ridged, a back so hard, and sculpted as if it were cast in bronze. She hadn't realized springy brown hair could look so appealing on a man's bare chest.

"Keep looking at me as you are and my promise will be as worthless as a bent ten-penny nail."

She hurriedly glanced away, her face hot as she slipped from the bed and started for the door and her own room across the way.

"Kitt?" She stopped and slowly turned. "Thank you for taking the risk."

She flushed again, feeling strangely warm inside. "Thank you for keeping your word." That he had done so gave her hope—more than she'd had in years. If she was honest with herself, she had liked waking up curled against him. When she was younger, she had imagined lying next to a husband she could love and respect.

Love. The girlish fantasy had died at sixteen. And even if she believed it could happen, it would never happen with Clay. The man she had wed wasn't the sort to fall in love, and yet she had a chance to make something of the tentative friendship that did exist between them. And if Clay could succeed in his efforts, if he could teach her to accept him in her bed, she could have the children she wanted.

As she reached the door to her bedchamber, she took a last look at Clay. He was leaning over the mattress, holding a small penknife in his hand. She gasped as he sliced it across his thumb, then trailed drops of blood on the sheets.

"Wh-what are you doing?"

"The servants will gossip should they find no blood the morning after the bedding."

Her face went bone white and she swayed a little on her feet. She remembered the blood that night, all over the bench, spots of it ruining her pretty embroidered chemise. She'd had to hide it so the servants wouldn't know what she had done.

"Kitt?" She felt Clay's presence beside her. "You're shaking." He tried to make her smile. "If you're worried about my injured hand, you needn't be. I promise it didn't hurt all that much."

She saw the concern in his eyes and guilt assailed her. He didn't deserve a wife who didn't want him, a woman unwilling to submit, even in order to bear him a child.

But as he had said, they were married. She had to make the best of it for both of their sakes.

By the time Tibby arrived in her bedchamber on the opposite side of the sitting room, Kitt was already dressed, and except for the buttons at the back of her gown, ready to go downstairs. The dark-haired woman frowned. Having never been married herself, Tibby apparently believed, after a night of making love, Kitt should spend the day abed.

"Are you sure you're up to it, milady? Perhaps I should fetch you some bread and cocoa. 'Twould settle your stomach a bit."

"My stomach is fine, Tibby. I have a number of things to do this morning. I should very much like to get started."

Tibby still looked chagrined. "At least let me do up your hair."

She had brushed and braided it. Kitt started to tell her to simply pin it up out of the way, that she didn't need anything fancy. But for some reason, she decided to let her maid arrange it in the crown of curls she had fashioned the day before. It made her feel pretty when she wore it that way, and Clay seemed to approve.

Seated on the tapestry stool while Tibby completed the task, Kitt ignored the woman's furtive glances into the opposite bedchamber.

"What does it feel like, milady, bein' a married woman now?"

How would she possibly know? "Not much different, I'm afraid."

"I'm sure it takes a bit of gettin' used to."

"Yes, it certainly does." Like knowing she had a husband waiting for her downstairs. Assuming he was, that he hadn't gone off somewhere without her. It wasn't acceptable for a newly married man to abandon his wife so soon, but then they weren't really married, not in the biblical sense.

Still, she was relieved to find him in the breakfast room, looking sinfully handsome and far more relaxed than he had been earlier that morning.

He rose at her approach. "Good morning, my lady. You're looking exceptionally pretty today. Apparently a night spent in my bed didn't leave you any the worse for wear."

She glanced around, praying the servants hadn't heard, trying to ignore her embarrassment. "I slept well enough, I suppose. Considering . . ." Considering, it had taken endless hours to fall asleep. Considering the fear she'd had to battle. Sweet God, if she had known she would snuggle against him in the night, she would never have been able to close her eyes.

"As soon as you've eaten, I'll introduce you to my staff." He seated her in a high-backed chair next to his, then pulled out his own chair and sat down. "Then I'll show you the house and gardens. Afterward, since it's such a nice day, I thought you might enjoy a boat ride."

Pleasure filtered through her. "A boat ride sounds lovely."

"I know a little inn where we can luncheon and there are always interesting things to see along the shore. I thought you might like to take your sketch pad along."

Draw right out in the open? In front of God and the rest of the world? She had sketched in Anna's garden, but that was scarcely the same. Anna approved of her drawings and no one else but Clay had got near enough to see what she had drawn.

Kitt grinned, excited by the prospect. "I'd love to."

Clay looked pleased. "Good. In the meantime, Cook has prepared eggs and kidneys. If there's anything special you need, just let her know and she'll see that you get it."

"I'm sure I'll be fine. I'm not a particularly fussy eater. God knows how much I'll weigh when I get older."

Clay flashed her a roguish grin. "Then I shall have to make sure you get plenty of exercise."

Her face went warm. She started in on her eggs and didn't look at him again until the footman appeared to refill her cup of chocolate.

As promised, Clay took her through the house and introduced her to his staff. She especially liked the housekeeper, an Irishwoman named Molly Black. Mrs. Black was perhaps in her fifties, plump and blue-eyed, with hair even redder than Kitt's.

"It's a pleasure to be meetin' ya, yer ladyship." She smiled, cocked her head toward Clay. "Ye've yer hands full with the likes o' himself, but I'll wager you're up to the challenge."

Kitt laughed, but her smile slowly faded. Was she up to the challenge of a man like Clay? She knew what he wanted from her, but even if he got it, it would never be enough for him. Clay was an extremely virile man. Women were wildly attracted to him and it was no secret how many of them had warmed his bed. One woman—even if she was his wife—would never be enough for him.

As she walked beside him through the house, she told herself it didn't matter, that she might as well re-sign herself, that Clay was no different than the rest of the men in the *ton*.

He would do whatever pleased him and she would have to find a way to please herself.

By the time they left for the barge trip down the Thames, she had almost convinced herself.

And the beautiful, sunny day began to brighten her mood. Buoyant white clouds drifted by overhead and a pleasant breeze rippled across the water. They perched on deck chairs set out for the passengers who could afford to pay the first-class fare, sipped lemon-ade, and simply enjoyed the afternoon.

Clay was his most charming, entertaining her with tales of his misguided youth, years he and Justin had been students together at Oxford, though she imag-ined, out of deference to her newly acquired status as his wife, he had left out the most interesting parts.

"I used to box a little back then," he said. "I was pretty good at it, too, which was why I got so cocky. One of the upperclassmen was a good fifty pounds heavier than I, but I was sure I could take him. We got into an argument and I suggested we settle it with our fists."

Kitt arched a brow. "An argument over a woman, no doubt."

Clay shrugged. "A girl named Betsy McDaniels, I believe it was, but I'm not really certain. At any rate, by the time the fight was over, I had acquired two black eyes and a hard lesson in underestimating one's opponent. I haven't done it since."

"Then perhaps it was worth it. Life seems to be a series of lessons. The important thing is to learn from our mistakes."

"True, I suppose. And in the long run, my opponent Michael Boswell and I became close friends."

Kitt had discovered that about him, that he liked most people and they liked him.

The barge reached the hamlet of Tinkernon at the edge of the city, where they luncheoned in the garden of a quaint little inn called the Swan and Sword. On the trip back to London, they rode along in comfortable silence, Clay sitting beside her as she sketched.

She was exhausted by the time they returned home, far later than she had expected. Clay had insisted on supping at one of his favorite Piccadilly restaurants before returning to the town house, though Kitt still wore her day dress and night had begun to creep in.

A single change of clothes for one entire day? It was unheard of in Society but Harcourt seemed not to care.

"A little spontaneity is good for the soul," he'd teased as he led her into the slightly raucous tavern. Kitt agreed, feeling utterly liberated in her rumpled boating garments, nearly as good as wearing her cousin's clothes.

Returning at last to the town house, her sketch-book tucked under her arm, she wearily climbed the stairs, Clay right beside her.

The old tension returned. It was bedtime again, and she knew Clay intended for her to sleep in his bed. Her heart set up a clatter. Her palms began to sweat. She jumped as they stepped into the sitting room of the master suite and Clay closed the door.

Steeling herself, careful to keep her eyes straight ahead, she started walking toward her bedchamber, prepared to ring for Tibby to help her undress.

"Kassandra . . . ?" Clay's deep voice came from behind her, forcing her to turn and face him.

"Yes . . . ?"

"I realize you're tired, but after you change, I was hoping you might join me for a glass of sherry in front of the fire."

Part of her wanted to. It had been such a wonderful day, and Clay had been so charming she hated to see it end. But another, deeper part of her yet remained wary.

"I-I should really prefer to get some rest. I thought perhaps tonight you would allow me to sleep in my own bed."

His expression turned dark. His mouth thinned into a cool, determined line. "You slept in your own bed last night. That is where you will sleep every night from now on. You might as well get used to it."

Her jaw tightened but she didn't argue. She had made a bargain. As long as he kept his end of it, she was honor-bound to keep hers. "As you wish."

"As I said, I'd like you to join me for a while."

She simply nodded. Why not? It was a reprieve of sorts, time she wouldn't have to spend in his bed.

Tibby was waiting when she entered the bedchamber. Silently, the older woman helped her undress, then walked over to the armoire to fetch her nightclothes.

"You didn't wear the lavender gown last night." Tibby's voice sounded almost accusing. "Are you plannin' to wear it tonight?"

"A cotton gown will suffice for now."

Tibby turned toward the armoire, disapproving lines across her forehead. "A woman should dress to please her husband," she muttered as she returned with a plain cotton night rail and helped Kitt pull it on.

"In case you've forgotten," Kitt said crisply, "I am mistress here." Though where Tibby was concerned, she often wondered. "I'll wear what pleases me."

Tibby grumbled something she couldn't hear. Ignoring her maid's put-out expression, Kitt sat down on the tapestry stool in front of the dresser and fidgeted while Tibby brushed out her hair.

"I'd like it braided, please."

"Braidcd? But you've such lovely curls, so thick and springy, they are. Surely your husband would rather—"

"Tibby, please, just do as I ask."

The older woman sighed, used to Kitt's independent nature. "As you wish, milady."

Dressed in her cotton night rail and a thick quilted wrapper, her hair in a long single braid, Kitt made her way into the sitting room while Tibby headed for her room upstairs.

Clay rose from the sofa in front of the fire as she walked in. From the look on his face, he wasn't any too pleased.

"You look like a nun. Perhaps you should have gone into the convent, after all."

Kitt clamped down on an unladylike retort. "I'm sorry if you find what I'm wearing offensive."

"Actually, I do." He strolled toward her with non-chalance, but his face was set in hard, unbending lines. "From now on I'll expect you to wear the lavender gown Ariel and Anna bought for you. And I want you to leave your hair unbound."

The nearly transparent lavender gown? The blood seeped from her face. "Why should I? If you don't intend to make love to me, what difference does it make what I wear?"

"I want you to learn to feel comfortable with your body, to enjoy being a woman instead of being afraid of it."

A dozen emotions flitted through her head. Was she really afraid of being a woman? In some ways she knew that she was. A more immediate thought occurred: Clayton Harcourt seeing her all but naked. She could almost envision the heat in his eyes, the way his lips would slowly curve.

A lick of heat slid into her stomach that had nothing to do with being afraid.

"All right," she said softly. "If you think it's that important, tomorrow I'll wear the lavender gown."

He gave her one of his most charming smiles. "Thank you. Now, how about that sherry?"

Joining him in front of the fire, she accepted the glass he held out to her and both of them sat down. They sipped their drinks in silence for a while, the warmth of the liquid spreading out through her limbs, mixing with the gentle heat of the flames. Little by little she began to relax.

"Feeling better?" Clay asked, watching her over the rim of his glass.

Kitt smiled softly. "Much better. This was a very good idea."

"I'm glad you think so. I hope you like the next one even better."

She took a sip of sherry, more relaxed than she'd been in days. "What is it?"

"I'm going to kiss you. Nothing more than that. Just a kiss. If that's all right with you."

Was it? So far he had kept his word. And kissing him before had been rather pleasant. He moved closer on the sofa, reached out and caught her chin. This time she remembered to close her eyes.

A feather-light brush of his lips, once, twice, and again. Soft little nibbles at the corners of her mouth, then a deepening subtle pressure that sent little shivers across her neck and shoulders. A long, slow kiss followed, then another. Her tension eased, her body softened, turned warm and languid. He tilted her head the opposite way, kissed her again, and heat filtered into her stomach. Another lingering kiss and it radiated out through her limbs.

Her hands trembled. She rested them lightly on his shoulders. His tongue slid along the seam of her mouth, urging her to open for him, sliding gently inside. Heat sank low in her belly. Her nipples tightened and began to grow hard.

His shoulders felt like iron bands beneath her fingers, and she remembered the way he had looked that morning, the muscles beneath his skin so beautifully sculpted.

Her arms slid around his neck and she leaned toward him. Her breasts grazed his chest and she fought an urge to rub them there, to ease the tender ache against that solid wall of flesh. She thought she heard him groan.

Clay deepened the kiss, claiming her more fully. His tongue swept in, stroking softly, possessively, and she moaned into his mouth. His arms came hard around her, locking her in his embrace, his kiss more passionate, more taking. Out of nowhere the past rose up, slamming into her with painful force. She was back at Greenlawn, lying on the hard wooden bench in the gazebo at the far end of the garden, Stephen's heavy weight pinning her down.

Let me go! Stop, Stephen, please—you're hurting me! Please—you mustn't—

His hand clamped over her mouth, shutting off her protests. His other hand found her breast and he squeezed it roughly, twisted until she cried out in pain. Kitt struggled harder, tried to pull away.

Clay's kiss ended but still she fought him, trying to tear herself free, to end her desperate struggles. His sharp tone snapped her to her senses.

"Easy! Take it easy, sweeting. I'm not going to hurt you."

She was trembling, she realized, the fog of her mind beginning to clear, the soft warmth of his kisses long faded, her body now rigid with tension.

She swallowed and glanced away. "I'm s-sorry. I don't know what . . . what happened, I . . ." She looked up at him, fighting to hold back tears. "I warned you. I told you I was different. That I couldn't . . . that I couldn't . . ."

"You did just fine. I rushed you a little, that's all." He smiled, but it looked tight and forced. "For a while you enjoyed it. Next time—"

"*Next time?* How can there be a next time? Surely you can see this isn't going to work."

"Tell me you didn't like it in the beginning. Say that and mean it and perhaps I'll agree."

Kitt stared down at his powerful chest, watching it rise and fall a little too quickly. She remembered the warm, pleasurable sensations when he kissed her, how good it had felt to touch him. She *had* liked it, just as he'd said, and she refused to lie about something so important.

"I enjoyed it. For a while it felt . . . wonderful."

He was smiling when she looked up, his expression full of relief. He leaned over and kissed her, quick and hard. "Tomorrow we'll try again."

"Tomorrow?"

"And every night until you get used to my touch."

But what if she never did?

"Come," he said, standing up from the sofa, reaching a hand down for her. "It's time we went to bed."

She hesitated only a moment. Then she placed her hand in his and let him lead her into the bedchamber. As she climbed onto her side of the mattress, it occurred to her for the very first time how much she wanted to succeed in this endeavor. She wanted to be the wife Clay wanted. She wanted to learn to be a woman.

A month ago, she wouldn't have believed it. Now it seemed so right. If only she could succeed.

Tomorrow night they were attending a party Anna was giving here in the city. Afterward, when they returned home, Clay would kiss her again, and this time she would try harder.

And she would wear the lavender gown.

The royal suite at the Hotel Clarendon occupied the entire top floor of the fashionable brick building in which it was housed. Gowned in sapphire silk, Anna Falacci greeted guests in the entry, perhaps fifty or sixty friends and acquaintances. Anna especially looked forward to seeing Clayton and Kitt, now that they were married. She bit back a grin as she imagined the pair even more enamored of each other than they had unknowingly been before.

Instead, as she looked across the room full of familiar acquaintances, easily spotting Clayton, who was taller than most of the guests, she saw that his face looked tense, his body too rigid, too tightly strung. Though he smiled whenever he looked at his wife, instead of the pleasantly relaxed expression of a contented, newly married man, the restless hunger in his eyes yet remained.

And Kitt appeared equally tense. *Santa Maria,* whatever was happening between her friends did not bode well.

"What can I do to erase that frown from your beautiful face?" Bradford Constantine stood beside her, bright blue eyes focused in the direction she had been gazing. "If you're worried about your friend Kassandra, don't be. Where women are concerned, Clay has a world of patience—at least when the occasion calls for it. He'll take great care with your innocent young friend."

"I hope you are right. But I have never known Clayton to be a patient man."

Ford chuckled softly. "Nor am I . . . generally speaking, yet I have been beyond patient with you."

Anna arched a pale eyebrow. "As I recall, Lord Landen, I have told you on a number of occasions that I am not interested in playing your games of seduction. Nor will I be interested at any time in the future."

He took a sip of his champagne. "Perhaps not." He reached up, brushed a strand of her short blond hair away from her cheek, caught her softly indrawn breath. "But I believe you're attracted to me. As I am more than attracted to you."

Anna felt a flush rising into her cheeks. Unlike Kassandra, she wasn't an innocent young girl, yet Ford could make her blush as if she were.

She steeled herself to appear indifferent. "I am a woman. You are a very attractive man. If I were interested in a dalliance, I would place you at the top of my list."

A corner of his mouth curved up. He had a very beautiful mouth, she thought. "I'm not at all certain that's a compliment."

Anna's sigh held a hint of exasperation. "I have told you, my lord, that I am in mourning. I cannot help it if I still grieve for the man I loved."

"Perhaps that is so. But I believe I can do something to change that, and I shall continue to try. There's a new Mozart opera opening tomorrow night at The King's Theatre. I should be pleased if you would accompany me."

Anna shook her head. Though she dearly loved a good, tear-inspiring opera, she couldn't possibly go with the marquess. "I do not understand why you continue your ridiculous pursuit when it is clearly doomed to failure."

Ford grinned, etching a dimple into one lean cheek. *Mio Dio,* the man was handsome.

"I suppose I'm simply too stubborn to quit," he said, "not unlike a certain lady of my acquaintance. Now, will you agree to go with me, or must I show up on your doorstep every day until you do?"

Anna rolled her eyes. How could she fight a man with such devastating charm? *"Sì,* I will go with you to the opera, but that is all. If you are determined to waste your time in pursuit of a woman who hasn't the least bit of interest in you, then who am I to dissuade you?"

Ford laughed softly. "Certainly not anyone I would listen to." He bowed elegantly over her gloved hand, pressed a kiss against the back, and little shivers ran up her arm. Very firmly, she ignored them.

"Until tomorrow night, contessa." With a last, cheek-dimpling smile, the marquess walked away.

Anna watched him bid a last farewell to friends in the drawing room, then disappear out the front door. The Marquess of Landen was one of the most determined men she had ever met. He wanted her in his bed and he had pursued her to that end with relentless force. And he was right—she was attracted to him, more than any man she had met since Antonio.

But she had been honest. She still grieved for the only man she had ever loved, ever *would* love. Her heart wasn't yet ready for another relationship, not even one of the most basic sort.

Perhaps in time, Ford would realize that.

Anna ignored the secret, inner part of her that was terribly afraid he would.

14

With the crush of people in the contessa's magnificent suite, Kitt found herself separated from her husband. She spoke to several acquaintances she had met during her stay at Blair House, talked a moment to Franklin Heridan about the opening of *The Stranger*, his latest play, and renewed her friendship with the young physician, Peter Avery. All the while, her gaze kept searching for Clay.

Wherever she went, she found him not far away, watching her with a hot, unsettling look that left her slightly breathless. There was something in those dark, golden brown eyes that reminded her of the way he had kissed her last night and promised more of the same.

And yet he appeared to be enjoying himself. The fact that he was married seemed to have little effect on the women, who if anything seemed even more intrigued. Her friend, the pregnant Glynis Marston Trowbridge, Lady Camberwell, tittered like a schoolgirl when Clay bowed over her hand. Elizabeth

Watkins was there, aloof at first, but easily charmed by one of his smiles and was soon smiling back at him.

A stab of jealousy shot through her, sharp and unexpected. It made her want to tear every strand of gorgeous black hair from Elizabeth Watkins's head.

Instead she simply turned and walked away, ignoring the countess's interest in her husband and the fact that they had once been lovers. Peter Avery joined her and they chatted pleasantly for a while about Heridan's new play, but she couldn't seem to focus on the conversation. Excusing herself as politely as she could, she made her way toward the doors leading out on the balcony, hoping for a breath of fresh air.

Stepping round a liveried servant carrying a heavy tray of food, she glanced back toward her husband but didn't see him and collided instead with another of the guests, who caught her to keep her from falling. Kitt flinched at the pale, thin hand Stephen Marlow curled around her waist.

"Lady Kassandra . . . As always, a pleasure to see you."

She took a step backward, repelled by the lascivious glint in his ice blue eyes. "I'm sorry I can't say the same for you, my lord. Will you excuse me? I believe my husband is looking for me."

He made no effort to move. "Are you certain? I believe he was otherwise occupied with the lovely Lady May."

The color leached from her cheeks. She wanted to slap that smug expression off his face. "Get out of my way."

Stephen made no effort to move. She had just started round him when she heard Clay's voice.

"Kassandra—there you are. I wondered where you had got off to."

A rush of gratitude spread through her, so strong it made her dizzy. When she turned to look up at him, a frown replaced his smile and she wondered what he read in her face. His gaze swung from her to Westerly, whose expression remained bland and disinterested.

"I hear congratulations are in order," Stephen said.

"Yes . . . thank you," Clay said a bit stiffly.

"You're a very lucky man, Harcourt. You can't imagine how many of us poor sods have envisioned the fiery Kitt Wentworth in our bed."

Clay's jaw hardened. "Actually, I can."

"It was certainly well done of you, old sport, what with the size of the lady's dowry and the keen competition."

Clay's eyes darkened to nearly black and a muscle jerked in his cheek. "As you said, I'm a very fortunate man. Now, if you'll excuse us, the hour grows late. It's time my wife and I went home."

"Can't blame you," Stephen went on, ignoring the dark look on Clay's face. "Why, you've scarcely had a chance to sample—"

"That's enough," Clay cut in with dark warning. "From now on I'd advise you to keep a civil tongue in your head when you are in the presence of my wife."

Stephen looked not the least bit contrite. "Sorry. I meant no offense."

Clay gathered her a little closer and guided her toward the door. He paused when they reached the entry, a last hard glance flicking back toward where Westerly stood.

"He didn't do anything to offend you? The man has a habit of—"

"No! I mean, no, of course not. I have simply never been fond of him." That was hardly the truth. There was a time she thought Stephen Marlow the handsomest, most charming man she had ever met. God, what a fool she had been. "I'm grateful, however, that you arrived when you did."

He nodded. "He's never been a favorite of mine, either."

Clay was quiet on the carriage ride home. Kitt wondered at his thoughts; her own were in such turmoil. Westerly's presence tonight had stirred up ugly memories of a dark, painful past. She wasn't sure she could follow through with her intention to please her husband, once they reached the privacy of their suite.

But the fact remained, she didn't want to be afraid of being a woman. She wanted to be a wife to Clay, the sort he had promised to make her—a woman in every sense of the word.

After so many years of convincing herself that marriage in any form was the last thing she wanted, it was a difficult fact to accept, but now that she had, she intended to give it her very best effort.

If she failed . . . well, she would cross that bridge when she came to it.

Upstairs in her bedchamber, she stood nervously as Tibby helped her to undress and comb out her hair. When the woman started to braid it, Kitt caught her wrist.

"I'll be wearing it down from now on. My . . . husband prefers it that way."

Tibby grinned, displaying a row of crooked bottom teeth. "Right you are, milady." She started for the armoire, stopped, and turned. "Will it be the lavender tonight?"

Kitt couldn't help but smile. "Yes, I believe it will."

She was dressed in a thrice, Tibby quietly escaping out the door. Her pulse thrummed. Her palms felt damp as she walked in front of the cheval glass. For a moment, she just stood there, staring.

Was the woman in the mirror really her?

The creature with the fiery untamed curls and voluptuous woman's body was no timid, frightened mouse. She was a siren, a seducer of men, a bold, evocative temptress who took what she wanted and gave a man no quarter.

And yet it was her own face staring back, her own body outlined beneath the sheer layers of lavender silk. Perhaps some hidden part of her really was like the woman in the mirror, or perhaps, sometime in the past, she had been capable of becoming that woman.

Which of the two would face Harcourt tonight?

The frightened mouse—or the temptress in the mirror?

Instead of reaching for her thick, quilted robe, Kitt left it at the foot of the bed and crossed to the door just as she was, her bare feet padding softly, the lavender silk gown all that hid her nakedness.

Clay stood in front of the fire when she walked in, leaning nonchalantly against the mantel, a brandy snifter cradled in one big hand. He had shed his coat, waistcoat, and neckcloth, and wore only his white shirt, opened at the throat, and snug-fitting, dark brown breeches.

He straightened at the sight of her, set the brandy glass down on the mantel. "God have mercy."

There was frank approval in his expression, and the undisguised heat of desire. The knowledge gave her courage, made the last of her uncertainty disappear.

Perhaps she could be the siren. If she only had the nerve.

She paused a few feet in front of him. "I hope my attire tonight is more to your liking."

His eyes ran over her, the centers dark, the gold around the edges glowing like embers. His slow perusal began at her toes, stopped when he reached her breasts, and a soft throbbing started in the tips.

"Yes . . . very much to my liking."

She dragged in a steadying breath, forced it out slowly. "I won't tell you I'm not nervous because I am. I feel . . . I feel utterly exposed and totally . . ."

"Beautiful?"

It was true. She felt womanly as she never had before, as she had been afraid to feel since the day she turned sixteen. "Yes . . ."

"Since it would only unsettle you more, I won't tell you how much I want you." He smiled, a lazy, sensuous smile that made her heart beat faster and the breath catch in her throat. "Just know that whatever happens between us, it will be what both of us want."

Such precious words. She prayed they were true. She was risking so much and yet she had begun to believe in him, believe the risk she was taking would be worth it. He had kept his word when she had been certain he would not, had treated her with a care and kindness that went far beyond her expectations.

He came away from the fire with an easy grace, reached out, and took her hand. Very slowly, he drew her toward him, straight into his arms.

His kiss was soft and tender, a gentle meeting of lips. Then slowly, subtly, it shifted, changed to something more. His mouth moved over hers with exquisite care, and small fires sparked to life inside her. His tongue swept in, stroked her deeply, and she touched it with her own. His hand found her breast and he began to caress her, his fingers closing lightly around the fullness, testing the weight, sending a jolt of heat to the pit of her stomach.

He teased her nipple, pebbled the end, stroked a hand down her back until he cupped her bottom and drew her more firmly against him. All the while he kissed her. Deep, drugging kisses that made her tremble; wet, hungry kisses that melted her insides. Kisses unlike any she could have imagined.

A flood of sensation washed over her. Her body felt tight and limp all at once, hot and cold and needy.

Clay lifted her a little, drawing her closer still, pressing his hardness into her softness. She could feel his arousal, thick and rigid, knew what he wanted to do with it, and a tremor of the old fear ran through her. She fought it determinedly, forcing her mind back to the present, back to the heat pulsing through her, the need that continued to build. She swayed toward him, slid her arms around his neck, told herself it was Clay who held her, not Stephen. Clay, who had become her friend and was her husband.

He deepened the kiss and she let him, caught up in the desire building inside her. It bubbled like hot, slick oil through her veins, ran like a river of fire through her blood. Perhaps she wasn't so different after all, perhaps she could yet become the woman that she wanted to be.

She felt Clay's hand on her belly, sliding downward, over the gossamer lavender silk, moving lower, over the dark red curls at the juncture of her thighs, cupping her there, stroking her through the delicate fabric.

She closed her eyes, trying to absorb the heat, fighting not to remember, telling herself this was Clay's strong hand caressing her like a lover, not Stephen's long, thin fingers, probing her roughly, forcing her legs apart, holding her down so she couldn't move, forcing her to endure the painful burning as he pushed himself inside her.

She didn't know when she started to scream.

She simply could not stop.

Not until Clay roughly shook her, his fingers digging into her shoulders, his voice harsh and gruff. "Stop it! Dammit, stop it right now!"

She looked up at him through a blaze of tears, saw that he was trembling nearly as badly as she. Then he pulled her into his arms.

For a moment, he just held her, his arms wrapped tightly around her, his jaw like iron as she sobbed against his chest, soaking the front of his white lawn shirt.

His hand stroked gently through her hair. "God, I've been a fool."

Kitt barely heard him. She was trying to stop the memories, to control the trembling that still shook her body. She looked up at him through tears. "What . . . what do you mean?"

He brushed damp hair from her cheeks. "I should have known. I should have guessed from the way you behaved when I touched you." His expression, though still full of tenderness, held an edge of something grim. "You didn't lose your innocence making love, did you? Someone took it from you."

Kitt didn't answer. Whatever she might have said jammed tightly in her throat.

"It's true, isn't it? I'm not wrong about this."

She swallowed, opened her mouth, but no words came out.

His look turned even harder. "Who did this to you? Tell me his name and I swear I'll kill him." She had never seen him this way, a pulse throbbing in his neck, his eyes like blackened pits.

She knew she should say something, but she simply started to cry again. She didn't resist when Clay lifted her into his arms and carried her over to the sofa. He sat down with her in his lap, soothing her with the warmth of his body.

"Tell me what happened."

"I . . . can't."

"You can. You have to. If you don't you'll never be free of it. It will haunt you the way it has for God only knows how long."

She leaned toward him, slid her arms around his neck, and for a moment simply clung to him, her face pressed into his shoulder. Her body heaved with sobs, but he didn't try to quiet her, just held her for seconds that stretched into minutes, for minutes that collected into nearly half an hour. Finally her crying eased.

"All right?" he asked gently, ignoring her unlady-like hiccups as she knuckled away the wetness clinging to her cheeks.

"Yes . . . I'm all right." She did feel better. And the fact was, Clay was her husband. He deserved to know the truth. "What happened that night . . . it wasn't really his fault. It was mine. I led him on somehow. I didn't mean to but I did. I made him think I wanted him to make love to me."

"Is that what he told you?"

It was exactly what Stephen had said. "Yes."

"How old were you when it happened?"

"It was my birthday. I'd just"—she dragged in a shaky breath of air—"I'd just turned sixteen."

Clay swore softly. Though his voice sounded calm, beneath his shirt, the muscles across his chest strained with tension. "Tell me what happened."

Kitt clamped down on her trembling lip, wishing she didn't have to relive the painful memories, hoping he was correct and finally talking about them would help in some way.

"Father threw a party at Greenlawn in honor of my birthday. I knew . . . I knew *he* would be coming and I . . . I was so excited. Glynis and I . . . we both thought he was wonderful, so handsome and charming. He was years older than we were, a man instead of a boy." She swallowed past the tightness in her throat. "For months, I had carried a secret *tendre* for him. I think Glynis had, too. But I was the one foolish enough to believe he actually cared for me in return. I dreamt . . . I dreamt that someday we would marry."

When she didn't say more, just stared down at her lap, Clay caught her chin, forcing her to look at him. "Go on, love. Get it out in the open where it can no longer hurt you."

Kitt trembled, collected herself, took another long breath. "We danced together that night. When the dance . . . when the dance was over, he asked me to meet him out in the gazebo . . . at midnight, he said. It sounded so romantic . . . how could I not agree?"

She moistened her lips, felt Clay's concerned gaze urging her on. "He was waiting when I got there. I remember the way he smiled at me. I remember him reaching for my hand. He started . . . started kissing me and at first I liked it. I had never been kissed before but I had imagined what it might be like. Then . . . then he got rough. He started putting . . . putting his hands on me. He pressed me down on the bench in the gazebo and began . . . began to shove up my skirts. I begged him to stop. I told him he was hurting me, but he wouldn't listen. I tried to fight, but he was bigger and stronger than I was. He covered up my mouth so I couldn't scream and he . . . he—"

She started weeping again and Clay gathered her close, holding her tightly against him. His hand stroked over her hair.

"It's all right, sweeting. It's over. No one's going to hurt you again—not ever. I promise you that. And it wasn't your fault. You were sixteen years old. He knew that. The bastard knew exactly what he was doing. He set out to seduce you and that is exactly what he did."

Unconsciously, his hold on her tightened. "Tell me his name." The chill in his voice could have frozen stones. She didn't want to tell him. Not now. Not ever.

"I can't, Clay. I won't. I don't want any more trouble. I just want to forget."

Clay said nothing for the longest time. He drew in a steadying breath and slowly released it. "Why didn't you go to your father?"

She stared down at her lap. "I couldn't. After it happened, he said if I told anyone, his friends would say they had also . . . had also . . ." She swallowed, trying to block the memory of Stephen's cruel words. *My friends will all say they've had you, that you asked for it. They'll tell everyone what a hot little piece you are.*

"More importantly," she continued, shoving the ugly memory away, "if I had told my father what had happened, Father would have made me marry him. I would rather have died than be forced to wed a man like that."

Clay's face looked hard as granite. Lifting her into his arms, he carried her into the bedchamber and settled her in the bed. Wordlessly, he removed his shirt and breeches, then climbed up on the mattress beside her. Instead of keeping his distance as he had done before, he pulled her against him, cradling her in the crook of his arm.

"I'm only going to hold you."

Kitt didn't fight him. Tonight she needed the comfort of his big solid body. Lying there beside him, she felt cherished and protected, and it occurred to her how much she had come to trust him. No matter what, Clay would never treat her the way Stephen had.

"It took a great deal of courage," he said softly, "for you to come to me as you did tonight." He lifted a damp curl away from her cheek. "We aren't going to let him win, you know. We're not going to let him ruin our lives."

Kitt looked up at him, a thick lump rising in her throat. "I'm not sure I can ever—"

"I am. We have time. We'll simply go on as we have been." His eyes moved over her breasts, barely concealed by the lavender silk, and a corner of his mouth edged up. "Look at the progress we've made already."

It was true, she realized. She was lying half-naked in bed with him and she wasn't the least bit afraid.

She managed a watery smile. "You're right. We have come a very long way." To prove it, she leaned over and kissed him softly on the mouth. "Thank you for what you said tonight." Words that dissolved her guilt, words that placed the blame on Stephen instead of her. She thought they might even be true. She settled back in the circle of his arms. "Good night, Clay."

He kissed her temple. "Good night, my love."

The endearment washed over her. She closed her eyes, feeling safer than she had in years. It was amazing, how quickly she drifted to sleep.

Seated across from Justin in the comfortable book-lined study of the Earl of Greville's spacious town house, Clay leaned back in his chair. Two days had passed since Kitt had confided her dark, heartbreaking secret, and he couldn't get it out of his head.

"I have to know who it is," he said to the only man he trusted enough to divulge such a confidence. "I'm going to find out and I'm going to kill him for what he has done."

Justin uncrossed his long legs and sat up straighter in his chair. "You can't do that. The man was invited to Greenlawn. He has to be a friend of the viscount's, likely a member of the aristocracy. You can't kill him without a reason and you can't say what that reason is without hurting Kassandra even more than she has been already."

Clay swore foully. "What would you do if it had happened to Ariel? I can't imagine you would simply ignore it."

A harshness crept into the planes of Justin's face. His eyes, a cool blue-gray, glittered like shards of ice. "No, I wouldn't ignore it. I'd find a reason to see him dead that had nothing to do with the past. Just be certain you've got the right man."

Clay clenched his jaw. Oh, he would make certain of that. He wanted the vicious bastard who had stolen a young woman's innocence and very nearly ruined her life. He wasn't going to let it happen—not to Kitt. Little by little, his wife was becoming more sure of herself and more trusting of him. It took the patience of a saint to hold her through the endless hours each night, his muscles screaming in protest, his shaft rock-hard and throbbing. But Kitt was strong and determined, and she was no longer afraid.

And he believed she was beginning to want him, too.

Clay rose from his chair. "Thanks for listening. I knew I could count on you for that . . . and for the advice."

"How do you plan to discover the man's name?"

"I'm not exactly certain. I'll make a few discreet inquiries, keep my eyes and ears open. Perhaps, in time, my wife will tell me who he is."

"Perhaps. And if you never find out?"

"Then I suppose I'll learn to live with it, just as Kassandra has done."

The conversation wound to a close. Clay left the town house, bidding farewell to Ariel on his way out the door. All the way home he kept thinking, wondering what man of his acquaintance—for there was every chance they had met—would be cruel enough to force himself on a sixteen-year-old girl.

No image came to mind and yet, he believed, in time, he would find out. A man like that didn't change. Likely there had been other young girls and there would be more still. Sooner or later, the truth would come out. Clay meant to be there when it did.

15

❦

The days slid past. Clay was solicitous but distant. He held her for a while each night, kissed her goodnight, but made no move to carry his seduction any further. Kitt had been afraid her confession had ended his desire for her, but he had assured her that wasn't true.

"The fact is, love, whatever has happened, you remain an innocent. Knowing I'll be the one to show you the pleasure a man can bring a woman only makes me want you more."

But he didn't press her and in a way she was glad. He was giving her time, she realized, a chance to grow more comfortable with him before he tried to make love to her again. The morning of the fifth day, he had a meeting with his solicitor and asked if she wanted to join him.

"It shouldn't take long. We can luncheon and afterward there is an exhibit of some of Hogarth's more notable drawings at an opening at the Hatton Gardens. I thought you might like to see them."

She ignored the reference to business that reminded her of the money he had received through their marriage. He deserved it, she believed. Her recklessness had ensnared him in the first place.

Instead she thought of the Hogarth exhibit and flashed him a sunny smile. "That sounds wonderful, Clay." Fifty years ago, the artist was famous for his sketches of everyday people, caricatures that caught the gritty side of life Kitt also loved to draw. "I should really love to see his work."

Straightening her peach silk gown, tying a matching silk bonnet beneath her chin, she accepted Clay's arm and they set off in his snappy high-seat phaeton. They were conversing pleasantly, rolling along through the crowded London streets, when a flash of color at the entrance to an alley caught Kitt's attention. Her artist's eye zeroed in on the red sash tied around the little boy's waist and the yellow scarf at his neck. She saw the small bare feet, the shaggy black hair, and realized the child was a Gypsy.

"Look, Clay—over there!" A well-dressed gentleman stood in front of him, holding out a shiny silver coin.

Clay hauled back on the reins, slowing his high-stepping horse. "Isn't that one of the children we saw the day we went out to the Gypsy camp?"

She looked harder, recognized the soulful brown eyes and full, gently curving lips, and recognized the little boy who had been playing with Tonio and Izzy. "Why, yes. What do you suppose he is doing here all by himself?"

Clay pulled harder on the reins, steering the carriage over to the side of the street out of the traffic. "I can't imagine." As the phaeton rolled to a stop, Kitt searched both sides of the road, looking for any sign of the little boy's parents, but no other Gypsies were in sight. She returned her worried gaze to where the child stood in front of a tobacconist's shop, shaking his head, trying to back away from the man who had given him the coin. Kitt thought that he looked frightened.

Clay must have noticed it, too. The bay horse pranced in its harness as he set the brake and wrapped the reins around it. "Stay here."

He jumped down from the phaeton, leaving her behind, but of course she wasn't about to stay. Her heart squeezed with worry for the child, who appeared to be no more than six or seven and looked more and more frightened as the man gripped his hand and started tugging him off down the street.

Jumping down from the wheel of the phaeton, Kitt started after them, walking as fast as she could without running, praying Clay would reach them before they disappeared.

She caught up with the three of them at the corner, where she heard her husband's oddly soft drawl.

"Good morning . . . brother."

The man stiffened, turned, saw that it was Clay at the same moment Kitt recognized Richard Barclay, Clay's older half-brother, the duke's legitimate son and heir.

Richard's look turned smug. "Well, if it isn't the prodigal . . ." He was attractive in a different way than Clay, lean and fine-boned, five years older, with light brown hair and a faint cleft in his chin.

The boy stared up at Richard, said something in Romany, then turned to Kitt. "I want to go home." His bottom lip trembled and fat tears glittered in his eyes, but he thrust out his chin, determined not to cry, and Kitt's heart turned over.

"The boy is lost," Richard said to Clay. "I'll take care of him, find his parents. You needn't trouble yourself."

Kitt knelt beside the child. "Do you remember me? I came to your camp a few weeks ago." She untied her bonnet and pulled it off, showing the child her dark red hair. "I danced by your fire."

The boy reached out, touched the curls almost with reverence. "Do you know where my mother is?" he asked and she couldn't miss the hope in those pitch-black eyes.

Richard tugged on the small hand still clasped tightly in his. "As I said, I'll see to the child. You needn't trouble yourself." He turned and started to walk away, but Clay stepped in front of him.

"My wife knows the boy. We'll take him home and care for him until his parents can be found." There was iron in his voice, though his words came out smooth and his expression remained carefully bland. It was no secret, the animosity between the two men, though Kitt had never realized how strong it was until now.

A muscle ticked in Richard's cheek. Clearly, he wasn't happy with Clay's interference. His long fingers tightened for an instant around the small dark hand. At the implacable look on Clay's face, his fingers slowly uncurled. He released the child and stepped away.

"I felt sorry for him, that's all. I was only trying to help."

"I'm sure you were," Clay said, but there was something in his eyes that made Kitt uneasy.

Richard's lips curved in a faint, nearly nonexistent

smile. "Well then, since my help is no longer required, I shall bid you and your lovely wife good day." Turning, he walked briskly down the paving stones, disappearing a few seconds later in the throng of people that passed along the street.

Kitt took the small boy's hand. "It's all right, sweetheart. We're going to help you find your mother. What's your name?"

He studied her with those big dark eyes and the muscles in his straight little shoulders relaxed. "I am Yotsi," he said.

"What happened to your mother, Yotsi? How did the two of you get separated?"

The boy turned, pointed back toward where she'd first seen him. "I followed a gray cat into the alley. She had a litter of kittens behind some empty boxes. I played with them for a while. I looked back and my mother was gone."

Just like Richard Barclay, Kitt saw, watching his high beaver hat disappear around the next corner followed by Clay's uncertain scowl.

"Your brother was only trying to help," she reminded her husband, hoping to dispel his oddly pensive mood.

Clay reached down and hoisted the boy up into his arms with the ease of a man who had a dozen small children at home. "Yes . . . I'm sure he was."

Taking Kitt's hand, he started walking back toward the phaeton, the boy resting comfortably against his chest.

"Still, I'm glad we brought Yotsi with us," she said, "since Richard has no wife at home to take care of him."

Clay made no reply, just kept walking until they

reached the phaeton and he lifted them both up onto the seat. He climbed up on the opposite side, settled himself beside the boy, and took up the reins. For the next half-hour, they drove through the busy streets, looking for a bright-painted Gypsy *vardo* or a band of Gypsies milling through the crowds walking in front of the shops. The little boy seemed worried, but no longer frightened, though he clung to Kitt's arm and still clutched the shiny silver coin Richard had given him.

"Piccadilly isn't far," Clay said. "I've seen Gypsies there before. At least it's a likely place to look."

He turned the phaeton off Old Bond, and they started searching up and down the streets, passing another quarter hour. "If we don't find them soon, we'll take him home with us. I'll speak to the night watch, see if they've seen any sign of Gypsies about."

In the end they didn't have to.

"Yaya!" the child suddenly cried out, pointing and jumping up from the seat. Kitt spotted an ancient Gypsy woman and the big dark Gypsy named Demetro she had encountered the night she had gone to the Gypsy camp. A well-dressed man stood in front of them, his eyes fixed on the makeshift table the Gypsies had set up at the side of the road.

"They're playing the shell game," Clay said. "The fool will lose every cent in his purse. Gypsies know every way in the world to fleece a *gadjo*." He pulled the phaeton to a halt and set the brake.

"Yaya!" the boy cried again, and it seemed likely the half-crippled old woman was Yotsi's grandmother.

"Perhaps his mother is out looking for him." Clay halted the phaeton and climbed down, reached up and lifted the little boy down. As soon as his feet hit the ground, he started running. The old woman spotted him, made some sort of sign toward the heavens, and grinned, flashing pink gums and a few rotten teeth.

Clay swung Kitt down as Demetro intercepted Yotsi. The stout Gypsy grabbed the boy's arm, shook a finger in his face, then cuffed him soundly on the ear. He said something in Romany and Yotsi's face went pale. The boy shuffled backward until the old woman formed a buffer between them.

"We are in your debt," she said, waddling forward. "My daughter has been sick with worry for him."

"Where is she?"

"She and Pito, her husband, search the streets. They will be grateful you have found him."

"I'm glad we were able to help," Clay said. Demetro had returned to his game with the gentleman, who, as Clay predicted, seemed intent on losing his coin. The Gypsy said nothing to either of them, but his black eyes moved over Kassandra in the same disturbing way they had that night at the camp.

"Good-bye, Yotsi," Kitt called out, waving farewell to the child as Clay led her back to the phaeton.

"He'll be all right. He's back with his family, and Gypsies are very protective of their young ones."

Kitt said nothing to that, thinking of the thin, ragamuffin children she had seen at the camp. She rode quietly as they continued their journey to Clay's solicitor, thinking of Yotsi and the Gypsy life, viewing it in a way she hadn't before.

"When I saw them in the camp that day," she said, "they seemed so free. Now . . . I don't know . . . they just seem sad and poor and homeless."

Clay reached over and caught her hand. "Freedom comes with a price, love, and that price is never cheap."

It was true, she thought. She had gained a certain freedom when she had married Clay. In return, he expected to gain a wife. Not for the first time she wondered what the cost would be in giving him what he wanted.

Another week passed. An unexpected business matter arose and Clay left for Portsmouth. He didn't ask Kitt to accompany him. She thought that perhaps the strain of sleeping together and not making love was simply too much of a burden.

Which meant there was every chance that while he was away he would seek relief in the arms of someone else.

A queasy ripple skittered through her stomach. She didn't want Clay making love to another woman. She didn't want him touching her, kissing her, whispering soft, sensual words. Yet she knew it was the way of most married men, and Clay was no different. In truth, since she wasn't allowing him to bed her, he had even more need of a woman.

After a night of tossing and turning, she awakened at dawn, alone in her tester bed, missing his warmth. When had it happened that she had come to want him in her bed? When had it happened that she wanted him to kiss her, hold her, to feel those hard muscles pressing against her back as she slept? When had she started to wonder what it might be like to have him make love to her?

Unable to return to sleep, Kitt tossed back the covers and climbed out of bed. Pulling on her quilted wrapper, she took her sketch pad out of the drawer and curled up in the window seat.

In the days Clay had been gone, she had spent endless hours drawing: scenes from her journey down the Thames along with random images of the servants at work in the household. Clay's cook made a particularly interesting subject. Matilda Weeks, the tiny, toothless old woman with the ancient eyes and wise, all-knowing smile ran the kitchen like a tyrant and, at seventy, commanded the respect of everyone in the house.

Yesterday Kitt had drawn several sketches of Yotsi, the little Gypsy boy they had rescued on the street. Now, as she sat in the window seat, she drew another, catching his smile of relief when he had first spotted his family.

Her mind wandered. Bold strokes drew an image of Clay the day they were married. She thought of the night she had told Clay the truth about Stephen, though she had never divulged his name. Her fingers began to move, sketching faster, harder, across the page.

Dark clouds formed above a thickly brambled garden. The lines of a gazebo appeared, nearly covered by vines and dark, sinister growth. Her hand moved fiercely, sketching rapidly, her mind lost in bitter, painful images of the past. The features of a man appeared near the top of the page. The charcoal in her fingers flew wildly across the paper, forming the lines of a nose and mouth. Eyes appeared, crinkled at the corners. She tried to capture their too-pale hue.

A pair of hands appeared, the fingers long and thin, curving like talons, the nails at the tips perfectly manicured, yet somehow repulsive.

The charcoal suddenly crumbled and her frantic movements stilled. She was doing it again, letting the past sneak into the present. Yet each time she had drawn the picture, she felt freer, a little more able to let it go.

This time, as she stared down at the drawing, she felt detached from the pain, as if it were no longer a part of her.

Clay had done that. With his gentle seduction and comforting words, he was making the past fade away.

With a soft sigh, she closed the sketchbook and put it away, missing Clay as she hadn't believed she would. She rang for Tibby, dressed, and headed downstairs. Reading, she hoped, would provide a diversion, but once she reached the oak-paneled interior of the library, she realized it wasn't going to work.

She'd been cooped up for too long. She needed to get out of the house, enjoy the fresh air and spring sunshine. Now that she was married, at least she had gained a certain amount of freedom. Clay had been right about that.

"Beg pardon, my lady." The butler, a spare, bald-headed man named Henderson with bushy gray eyebrows and an astonishing dedication to his employer, stood in the open doorway.

"The Contessa di Loreto is arrived to pay a call. I've shown her into the drawing room. Do you wish to receive her or shall I tell her you are otherwise occupied?"

Kitt grinned. "Tell the contessa I very much wish to see her. I'll be right in."

She found her friend pacing in front of the green-striped sofa, apparently as restless as she.

"I am sorry," Anna said with a smile. "I should have sent word, I know, but I was eager to see you. I hope I am not intruding."

Kitt grinned. "You know better than that. Actually, I was frantic to get out of the house. I had just about decided to come over and visit *you*."

"Then we are both of the same mind today." For the first time, Kitt noticed the newspaper Anna held in a slim gloved hand. "I came to bring you this, in case you have not had a chance to see it."

Kitt reached out and plucked the paper from Anna's fingers. "What is it?"

"Open it and you will see."

She did so with a hint of trepidation, then her eyes widened in surprise at the engraving prominently displayed on page two of the *London Times*—her drawing of the Cossack! Below it was an article about the man's adventures since his arrival in London.

"How on earth . . . ?"

"Your Clayton must have sent it to them. You see—there are your initials down at the bottom. K.W.H. And since no one knows you draw, you need not worry about anyone guessing it was done by you."

Kitt studied the drawing, her finger running over the engraving and her initials beneath—Kassandra Wentworth Harcourt. She had never felt such a sense of accomplishment and self-worth. She marveled that Clay would have done such a thing and felt a soft swell of affection for him. She remembered the way he had looked lying next to her the morning he had left, his body hard with desire for her, his eyes dark as they traveled over the lavender gown.

Again she wondered if his sudden trip out of town involved another woman.

Anna's voice drew her attention. "I thought you would be happy, *cara.*"

She managed to muster a smile. "I am happy, Anna. It was extremely thoughtful of Clay to do something like that."

Anna eyed her shrewdly. "You cannot fool me,

cara. I can tell by your face that something is wrong. I have seen you and Clayton together. I have been worried that everything is not as it should be."

Kitt glanced away. She didn't want to lie—her friendship with Anna was simply too important. Yet it was hard to admit the truth. "Clay and I . . . we haven't . . . consummated our marriage."

"What!"

"When he asked me to marry him, he promised to give me time if I would agree. He said he would give me a chance to get to know him."

"Santa Maria. You are in love with him. He will show you the pleasures of a man and woman. That is all you need to know."

If only it were that simple. "I'm not in love with him."

Anna arched a golden eyebrow. "No?"

"I realize you like him, and I . . . I'm beginning to see his good side, as well. But I'm certainly not in love with him."

Anna didn't argue, though she didn't look convinced, and the more Kitt thought about it, the more she worried that the contessa might be right. Clay was a powerfully attractive man. Incredibly handsome, beautifully built. True, he could be arrogant and demanding, but he could also be gentle. She thought about the little Gypsy boy he had rescued. He was charming and intelligent, and, she had learned, exceedingly protective. It was hard not to love such a man.

And dangerous beyond imagining.

Her stomach tightened at the thought of giving her love to someone whose affections would never belong soley to her. He'd had dozens of women. He would do so again.

"Where is he?" Anna asked, breaking into her thoughts. "I did not see him when I came in."

"He's off on a trip to Portsmouth. Some business he's involved in with Greville." Now that he controlled her money, he could invest in any number of ventures. Though she told herself it wasn't important, that it was only fair, given the circumstances of their marriage, it bothered her to know he had married her in good part for her dowry and inheritance.

Kitt ignored the soft ache that rose in her chest. Unlike the others, at least Clay had been honest about it.

"Shall I ring for tea?" Kitt asked. "Or shall we get out of the house, perhaps do a bit of shopping?"

Anna grinned. "Shopping or tea? Do you really need to ask?"

They left the house in the contessa's shiny black carriage, headed for the Bond Street shops. Along the way, Anna seemed pensive.

"I am surprised your Clayton has waited," she said, returning to the subject Kitt wished least to discuss. "He has wanted you for a very long time."

Kitt stared out the window at the throng of well-dressed people strolling along the street. "We made an agreement. He is bound to honor the terms."

"*Sì,* but you are the one who wished to wait. You can free him from his promise, no?"

"I suppose I could if I wanted."

Anna reached over and took her hand. "Then listen to your friend. Welcome your husband into your bed. Do not wait a moment longer."

Uneasiness knotted her stomach, yet her instincts agreed. Kitt wanted this marriage to work. There were no more dark, fearsome secrets between them. It was time she became Clay's wife in truth.

Their conversation continued, but wisely Anna dropped the unwelcome topic of the marriage bed. They spent the day shopping, Kitt ordering several new gowns from Madame Delaney's, one of the most fashionable dressmakers in London, and amazing herself with the purchase of a white lace nightgown from Paris that was even more scandalous than the lavender silk.

Clay would be home sometime tomorrow. She would thank him for getting her drawing printed in the paper and tell him her decision. Tomorrow after the ball they were scheduled to attend at Lord and Lady Camberwell's, she would let him make love to her.

She wanted to be a wife and mother. She trusted him not to hurt her. Surely she could submit to him, allow him to take what he wanted, what he rightfully deserved as her husband.

Determination surged through her.

She would succeed this time, no matter the cost.

It was the price of the freedom she had gained. It was past time that she paid it.

16

A bright late afternoon sun slanted in through the open carriage windows, heating the interior to an uncomfortable warmth. Clay ran a finger beneath his neckcloth, loosening it a little, finally giving in to temptation, untying it and tugging it off.

He felt restless, his energy bottled up with no way to release it. He needed a woman. Badly. A circumstance he had intended to remedy on his journey to Portsmouth. In Drayton, he knew a little inn just off the road, the Wayfarer Tavern. In the past, for a few silver coins, a buxom little wench named Mandy had been more than willing to satisfy his needs.

Unfortunately, by the time he had nearly reached the inn, his conscience began to nag. He was only newly married, his wife not yet bedded. It felt wrong somehow, to take another woman before he'd accomplished the task.

And so, with a great deal of reluctance and no small amount of regret, he'd instructed the coachman to continue down the road, refusing to give in to temptation.

At least the business portion of his journey had been successful. He had gone to the seaport to investigate the purchase of a ship. The *Aurora* needed costly repairs the present owner, Martin Biggs, couldn't afford, though the ship had performed quite profitably in the past. The *Aurora* was for sale at a well-below-market price, since Biggs desperately needed funds to repay his gaming markers and stay out of debtors' prison.

Clay thought he and Justin might oblige the poor fellow and, as an added bonus, he could stop at the tavern, end his self-inflicted celibacy, and return home a far saner man.

Instead, five days later, he was returning to the city just as restless, just as needy, as he had been before.

Bloody hell. He wanted the prize he had earned the day he married. But Kassandra had been deeply wounded, and as with any injured creature, he had to go slowly, no matter how painful it was for him.

How much longer would it take to gentle her, to convince her to let him make love to her?

Clay sighed into the silence inside the carriage, his body going hard just thinking about it. Tonight would be another endless night without relief, and yet, as torturous as it was sleeping beside her, unable to touch her, he had missed her. He'd grown used to the feel of her small body snuggled against him. He missed the sound of her laughter and her impudent grin.

He thought of the night she had shared her darkest secret. How terrible it must have been for a strong, independent young woman like Kitt to be so completely helpless, so utterly at someone else's mercy.

Unconsciously, his hand fisted. Damn, he wished he knew who the rotten bastard was.

The hours slipped by. Clay continued to think of Kitt, wanting her, pondering his next move. Eager to see her, he shifted on the uncomfortable seat, wishing the coach could go faster. To make matters worse, just outside Tooting, a rear wheel broke and it took two long hours for the footman to get it fixed at the local blacksmith's shop.

It was dark by the time he reached his town house and saw the whale oil lamps lit and glowing warmly in the windows. Stepping down to the walk out in front, he strode toward the house, every bone in his body aching from the long confining hours in the coach. Worse than that, as late as it was, Kitt had undoubtedly gone on to the Camberwells' ball with one of her friends.

Wearily he climbed the stairs, disappointed to think she wouldn't be there waiting, determined to change out of his dusty traveling clothes and join her, no matter how tired he was. When he reached his upstairs suite, he crossed directly to the sideboard in the sitting room, poured himself a stiff shot of brandy, and drained the glass. He poured himself another, carried it into his bedchamber and reached for the bellpull to ring for his valet.

A glance across the room, and his hand stilled on the gold satin cord, his eyes fixed on the vision of near naked loveliness coming to her feet from the chair beside the bed.

His mouth went dry. His body hardened almost painfully. He worked to make his voice sound normal. "I thought you had gone on to the ball."

Kitt smiled softly. "I thought about it. As the hour grew late, I realized how tired you must be. I decided I would wait for you here."

His eyes ran over her, taking in the lovely white lace nightgown that clung to every curve. "So I see."

"You already have a brandy. Shall I freshen it for you?"

He shook his head. "I don't need any more brandy. I'm happy just to stand here and look at you."

She flushed prettily, as he had known she would. The lacy white confection she wore was nearly invisible, allowing him to see the shadowy patch of dark red curls of her womanhood, the ripe, heavy swell of her breasts. Her nipples were covered by circles of delicate lace, but he could see the pink areolas, and a surge of blood sank straight into his groin. With her hair left unbound, a cloud of wild curls clustered around her shoulders.

Perhaps she intended that tonight they would make love and— He broke off the thought, afraid it would only lead to disappointment. He knew what Kitt had suffered. It was bound to take time. . . . But God's blood, how the devil would he sleep with her and not do more than kiss her?

"You look tired," she said. "Shall I have a bath brought up?"

He nodded, finding it difficult to speak. She crossed the room and disappeared into the adjoining room. He heard her pulling on her thick quilted wrapper, speaking to the servants, instructing them exactly the way she wanted the bath prepared.

She returned still wearing the robe, and the disappointment he had feared reared its head. Another part of him was glad that her luscious body was covered. It was torture wanting her and not being able to have her. Inside his breeches, his arousal throbbed with an aching heat.

"I presume your trip went well," she said.

He nodded, praying he could keep his mind on the conversation instead of thinking how little she wore beneath the robe. "The ship looks salvageable and the price is better than good. Once she's been refitted, with Justin's reputation for managing successful endeavors, we should be able to secure any number of shipping contracts. The venture should turn out to be quite lucrative."

He caught the hint of a frown. Whenever he mentioned business her mood seemed to darken so he let the subject drop.

She looked up at him and began to unbutton her robe. "While you were away, I had the chance to do some thinking. I'm no longer afraid of you. I suppose I never really was. It's time I accepted my wifely duties. I thought I would ... I'm ready to submit to you tonight."

A surge of lust jolted through him, followed by a flash of irritation. "That's very noble of you."

Her expression shifted. For a moment she looked uncertain. "That is, of course, if you still want me."

He forced the corners of his mouth into a smile that really wasn't. "Oh, I want you—you may rest assured of that." But he didn't want her merely submitting. He wanted her writhing beneath him, her nails digging into his shoulders, her body tightening around him as she reached her release.

"Then it's settled," Kitt said, her chin going up with determination as she tossed the robe across a nearby chair. "I shall await you in your bed."

She started to turn, but he reached out and caught her wrist. "I don't think so. Not yet."

"But you said you still wanted me."

"And believe me, I do. But first I'll need your help with my bath."

"Surely, your valet can—"

"I don't want my valet—I want you." He ran a finger along her jaw and captured her chin. "You've obviously put a good deal of thought into this and I'm grateful you wish to please me. But I've had time to think as well." Hours, in fact, on the long, hot, dismal ride back home, though the notion had not completely formulated until now. "I've an idea that might please us both."

She looked up at him with eyes that were big and a little uncertain. "What is it?"

"Tonight you'll be in charge of what happens—not I. It'll be your turn to explore my body, to do whatever you wish. If you want to make love, that'll be up to you, as well."

A spark of interest lit those leaf-green eyes. "You mean I can see . . . all of you?"

He smiled. "Exactly so. You can touch me, kiss me, do whatever you feel like doing."

Myriad emotions flickered across her face. Curiosity, trepidation, a hint of suspicion. Curiosity won out. The eager look she gave him made his shaft go harder still.

"When do we start?"

"How about right now? You can help me get out of these clothes."

She hesitated a moment, then nodded. "All right." Moving closer, she slid his jacket off his shoulders and carefully draped it over a chair. Undoing each silver button on his waistcoat, she slowly drew it off, then helped him pull his shirt over his head. Naked to the waist, he stood in front of her.

Kitt's eyes fixed on his chest. "You're very solidly built. From boxing, I suppose."

A corner of his mouth kicked up. "It's definitely good exercise." But not the kind that he enjoyed most.

Tentatively, she touched him, testing the hardness, the flatness of his stomach, running a finger along the ridge above each of his ribs. Every light touch, each tentative exploration, burned like the brush of a flame. His skin felt hot and tight and the ache in his groin grew nearly unbearable.

When she reached for the buttons on the front of his breeches, he gently caught her hand.

"You might want to take my shoes off first." Anything to slow things down a little.

"Yes ... of course."

Bending, she helped him out of his shoes, then returned to unbuttoning his breeches. She removed them with care, her hands sliding over his thighs, over his hair-roughened calves. Clay steeled himself, bit back a groan.

She was staring at the thick ridge of muscle hidden only by his small clothes. Tentatively, she reached out to touch him. She stroked him gently, testing the thickness and length. His loins tightened with violent force and she squeaked in surprise as his shaft leapt toward her hand.

"My ... You're very large, I think."

He swallowed. "We'll fit together perfectly. I promise."

She glanced around, fiddled with the lace at the neck of her gown. "It's terribly warm in here, isn't it?"

At least a thousand degrees. "Perhaps you should open a window."

She turned away, walked over, and shoved the window open a little, letting in a soft evening breeze. God, she was lovely, her burnished hair framing her face, her body made for a man's pleasure. He couldn't remember wanting a woman so badly.

"I can't bathe until I'm completely undressed," he reminded her.

Kitt moistened her lips. "Yes ... of course." Leaning down, she slid off the final garment, leaving him totally naked, his member swollen and riding high against his belly. Slowly reaching toward him, she circled it with her fingers, her touch like the brush of wings. Pleasure streaked through him, so intense, so incredibly erotic, that for a moment he thought he would disgrace himself like a schoolboy.

"Easy, love. We have plenty of time. Perhaps I should bathe before we continue."

She slowly nodded. Moving ahead of him, she crossed to the bathing room and he followed her in. Once he was seated in the tub, his knees folded up, his arousal hidden beneath a layer of frothy bubbles, she soaped a cloth and began to wash his back. His muscles contracted. His breath came a little too fast. Damn, but this was even more difficult than he had guessed.

She lathered his chest, rubbing soap through the springy curls across it, moving lower, over his abdomen, lightly brushing his groin. Heat exploded like fire in his blood and he struggled to maintain control.

"See what you do to me?" He caught her wrist, wrapped her fingers around his hardness, felt it swell into her palm. "How does it feel to be the one in control?"

Her hand trembled but she smiled, her confidence growing by the minute. "I discover I like touching you. I like it very much."

Sweet God, he liked it, too, more than she could begin to guess.

He finished his bath, toweled himself dry, drew on his brown silk dressing gown, and they returned to the sitting room. He stopped in front of the sofa.

"You're in charge. What would you have me do?"

She glanced toward the door leading into the bedchamber. "The hour grows late. I think it's time we went to bed."

Another shot of lust slithered through him. *Far beyond time,* Clay thought, praying tonight wouldn't end like those in the past. He wasn't sure how much more of this he could endure. And he knew he would leave before he would take her against her will.

She wanted to kiss him. Sweet God, she wanted it so badly. She knew how soft his lips would feel, how they would gently take control and start moving over hers, how little licks of fire would ignite in her stomach.

Lying in the middle of the big four-poster bed, she leaned over and pressed her mouth to his in a tentative kiss. His lips found hers, fit them perfectly together. Almost at once, he opened for her, allowing the sweep of her tongue. Her breasts pressed into his chest, the white lace chaffing her skin. She wanted to feel his warmth against hers, to absorb his heat and strength. She wanted to rub her sensitive nipples against his curly dark chest hair.

She hesitated only a moment. He had given her leave to do what she wished—anything that she wished. She had made up her mind to submit to him, but it never occurred to her that he might submit to her.

Somehow it changed things between them, gave her the freedom to explore her feelings, her body's wants and needs.

She ended the kiss and felt him tense as she withdrew. Sliding the straps off her shoulders, she shed the white lace nightgown, let it fall on the floor beside the bed. Now as naked as he, she could feel his eyes on her, dark and hot, fastening on the swell of her breasts.

"Lovely," he said. "So pale and perfectly curved." His hand reached out, paused just inches from touching her. "With your permission, my lady."

Her nipples tighted, ached. Dear God, she wanted him to touch her, craved it suddenly, almost like a favorite sweet. "Yes . . . please . . ."

He did so gently, cupping the weight, his thumb stroking over her nipple. Pleasure seeped through her, spread out through her limbs.

"Do you want me to kiss you?"

Dear Lord, more than anything in the world. "Yes . . . I should like that very much." He cupped the back of her head and kissed her sweetly, then more forcefully. She parted her lips and his tongue swept in. He stroked her deeply, once, twice, then eased away.

Frustration tore through her. Sweet Lord, she didn't want him to stop.

She leaned toward him, kissed him long and thoroughly, ran her fingers over his chest. His muscles were so taut they quivered. He wanted her, she knew, and yet he would not take her. Not unless she wanted him to.

"What . . . what should I do next?"

His voice was deep, rough with restraint. "Would you like me to show you?"

It was amazing how much she wanted exactly that. She never would have imagined. "Yes . . ."

He kissed her again, a fierce, erotic kiss that turned hard, possessive, demanding. Instead of being frightened, a soft throbbing started in the place between her legs. She was wet there, she realized, damp and aching. He trailed kisses along her throat, across her shoulders, then moved lower. Taking a nipple into his mouth, he gently bit the tip, and Kitt arched upward, begging him for more.

His hand moved down her body, skimming across her skin, leaving gooseflesh in its wake. Over her rib cage, the flat spot below her navel, lacing through the curls at the joining of her legs, parting the damp petals of flesh there, sliding easily inside.

Heat rolled through her. The ache there grew intense. He stroked her slowly, skillfully, and sensation rushed over her. She thought she would be afraid, but there was no fear, only a desperate need to be closer to Clay.

He eased her legs apart and continued his skillful attentions. Something hot and sweet began to unfold inside her, something she wanted but couldn't quite grasp.

"Clay . . . ?" she whispered, clutching his shoulders, arching against his hand. Behind her closed eyes, pinpricks of shiny silver light hovered just out of reach. *More,* she silently pleaded. *Please, don't stop yet.* She nearly cried in frustration when his hand went still.

Shifting his position, he moved above her, settling himself between her legs. His kissed her long and deeply, began to stroke her again, and a fresh wash of pleasure rolled through her.

Heat and need seemed to swell with every heartbeat, beckoning her toward the distant silver light. She had almost reached it when she felt his hardness probing for entrance, then sliding deeply inside. He buried himself completely, yet the pain she feared never came, only a sweet, pleasurable fullness that made her shift restlessly beneath him.

"All right?"

"Yes, but . . . is it . . . over?"

A rumble in his chest. "No, love, not hardly."

And then he started to move.

Dear God in heaven. The sweet ache returned, deeper this time, stretching her nerves, sending ripples of heat rushing over her skin. With every deep thrust, the pleasure heightened, carried her upward toward the shiny silver light. She clung to his neck and arched toward him, taking more of him, wanting more of him still.

The light moved closer. It beckoned her to reach it and this time she did. She cried out as her body tightened, shattered, seemed to fly apart.

Clay drove into her again and again, his muscles straining, contracting, snapping to rigid attention. He hissed in a breath and held himself above her, his body shaking with the impact of his release.

Seconds passed. A soft, low groan escaped and the tension in his body began to ease. Rolling to her side, he drew her into the circle of his arms.

"My God," was all he said.

Kitt lay beside him, her breathing ragged as she waited for her heartbeat to slow. She turned her head a little to study his profile, strong and chiseled, so incredibly handsome, his expression relaxed now as she hadn't seen it in weeks.

"It was nothing at all the way I imagined it would be," she softly admitted. "Not with you . . . I'm so sorry, Clay."

"Sorry?"

"Sorry I kept you waiting for so long."

He leaned over and kissed her forehead. "You were worth every torturous minute."

Kitt smiled. She couldn't help it. She'd been right to put her trust in Clay. "We might have made a child."

He chuckled softly. "Yes, we might have."

"Then again, probably not. Undoubtedly it takes a great deal of effort."

The heat returned to his eyes. "Undoubtedly."

"I'd like a child, wouldn't you?"

His body quickened. She watched his shaft rise up, become thick and hard.

"I'd like a child very much," he said gruffly, reaching over to caress a breast. "Since we are both of that same mind, perhaps we should try again."

Heat slid into her stomach. It spread all the way to her toes. "Yes . . . perhaps we should." She didn't balk when Clay gave her a very thorough kiss and slid himself inside her.

The fear was gone. As Clay had promised, he had made her a woman—in the truest sense of the word. It was a wild, heady sensation that filled her heart with gladness.

But as the hours slid past and they made love for the third time that night, a new fear began to take root. As Anna had believed and Kitt could no longer deny—she was in love with him.

She had known Clayton Harcourt for years, knew of his voracious appetite where women were concerned, knew how fleeting were his affections.

Knew he wasn't the sort of man who could ever love her in return.

17

Clay let her sleep late the next morning, keeping the servants away, telling them she'd had a fitful night and needed a little extra rest.

He was gone from the house when Kitt finally managed to rouse herself just before noon, surprisingly disappointed not to find him still sleeping beside her. Still, she needed time to sort things out, to get used to the fact that she was truly a wife, a woman wedded and bedded, that in the past few weeks her life had completely changed.

What kind of life would she face, married to a man like Clay? What sort of future could possibly be in store? Dear God, she had never expected to fall in love, and especially not with a man like Clay.

Kitt bit her lip as she gingerly swung her legs to the floor, tender in places she had never been before. Clay might be infatuated with her, might enjoy her in bed—for a while. But he had felt the same about dozens of different women. None of them had held his interest for more than a couple of months. For years, the *ton* had gossiped about his virility. Even Ariel had laughed about the foolish women who threw themselves at his feet.

Now that he'd had her, he was sure to grow tired of her. Sooner or later, he was bound to take a mistress. It was only a matter of time.

Kitt shivered as she rang for Tibby to help her bathe and dress. Life was what it was, she told herself firmly; she would have to learn to accept it. She didn't know much about being in love. Perhaps the love she felt for Clay would wane and she would grow tired of him as well.

Whatever occurred, she would make the best of it. She was strong. She could handle whatever lay in store.

In the meantime, she had her own life to live and being a wife didn't change that. Clay would be busy with his business ventures and she would be left on her own. She wasn't the sort to sit around the house and embroider. She had no interest in spending hours preparing the menu for the week, or planning lavish balls. In most ways she was the same woman she was the day before, a woman who wanted to experience life, not simply read about it in books.

She spent most of the morning pondering her future, trying to convince herself it would be better than what she imagined.

She was fidgeting, pacing to and from the window in the drawing room when she heard Clay coming through the front door. Ignoring the way her pulse leapt at the sound of his voice, she went to greet him in the entry.

Dressed in snug buff breeches and a dark brown tailcoat, he looked even more handsome than he had the night before. His smile was so warm her pulse shot up a notch. She hadn't expected the restless hunger that flashed in his eyes.

"My lady wife," he greeted her, tugging her down the hall into his study and firmly closing the door. She hadn't time for a reply before he hauled her into his arms and gave her a knee-weakening kiss. She was breathless by the time he stopped.

"Good heavens—what will the servants think?" Not that she cared in the least.

Clay grinned wickedly. "They'll think I'm a newly married man, enamored of his very desirable wife."

Was he? Perhaps for now. Her heart twisted at the thought of Clay and his legion of women, but she forced the painful thought away. Cheeks flushed, she reached up to re-pin a lock of her tumbled-down hair. "I trust your morning was pleasant."

"I had business with Greville." He smiled. "You may believe it was a matter of some importance or I would still be abed with my wife." His gaze moved over her as if he debated taking her there on the sofa, and a little sliver of heat trickled through her. Then his eye caught the stack of papers on his desk and he gave up a defeated sigh.

"Unfortunately, at least for the next few hours, I will be otherwise occupied." So saying, he gave her a quick hard kiss and strode off toward his desk. He began to work, riffling through his papers, sorting them into stacks in order of importance. Where business was concerned, she had noticed, he seemed an extremely efficient man.

"You said Greville was in town. Did Ariel come with him?"

"Yes, as a matter of fact, she did. They'll be staying through the end of next week. The Duke of Chester's birthday ball is coming up. I presume we're still planning to attend."

"Of course." But balls and soirees had never been enough for her. They never would be.

"How was your morning?" Clay asked, mischief sparkling in his eyes. "Catch up on your sleep?"

She smiled a little shyly. "Thanks to you, I slept wickedly late."

Clay's grin held no remorse. "Tomorrow, I won't let you out of bed at all."

Her cheeks went hot and she glanced away. Searching for a safer subject, she crossed the room, reached over and picked up the copy of the *Times* she had left on the table beside the sofa.

"Anna stopped by yesterday. She brought this with her. She was afraid I might miss seeing it." She opened the paper, turned to the page displaying the engraving of the Cossack, and handed it to Clay.

He flashed a cocky grin. "I wanted to surprise you. I'm sorry I wasn't here when the paper arrived."

"Thank you, Clay. That's one of the nicest things anyone has ever done for me."

"You're a marvelous artist. You deserve to have your talent exposed. You might not be able to claim credit for your work, but at least you have the satisfaction of knowing your art is appreciated." He dug among the papers he had been studying, dragged out a letter, and handed it over.

Kitt broke the seal and stared at the bank draft inside. "It's a payment for services rendered."

He grinned again. He had been doing that since he'd walked through the door, proud of himself, no doubt, for his success last night in the bedchamber. "Now you're a bona fide professional."

Kitt looked down at the paper she held in her hand. The amount was only six shillings, yet it meant so much to know that her work was of value to someone. "This brings up a subject I've been thinking a lot about since my drawing was published."

He reached for her, drew her into his arms. "That's a very dangerous habit for a woman like you. What exactly were you thinking?"

"I was wondering. . . . Do you think there's any chance the paper would consider printing other pieces of my work?"

"They might. It would depend on the subject matter. The Cossack's visit was a very important topic. Everyone wanted to read about him. Your sketch gave people a chance to see what he actually looked like."

"How could I find out what else they might need? It wouldn't have to be work I've already done. It could be something new, something pertinent to a story they were working on."

"You can hardly ask Pittman yourself. He has no idea the drawing was done by a woman. I told him simply that the artist was a friend of mine."

"You could find out for me."

Clay turned away, went back to shuffling through the mail on the corner of his desk. "You're a wife now, Kitt. Soon you'll have children. You can't go traipsing around the countryside the way you did before."

A fine thread of anger filtered through her. "That isn't what you said when you asked me to marry you. You said you would take me places, show me the things I wanted to see."

Clay looked up, raked a hand through his hair. "I know I did, but—"

"So you're going to break your word. You're going

to turn into a typical male and forbid me to do anything but sit around and work on my embroidery."

A reluctant smile pulled at his lips. "Actually, I had far more interesting things planned for you to do."

Kitt blushed and glanced away. "We can't stay in bed all of the time."

"Perhaps not." He flashed a wicked grin. "But we can certainly make a valiant effort." She gasped as he scooped her into his arms and started striding across the room toward the door.

"Are you insane?" Kitt slid an arm around his neck to steady herself. "It's the middle of the afternoon!"

"You issued a challenge, my lady. I am merely taking you up on it."

We can't stay in bed all of the time. Kitt laughed. She couldn't help it. "You're incorrigible."

"And you are a temptation no sane man could resist."

Striding past Henderson, who discreetly busied himself hanging an umbrella in the coat closet, he carried her up the stairs and into their suite. Kicking the door closed behind him, he set her on her feet, bent his head, and kissed her.

For a moment she kissed him back, enjoying the warm sweep of pleasure spearing through her. Then she remembered her mission and pulled away.

"I won't let you distract me. Not until I get an answer. Will you do it, Clay? Will you find out if there is any subject I might draw that the paper would like to reproduce?"

He drew her back into his arms. "I'll find out on one condition."

"And that is?"

"If there is a drawing they want you to do ... somewhere you need to go, I go with you." He kissed the side of her neck. "You no longer need to sneak off on your own. You have a husband to get you there safely."

"All right," she murmured, between soft, nibbling kisses. "If there is something they wish me to do, you can go with me."

Then he found her mouth again. The kiss turned fierce and hungry, his big hand caressed her breast, and she forgot about her drawing, forgot everything but the feel of his hard body pressing against her.

Her senses didn't return until several hours later, when she awakened from their afternoon lovemaking in the middle of his big four-poster bed. Again the thought occurred: dear God—I'm in love with him.

Considering the man he was, the sort of man he always would be, it was truly a terrifying thought.

The week passed swiftly. Clay had never imagined being married would bring him such a feeling of contentment. Not only did he enjoy his wife in bed, he actually liked talking to her, simply being with her.

Unlike most of the women he knew, Kitt was well-educated—thanks to a fierce determination on her part and her father's desire to keep her in school and therefore out of his hair. She was intelligent and blessed with a deep-seated curiosity that included just about everything. Her laughter and enthusiasm filled his days with joy, while her newly awakened passion filled his nights.

Still, in that regard, he trod softly. As much as she enjoyed the pleasures he had shown her, she retained a wariness that stemmed from her earlier mistreatment. In time, she would blossom, be ready to accept his more ardent, more passionate nature, a side of himself he had kept under careful control.

Smiling as he thought of her, wishing Kitt were at

home this afternoon instead of out shopping with Ariel so that he could make love to her again, he climbed the stairs to the master suite. He had told her he would find out if there were other sketches the newspaper might want or some they might want commissioned and he was determined to do so.

Interested in what she might have drawn while he was in Portsmouth, he opened the bureau drawer, pulled out her latest sketch pad, and began to flip through the pages. He smiled at the pictures of his cook, Mattie Weeks. With her endless wrinkles and dramatic dark eyes, the old woman made an excellent subject. There were sketches of the little Gypsy boy they had found on the street, and the obvious love she felt for children pleased him.

He flipped through the next few pages, which contained more of the same and probably nothing the newspaper could use, then his fingers tightened around the edge of the page. He had seen a drawing much like this one before. Since Kitt had confided her dark secret, he now understood what it meant. He recognized the gazebo she had gone out to that night. He knew the pale, fine-boned hands in the sketch belonged to the man who had taken her so cruelly, knew the eyes were those of the villain who had brutally stolen her innocence.

He stared at the drawing for long, bitter moments, memorizing the features, finding them somehow familiar. At the edge of his mind an image surfaced, but before he could see it clearly, it dimmed and faded away.

Damn. He had seen those eyes before. Somewhere in the back of his mind, he knew who those distinctive eyes belonged to. If only he could recall.

So far his subtle questions and delicate probings had turned up nothing that might be of help. But time was on his side. The weeks it had taken to accomplish his wife's seduction had taught him patience. Until he'd met Kitt, he had never been a patient man.

He closed the sketch pad, drew out her portfolio, and thumbed through it, withdrawing several sketches he thought the paper might find of interest. Tucking those under his arm, he left the town house, heading down to the big brick building that housed the *London Times*.

Kitt was home by the time he returned.

She blanched when she saw the sketches. He knew she worried he had seen the dark, painful drawing she had done of the night she had been attacked.

He kept his voice carefully even. "I spoke to Edward Pittman of the *Times* this afternoon. I thought he might enjoy seeing some of your work."

She reached for the sketches with a hand that trembled and began to shuffle through them. "What did he say?" She finished checking the stack, saw that the dark drawing wasn't among them, and slowly relaxed.

"He thought they were extremely good. Unfortunately, none of them is pertinent to the stories they're working on at present."

She looked more resigned than disappointed. "Is there anything else I might be able to draw for them?"

Clay shook his head. "The only thing they're currently interested in is the four men scheduled to be hanged outside Newgate on Monday afternoon. The public's so ghoulish, Pittman figured a picture of the proceedings would definitely help spark sales. I told him you wouldn't be interested in anything so—"

"Oh, but I am."

He frowned. "What are you talking about?"

"I'm talking about the hanging. It hadn't occurred to me, but now that you bring it up, I want to draw it."

He clamped down on his temper. She couldn't possibly understand what she was saying. "I realize you're curious about the darker side of life, but you can't possibly wish to attend a hanging."

Kitt smoothed the folds of her yellow muslin day dress, hesitant yet determined. "Believe me, I haven't the slightest desire to watch a man being put to death—not in any manner. But perhaps if I were to draw what it's like . . . if people could see how very awful it is, they would think before they committed a crime that deserved such a terrible penalty."

"No."

"No? That's it? You're simply telling me no?"

"That is what I said. I'm not taking you to a hanging and that is the end of it."

"Oh, so now that we're married, you're forbidding me to do anything you don't happen to approve."

"There are any number of things you can do besides watching someone hang. And if you even think of sneaking off by yourself, I swear I will put you over my knee."

Her chin inched up. "I'm a grown woman, Clay, not a child. You can't treat me as if I were one."

A shot of anger heated the back of his neck. "I'm your husband. It's my duty to keep you safe. Since you've never had the least regard for what might happen to you on one of your misadventures, I'll do whatever it takes to accomplish the fact."

Her cheeks bloomed. "I'm going."

"No, you're not."

"You aren't my father—nor my jailer."

"That's right—I'm your husband. And should you wish to see how serious I am about this, I will be happy to give you that thrashing right now."

"You wouldn't dare!"

"Wouldn't I? You've needed a man's strong hand on your lovely little bottom for years. It would be my pleasure to see it done." He started toward her and Kitt backed away, knocking over a piecrust table, barely catching it before it hit the floor.

"You'd do it, too, wouldn't you?" She set the table upright. "You'd beat me rather than keep your word."

Some of the fight went out of him. She might be a headstrong little chit, but he would never hurt her. "Dammit, do you have any idea what will happen to those men that day? It isn't something a woman—or a man, for that matter—should ever have to see."

"We wouldn't have to stay. Only until I've seen enough to do a sketch. I could contribute something, Clay, something important."

"Ask me to take you somewhere else—a boxing match—there's one on Friday night just outside the city."

"I've been to a boxing match."

"Well, you aren't going to a hanging. You might as well accept the fact."

Kitt set her jaw but didn't say anything more. With a last disdainful glare, she turned and walked away.

Bloody hell! He never should have mentioned the damnable hanging. It simply didn't occur to him she would actually want to go.

"We'll be busy on Monday," he called after her before she reached the door.

Kitt whirled to face him. "Doing what?"

"Anything that will keep you away from Newgate."

"You're despicable. On top of that, you're breaking your word."

"Dammit, Kitt, a hanging was never part of the bargain."

She simply ignored him and continued to walk

away. Swearing, knowing he would face an empty bed that night, he strode to the sideboard and poured himself a brandy.

Damn her, she wasn't getting her way in this. He had been to a hanging. The ghastly sight of four men swinging from the end of a rope would be worse than she could imagine. No woman should see such a thing, and especially not his Kitt.

Christ, would refusing her really be breaking his word? It didn't matter. Under absolutely no condition was he taking his wife to a hanging!

The carriage moved slowly forward, just one in a long line of coaches and wagons that rolled toward the high wooden gallows set up between the courts at Old Bailey and the walls of Newgate prison.

Inside the conveyance, Kitt sat across from Clay, whose mood was black and churlish, his golden eyes dark and disturbed. As they neared their destination, Kitt's own mood began to darken. She'd been determined to come, and finally, amazingly, Clay had relented and agreed.

He had given his word, he'd said, as she had rightly pointed out. He would hold to it, no matter how strongly he disagreed.

Few men of her acquaintance would have behaved so honorably and Kitt was inordinately pleased to discover that her husband was among those few who would. The drawing she intended to make was important. Most people had never seen a hanging, nor were they educated enough even to read about it in the paper. Perhaps they couldn't imagine how terrible it was. But even the poorest beggar on the street leafed through discarded newsprint, looking at the drawings inside. An engraving done from the sketch she made could show them exactly the horrible consequences, should they be foolish enough to break the law.

She stared out the window at the sea of people moving like a giant wave toward the gallows. She had known the afternoon would be unpleasant. It never occurred to her that hundreds of people would find it entertaining.

A gust of wind blew in through the open carriage windows and Kitt shivered. The day was as dark and dreary as the occasion, flat gray clouds obscuring the sun, a stiff, biting wind slicing in off the Thames. Drawing her cloak more closely around her, ignoring her husband's scowl, she leaned forward to peer outside.

Through the building throng milling outside the prison, traffic inched slowly forward. The notorious highwayman, Bart Robbins, and three other members of his gang, would be facing the gallows this day. It had been years since there had been a multiple hanging and apparently the occasion had become a major event. Londoners, from the lowliest pickpockets, chimney sweeps, and doxies, to the highest members of the *ton* were among those walking along the street.

Industrious souls lined both sides, determined to make the most of it. A puppet show captured an audience near the corner. A ragpicker hocked his wares from a rickety wooden cart, and an ancient, wrinkle-faced woman sold apples from an apron tied round her waist.

Kitt looked at them and her stomach began to churn. "What's the matter with all of these people? This isn't a picnic. It is not some sort of celebration. Four men are going to die here today."

Clay followed her gaze out the window. "What you

see out there is only the beginning. There's a very unpleasant side to human nature, I'm afraid. That side will be more than evident today."

Kitt suddenly found it hard to breathe. "I don't understand it."

Clay eyed her pointedly. "And yet you are also here to watch the hanging."

Her head snapped up and she turned away from the window. "It isn't the same and you know it. I came here for a reason."

"Did you? Or is the sketch merely an excuse to observe the darker side of life you seem to find so fascinating?"

Was it? Kitt bit down on her lip. In truth perhaps it was—in the beginning. Now that she had seen the circuslike atmosphere, had begun to imagine what lay ahead for those four men, she hadn't the least desire to be there. But she had made a commitment, to the *Times* and to herself. She meant to make a visual record of the event, no matter how painful it might be.

"Let me take you home." Clay's deep voice drifted toward her across the carriage. "You didn't know what you were letting yourself in for. Now you do. Let me take you back before this gets any worse."

She only shook her head. "I made a promise to Mr. Pittman at the newspaper." In a message delivered by Clay. "I mean to see this through."

Clay softly cursed. Rapping on the top of the carriage, he ordered the coachman to bring the vehicle to a halt, and the horses sat back in their traces. "We may as well get out here. I don't think we'll be able to get close enough to see unless we do."

She hadn't planned on this. She had hoped to stay

inside the carriage, watch the hanging from a safe distance away. Her hand shook as she descended the stairs, took Clay's arm, and let him guide her along the street. The crowd surged around them, some in rags, others in silk and jewels. A strange mix, she thought. Obviously the morbid fascination with death had nothing to do with one's social status or the size of his purse.

They meshed into the crowd. Surprisingly, she recognized several faces. Lord Percy Richards escorted a young woman in a slightly garish, obviously expensive silk gown. She clung to him so possessively she had to be his mistress. Miles Cavendish and Cedrick Claxton, two young dandies, friends of Stephen Marlow's, made bawdy remarks as they shoved through the crowd up ahead. Off to the left, she caught a glimpse of the young physician, Peter Avery. From the grim set of his features and the purposeful way he walked, she thought he must be there in an official capacity.

The gallows loomed in front of her, a huge wooden platform constructed of thick, sturdy timbers. Suddenly, Kitt's feet refused to move. Someone jostled her from behind, but still she simply stood there.

"We can still go back," Clay said softly from beside her.

Kitt wet her lips. "I'm staying."

"Don't say I didn't warn you." Jaw set in disapproval, he tugged her forward. A sudden gust of wind tipped her straw bonnet backward. She caught it, clamped it back down on her head, tied the ribbon tighter beneath her chin, and kept on walking. Knowing what the gossips would say if they saw her drawing such a scene, she had left her sketch pad in the carriage. It didn't matter. She was certain this was a sight she would never forget.

They reached a spot at the rear of the crowd, still some distance from the gallows. Clay led her up a low flight of stairs that led into a nearby red brick building. "Close enough for you?" She didn't miss the cool edge to his voice.

"Yes. This should be fine." She leaned against the rough masonry wall, her hands gripping the cold iron stair rail, grateful for its support.

As the proceedings began, Clay stood stiffly beside her, the chill wind ruffling his thick dark brown hair. Speeches were made, lengthy prayers spoken.

"Stay here," he said, his eyes on someone in the crowd. "I believe I see a friend."

Hoping he wouldn't tarry, she watched him descend the stairs and followed his progress to a tall, cloaked figure standing in the shadows at the back of the crowd. Dressed as a gentleman in tailored, austere black coat and breeches, the man was lean and dark-complexioned, his hair raven-black, his features sharply defined in angles and planes, a handsome face that was harsh, yet oddly beautiful in some indefinable way. She wondered why he was there, since his manner was somber, reflecting none of the gaiety of the rest of the crowd.

She watched him a moment more, then returned her attention to the platform, the morbid spectacle catching her interest again. Her mind spun, gathering images, collecting the collage of lines and angles she would use to produce the picture she had come here to get.

Only the prisoners were missing. Kitt stared at the four dangling nooses awaiting their unlucky victims and prayed Clay would return before the hangings actually began.

18

❧

"I thought that was you." Clay extended a hand and his friend, Adam Hawthorne, shook it. "I thought you were still on the Continent, doing your best to rout the French."

Adam smiled thinly and Clay noticed the fine scar running beneath his hairline, down along the edge of his jaw. "I was wounded. For me, the fighting is over."

Clay flicked a quick glance the length of him. "At least you're still in one piece." They had known each other since Oxford. The second son of the Earl of Blackwood, Adam had been a serious youth, worried more than most about his future. With an older brother in line to inherit the Blackwood title and fortune, and few other appealing prospects, at one and twenty, he had entered the British army. The last Clay had heard, Hawthorne was a major in the cavalry. Apparently, that was no more.

"Are you permanently returned to the city?" Clay asked.

Adam nodded. "It would seem so. There are matters I need to attend. Several weeks ago, my brother Carter died of the pneumonia."

"My condolences. I hadn't heard. I always liked your brother." He arched a questioning brow. "If memory serves, that puts you in line for the title."

Adam made a brief formal bow that came off as vaguely cynical. "Adam Hawthorne, newly titled Earl of Blackwood, at your service."

"Congratulations."

"I would rather Carter still lived. But that is the way of things, is it not?"

"Yes, I suppose it is."

"I hear you've recently married."

"Apparently you've been back in town longer than I thought."

Adam gazed toward the place Kassandra stood at the top of the back porch stairs. "That little hellion of Stockton's, I gather. An interesting choice. I always thought—if the right man came along—the lady would make a good wife."

Clay fought both surprise and an unexpected twinge of jealousy. Tall and lean, with broad shoulders and slim hips, the recently titled Earl of Blackwood was intelligent and handsome, in a hard-edged, brutal sort of way. The scar he now carried added a dramatic flair that, where women were concerned, would only make him more attractive.

"Not that I was ever interested," Adam went on, as if he had read Clay's mind. "I've never been the sort for marriage. I'll leave progeny to my more than capable cousin, Willard."

Clay relaxed a little. Adam had once been a very close friend. They had seen each other on occasion over the years and Clay had noticed the changes. Still, hardened from his years in the military and jaded though he was, he had always been a man of honor, someone Clay had trusted completely.

"So what are you doing here today? You never struck me as the sort for a hanging."

"Nor you," Blackwood said simply.

"My wife has a penchant for art. She's here to do a drawing of the event. She's convinced she is helping save mankind from his baser instincts. And you?"

Blackwood stared back toward the gallows, where four empty nooses swung in the afternoon breeze. "One of the men is Gordon Rimfield. He was a sergeant in my regiment for a number of years, a damned fine soldier and a very good friend. Some months back, he was seriously wounded and forced to retire from the army. After his return to England, he fell on hard times, but according to Gordon, he was never a member of Bart Robbins's gang. He was simply in the wrong place at the wrong time."

"You believe him?"

"Gordon was a lot of things, but he wasn't a liar. Unfortunately justice isn't always just."

"Then you're here to take care of the body."

"It was all he asked."

Clay just nodded. He heard a commotion and his gaze swung back to the gallows. "They're bringing in the prisoners. I need to see to my wife." He glanced in her direction and smiled. "She isn't nearly as tough as she'd have me believe."

Adam's mouth curved faintly. He returned his attention to the gallows, and Clay continued toward the stairs. Kassandra stood waiting exactly where he had left her, her gloved hands still clutching the stair rail. Even from a distance, he could see how pale she was, and he cursed himself for letting her convince him to come.

By the time he reached her side, all four prisoners had arrived on the platform. Each one now stood in front of a swinging noose.

Kitt turned huge green eyes up to his face. "Surely they aren't . . . aren't going to hang all four of them at once."

He frowned, not liking the nearly bleached color of her skin. "I thought you knew."

She barely shook her head. "I thought I would watch the first and then leave. I never intended to stay any longer than I had to. But four men all at once . . . it's practically inhuman."

He gripped her arm. "All right, that's it. You've seen enough. It's time for us to leave."

Kitt yanked free of his hold. "I'm staying. I gave my word. This needs to be done and I am the one who agreed to do it."

He clamped down on his anger, let her hands return to their death grip on the rail. On the platform, four guards walked forward, one to each of the prisoners who faced the jeering crowd. They urged each man up on a heavy wooden block, then climbed a set of stairs to pull black hoods over their heads.

For the first time Clay noticed one of the men wore a bright red, full dress army uniform, Sergeant Rimfield, no doubt. When the mask was offered, the sergeant shook his head, his manner quiet and dignified, his bearing perfectly erect.

"One of them is a soldier," Kitt whispered bleakly.

"Blackwood's friend, Sergeant Rimfield."

"Blackwood?"

"The man I was speaking to earlier. Adam Hawthorne, Earl of Blackwood. Adam seems to think the sergeant is innocent."

"What?" At the look of horror on her face, he could have cut out his tongue. "But surely that's not possible."

"Don't let it bother you—they all claim they're innocent. Wouldn't you?"

"But what if it's true? What if—"

The crowd fell eerily silent and she whirled back toward the gallows. The sound of one man's weeping rose up; another man muttered a prayer. An instant later, the guard positioned beside each prisoner kicked the block of wood out from under his feet. In unison, all four men dropped hard on the end of his tether.

No one said a word.

The wind kicked up. Two of the bodies just swung there above the platform, the rope creaking in the icy breeze. The other two jerked and spasmed in the final throes of death.

Clay's attention fixed on Kitt, who stared in frozen horror. Several moments passed, then stiffly, she turned to face him.

"Would you . . . take me home now . . . please?" Beneath the brim of her straw bonnet, she looked as pale as the death that lurked on the gallows, and he cursed himself, cursed all stubborn, headstrong women, and especially his wife. Bloody hell—why had he ever let her come?

Fighting an urge to scoop her up and carry her back to the carriage, knowing it was the last thing she would want him to do, he simply extended his arm. "Just hang on and I'll get you out of here."

It took sheer force of will to merely guide her

through the crowd when he wanted more than anything to erase the last few minutes as if they had never occurred. He felt her fingers digging into his coat sleeve, trembling faintly, holding on a little too tight. With rigid, jerky movements, she walked next to him through the once-again buoyant crowd, looking neither right not left, her eyes fixed straight ahead.

A gust of wind swept her bonnet off and it dangled by the ribbon around her neck. She made no move to right it. When they finally reached the carriage, he opened the door and waited while she climbed inside and sat down woodenly on the seat.

His worry increased. Ignoring the seat on the opposite side, Clay settled himself beside her, reached out and caught hold of her chin.

"Kassandra ... love, are you all right?" Her skin felt icy cold. She seemed to stare right through him. Slowly her eyes filled with tears. With a sob, she turned her head into his shoulder and quietly began to weep.

Clay gathered her into his arms, holding her gently, wishing he knew how to soothe her. "I never should have let you come. God, I wish I hadn't."

She drew back and looked up at him. "I had to, Clay. Don't you see? I've always wanted to do something important, but I never thought I would. My drawing could actually make a difference. If it saves one man from so terrible a fate, whatever pain it costs is worth it."

He tightened his hold around her. Perhaps she was right. He didn't really know. He only knew she was different than any woman he had ever met. Smart and brave and determined. It occurred to him that he was proud of her, and very glad that he had married her.

The feeling unnerved him a little. Kitt had always

been impulsive and completely unpredictable. He had no idea what feelings she held for him, aside from enjoying the pleasure he brought her in bed. For himself, with every passing day, he was becoming more and more enamored of her. It worried him, but the feeling continued to build, settling deeper into his bones.

As the carriage rumbled home, she rested her head on his shoulder and he held her that way until they reached the town house. As the footman pulled open the door, she straightened away from him, borrowed his handkerchief, and dabbed away the last of her tears. Righting her bonnet, she retied the strings and followed him down the carriage stairs.

"Feeling better?" he asked when they reached the entry.

Kitt nodded but her slight smile looked wobbly. "Yes, thank you." She said no more, just excused herself and climbed the stairs to her bedchamber. Clay wished he could follow. He was worried about her, yet something told him that she would be all right. She would make her drawings and it would help to erase the awful things that she had seen today, just as her dark, stormy sketches had helped her other painful memories fade away.

Fleetingly, his thoughts turned in that direction. As he had a hundred times, he wondered which man it was who had hurt her. As always, a quiet rage welled inside him.

Whoever it was deserved the wrath he intended to rain down on him once he knew the man's name.

In a way, Clay hoped he would never find out.

Kitt finished a series of drawings of the four hanged men that same day and Clay turned them in to the *London Times* the following morning. One of them appeared in the paper soon after, above an article extolling the virtues of a life free of crime.

"Perhaps you were right," Clay said, surprising her as he set the newspaper down in front of where she sat at the breakfast table, sipping a cup of chocolate. "I've never seen such a portrait of angst as the one you have drawn. Anyone who looked at this would think twice before he committed a crime."

She smiled, pleased at his words. "I truly hope so." What her small contribution actually amounted to she would probably never know, but she felt good about doing it, as if her life was worth something more than simply living well.

"Mr. Pittman was pleased, to say the least," Clay continued. "He wants to meet you."

"Meet me? Dear God, Clay, I couldn't possibly. If anyone found out—"

"It's all right." He grinned. "I told him my friend guarded his privacy, that he was rather sickly and rarely got out. I said that if he wanted your services, he would have to continue working through me. Pittman seemed satisfied—at least for the present."

"Thank you." More than a little relieved, she took a sip of chocolate. "Tonight is the Duke of Chester's birthday ball. You haven't forgotten, have you?"

"How could I, with the amount of shopping you and Ariel have been doing?"

Kitt glanced away, unwilling to meet his eyes. She had shopped almost frantically, determined to find exactly the right thing to wear. The Duke's ball was a huge social event and all of Society—and a number of Clay's former paramours—would be there. She tried to tell herself it didn't matter, that he was married to her, not to them, but it didn't make her feel any better.

Time for the ball arrived and Kitt was a bundle of nerves. With Ariel's help, she had chosen a gown of gleaming copper silk, embroidered in gold in a Grecian motif. An overskirt of sheer, gold-shot tulle floated around the narrow skirt, which was slit up the side almost to the knee.

When she descended the stairs, her hair done up in a braided coronet, her feet encased in gold kidskin slippers, Clay stood waiting at the bottom. Dressed formally in tight brown breeches, a gold flecked waistcoat, and a sienna tailcoat, he watched her, his golden eyes moving over her from head to foot. His gaze lingered on her breasts, and the air in her lungs seemed to heat.

"Beautiful," he said, his voice deep and rough. "I'm hard-pressed not to ignore the damnable ball, carry you back upstairs, and make love to you for the balance of the evening. But then, since the moment you started down those stairs, I have simply been hard."

Her cheeks warmed. He wasn't jesting, she saw, as her gaze traveled over his magnificent, broad-shouldered build to the thick ridge pressing against the front of his breeches. For an instant, she was tempted. She wouldn't have to go to the ball, wouldn't have to watch a dozen different women fawning over him, gushing for his attention the way they always did.

"This gown cost a very small fortune," she said with a smile that was only slightly forced, refusing to let thoughts of other women intimidate her. "For that reason alone, we had better wait until we get home."

The corners of his mouth edged up, but his eyes remained hungry. "I shall hold you to it, my lady."

Ignoring a thread of anticipation, she took the arm he offered and let him guide her toward the door. Had it really been mere weeks ago that the thought of making love seemed utterly repulsive? With the right man, she now knew, it could be a glorious experience.

Her stomach tightened. Clay was the right man for her. She knew that now, without the slightest doubt. But even if she were the right woman for him, she didn't believe for a moment that he could be faithful. He enjoyed the passion they shared, but for exactly how long?

He didn't love her.

What would happen when he tired of her and went in search of someone else?

Kitt shuddered, her insides twisting into a knot. It would happen, sooner or later, and when it did, she'd have no one to blame but herself. She had known the consequences when she had married him. She'd been willing to accept his affairs—at the time she had actually believed she would be grateful for them.

But that was then and this was now.

Seated across from him in the carriage, she watched him from beneath her lashes. She had made a devil's bargain the day she'd agreed to wed him. She would have to accept what lay ahead, enjoy the fleeting happiness she felt with him now and try not to think of the future.

Clinging fiercely to the notion, determined to enjoy herself, she returned her attention to the landscape on the outskirts of the city that passed outside the window and spotted the Duke of Chester's mansion around a bend in the road up ahead, looming like a fortress in the night.

Three stories high and built of stone, it was magnificent. A lamp glowed in every window, welcoming arriving guests, and as the row of carriages rolled down the long gravel drive, a throng of elegantly dressed men and women flowed up the broad stone stairs and in through the gilded front doors.

Clay smiled as he took her arm and laced it through his. "Ready?"

In the entry, where a domed ceiling with a huge stained-glass window rose overhead, the crush of people seemed to go on without end. They made their greetings to the duke, a portly gray-haired man with a congenial smile, and his duchess, a woman several years younger who had borne him ten children, yet remained attractive and vital.

Not far away, they encountered another duke, this one more familiar—the Duke of Rathmore, Clay's father. He was standing beside his wife, and the smile he gave Clay, though pleasant, seemed to hold a note of warning.

Clay smiled back, made a polite inclination of his head, and simply kept on walking. Thinking how painful it must be to have a father who behaved as such only part of the time, Kitt's heart went out to her husband. When she looked at him, she saw that his jaw was tight, yet his expression seemed one of resignation.

They continued down a wide marble hall that led to several spacious drawing rooms. Hoping to find Ariel in one of the sumptuous chambers, Kitt craned her neck in search of Justin, whose tall figure always stood out above the rest. She spotted him in the Silver Salon, Ariel beside him, her blond hair gleaming like the tip of a flame.

Justin smiled and bowed over Kitt's hand. "Lady

Kassandra . . . you're looking exceptionally lovely tonight."

She made him a very deep curtsy. "Thank you, my lord."

Clay greeted Ariel in an equally flattering manner and they made small talk for a while: the weather; the roads; who might or might not have been invited.

Kitt flicked a glance at Clay and flashed Ariel a mischievous grin. "I wasn't completely certain we would make it tonight ourselves. You see, my husband thought that perhaps we should stay home and—"

Clay suddenly cleared his throat and cast her a look of warning. "I'm sure Lady Greville has little interest in why we might have been delayed."

Kitt suppressed a grin, enjoying his rare discomfort.

"I imagine you took one look at your wife in that gown," Ariel said, closing her painted fan, "and thought of something you would far rather do than attend another tedious ball." She winked at Clay, and Kitt actually saw him blush.

It was so unusual in a worldly man like Clay, Kitt found it absurdly endearing. Taking pity on him, she changed the subject. "Has anyone seen Anna?"

"She's dancing with Lord Constantine," Ariel said. "I certainly give that man credit for persistence."

"Meaning?" Kitt asked.

"Meaning he has a better chance of defeating Napoleon's army singlehanded than of making Anna Falacci his mistress."

"From what I've seen," Clay drawled, "Landen isn't the sort to give up. Perhaps he'll offer marriage."

"Perhaps. I don't think it would make any difference. The marquess may be determined, but Anna is equally so. She has lost one man she loved. I don't think she's willing to take the risk again."

Kitt pondered that, a faint chill creeping through her. Anna had spoken of the grief she had suffered in losing Antonio Pierucci. Kitt thought of Clay and wondered what sort of pain there would be in loving a man and losing him to another woman.

Unconsciously, her gaze went in search of him. He had wandered a few feet away and stood speaking to the Earl of Winston, who introduced him to his daughter, Lady Claire. Plump and fair, with honey blond hair and a round, voluptuous bosom, she was enjoying the year of her come-out. Rumor had it she had already received several offers of marriage, yet when Clay smiled and made a very proper bow, the girl smiled back so brightly that dimples appeared in her cheeks.

Along with half the women in the *ton,* she was enamored of him after only a brief introduction. Watching him charm her without the slightest intent, a heaviness settled in Kitt's chest.

It was ridiculous, she told herself. Clay was merely being polite. Claire Sloan was barely out of the schoolroom and deeply in the marriage mart, hardly of interest to a man like Clay. But the heaviness in her chest remained, along with the terrible insecurity.

Clay bid the pair good-bye and Kitt turned away, disgusted with her unfounded bout of jealousy. Yet she couldn't quite get the picture of Clay and the dimple-cheeked Lady Claire out of her head.

Guests continued to arrive. Once more on Clay's arm, she accompanied their small retinue up the sweeping staircase to join the dancing. The gilded, mirror-lined ballroom blazed with candles in magnificent crystal chandeliers. Huge silver urns held sprays of white ostrich feathers and elegant bouquets of white orchids. Servants in silver bagwigs and royal blue livery carried trays of hors d'oeuvres and champagne.

Kitt danced a country dance with Clay, then he spotted a friend and guided her in that direction. It was Blackwood, she saw, recalling his tall, lean frame and dark, exotic good looks from the day of the hanging.

"I'd like to present my wife, Lady Kassandra Harcourt," Clay said to the earl, gracing her with an intimate smile.

"Lady Kassandra . . ." The earl made an elegant bow over her hand. Now that she saw the man up close, she realized he was breathtakingly handsome. And yet there was something about him, a hardness, a ruthless quality that made her take a step closer to Clay.

"I'm acquainted with your father," he said to her. "I'm glad we've at last been formally introduced." It was obvious he had known who she was even before the introduction. She tried to recall seeing him somewhere in the past, imagined him in the bright red uniform of a British major, as Clay had told her he was, and realized that if she had ever seen him, she would have remembered, no matter what he had worn.

They spoke for a while, then Anna appeared. The women started to converse and the two men wandered away. She danced with the Earl of Winston; her host, the Duke of Chester; and once with Peter Avery. The evening was progressing fairly well, her worries about Clay once more firmly tamped down, when she saw Elizabeth Watkins walking up to Clay.

Gowned in white and silver-shot silk, her black hair pulled up and gleaming in the candlelight, she looked like a pale-skinned goddess. She said something to Clay and he smiled. He laughed at some clever remark Elizabeth made, his head bent close to hers, and Kitt felt sick to her stomach.

Her husband made love to her every night and he never seemed to grow tired of her, yet in time it was bound to happen. She spotted Lord Percy Richards standing next to his wife and remembered the mistress who'd been with him the day of the hanging. How could Lady Percy stand sharing her husband with another woman? Perhaps she didn't know about the affair, but more likely she simply pretended not to.

It was the way of the *ton,* the way any well-bred wife was expected to behave. A wife ignored her husband's infidelities, and though Ariel had been blessed with a man who was faithful, Kitt couldn't imagine that happening with Clay. Between snatches of conversation with Peter, she watched him bid farewell to Lady May and a few minutes later, dance with the Duchess of Chester. Kitt noticed the way the woman blushed and fanned herself, the way she laughed at whatever it was Clay said. Women loved him. They always had.

It occurred to her that she was no different than the rest—except that she was married to him.

Kitt bit down on her suddenly trembling bottom lip. Dear God, she was a fool. She had known from the start the way Clay was with women. How could she have let herself fall in love with him?

"Good evening . . . my lady."

Her attention shifted. She stiffened at the familiar male voice and a shiver went down her spine. "Good evening, Lord Westerly."

He looked down at the dance card she held in a

stiff, gloved hand. "I see this spot is still open. Why don't we dance?"

Her stomach twisted. She thought of his thin white fingers and too pale eyes and the bile rose up in her throat. She wanted to tell him to go straight to hell, but the room was filled with people.

She worked to keep her voice carefully even. "I'm afraid I'm beginning to feel fatigued. I believe I shall sit this one out, if you don't mind."

"Oh, but I do." He turned to the duchess, who walked up just then with Clay. "What do you say, Your Grace? The lady pays far too much attention to her husband. 'Tis highly unfashionable. I offer her a chance to redeem herself."

The duchess laughed. "Stephen is a very fine dancer. Of course you should dance with him."

She wanted to refuse. Sweet God, she wanted to slap the satisfied smirk off his face. If she did, there would surely be a scandal and dear Lord, she didn't want that. Instead, with a beseeching glance at Clay, who had begun to scowl, she accepted Westerly's arm and let him guide her onto the dance floor.

The roundel seemed interminable. Each time the line moved forward and she was obliged to take Stephen's hand, her stomach swirled with nausea. She forced herself to look at him, but her mouth felt dry, and inside her elbow-length gloves, her palms began to sweat.

"Smile, my lady. You wouldn't want anyone to know what you are thinking."

God in heaven, that was the last thing she wanted. "As long as *you* know, that is all that matters." Feeling a surge of triumph at the tightness in his face, she forced her lips up at the corners, but that was the best she could do.

She saw Clay watching them from his place beside the duchess. If Stephen returned her there, he might remain to speak to the duchess and she would be obliged to endure his company even longer. Instead of going back, the moment the dance was ended, she headed for the French doors leading out to the terrace. Making her way to a place where she could once again breathe easy, she leaned back against the cool stone wall.

Dear Lord, would the man never leave her alone? What did he want from her? Why did he continue his pursuit? But deep down, she knew. He enjoyed the power he held over her, enjoyed silently taunting her with the cruel secret of what he had taken from her four long years ago.

And indeed, a few minutes later, he appeared on the terrace, his tall slender frame outlined in the light of the torches, his blond hair glinting like slightly tarnished gold.

Spotting her there among the shadows, he began walking toward her. Kitt glanced wildly around, saw that the terrace was empty, and for a single brief moment, fear rose up inside her. She was back at Greenlawn, just turned sixteen, in love with Stephen's gallantry and pale good looks—ripe for ruination.

For an instant, Kitt thought she might actually faint.

19

❧

Clay watched his wife disappear through the French doors and something about her hurried departure caught his attention. He knew she disliked the Earl of Westerly, would have refused his request to dance if the duchess hadn't insisted.

From the corner of his eye, he spotted the tall blond earl slipping outside through another set of doors, and his senses went on alert. Westerly had always been fascinated with Kitt, while she went to a great deal of trouble to avoid him.

Perhaps Stephen believed, now that Kitt was married, she would be interested in having an affair. It was possible he had already approached her.

Clay's jaw hardened. Perhaps it was fashionable for a married woman to take a lover—once she had given her husband a child—but then or now, Clay had no intention of sharing his wife with another man.

Setting his champagne glass down on a marble-topped table, he made his way through the crowd and stepped out on the terrace. A few feet away, Kitt's voice drifted up from the shadows. He thought he caught a faint note of alarm, but forced himself to remain where he was. His mind was spinning, churning up possibilities, racing backward over other encounters between the pair. Westerly and Kitt. A terrible suspicion arose. He had to know if it might be correct.

"What are you doing out here, Stephen?" he heard Kitt ask, a quiver in her voice. "Surely you know you're the very last person I wish to see."

"So you say, my lady, but somehow I wonder. There was a time we meant something to each other. Perhaps it could be so again."

"You're insane. I loathe the very sight of you. You're vile and despicable—the lowest excuse for a man I have ever had the misfortune to meet."

"And you, my dear, are a choice little morsel I should very much like to taste again."

Kitt muffled a shriek as he reached for her. At the same instant, Clay moved out of the darkness, stepped between them, and grabbed hold of the man's lapels. He slammed Westerly up against the wall with all the strength he could bring to bear. Fury swept through him in blinding waves.

"It was you, wasn't it?" He stared hard at Westerly, whose pale blue eyes looked even paler in the light of the torches. He knew those eyes, he realized, knew the long thin fingers trying to pry loose his hand. He had seen them in Kitt's dark, pain-filled drawings.

"Let go of me," Westerly demanded. "Who do you think you are?"

Clay slammed him against the wall again, even harder than before. It took all his will not to accuse the man outright, but one look at his wife's bloodless face and he clamped down on the urge, knowing how badly the scandal would hurt her.

Instead, he released the man's jacket and stepped away, took off one of his kidskin gloves and slapped him hard across the face. "You've insulted my wife. I'll expect satisfaction. The choice of weapons is yours."

Kitt gasped and grabbed his arm. "Dear God, Clay—what are you doing?"

He simply ignored her, his gaze fixed on the earl.

Westerly straightened, his mouth a flat, ugly line. He made a curt, perfunctory nod, barely controlling his anger. "Pistols," he said. Very carefully, he adjusted the lapels on his coat. "Dawn on the morrow, if that suits. Grantham Park. I shall be there with my seconds."

The earl's composure had returned, his air of confidence settled firmly back in place. Westerly was no novice at dueling. Rumor had it, he had killed a man once, over a horse.

"Dawn," Clay repeated. "Grantham Park."

With a final stiff nod of his head, Westerly turned and walked away.

As soon as he was gone, Kitt gripped Clay's arm. "For God's sake—what are you thinking? You can't do this. Stephen could kill you!"

A corner of his mouth edged up. "Or I could kill him."

"I don't understand. Why are you doing this? Why are you risking yourself this way?"

His eyes fixed on her face. "It was Westerly, wasn't it?"

Kitt blanched bone white. "I don't . . . don't know what you're talking about."

"Tell me he wasn't the one. Look me in the eye and say it, and I'll call the whole thing off."

She stared up at him, her eyes huge green pools. Very slowly, she moistened her lips. "Stephen wasn't . . . he wasn't . . ." But the words faltered, her lips trembled, and a sob caught in her throat.

Clay caught her hard against him, holding on tight, cradling her head against his chest. "It's all right, love, don't cry. By tomorrow, this will all be over."

Kitt turned glistening eyes up to his face. "Please don't do this. I'm begging you, Clay. If you care anything for me at all, you won't go through with this."

Clay didn't answer. Instead, he said, "Come . . . I'm taking you home."

They left through the formal gardens skirting the big stone house and made their way out to the front. Clay sent a footman to fetch their wraps and called for his carriage. Kitt said nothing along the road home and neither did Clay. All he could think of was killing Stephen Marlow.

He only wished the man had chosen sabers. He relished the thought of carving the sonofabitch into little tiny pieces.

Kitt was frantic. Clay was fighting a duel and it was all her fault! There was no way to deny it, no way to rationalize it as anything else. He wanted vengeance against Stephen for what he'd done to her that night in the gazebo.

And yet Clay had very cleverly managed to disguise the fact, claiming the earl had made improper advances out on the terrace. Since he had, it was the truth.

Stephen might know it was something more, but even he couldn't be certain, and exposing the past would only make matters worse for everyone.

Still dressed in her copper silk gown, Kitt paced the floor of the sitting room in the master's suite, waiting for Clay's return, knowing he had gone back to the Duke of Chester's mansion to find Lord Greville and ask him to act as his second.

She prayed the earl would refuse, that he would see the folly of dueling with a conscienceless man like Stephen and convince Clay to let the matter drop.

Unfortunately, half an hour later when her husband arrived back at the town house, one look at the grim purpose etched into his face and she knew that Greville had agreed. Fighting to control her trembling limbs, she walked up behind him as he stood in front of the sideboard, pouring himself a brandy.

"Tell me you've changed your mind," she said. "Tell me Greville convinced you not to do it."

Clay slowly turned to face her. "Justin is my friend. He'll stand by my actions, as I knew he would."

She moistened her trembling lips. "Please, Clay—I'm asking you again—don't do this. Tell Westerly you mistook his words. Tell him whatever you wish, just please don't go through with this."

He stared at her and his eyes were hard, without the warm golden glow she usually saw there. "It has to be done. God knows how many other young women the man has ruined without the least remorse."

"Let someone else do it, then. There is no reason for you to risk—"

"There is every reason! You're my wife. What Westerly did to you is unconscionable. I won't rest until he pays for what he has done."

She stared up at him, for the first time realizing exactly what Clay meant to do. "Oh, my God—you're going to kill him!"

He tossed down the brandy, set the glass down hard on the table. "Why would you care what happens to Stephen Marlow?"

"I don't. I've wished him dead a thousand times. I care what happens to you."

Some of the tension eased from his shoulders. He cupped her face between his palms, leaned down, and very gently kissed her. "I'll be back in a couple of hours. By then this will all be over." Turning, he strode toward the door.

"If you're bound to do this, I'm going with you."

Clay stopped and turned. "Like bloody hell you are. You're staying right here." He walked back to where she stood, his tone more gentle than before. "This is something I have to do, Kitt. It's between Westerly and me. I want you here, waiting for me when I get home. Will you do that for me?"

She wanted to say no—not in a thousand years was she letting him go off to face Stephen Marlow, perhaps get shot or even killed, not when she was the cause. But she could see by the look on his face what would happen if she tried to defy him.

"Just be careful," she said instead, hoping he couldn't hear the fear in her voice, careful to avoid the lie. "Don't trust him to act as honorably as you do. Stephen doesn't have any honor."

Clay kissed her gently, then deeply and quite thoroughly. She was clutching his lapels by the time the kiss was over.

"I'll be careful," he said a little gruffly. His mouth curved into a provocative half smile. "Keep the bed warm until I get home. I plan to join you there."

Kitt tried to return the smile, but it simply would not come. She listened to Clay's footsteps as he strode down the stairs, paused to retrieve his greatcoat, then headed out the door to his carriage. It was almost dawn, and she was frantic. The minute Clay was gone, she went into motion, ringing for Tibby, dragging her little maid out of a very deep sleep, spinning herself around so Tibby could unfasten the buttons at the back of her gown.

When she raced to the armoire and dragged out the satchel that held her young cousin's clothes—the breeches, loose-sleeved shirt, and jacket she'd vowed not to wear again—Tibby's sleepy blue eyes snapped wide open.

"What on earth do you think you're doin'? You can't be meanin' to go out like that—not this time of night."

Kitt didn't bother to answer. "I need you to go to the stable, Tibby. Rouse one of the grooms. Tell him to saddle me a horse."

"You can't be meanin' it."

"Go—dammit! I haven't got very much time!"

Grumbling beneath her breath, Tibby shuffled out of the bedchamber and headed down the servants' stairs out to the mews at the back of the town house. By the time she returned, Kitt was dressed in breeches and boots and ready to leave.

She pulled a soft, brown felt hat out of the satchel, jammed it over her braided hair, and raced for the stairs. Ten minutes later, she was mounted on a tall gray gelding and riding like thunder through the deserted London streets toward Grantham Park.

How much time had she lost? Would she be able to get there in time to stop them? She didn't know how she would do it. She only knew she had to try.

The sun was beginning to rise, casting a harsh orange glow against the horizon by the time she spotted the line of carriages resting on the road beside the park. Slowing the gray, she reined the animal to a halt beneath the overhanging branches of a sycamore tree and quietly slid down from the saddle. Careful to stay in the shadows, her heart slamming madly, she rushed toward the men who had already taken the field.

They stood back to back, their pistols pointed skyward, Clay's expression deadly grim. Her stomach knotted. With each step forward, her feet felt encased in lead. From the corner of her eye, she saw Justin not far away, and two men she didn't recognize, there on Westerly's behalf. Justin saw her an instant before Clay. She heard his muttered curse as he started running in her direction, neatly cutting her off, slamming her hard against his chest.

"Let me go!" She struggled to break free, her terrified gaze fixed on Clay, her whole body trembling with fear. "I have to stop them. Help me! We have to do something!"

Justin shook her—hard. "For God's sake, Kitt—stop and think what you are doing! Do you want to get him killed!" She could feel the tension in his broad-shouldered frame, the fear that gripped him nearly as much as it did her.

She stopped struggling and her body went limp. "Surely there is something we can do," she said weakly, knowing he was right, that it was already too late.

"I'm sorry, love," he said, flicking a glance at Clay, who returned his attention to Marlow. "I'm afraid it's out of our hands."

Though she made no further attempt to escape, Justin didn't release his hold and in a way she was glad. She needed his solid support. Sweet God, she knew Stephen's reputation as a marksman. He had always been proud of his expertise.

Clay cast her a last unreadable glance and the men started counting. Two. Three. Four. At five, a fresh jolt of fear ran down her spine. *Please, God, don't let Stephen kill him!* Seven. Eight. Nine. Stephen whirled before they reached ten and raised his weapon. Clay must have expected the move, because he turned nearly at that same instant, his body going sideways, flattening out, making a more difficult target for Stephen's lead ball to hit.

Her stomach clenched at the sound of the hammer slamming down on Westerly's gun. It exploded with a roar. Kitt cried out as Clay winced and a blossom of bright red blood appeared on the side of his coat. She tried to tear free of Justin's hold, but his arms were steel bands around her. "Easy."

For an instant Clay's eyes locked with hers. Then he raised his pistol, pointed it toward Stephen, and took careful aim.

Westerly bolted. For several long strides, Clay let him run. Then he lowered the pistol, aimed at the back of Stephen's knee, and carefully squeezed the trigger.

The moment the earl went down, Kitt started running toward Clay. "Clay!" Inside her chest, her heart beat madly, battering itself against her ribs. Her palms were slick with sweat and her mouth was so dry she couldn't swallow. *Please, God, don't let him be hurt too badly.*

Clay remained on his feet. His attention swung in her direction and he started walking toward her, one of his big hands pressed against the growing red stain on his side.

The moment he reached her, she flung herself against him, her body trembling as his arm went around her and he held her with all of his strength.

"I thought I told you not to come," he said against her ear. But there was no heat in his words, just worry for her, and something else she could not name.

Kitt untangled herself from his embrace and jerked open his coat with shaking hands. "How badly are you injured?"

"I don't think it's as bad as it looks." He shrugged out of the coat with only a hiss of pain and she started on his waistcoat, unbuttoning the shiny gold buttons, tossing the expensive fabric haphazardly down on the grass beside his jacket.

Justin reached them just then. "How bad is it?" he asked, his face full of concern.

"The ball glanced off a rib," Clay said, sucking in a breath as Kitt tore open his white lawn shirt. "Took a healthy bite of flesh, but the wound isn't all that deep."

Not trusting his assessment, Kitt gently examined the injury. A long bloody gash ripped across the hard flesh between his ribs, gouging a path from front to back. It was jagged and ugly, but as he had said, the wound wasn't terribly deep.

Some of her fear receded. Behind them, Westerly's seconds worked over the earl, tying a neckcloth around his leg to help stop the bleeding, helping him up on his feet. They draped one of his arms over each of their shoulders and started dragging him off toward his carriage.

With a still-shaking hand, Kitt reached for the white stock Justin handed her as a bandage, wrapped it around Clay's ribs, and tied it snugly.

"Can you make it?" Justin asked.

Clay slid an arm around Kitt's shoulders. "I'll be all right. Or I will be, as soon as I get home." They reached his carriage a few minutes later and the coachman opened the door.

"Thanks for coming," Clay said, extending a hand to Greville.

Justin clasped it firmly. "Why didn't you kill him?"

Clay's smile slid away. "Perhaps I would have . . ." He cast a look at Kitt. ". . . if my wife hadn't arrived when she did."

"Perhaps it is better this way," Justin said. "That shot of yours took out his kneecap. Assuming putrefaction doesn't kill him, he'll never walk again without a limp. Wherever he goes, for the rest of his life, he'll remember this day and the lesson you taught him."

Clay said nothing, but his grim-set features held a note of satisfaction.

"I'll drop by later in the day to make sure that you're all right," Justin said.

Clay just nodded. He had lost more blood than he wanted to admit and Kitt worried that his strength was waning. And as Justin had said, there was always the worry of putrefaction. Once she had him settled in the carriage and her horse tied on behind, they set off through the slick, mist-dampened streets. Outside the window, the early morning hustle was just beginning. Fishmongers and vegetable merchants, milk sellers and coal vendors all swarmed around them, ready to begin their long day's work.

Kitt barely noticed. Her entire concentration focused on Clay. By the time they reached the town house, she was numb with fatigue, suffering the exhaustion of a sleepless night and the heavy weight of spent fear. They sent for a physician, who arrived

within the hour, dressed Clay's wounds, and prescribed daily leeches, which Clay flatly refused the
moment the man left the house.

Nearly asleep on her feet, Kitt was standing in front
of the bedchamber window in her quilted blue wrapper, brushing the tangles from her hair, when she
heard Clay calling.

Fighting down a fresh stab of fear, she hurried to
his bedside. "Are you in pain? Is there something I can
get you? I thought by now you'd be asleep."

His mouth edged up. "I'm fine." There was something in his eyes, a look so dark and hot it made her
breath catch. Slowly, he drew back the covers. "I was
hoping you would join me."

Her hands shook. Her throat went dry. She knew
that smoky, sensual tone of voice. He was naked, she
saw, and the sight of all that hard male flesh made her
knees go suddenly weak.

"What . . . what about your injury? You need to rest
and take care of—"

"What I need most right now is you."

The bottom slid out of her stomach. Her gaze ran
the width of his shoulders, over the muscles across his
chest, down to the hard flesh rising against his flat
belly. She'd been so frightened, terrified she would
lose him. Tonight he had almost been killed. She
needed to touch him, hold him, feel him inside her.

Dear God, she loved him. Tonight, she realized just
how much.

It was the most frightening realization she'd ever
had in her life.

Clay felt the mattress dip beneath his wife's small
weight. She still looked pale and shaken. Faint purple

smudges betrayed her lack of sleep. Yet when she looked at him, he couldn't miss the worry in her eyes.

She needed him this night, just as he needed her.

He allowed his gaze to run over her, taking pleasure in the soft curves and valleys. She had removed her heavy robe and the silky little nightgown she wore underneath. He had forbidden her—if there were such a thing with Kitt—to wear the bulky white cotton night rails she had previously worn to bed, and secretly he believed she was glad.

As she settled herself on the mattress, careful not to disturb the wound in his side, he thought how much he had come to enjoy making love to her. It was strange, but he wanted her more now than he had before they were married. He had thought that having her would end his obsession, his unquenchable desire for her, but in the weeks they'd been together, his need of her had only continued to build.

She leaned toward him. Her fingers brushed lightly over his chest, and a jolt of pure lust shot through him. He wanted to drag her down on the bed, spread her pretty little thighs, and plunge himself inside her. He wanted to suckle her luscious breasts until the tips went diamond-hard, wanted to kiss her beautiful body in places that would shock her—as one day he fully intended to do.

There were so many things he still wished to teach her, so many ways to pleasure her that he had yet to show her. Instead he held himself back, always going slowly, afraid if he unleashed the passion he held in check she would be frightened or repulsed.

The thought made a knot curl in the bottom of his stomach. He didn't want to lose her. Now that she belonged to him, he couldn't imagine life without her.

"Are you certain you're not in pain?" she asked again, tentatively touching the thick white cotton bandage stretched round his ribs.

He smiled. "No, love, not the sort you mean." A far worse pain was the hot need throbbing in his groin. Desire swelled with every heartbeat. When she leaned over and smoothed back a lock of his hair, he slid a hand behind her neck and dragged her mouth down to his for a kiss. He tried to be gentle, but he wanted her so badly it was nearly impossible to do.

At last he gave in to the passion beating through him and kissed her deeply, taking her with his tongue. He felt the tentative touch of her tongue in return, and the slick, wet feel of it inflamed him. He wanted to roll her beneath him and bury himself to the hilt, to pound into her until he found release.

Another hot kiss, deeper, more probing. His control was slipping. He took one of her soft round breasts into his mouth and desire welled up, blinding hot, sapping a little more of his restraint. He told himself to go slow, but the bloodlust was still fresh in his mind, the fight still pumping through his veins. He needed to take her swiftly, fiercely, thrust into her until he drove them both to frenzy.

Kitt would recoil in terror, he was sure. She would be frightened to let him touch her again.

Swearing a silent curse, fighting for control, he gripped her waist and lifted her up. Kitt gasped as he settled her astride him. For a moment their eyes met and held.

"Won't . . . won't this hurt your side?"

His shaft pulsed, throbbed. "There are worse sorts of pain."

Kitt shifted, her body tightened around him, and

every movement, every simple twist of her hips sent flames fanning over his skin. He clenched his jaw, bit back an urge to roll her beneath him and take her as savagely as he wanted. Instead he let her lead the way, let her set the pace, and in minutes both of them reached their release.

Vaguely, he wondered if this would be the time they created a child and thought how much he wanted that to happen.

Exhaling a satisfied breath, he eased her down beside him and she curled against his chest.

"Clay?"

"Yes, my love?" His voice sounded thick and deep with the onset of sleep.

"Thank you for what you did."

He frowned into the darkness. "What? Wounding Westerly instead of killing him?"

"No. Fighting for my honor. No one has ever done that before."

Something squeezed inside his chest. He made no reply, just watched as her smile slipped away and her eyelids grew heavy. Ignoring the wound in his side that had begun to hurt like the bloody devil, he lifted a curl away from her cheek and watched until she finally fell asleep.

Stephen Marlow, Earl of Westerly, clenched his fist against the mattress and groaned in pain. His bony physician, Artemus Perth, worked over him, examining his leg, clucking his tongue and looking for all the world like a skinny, whey-faced chicken.

"Well, what is it, man? Don't just stand there frowning and making those disgusting noises, spit it out."

The old man straightened, plucked the wire-rimmed spectacles off his nose, and unhooked them from behind his cup-size ears. " 'Tisn't good, milord, I'm afraid. Not a'tall. The knee cap is shattered. Can't be mended, you see. At present, however, our biggest concern is putrefaction."

Stephen paled.

"I've dosed the wound with milkweed powder, which I've used with some success in the past. Hopefully the injury will heal without complications. Unfortunately, as I said, the damage to the kneecap is permanent. There is very little chance you'll be able to walk as you once did."

Stephen's stomach churned with fear, making him suddenly nauseous. For a moment, he was afraid he would embarrass himself. "You're not saying . . . you're not telling me I'm going to be a cripple?"

The old man flashed him a look of pity that only made Stephen more afraid. "Please, milord, you mustn't fret yourself. At present, you need to rest and heal. In time, we shall better be able to assess the damage."

Assess the damage. The words had the ring of a death knell. His fist slammed down on the mattress so hard another shot of pain ripped through him. He swallowed, fighting to keep the swirling black circles of unconsciousness at bay.

"The laudanum will take effect soon, milord. Rest is always the best medicine." The old man creaked over to his tapestry satchel and began to put his instruments of torture away. "I shall return on the morrow to change the dressings. Until then, sleep well, milord."

Stephen said nothing. The pain had begun to fade beneath the heavy dose of laudanum the doctor had given him. It dragged him down, beckoned him to the soothing relief of slumber. Still, he lay there for several long minutes, awake enough to recall the duel, to imagine the triumph in Harcourt's face as he saw Stephen lying there, bleeding on the grass.

At least there would be little fear of scandal. He had threatened his two sycophantic friends, warning them to keep their mouths shut. Cowardice was unacceptable in the *ton,* and he refused to be shunned from Society merely for attempting to rid the world of another unwanted bastard. So what if he had turned an instant sooner than he should have? So what if he had run, hoping to save himself?

Harcourt wouldn't say a word. He'd be too worried about his wife's already less than sterling reputation and Greville would be worried about his friends.

Beneath the thick layer of laudanum, images of Harcourt's too-handsome features blurred into those of Kassandra. He could still see her racing across the field, terrified at the inconsequential crease in Harcourt's otherwise perfect torso. The jolt of hatred Stephen felt in that moment was nearly as painful as the bastard's lead ball.

The two of them had schemed this—he had never been more certain. They'd hoped to destroy him. But Stephen still lived, and as long as he did, he wouldn't rest until he got even.

With Harcourt for shooting him.

With the bastard's precious little wife for being such an irresistible temptation when she was just sixteen.

20

It was nearly noon when Kitt left Clay sleeping upstairs in his big featherbed. He was resting comfortably and his wound no longer bled; it looked, thank God, as if he was going to be all right. Still, the terror she had felt last night, combined with only a few hours of fitful slumber, left her in a state of near exhaustion.

She needed to rest but her mind whirled with disturbing thoughts and she could no longer remain abed. Careful not to wake Clay, she returned to her own bedchamber and rang for Tibby to help her dress, then wearily made her way downstairs. Perhaps some tea and toast would make her feel better.

She had almost reached the entry when she heard a knock at the door and paused on the bottom stair to discover who it was. Henderson hurried to pull open the heavy portal and the moment he did, his bushy gray eyebrows shot up. A woman stood on the porch across from him, and Kitt recognized her long-time friend, Glynis Marston Trowbridge, Lady Camberwell, looking a little bit worried and very, very pregnant.

"Good heavens, Glyn, come in before you teeter right over on your nose."

Glynis laughed good-naturedly and waddled in out of the chilly late May wind. Brown-haired and green-eyed, she was pretty in a simple, unobtrusive way. She scarcely looked the type to sneak out with Kitt to a boxing match, but then Glyn had always been full of surprises.

"I hope I'm not intruding," she said. "I meant to send a note, but time slipped away. I'm a bit of a scatterbrain lately."

"Don't be silly," Kitt said, though she was hardly in the mood for visitors. If it had been anyone but Glynis, she would have made her excuses and escaped. "You know I'm always glad to see you."

"I realize it's hardly the thing for a woman in my condition to be toddling about the city, but I knew you wouldn't mind and I was about to go mad in the house."

"Come on. Let's go into the drawing room. I imagine we could both use a cup of tea."

Henderson saw to the task, carrying the heavy silver tray into the salon at the front of the house with the lovely green-striped sofas. Glynis sat in a matching overstuffed chair while Kitt finished pouring the tea.

"Aside from escaping my confinement," Glynis said, taking a sip of the flavorful brew, a faintly sweet blackberry and currant tea Kitt knew her friend particularly enjoyed, "I had an ulterior motive for coming. Thomas dropped by the Duke of Chester's ball last night to wish him felicitations on his birthday. When he returned, he mentioned he had seen you. He said that you and Clay left rather abruptly and he hoped that nothing was amiss. Since I've scarcely seen you since your wedding, I wanted to be certain that you were all right."

Kitt's teacup remained in the air halfway to her lips. She thought of her husband lying upstairs with a bullet wound in his side. She thought of how desperately she had fallen in love with him and what a disaster it was certain to be. She thought of Clay and Elizabeth Watkins and set the cup back down, untouched, in its saucer.

"I had a bit of a headache last night, is all. Clay thought it would be best if we went home."

Glynis studied Kitt's face, assessing the faint purple smudges beneath her eyes. "You look a little pale, Kassandra. Are you certain that you're all right?"

Kitt didn't answer. Instead her glance went to her friend's protruding stomach, the mound that would soon be Glyn's child. "You're about to become a mother. Surely you must be pondering any number of things. Have you ever thought . . . have you ever worried that your husband might . . . that someday Thomas might stray?"

Glynis sighed and leaned back in her chair, trying to get comfortable though it seemed an impossible task. "Every woman wonders, I suppose, though I do my best not to think about it. Tom is rather quiet and a little bit shy. He often prefers being at home to going out. That is one of the reasons I married him."

"Because you believed he would make a good husband."

"Yes. A good husband and father. I hoped he would be content with me as his wife."

"Do you love him?"

"Of course. Tom is kind and gentle. He's a good provider and—"

"No, what I meant to say is are you *in love* with him?"

Glynis set her teacup back in its saucer. "I care a great deal for Thomas and he cares about me. To be honest, that is all I want from our marriage. Soon I'll have a child and in time there will be others. If Tom should stray, I shall endure it, as any wife must."

"But if it should happen, your heart won't be broken."

"If he does seek another woman's company, I hope I never find out, but the fact is, most men do, and no, my heart will not be broken." Glynis eyed her with scrutiny. "Is that what has happened? Is Clayton having an affair with Elizabeth Watkins?"

Kitt sat upright and quickly shook her head, but the image of Clay last night with the beautiful Lady May refused to disappear. "No, it's nothing like that. But I won't deny it worries me. I couldn't be as accepting of a mistress as you, Glyn. It simply isn't my nature." *I love him far too much.*

Glyn smiled, but it seemed to take a little too much effort. "Well then, you will simply have to keep him content. Some men are faithful, you know. Not many, of course, but a few."

"Yes . . . of course, there are always a few." But Clay would never be one of them. Ignoring the sick feeling that burned like acid in the pit of her stomach, Kitt smiled and changed the subject. "So, when is the baby due?"

Her friend's entire face lit up, brightening to a rosy glow. She began to speak of the child, of the names she and Thomas had chosen, Alice for a girl, Jason Thomas if the infant was a boy. She talked about the nursery that had recently been completed, and plans for a christening that were already underway. Kitt listened with only half an ear, a smile pasted firmly on her face.

She was thinking of the man upstairs, thinking how much she loved him ...

... and more certain than ever it was the worst thing she could possibly do.

Sitting in the window seat of the drawing room, Kassandra set aside her sketch pad and slowly came to her feet. It was impossible to concentrate. She had been trying for hours and only accomplished a few, meaningless scribbles on the page.

Ever since the shooting, all she'd been able to think of was Clay. The way he had stood up for her, and so fearlessly put his life in danger. Sweet God, when she'd seen the blood on his shirt, she had been nearly paralyzed with fear. It was the moment she had known how totally and completely she was in love with him.

His tall handsome image rose in her mind and a painful lump formed in her throat. She loved him as she never thought she could, loved his loyalty, his gentle concern, his fierce protectiveness. In truth, she loved nearly everything about him. It made her heartsick to think how deeply she had fallen, and to make matters worse, since the night of the duel, he had been more solicitous than ever and even more charming.

Her love for him was swelling like a tumor in her heart—one she desperately needed to cut out.

Kitt crossed the room, her mind on her conversation with Glynis, her chest aching dully. *If he does seek another woman ... most men do ... I shall endure it, as any wife must.*

Her heart throbbed. She wasn't like Glynis. If Clay

took a mistress, she wouldn't be able to bear it. Not the way she felt about him now.

Since the morning Glyn had come to visit, Kitt had tried to put some distance between her and Clay. She had argued with him, goaded him, tried to make him lose his temper as he'd so often done before, but all he had done was shake his head, grin and kiss her, or carry her off to bed.

His side was rapidly healing and he had refused to remain locked in the house. Instead he had taken her for long rides in the park, taken her to the theater, taken her to the opera. He had brought her presents and armloads of flowers.

God above, every day she fell a little deeper under his spell—and more terrified than ever of the perilous road that could only lead to heartbreak.

The heaviness in her chest expanded and tears collected in her eyes. Sweet God, she never should have married him. She knew the way he was. The way he would always be. She had known Clay for years. His reputation as a lover was legend. The number of women he took to his bed was the talk of the *ton*. He charmed them with a single glance, won their hearts with only a smile. Clay made each of them feel as if she were the only woman in the world.

Now *she* was his latest conquest, the woman he was currently enamored of, the one to receive his undivided attention. But as surely as the sun came up, that would change. The day would come that he grew tired of her and went off in search of someone else.

For God's sake, the man's own mother had been mistress to a duke! Clay had been raised to believe keeping a woman as well as a wife was perfectly acceptable. She thought of him making love to Elizabeth

Watkins and a dozen other women and a painful lump thickened in her throat. Dear God, how could she have been such a fool? How could she have allowed him to insinuate himself so deeply in her heart?

She paced back and forth before the window, her chest hurting, love for Clay gnawing away at her like an abscessed wound.

You've got to do something! a voice inside her shouted.

You've got to find a way to protect yourself!

It was the truth. Dear Lord, it was the truth. Whatever it took, she had to stop this insane infatuation before it completely destroyed her. But there was no easy way to accomplish the task, at least none she had thought of so far.

Her heart felt leaden as she crossed her bedchamber and pulled open the drawer to put away her sketch pad. Her portfolio lay inside and impulsively she began leafing through her more recent drawings, those of Clay's servants and the ones of the hanging, pausing when she reached the pictures she had made last year in Italy.

A drawing of her cousin Emily surfaced, laughing with her three children, Marcus, Geraldine, and Harrison, on the veranda of her villa in Ostia, not far from Rome. She'd been happy there, carefree in a way she had never been before. If only she could go back there. She could forget about Clay, forget her unwise marriage. In a few months' time, she would be able to put him at arm's length again.

The notion began to change from a wistful longing to a desperate possibility, and with it came a surge of hope. Emily would welcome her with open arms. She and her husband loved to entertain visitors and especially family from home. Kitt received a very large monthly stipend, a goodly portion of which sat untouched in her personal account, money enough for the journey and any incidentals she might need while she was away. She would simply tell Clay—

Her planning abruptly ended and her rising spirits crumbled.

The moment she mentioned leaving, Clay would forbid her to go. He would expect her to play the role of wife exactly as he saw fit, and that didn't include a lengthy time apart. But now that the idea had taken root, she simply couldn't ignore it. It was the answer to her prayers, a means of saving herself.

What to do . . . ?

Even as the question formed, the answer came with it. Clay was planning a business trip with Justin at the end of the week. Something about a mine in Derbyshire and a problem that had arisen. The men would be gone for six or seven days. If she could book passage on a ship, she could be gone by the time Clay returned.

He would be angry, of course, but in a few days' time, he would get over it.

And she would have time to get over him.

Her pulse accelerated with a fresh shot of hope. Once she was away from him, she'd be able to put their relationship back in its proper perspective. She could bring her emotions under control and accept things the way they were. Do as Glynis would do.

Memories arose of the days they had shared since their marriage, of his gentleness and caring, his laughter and passionate lovemaking. Once she left, those days would be over forever. She would lose him completely, she knew, and a sharp pain stabbed through her. She had never imagined what it might be like to fall in love and especially not with a notorious rogue like Clay. Every time she thought of how hopeless it was, her heart just simply shattered.

Kitt dragged in a shaky breath and wiped the tears from her cheeks.

She considered speaking to Ariel, explaining why she had to leave, but her friend was forever scolding her about running away from her problems. Ariel believed it was better to stay and face up to them—and she would, Kitt vowed, once she had her life back in control.

Sitting down at her small French writing desk, she quickly penned a note to Emily of her pending arrival. Then she rang for Tibby to help her change into something appropriate for a trip down to the docks. She would locate a ship to carry her abroad, and in a very few days, she would be gone.

Just thinking about it made her feel better.

It was with a sense of relief and not the heartbreak she expected that she wrote her husband a brief farewell message the day after he and Justin left for the country, bundled her steamer trunks into the carriage, and set off with her maid for the ship that waited at the docks.

In the long run, she told herself, Clay would be glad for what she had done. After a few months apart, she could return to London with a completely different attitude, and be as cavalier about her marriage as the rest of the women in the *ton*. Clay could have his mistresses and she wouldn't give a damn.

As the ship set sail, Kitt ignored the tearing pain in her heart and vowed she would see it done.

* * *

He couldn't believe it, he simply could not. Standing in front of the dresser in his bedchamber the afternoon of his return to the city, Clay read for the third time the message Kassandra had left for him.

Dearest Clayton,

In your absence, the air in the city has become quite abominable. It is past time for a change of scenery and a little fresh air. With that goal in mind, I have decided to pay a visit to my cousin. As you may recall, Emily and her husband, Lord St. Denise, own a villa outside Rome. As I remain uncertain the length of my stay, I shall inform you of such at a later date.

With regards,
Your wife, Kassandra

He read the letter one last time, assessing the coldly impersonal words, trying to find some hint of emotion, some thread of feeling. Surely the iron-hearted bitch who wrote it couldn't be his adorable little wife. She couldn't be the same woman he had made love to the night before he'd left, the soft, responsive creature who had wept his name in passion and slept sweetly in his arms.

Fury engulfed him. He had imagined the months after his marriage in a dozen different ways, but he had never imagined Kitt would abandon him just weeks after they had wed.

Wadding up the note, he slammed it into the waste bin and strode toward the bellpull to ring for his valet. Damn her to hell, she was his wife! A wife belonged with her husband! He would track her down and drag her home by her lovely red hair!

The thought slid away even as his fingers closed

around the silken bellpull. He might have made love to a number of women, but he had never made a fool of himself chasing after one. He didn't intend to start now. Dammit, he wasn't some randy stallion, running after a mare in heat!

He thought of the weeks since his marriage, the gut-wrenching anger he had felt when he'd discovered what Stephen Marlow had done, the care he had taken to bring her gently to his bed, the concern and respect he had always shown her. He had done everything in his power to be the sort of husband Kitt deserved. If that wasn't good enough for her, there was nothing more he could do.

Stalking out of the room, he stormed down the stairs to his study and poured himself a brandy. He remembered the coolness of her note and anger rose up once more. He tried to recall every moment they had spent together in the past few weeks. Had he done something to offend her? Had something happened in the days that he had been gone?

As furious as he was, he couldn't rest without knowing why she had left him, and if anyone would know, it was Ariel. Clay tossed down the brandy and returned upstairs, shouting for his valet to pack him a bag. He would go to Greville Hall to discover the truth of Kitt's departure. She had always been reckless and unpredictable, but surely there was more to it than that.

Gripping his valise a little harder than necessary, Clay pounded back down the stairs, determined to discover the reason his wife had run away.

"She's gone." Standing in the open doorway of the Blue Room at Greville Hall, Clay watched the confusion spread across his two friends' faces.

Seated on a sofa in front of the tall mullioned window, Ariel's gaze caught his and for a moment, she simply stared. "You're not talking about Kassandra? What do you mean she is gone?"

"I mean exactly that. Gone. Departed. Left. Fled the country."

"Fled the country?" Ariel came to her feet. "For God's sake, where did she go?"

Clay still stood in the doorway. He had yet to make it completely into the room. "According to the very brief note she left me, she has gone to visit her cousin. That's why I came. I'm here to discover why my wife has run away."

Ariel's pretty blue eyes darkened with distress. "I don't know. She never mentioned anything about leaving. I have absolutely no idea why she would go, but she must have had a reason." She cast an accusing glance at Clay. "What did you do to her?"

Fell in love with her, he almost confessed, the thought forming painfully, though he had known the truth since that morning at Grantham Park, known it the instant he had seen her, pale and shaken, running toward him in the faint light of dawn. She had come there to protect him, afraid that he would be killed, and seeing her face bleached white with fear, he had recognized the gut-twisting emotion he suffered as love.

He hadn't meant for it to happen, never considered the possibility such an event might occur. Greville had fallen prey to a woman's charms, but he never believed it would happen to him.

Clay didn't utter the words. It was embarrassing enough that his wife had run away from him. He would look an utter fool if they knew how devastated he was.

"What did I do to her?" he drawled, strolling a little farther into the room. "Let me see . . . in the past few days, I've squired her all over London. I've bought her roses, a diamond brooch, and a pair of very noisy lovebirds she seemed particularly fond of. Oh, and lest I forget, I made love to her until she nearly passed out with pleasure. That sort of treatment is certain to make any woman flee into the night like a scalded rabbit."

Ariel stood her ground. "You must have done *something.*"

Clay shrugged as he wandered toward them, trying to appear indifferent when it was the last thing he was feeling. "Not as far as I can recall. We haven't quarreled. She made no mention of being unhappy. Like a fool, I actually believed we were getting on very well." Something was hurting inside his chest. He forced himself to ignore it.

He knew the way Kitt was, headstrong and reckless, often irresponsible. She hadn't wanted to marry him in the first place. What an idiot he had been to actually believe simply because he had fallen in love with her, she would fall equally in love with him.

Ariel must have read some of his thoughts. She walked toward him, slid her arms around his neck and gave him a sisterly hug. "Whatever has happened, Kassandra should have stayed and talked to you about it. Sooner or later, she'll reason that out." She stepped back a little to look at him. "How soon will you be leaving?"

"Leaving? Why would I be leaving?"

"Surely you're going after her."

He wanted to. Dammit, he wanted to find her and wring her pretty little neck. He wanted to drag her back to their bedchamber, tie her to the bedpost, and make love to her until she never wanted to run again.

"Kassandra is a grown woman. If she is happier in Italy than she was with me, there is nothing I can do about it."

The room fell silent. Ariel bit her lip and Justin stepped into the breach. "Kassandra may be impetuous on occasion, but she is not a fool. In time, she'll recognize her folly and return."

He smiled sardonically. "Perhaps." But something told him it wouldn't be soon.

He felt Ariel's light touch on his shoulder. "Give her a chance, Clay. Whatever is wrong, in time, she'll work it out. As soon as she does, she'll return."

He nodded. He really had no choice. He loved her. He wanted their marriage to work. Secretly, he had always envied Justin and Ariel their somewhat unconventional marriage. Unlike most of the *ton,* theirs was a love match, a bond that ran deep and true. Once he'd discovered how much she meant to him, Clay had hoped he and Kassandra would build such a bond. Now he wondered at the folly of such thinking, and, as the days slid past and he received no further word from her, the bitterness he was feeling continued to build.

Dammit, she owed him at least an explanation.

A letter arrived six weeks later. He ripped it open with an unsteady hand, praying the note would say that she was sorry for leaving, that she had missed him, that she was on her way back home.

Instead it was as brief and cool as the last. She was fine. Her cousin and her family were fine. The weather was warm. She was sketching a little. She still remained uncertain as to when she would return.

Clay crushed the letter in a tightly clenched fist, tossed it away, and stormed out of the study. He didn't bother to answer the message. That night he proceeded to get blind, falling-down drunk. He got into a fistfight outside his club and came home with his knuckles scraped raw and his heart hurting worse than it had before.

He had known that he was in love with her.

He hadn't understood that he was insanely, wildly, ridiculously head over the mark, and he hated himself for it.

And little by little, as the days crept slowly past, Clay began to hate Kitt even more than he did himself.

21

≈≈≈

Kitt sat on the veranda, her sketch pad lying carelessly open in her lap. Her cousin's villa overlooked the small town of Ostia, the closest seaport to Rome. From where she rested beneath a big, yellow-striped umbrella, the blue Tyrrhenian Sea stretched for miles off the white sand beaches along the coast. A cool breeze tugged at her hair, lifting it away from her cheeks, giving her respite from the late July sun.

"Kassandra—there you are. I wondered where I might find you."

She turned to see her cousin walking toward her. Dressed in a cool white muslin gown trimmed with pale blue satin ribbons, Emily Wentworth Wilder, Lady St. Denise, was nearly her same height, but her petite frame was far more fragile, her skin more pale, her hair a deep chestnut brown.

Emily's husband, Preston Wilder, Baron St. Denise, had accepted a post as advisor to the British Ambassador in Rome. His mother was Italian. Pres had spent a good deal of time in the country and spoke the language fluently. By now, so did Emily and all three of their very precocious children.

Kitt smiled at the cousin she loved like an older sister. "It's such a beautiful day I couldn't stand being indoors. I thought I might sit outside and do a little drawing."

Emily looked down at her open sketch pad, saw the odd little squiggles that were all she had drawn, and frowned. "I see you haven't finished."

Kitt merely shrugged.

Emily sat down in the chair beside her. "I'm worried about you, Kassandra. You've been here more than a month, and you still don't seem yourself. You smile and carry on a conversation but you never seem to say whatever it is that you are thinking. You pretend to draw, but you never get anything done. It isn't like you, dear."

Emily caught Kitt's hand, freckled across the back since she rarely wore her gloves. "I've hoped that in time you would talk to me about what's bothering you, but you never have. I'm your friend, you know. Why don't you tell me what is wrong?"

It was the first time Emily had actually pressed her. Until now, her cousin had apparently hoped she would work things out on her own. Kitt had hoped to hide her heartbreak, but it was obvious she hadn't succeeded.

She took a breath, slowly released it, tried to muster a smile and failed. "It's quite simple, really. I married the wrong man."

Emily's pale hand fluttered up to her throat. "Oh, my dear girl. Surely you don't mean that. In the letters I received after your marriage, you spoke so highly of

Clayton. What has he done to make you believe he is not the right man?"

She only shook her head. Tears were beginning to well and she refused to let that happen. She had come here to get over him. Simply put, she had come to fall out of love.

Unfortunately, after a voyage of several weeks and a month on the Continent, she loved him just as much as she had before.

"It isn't what he did. It is simply the man he is. I knew what he was like before I married him. I knew he would never be satisfied with only one woman. I thought I could live with that. At the time, I actually believed it wouldn't matter. I never meant to fall in love with him."

She brushed a stubborn tear from beneath her lashes. "I came here to forget him, but I can't seem to do it. I think of him every day, every minute. The letter I received yesterday from Ariel begged me to come home. She says I've hurt Clay dreadfully, that if I don't come back, I am certain to ruin my marriage. But I really never had a marriage, not the sort you and Ariel have. Clay never wanted to marry me in the first place. He doesn't love me. I can't go back until I stop loving him."

She started crying then, she couldn't help it. She had forbidden herself to cry since the day she'd left England and so far she had succeeded. Now a sob leaked from her throat and tears erupted like a geyser, streaming down her cheeks, dripping onto the front of her blue muslin gown.

Her face lined with sympathy, Emily reached into the pocket of her skirt and dragged out an embroidered handkerchief. She handed it to Kitt, who furiously dabbed at her eyes.

"I'm sorry . . . I didn't mean for that to happen."

Emily also blinked back tears. "I'm glad it did. You know you are welcome to stay here as long as you like. Preston and I enjoy your company and the children love you dearly. But I can see how unhappy you are. Perhaps you should consider going home. Perhaps it is time you talked to Clay, tried to work things out."

But there was no way to do that. Clay was Clay. Until she could accept him exactly the way he was, she had to stay away. She wrote him an occasional letter, but always kept it impersonal. She had received one equally terse correspondence from him and cried for the balance of the day.

Emily continued urging her to return, at least voice her concerns and clear the air between them. Kitt refused.

She was getting stronger, she believed, beginning to forget him. Just a little more time and she would be the strong, independent woman she had been before she met him. She could deal with him then on an equal footing—the way she had meant to keep things from the start.

But another week passed and she ached for him just as much as she had the weeks before. Dear Lord, she still loved him. What in God's name was she going to do?

Clay strode into the lavish marble entry of Rathmore Hall. Two weeks ago, Her Grace, Joanne Barclay, his father's wife, had succumbed to an illness that had lingered these two months past. Two days ago, his father had been shot in a hunting accident. Clay hadn't heard the news until this morning, when a footman appeared at his door with the unwelcome message and an urgent request for Clay to return with him to his father's bedside.

Clay had done so in all haste, worry gnawing at him every minute of the way. He loved his father. They were so much alike, and though they had never spent a good deal of time together, there had always been a special sort of bond between them. As a boy, more than anything in the world, he had wanted his father to claim him as his son.

It hadn't happened and for years, Clay had resented the fact. In truth, it was part of the reason he had gained such a wild reputation. It was certainly the reason he had never told the duke how successful he had become.

Let the old man believe the worst, he'd always thought. If he couldn't be a legitimate son like his older half-brother, Richard, he would be the rake, the gaming, womanizing bastard son.

Trying to calm his fears, he followed the butler up the sweeping grand staircase and down the hall into the duke's massive suite of rooms. He had never been in the house before. Rathmore Hall was the duchess's domain and his father always did his best to shield her from anything unpleasant, including his illegitimate son.

Not that she didn't know he existed.

Like most of the women in the aristocracy, she simply pretended not to care.

The butler shoved open the door and Clay walked past him into the room. At the sight of the pale, hollow-eyed man lying in the middle of the huge four-poster bed, his footsteps halted.

Surely this broken, shattered hull of a man wasn't the youthful, vital man his father had been just a few days before.

It took an effort of will to continue across the carpet. When he reached the bed, he went down on one knee, reached over and clasped the duke's cold, pale hand. "I came as soon as I heard, Father."

He barely nodded. "I'm glad ... you're here."

"What happened? The footman said only that there was an accident and you had been shot."

The duke dragged in a difficult breath and Clay's chest went tight at the pain he read on his father's face.

"We were ... pheasant hunting. Stockton ... Sir Hubert, Lord Winston ... and a few other friends. Something ... happened. Winston was laughing and suddenly ... his gun went off. Caught me in the middle of ... the chest." He coughed, wheezed in a breath, and Clay's fingers tightened around his hand.

He could see the wound. The bandage across his father's torso showed faint traces of dark red blood. Fear coiled in his stomach. He glanced around for the physician but didn't see him.

"Where's the doctor? Why isn't he here?"

"I asked him to wait ... outside. I wanted to ... speak to you ... alone." He began to cough again, wheezed in several hacking breaths, and Clay slid an arm behind his shoulders to help him sit up a little straighter. The coughing eased, but the wheezing sound continued with every breath and the wound had started oozing blood again.

"I'll get the doctor."

"Not yet. Not until I've said ... what I need to."

Clay clenched his jaw against a rising tide of fear. The wound was serious, perhaps even mortal, and there was nothing he could do. He had never felt so helpless in his life, never more alone, not even when his mother died. For an instant he thought of Kassandra, and desperately wished she were there. With ruthless force, he shoved the thought away. He would face this on his own, as he had faced most things in his life. He didn't need a wife who didn't want him.

"Let me fetch the doctor."

The duke shook his head. "There is something important . . . I need to say."

Clay fell silent. He couldn't imagine what it might be. He was barely able to think.

His father coughed once, cleared his throat. It was obvious how much effort it took to speak. "Since the day you were born I've . . . loved you. You will never know the joy . . . you brought to your mother . . . and to me. You were the son of . . . my heart, even though you never . . . carried my name."

A thick lump formed in Clay's throat. His chest felt as if it were encased in stone.

"I wanted to . . . claim you. You will never know . . . how much. Your mother understood. Rachael knew how much . . . I loved you both, but I had a wife to consider. I never loved Joanne, but I . . . respected her. Now Joanne is gone and there is nothing . . . to stop me from doing what I have wanted to do . . . for so long." He coughed, reached a shaky hand out for the handkerchief Clay handed him, pressed it against his lips.

"Last week," he continued weakly, "I took the necessary steps . . . to make you legally . . . my son. From this day forward, you are . . . Clayton Harcourt Barclay."

Tears burned his eyes. He hadn't cried since he was a boy and he wouldn't do it now, but it took every ounce of his will. "Thank you, Father. You'll never know how much that means to me." His voice cracked on the last. He cleared his throat, fighting to keep his emotions in check, uncertain he would succeed. Reaching into the pocket of his coat, he pulled out a folded square of paper.

"I have something for you, as well." He had taken it out of the safe before he'd left the house. He had done it on impulse, or perhaps some sixth sense had told him how seriously injured his father was. With a hand that shook, he passed his father the paper, pressing it into his icy fingers.

"What ... is it?"

"A bank draft for fifty thousand pounds. The wager we made. The money you gave me the day I married Kassandra."

His father's pale lips edged up in the faintest of smiles. "You never cashed it. I know. My banker ... told me."

"I didn't marry her for the money. I wanted her from the start."

His father's fingers wrapped around his hand. The skin felt as dry and cold, as brittle as parchment. "I heard she ... left London. Did the two of you ... ?"

"I was in love with her. I don't know why she left."

"She is ... young. She has always ... been impulsive. But Kitt is the right ... woman for you. Remember that, son. In time ... things will work out."

Clay said nothing. Things with Kassandra were never going to work out and he no longer cared. He had suffered enough at the hands of his errant wife. He was married to her, but he no longer felt like a husband. She had shown no loyalty to him, no caring. No love. He owed none to her.

He looked down at the duke's sunken, gauze-wrapped chest. "The bleeding's getting worse. Let me get the doctor." Determined this time, he started walking toward the door.

The duke's reedy voice followed after him. "There is one . . . other small thing."

He turned. "Yes . . . ?"

"I've disinherited . . . Richard. I've made you . . . my heir."

Clay couldn't have been more stunned if his father had told him he had just been crowned king. "What are you talking about?"

"There were things I discovered . . . things I cannot allow nor . . . forgive. As you are more of a son to me than he ever was . . . I cannot say I am sorry it has turned out as it has."

For a minute, Clay simply couldn't move. His thoughts were whirling, trying to make some sort of sense. The Rathmore title and fortune. His father was giving it to him, trusting him with all he owned, all he had built through the years. "Are you certain about this, Father? Are you absolutely sure this is what you want?"

He summoned a weak, pain-filled smile. "Absolutely . . . certain."

Clay clamped down on a fierce swell of emotion, his throat so tight he could barely speak. "I won't disappoint you, Father. I promise you that."

"I know you won't, son. You . . . never have."

Blinking rapidly, Clay turned and strode out the door, shouting for the physician, seeing him through a film of moisture.

Three days later, his father was dead.

Clay became the Seventh Duke of Rathmore, one of the wealthiest men in England. Bitterly, he wondered if Kassandra would find it easier to stomach a duke than a bastard son.

Kitt sat on the veranda, her sketch pad in her lap, watching her cousin's three adorable children playing on the grass below. It caused a bittersweet ache. She loved children. She had wanted children of her own—Clay's children—but the way things stood between them, that would never occur.

Before she'd left London, she had intended, on her return, to try again to conceive. By then she would be her old self again, able to accept Clay's notion of marriage and play the part of wife that he and the rest of the *ton* expected.

Unfortunately, that hadn't occurred. She was still in love with him, as wildly, as desperately as she had been the day she ran away.

Kitt dragged in a shaky breath of air. That was the way she saw it now, that she had run like a frightened child. After weeks of living apart from him, the stark reality was—Kitt had deserted her husband. Coldly, with utter calculation, giving no thought to his feelings or explaining the least notion why.

She had been so terrified of losing him that she had tossed away whatever chance she might have had of making their marriage work.

She looked down at the letter a footman had delivered just that morning, a message from Anna. Dated several weeks earlier, it began pleasantly enough, Anna talking about the weather, about her children, about the soiree she had held and who had been there. It was the passage on the second page, the portion Kitt had read a dozen times, that brought a sharp stinging wetness to her eyes.

I worry so for you, my dear friend, and my heart breaks for your Clay. He was so terribly in love with you, and he was so badly hurt. He has become a bitter man since you left him.

I think of you both very often. I wonder if you went because you were afraid of your feelings. I am one who knows about such things. After losing my Antonio, I was frightened of being hurt again, afraid to risk loving another man. But I have been a coward far too long. I have fallen in love with Ford and though he has not yet proposed marriage, he is a man worth any sort of risk. At last I see that, and I am no longer afraid.

I am no longer afraid.

The words seemed to throb bone-deep inside her. Like Anna, she had been the worst sort of coward. For months, she had been gone, hiding in Italy like a rabbit in a warren, waiting for the pain of loving Clay to go away. Instead it had festered and swollen, aching with every beat of her heart.

Ariel had written her, beseeching her to come home, to face her problems, to fight for what she wanted.

What she wanted, of course, was Clay.

He was so terribly in love with you.

Was it true? Had Clay really loved her?

With a hand that shook, she set the letter on the small wicker table beside her chair and flipped open the sketch pad she held in her lap. Clay's smiling face gazed back at her, the strong jaw and solid chin, the straight nose and full, sensuous lips. She thought of the way he had always protected her, always been so gentle, so caring and concerned. She thought of his passionate lovemaking, a fire that seemed to blaze hotter each time they were together.

Had he loved her?

She stared down at the drawing, one of dozens she had made of him over the past few weeks. She couldn't seem to draw anything else. Beautiful golden eyes stared back at her and there was something about them. . . . She flipped the page, studied a sketch of Clay propped up in bed, his muscular arms shoved behind his head. It was there again, the faint, soft yearning she couldn't quite define but always seemed present when she drew him, drifting among the treasured memories she carried.

Had he loved her? Dear God, what if he had?

Kitt picked up the letter. *He was so terribly in love with you, and he was so badly hurt. He has become a bitter man since you left him.* She shivered, though the sun slanted in under the big umbrella and the day was overly warm.

She didn't know what to believe where her husband was concerned, but the fact was, she still loved him. Wholly and completely, desperately and irrevocably.

And she wanted his love in return more than anything else on earth.

Ariel had won Justin's love. Anna was determined to win Ford's. Was it possible that she could win Clay's?

If the odds had been against her before, they were slashed to a pittance now. But time had made her stronger, able to see things more clearly. The pain of leaving him had forged an inner strength that she had never had. Now, reading Anna's letter, that strength coupled with a resolve that wrapped around her heart like a fist.

"Letter from home?" Emily stood a few feet away, a gentle smile on her face. Emily and Preston also had a solid, loving marriage. There actually were such things, she knew. They happened. Not often, but it wasn't completely impossible.

Kitt got up from her chair, the letter gripped tightly in her hand. "I've got to go back, Emily. I'm in love with my husband. It's taken me a while, but I've discovered that nothing is going to change that." She handed Emily the letter and walked over to the balustrade, bracing her hands on the rail. A crisp, salty sea wind whipped through her hair and fluttered the yellow satin ribbons woven beneath the bodice of her gown.

"Running away has cost me my husband," she said, turning back to Emily. "It's destroyed my marriage and caused me endless pain. Now I've got to go back and face what I've done. I've got to try to make things right between us."

Emily walked up beside her, the letter waving in her hand. There were tears in her light blue eyes when she returned it. "If you catch the first ship, you'll be home in a few weeks. When you get there, tell Clayton the way you feel. Tell him you love him, Kassandra."

She only shook her head. "I doubt he'd want to hear it. I don't think he would believe me, even if I did. I know I wouldn't."

"Then show him, my dear. If he is all the things you once told me he was, he'll understand why you behaved as you did. In time, he'll forgive you."

But she wasn't sure he ever would.

And now that she realized exactly what she had done, Kitt didn't blame him.

*   *   *

Sitting in the gaming room of the Earl of White-lawn's sumptuous town mansion, Adam Hawthorne, Earl of Blackwood, raked in his chips, piling them up with his sizable stack of winnings.

"Well, gentlemen, I'm afraid that's all the time I have for tonight." He shoved back his chair. "I've a previous engagement—one that is far more tempting than winning a hand of whist." That was the truth. The hot little redhead he had been seeing would keep him hard the rest of the night. She never offered much in the way of conversation. Then again, when he got her beneath him, there wasn't much need for words.

Across the table, Lord Percy Richards grumbled something beneath his breath. "You don't mean you're leaving without giving us a chance to win our money back?"

"I'm afraid so, Percy. I'll be happy to take more of your coin tomorrow night, if that is your wish."

Seated next to him, Clay Barclay, most recent Duke of Rathmore, slid back his chair and came to his feet. "I for one am damn glad you're leaving. You've the devil's own luck tonight. I've lost more than enough for one evening."

Adam's mouth edged up. Clay rarely lost. He was a very good player and never bet over his head. In the past few weeks, all that had changed. Clay had been drinking hard, engaging in deep play—and very often losing. Adam had heard the rumors. Clay's wife had left him, just weeks after their marriage. A trip to visit family abroad, it was said, but everyone wondered ...

And though it wasn't obvious to most, Adam could see how badly the girl's abandonment had hurt his friend. His jaw hardened. He had always liked Clay.

He was a damned good man, and he bloody well didn't deserve that kind of treatment.

Which was the reason, two weeks ago, Adam had introduced him to the tall, statuesque blond beauty, Lillian Wainscott, wife of the aging Marquess of Simington.

"I'm headed over to the Collingwood soiree," Adam said to Clay. "There's quite a crush going on over there tonight. Why don't you join me?"

Clay just smiled and shook his head. "I've an appointment tonight, myself, thanks to you. I'm meeting the lady right here."

As they descended the stairs, Adam spotted the marchioness standing in front of a gold-flocked wall in the long gallery.

"I gather the two of you are getting on well," Adam said matter-of-factly.

Clay shrugged. "Lillian's a beautiful woman."

"Yes, she is." Adam knew exactly how lovely she was. He and Lily had once been lovers but that had been years ago. Discovering the beautiful huntress was again on the prowl, Adam had introduced her to Clay.

He tipped a footman a vowel to fetch his hat and coat, then cocked his head toward the gallery. "I believe the lady has spotted you. Enjoy your evening, my friend."

"I imagine we both will," said Clay.

But Adam wondered. He knew the woman Clay really wanted, had known it the minute he had seen the two of them together.

A shot of anger slipped through him. He'd misjudged Kassandra Wentworth. Though he hardly knew her, he had sensed something about her. Against his better judgment and all his past experiences, he had mistakenly believed she was different from other women. Instead, she was merely another shallow, self-centered creature like the rest.

He cast a last glance at the blond beauty smiling at Clay and thought that at least a man knew where he stood with a woman like that. She wanted nothing but hot, mindless sex with no strings and no regrets.

Since that was exactly what Clay wanted from her, he figured they made a very good pair.

22

Exhaustion and nerves made her clumsy. The ship had arrived on the evening tide, but of course there was no one there to meet her. Kitt had returned to England as abruptly as she had departed, with only her steamer trunks and her loyal little maid. At any rate, since she'd caught the first packet bound for London, there hadn't been time for a letter to arrive there ahead of her.

Leaning back against the worn leather seat of the hack she had hired at the dock, Kitt closed her eyes and tried not to imagine what would happen when she reached the town house. What would Clay say? How angry would he be? Worse than that, what if he didn't care in the least?

Though the streets were crowded, it didn't take long to reach their residence off Grosvenor Square. Once they arrived, she paid the driver, then paid him again to help her and Tibby unload the trunks and carry them into the house. When the butler opened the door, his watery old eyes rounded in shock and he swayed on his feet.

"My lady! Er . . . I mean, Your Grace. We weren't expecting you. Here . . . let me help you with your baggage." He shouted for a footman and two of them raced over to pick up her trunks. "I'm terribly sorry. We didn't know you were coming."

"I left rather abruptly. There wasn't time for a letter to get here." From the corner of her eye she saw Tibby taking charge of the footmen and the baggage and leading the men upstairs.

"It's good you are safely returned," the butler said. "His Grace will be extremely surprised to—"

"For heaven's sake, Henderson, why do you keep saying that?"

"Saying what, Your Grace?"

"That. Why do you keep calling me Your Grace?"

"Because that is what you are. Oh, dear me. His Grace's letter must not have reached you before you left on your journey home. Oh, dear me." He straightened, drew himself up. "It is my most unfortunate duty to inform you that His Grace, the sixth Duke of Rathmore, died in a hunting accident. Your husband is the new Duke of Rathmore."

Her head spun. A sudden tightness settled in her chest. "The duke is dead?" She had always liked Clay's father. He had championed her any number of times when everyone else had condemned her.

"I'm terribly sorry, Your Grace."

Kitt shook her head, hardly able to believe the news. "I don't understand. Even if Rathmore is dead, Richard is the heir, not Clay."

"I'm afraid I don't know all of the whys and wherefores. I'm sure your husband will be able to explain."

She swallowed hard. Clay was a duke—and not just any duke—but Rathmore. The fortune that went with the Rathmore dukedom made him one of the wealthiest men in England.

Hope withered a little in her breast. If she'd had a fight ahead of her before, with the power and wealth he commanded now, he could have anything—anyone—he wanted. How could she possibly win him?

Kitt moistened lips that felt stiff and dry, and tried to sound nonchalant. "Where is he?"

"I'm afraid he is out for the evening. Gone to Lord Whitelawn's soiree, I believe."

She nodded. She would have to wait until he came home before she could talk to him. Part of her was disappointed, the other part relieved. She didn't have to face him. Not yet.

On the other hand, how could she stand to wait a moment more?

She made her way upstairs to change out of her clothes and found Tibby beginning to unpack.

"He's a duke," Tibby said with no little awe.

"Word travels fast."

"He's gone to Lord Whitelawn's soiree."

"So I've been told."

"I think you should go to him, my lady—I mean, Your Grace."

She flashed Tibby a look. It was difficult to get used to the idea that she was a duchess.

"It's late and I'm tired. I couldn't possibly face him tonight." But the thought refused to let go. It was insane. She was exhausted to the bone, and after nearly three weeks at sea, she looked an absolute fright. Still, he might not be home until morning and she had come so far, missed him so much. And there wasn't the least chance she could sleep until she had seen him.

"Are you sure you don't want to go?" Tibby pressed, reading her all too clearly.

She dragged in an uneasy breath. "What would I wear? I don't have anything—"

Before she could finish, Tibby raced off toward the armoire on the opposite side of the bedchamber. A few minutes later, she returned with an array of gowns Kitt hadn't taken with her when she left. One stood out among the others, an emerald green silk that glittered with golden beads, an incredibly beautiful gown Clay had picked out for her. Perhaps that was the reason she had left it behind.

"I'll need a bath," she said, her weariness beginning to fade. "And I should love a cup of tea." A stiff shot of spirits would probably be better, but she didn't dare indulge herself. She would need all of her wits about her when she first spoke to Clay.

It was late in the evening by the time her carriage waited out front and she was ready to leave for the Whitelawns' soiree. She could only imagine how angry Clay would be when he saw her. It terrified her to think of the scene he might make, but odds were he wouldn't want a scandal any more than she did.

Whatever happened, at least with a roomful of people, he wouldn't shun her completely.

Autumn had begun to color the landscape. The weather was chill, a damp wind blowing in off the sea, dark clouds hanging over the city, threatening rain. She drew her cloak a little tighter around her as she entered the three-story brick mansion and merged with the crush of people inside.

The house had been done in a Grecian motif, with ancient urns and rows of armless statues. Marble floors stretched into an endless number of drawing rooms. Steeling herself, Kitt began the search for her husband.

Standing beneath an elegant painted ceiling in the Flemish Salon, Clay absently surveyed his surroundings. Seventeenth-century tapestries hung at the tall mullioned windows, thick Persian carpets covered patterned marble floors, and hunting scenes in ornate gilded frames decorated the long expanse of wall. The Whitelawn mansion was beautiful in the extreme, but no more lovely than the woman who stood beside him.

Tall and fair, with pale blond hair swept up in a fashionable crown, a long, arched neck, and an elegantly slender figure, Lillian Wainscott, Marchioness of Simington, was one of the most beautiful women Clay had ever seen. Two weeks ago, at a rout at Sir Anthony Peppers's, Blackwood had introduced them. At Adam's urging, Clay had asked her to dinner and she had accepted. Tonight they would become lovers.

Clay studied the beautiful marchioness over the rim of his brandy glass as she conversed with the gray-haired Earl of Winston. Gossip was, Lily Wainscott was highly accomplished in the art of love. Tonight she would ease the needs that had been building in his body for the long months his wife had been gone.

It was past time it happened. Kitt had left him and even if she returned, it would never be the same between them. Lily was exactly what he needed, though he had been strangely reluctant to begin the affair. He remembered the night Adam had approached him.

"There's someone I think you should meet," Blackwood had said.

Clay just scoffed. "If it's a woman, forget it. That is the last thing I need."

"That, my friend, is exactly what you need. Your wife has made her choice. You owe her no loyalty now." The corners of his mouth lifted into a hard-edged smile. "Besides, the best way to cleanse your need of a woman is to find yourself another."

Clay agreed.

Ignoring the guilt and the ache in his heart, he was determined to make the only choice left to him. His relationship with Lily would be strictly sexual, of course, a shared need that went no further. It was enough for him. More than enough, though the notion left him feeling more empty than it should have, as if some elusive quality were missing.

Clay knew what it was. Making love and having sex were not the same. Loving someone was like sailing off the top of the world, or stepping off the edge of a cliff into thin air. It was an exhilarating, unforgettable experience—and he never wanted to feel that way again.

He gazed at Lily, knew that he would spend the night in her bed, and thought that when they were finished, at least he would finally be able to sleep. She looked at him, lifted a set of long, silky lashes, and her full mouth bloomed into a smile. There was no mistaking that smile. He knew women too well for that. It would soon be time for them to leave and Lily was looking forward to it.

By the time he took her home and got her in bed, he prayed that he would be, too.

Something shifted, stirred in the air around them. A soft murmur ran through the crowd. Lily lifted those beautiful, shrewd blue eyes to look over his shoulder and they sharpened as they fixed on the door.

"I believe someone is looking for you, darling."

He turned, saw the woman Lily referred to, and for an instant, his entire body contracted. She was wearing the emerald silk gown he had bought her, the bodice cut low, displaying the lovely white breasts he had caressed with such care. Her hair was swept up in fiery curls, and she wore a string of emeralds at her throat.

He imagined Lily's pale, elegant beauty and thought that it couldn't compare with Kassandra's wild, radiant fire.

She saw him in that moment, and her expression subtly altered. Her gaze ran over his face and the green of her eyes seemed to soften. She looked young and innocent and incredibly vulnerable. Her smile was so full of regret, it made the muscles across his stomach contract.

It was a lie, he knew. Kassandra didn't regret a thing. Still, it took sheer force of will to remain where he was, instead of striding across the room and dragging her into his arms.

Bloody hell.

He had convinced himself that he no longer cared about her, that when he finally saw her again, he would feel nothing. Now he recognized the power she still held over him, and fury streaked through him as hot as burning coals.

Kassandra must have noticed, for the soft look slowly faded. Bracing herself, she began to walk toward him, her steps only the least bit uncertain.

"I've never met your wife," the marchioness purred. "I believe I should like to."

He shoved down his rage and his lips edged into a cold, unforgiving smile. "Then by all means, you shall."

She settled a hand on his arm and he escorted her toward the woman he had married. They met halfway across the room, the focus of a goodly amount of observation.

"Good evening . . . Your Grace." Kitt sank into a curtsy, but her eyes remained on his face.

The cold smile never faltered. "Welcome home . . . Duchess."

Sadness surfaced in her eyes, softening the artificial curve of her lips. "I just heard the news about your father. I'm so sorry, Clay. I liked him very much. Everyone did. We're all going to miss him."

He ignored the sincerity in her voice. It made his chest feel tight, made him remember the day his father had died and how much he had wished that she were there with him.

"I'd like you to meet a friend of mine," he said smoothly. "Lady Simington, this is my wife, Kassandra."

Kitt shifted her gaze away from him, saw the proprietary look on Lily's face, and the faint smile she had mustered faded away. "A pleasure, my lady."

"The pleasure is entirely mine, Your Grace."

For an instant, Kitt's eyes flicked to his and he saw that she knew exactly the relationship he and Lillian Wainscott shared—or at least thought she did. Her spine slowly straightened. Her shoulders went square, yet it wasn't anger he saw in her eyes. Insanely, he could have sworn it was despair.

"I gather you've been away on the Continent," Lily said mildly. "Rome, wasn't it? One of my favorite cities. There is so much to do, so many parties to attend. One is never bored when one is in Rome."

Clay's jaw hardened. Bored? Kassandra? Hardly. He wondered how many handsome young Italians had squired her around the city.

"Actually," Kitt said, "I was staying in the country

with my cousin and her husband. They have three small children. Taking care of them requires a great deal of time. We rarely went into the city."

Lily ran a finger around the rim of her champagne glass. "Really?"

Clay cast a dark look in Kitt's direction. "I'm sure my wife was well entertained—wherever she happened to be."

Kitt looked straight into his eyes. "In truth, I was lonely. I missed my husband. I should have returned long before this."

She missed him? He wanted to laugh in her face.

"It's been a while since the two of you have seen each other," Lily said with exaggerated politeness, confident of her allure. "Why don't I leave you to get reacquainted?" She smiled slowly at Clay. "Besides, the hour is late and I grow weary. I believe I shall make my way home."

She cast him a meaningful glance as she walked away. The invitation remained. He would take it, he told himself. What better way to forget Kassandra than to make love to another woman just blocks from where she lay sleeping in her empty bed?

"Clay?"

At the sound of her voice, he turned, saw the uncertainty on her face.

"I shouldn't have gone," she said. "I know that now. It was wrong to run away. I'm sorry I did."

A muscle jerked in his cheek. He clamped down on a fresh shot of anger. "That's a very nice speech, Kassandra." Did she really believe a simple apology would erase what she had done? Did she think it would make him forget the long, empty nights he had spent without her, the hours he had worried for her safety, the embarrassment he had suffered in front of half the *ton?* Not bloody likely. "I presume you have transportation home."

"I . . . I asked my coachman to wait."

"Good, then if you will excuse me, I have plans with friends for the balance of the evening."

She straightened, her chin going up. She cast a glance toward the doorway Lily had just passed through. "Lady Simington, I presume."

He didn't deny it.

"Then forgive me for delaying your departure. I'm sure you wouldn't want to keep her waiting."

He made an exaggerated bow and gave her a last cool smile. "Enjoy the evening . . . Your Grace."

Kitt made no reply. He ignored the faint trembling of her lip as she turned and walked away, but the haunted look in her eyes stayed with him all the way to his carriage. In the end, he postponed his rendezvous with Lily and simply went to his club. He got drunk, gambled away a small chunk of his newly acquired fortune, and didn't go home until late the following morning. When he got there, Kitt was gone.

He wondered if she'd already packed her things and left him again.

Kitt followed Perkins, Greville's stoic butler, down the long marble-floored hall of the earl's town house. She had sent a note that morning to discover if Ariel was in residence and was relieved to discover that she was.

She heard her friend's voice in the drawing room. When Ariel saw Kitt walking toward her, she opened her arms and Kitt rushed into them, fighting to hold back tears.

"I'm so glad you're home."

Kitt tried to smile. "I'm so glad to be here."

"Come—we'll go someplace where we can be private." Ariel paused in the hallway long enough to order tea and cakes, then they made their way to a sunny yellow salon at the rear of the town house.

"When did you get back?" Ariel sat down on a yellow striped sofa and Kitt sat down beside her.

"The *Dolphin* arrived last evening. The voyage seemed endless. I thought I would never get home."

"I presume you know by now that you are the Duchess of Rathmore."

She pulled the strings on her bonnet, lifted it off, and tossed it on the end of the sofa. "I only learned when I arrived. I was terribly sorry to hear about the duke. He was such a kind man. I always liked him so much."

"I should have been here." Restless, she stood up and paced over to the window. "Clay needed me and I wasn't here."

Ariel stood up, too. "What has he said? Surely you've seen him by now."

Kitt swallowed past the lump in her throat. Tears burned behind her eyes, but she didn't want to cry in front of her friend. She had done enough of that last night. "I saw him. I went to the Whitelawns' soiree when I found out Clay was going to be there." She unleashed a bitter laugh. "He introduced me to his latest conquest. Lady Simington is quite a beautiful woman."

Ariel toyed with the lace on her gown and Kitt knew that she had been right—the woman was his lover. God, it hurt. It hurt so much.

She turned, stared out the window, watched the first light drops of rain begin to collect on the pane.

"Anna wrote me several times while I was away. She said that Clay was in love with me." She turned, looked into Ariel's face. "I wanted to believe it. I wanted to believe it so badly. Of course, it wasn't the least bit true."

Ariel reached over and caught her hand. "It is true—or at least it was."

She only shook her head. "Clay married me for my money—surely you realize that."

Surprise widened Ariel's eyes. "That is what you think? That Clay wanted your money? That isn't true, Kassandra. Clay had money of his own—a very sizable fortune, in fact. He has always been extremely private about it. I knew, of course. He and Justin have been partners in business for years."

"But I thought ... Clay never said anything. I merely assumed ..." She sighed. "The truth is I never asked him about his business dealings. Believing as I did, it simply hurt too much." She rested a hand on the windowsill, trying to sort out her thoughts. "If he didn't need my fortune, then I suppose he was merely being gallant. Father demanded it. If Clay had refused, Father would have sent me away—or tried to. I suppose Clay felt obligated in some way."

Ariel shook her head. "I don't think so, Kitt. I think he loved you even then, though perhaps at the time he hadn't realized it yet."

She remembered Clay last night, the presence and authority that surrounded him. It had always been so, even before he'd become a duke. She thought of him with Lillian Wainscott and a weight seemed to settle on her chest. "If he loved me, he wouldn't need other women. I knew when we wed that Clay could never be faithful. That is the reason I left."

Ariel's expression altered. "What has happened is not Clay's fault, Kassandra—and don't you dare try to blame him for it. You broke his heart when you left him. Even then, for months he remained a true and loyal husband. He waited for your return, waited for some sign that you cared even a little about him. I saw the letters you wrote. They were completely and utterly bereft of emotion. If you cared for him, how could you treat him that way?"

Her eyes filled. Dammit, she didn't want to cry. "I cared for him. I was so much in love with him I was sick with it. I couldn't stand the thought of losing him. I couldn't face the day that he would grow tired of me and go off in search of someone else."

"Oh, Kassandra, no."

"It's the truth. Oh, God, I loved him. I love him still."

Ariel's own eyes misted. "Dear Lord, if only you had said something, told someone what you were thinking. We could have talked about it, figured out what to do."

"He has a lover, Ariel."

"Yes, I've seen them together; I've heard the gossip about them. But what did you expect him to do? You made him believe you cared nothing at all for him. He has only been seeing Lillian Wainscott for the past two weeks. Until that time, he waited for you. A letter that said more than a sentence or two would have been enough, some sort of explanation, some sign that you still cared. He thinks you feel nothing at all for him."

She swallowed past the ache in her throat and the tears she'd been fighting slid down her cheeks. "Oh,

God, Ariel, I've made such a dreadful mistake. I love him so much. What am I going to do?"

Ariel hugged her, held on for a moment, then eased away. "Clay still loves you. I know he does. There has to be some way to mend things."

"It's hopeless. He'll never forgive me."

"People make mistakes. Justin made a terrible, dreadful mistake before we were married. It landed me in prison, as you well know, and nearly ruined both of our lives. But he loved me. In time I realized how much and I was able to forgive him."

"I wish I knew what to do."

Ariel started pacing, over to the window and back. "I'll tell you what to do. Fight for him. If you love him, you'll fight and you won't give up until you win."

Kitt stood frozen. Something like hope began to unfold in her chest. *Fight for him.* The words sounded solid and strong and exactly right.

"I've been such a coward," she finally said. "I've lost everything because of it. I'm tired of being afraid. I love Clay. I'm not giving him up—not to Lillian Wainscott or any other woman."

Ariel grinned. "There's my Kitt."

"Do you really believe I can do it?"

"I know you can."

It wouldn't be easy, she knew. But it couldn't be any harder than living without him. Kitt walked over and picked up her bonnet. "I've got to go," she said, setting the hat back on her head, tying the ribbons beneath her chin. "Suddenly, I have a great deal to do."

"What about our tea?" Ariel asked, hearing the rattle of the tea cart rolling down the hall.

Kitt smiled. "Next time. It seems I have a battle to

plan." As she reached the door, she stopped and turned. "Thank you, Ariel—for being my friend."

"I love you both—you know that. I want you to be happy."

But happiness—if she were smart enough to win it—hovered somewhere in a shadowy future. She said a silent prayer that beneath the anger, beneath the hostility and resentment, Clay wanted that happiness as badly as she did.

23

❧

Her campaign had begun. An hour ago, Clay had come home, changed into evening clothes, and left the house. As a duke and wealthy in the extreme, his invitations were endless. Fortunately, his valet, Cyrus Mink, usually knew which parties he planned to attend and with a little persuasion and an especially nice gift for his middle daughter's wedding, Cyrus had agreed to help her.

Tibby helped, too. Together, she and Kitt had carefully selected her attire for the evenings ahead, gowns that showed off her coloring to its best advantage, dresses with the bosom cut scandalously low. Clay had wanted her once. She would make him want her again.

Unfortunately, no matter where she went, no matter how many times she purposely ran into him, her husband simply ignored her. He was excruciatingly polite, bowing over her hand, introducing her to whomever he happened to be with at the time. Then he merely excused himself and left the affair.

She had no idea where he went. Though she had

encountered Lady Simington on several occasions, Clay was never with her. It made her sick with jealousy to think he might still be visiting the beautiful woman's bed—and more determined than ever to win him back into her own.

Tonight, she had learned, Clay was attending a house party at Lord Marley's. Kitt intended to be there. Gowned in dark blue silk heavily beaded with pearls, she arrived at the house with Glynis and her husband. Thomas Trowbridge, Lord Camberwell, was twelve years older than Glyn, a mildly attractive man with sandy hair and gentle blue eyes. Glynis had lost the weight she had gained with the birth of her daughter and looked smart and stylish in a gown of rose silk edged with green velvet.

As they began to mingle with the guests, Kitt scanned the room for Clay. She sipped her champagne, hoping to ease her nerves, trying with little success to concentrate on what Glynis was saying. A few minutes later, he strode in, tall and broad-shouldered, so handsome it made her heart lurch.

Notes of the orchestra floated in the air, but Kitt barely heard them. All she could think of was Clay and how miserable she was without him. A roundel ended and a waltz began. Clay had learned to waltz in Vienna, she knew, and he did so beautifully. The yearning to dance with him again was nearly overwhelming. He hadn't touched her since her return to London; now she ached to feel his arms around her, wanted it with near desperation.

Taking a breath for courage, she set her champagne glass down on a silver tray and started walking toward him, smiling as if they were lovers, instead of the strangers they had become.

"They're playing a waltz," she said when she reached him. "Dance with me, Your Grace?"

Clay said simply, "I'd rather not, if you don't mind." He stood next to his friend, the Earl of Blackwood, who gave her a cold, contemptuous stare. Kitt simply ignored him, turning her attention instead to the dowager Duchess of Woodriff, who stood on his opposite side.

"What do you think, Your Grace? My husband hasn't danced with me since my return to the city. I should like it very much if he did." The duchess was a crusty old woman and a terrible gossip, but Clay had always liked her and she very much liked him. "In fact, I think he should dance with both of us—not at the same time, of course."

The duchess's thin lips curved. She loved to dance and especially with Clay. Most women did. "Dance with your wife, Your Grace—and I believe I should enjoy a turn myself when you are done."

Clay smiled at Kitt, but it didn't reach his eyes. He turned a kinder smile on the dowager duchess. "If that is your wish, Your Grace, I shall make it a point to see it done."

Gripping Kitt's arm so hard she winced, he led her onto the dance floor. A strong hand settled at her waist and another closed over her fingers. She could feel the heat of his anger rolling toward her in powerful waves.

Kitt swallowed, worked to keep her smile carefully in place. As he swept her into the dance, she ignored the temper simmering beneath his surface calm and simply closed her eyes, remembering times he had danced with her before, wishing he would smile at her the way he had then.

Instead, when she looked at him, fury burned like torches in the gold of his eyes. "What did you mean to accomplish by this little stunt?" His movements grew less fluid, more rigid. She blanched at the barely banked rage darkening his cheeks.

"I just . . . I missed you. I wanted you to hold me. I remembered the way you made me feel when you danced with me before." She moistened her lips. "I wanted you to make me feel that way again."

Something flashed in his eyes, pain, hurt, a hint of the betrayal he felt . . . and a yearning so fierce and brief she wasn't certain she had really seen it.

"You want me to hold you as I did before?" he said. "You may be certain I will do so—sooner or later. I want an heir. When the time comes, I shall claim what is mine by right and plant my seed in your belly. Until that day, you would be wise to stay as far away from me as you possibly can."

Shock turned her silent. She stumbled and nearly fell. Clay's hard grip kept her upright and smoothly he eased her back into the steps of the dance. His mouth remained a hard, thin line as they finished the waltz, and Kitt's legs felt shaky. When he left her at the edge of the dance floor and returned to the duchess, her gaze unwillingly followed.

She buried her awful sense of failure beneath the memory of the yearning she had seen in his eyes.

For her it was the first faint glimmer of hope.

Sitting in a back room of Boodles, his gentlemen's club, Clay tossed back another glass of brandy. He'd been drunk every night for a week, ever since his wife had returned to the city. With her soft looks and inviting glances, he couldn't stop thinking about her.

He drank to forget what it was like to make love to her—and it took a goodly amount. Damn her to hell for the cold-hearted witch she was. At the rate he was going, he would wind up in an early grave.

He took a sip of his drink and thought of the waltz they had shared. As he'd held her in his arms, for a single, mad instant, all the old feelings had returned. He knew where they led, knew the misery of loving a reckless, self-centered creature like Kitt. She had left him without the slightest regard, grown bored and restless, he supposed, in need of a new adventure. Tonight, for an instant, she had stirred the emotions he'd once felt for her, but he had ruthlessly quashed them, leaving only the heat, the throbbing desire he couldn't seem to banish.

He had tried to quash that, too, but failed. When nothing he did seemed to work, he simply accepted the lust that wouldn't go away and determinedly ignored it.

As he worked so hard to ignore her.

It wasn't easy. She appeared wherever he went and no matter how hard he fought it, the moment he knew she was there, his gaze sought her out. She looked more beautiful than he remembered, older somehow, more of a woman.

The unpleasant thought crept in . . . *perhaps, while she was away, she found someone else.* Such a rush of fury swept through him, his fist slammed into the wall, knocking down a small oval portrait that hung over the sideboard. Silently he cursed as a footman walked over and picked it up, hung it back up where it belonged.

Clay ground his jaw, trying not to think of Kitt, trying not to remember what it was like to make love to her. He considered accepting Lily's open invitation as he hadn't yet done, and determined he would do so that night. But the hours slid past and somehow it was already dawn.

He returned to his town house, exhausted but unable to sleep. Instead of retiring to bed, he bathed and changed and headed for Rathmore Hall, the mansion at the edge of town that had belonged to his father and now belonged to him. Immersing himself in the business of being a duke, he had discovered, kept him occupied during the day, and at night he caroused, drank, and gamed, and tried not to think of his wife.

Tried to banish the bitterness he felt toward her.

Tried not to want her back in his bed.

Anna Falacci accompanied Ford Constantine up the steps of Kassandra's town house. Anna had received Kitt's message that she had returned to the city, and along with Ford, had traveled with great haste to see her.

"*Cara!* It is so good to see you! *Santa Maria*, I have missed you." Anna hugged her in the entry, and the three of them proceeded down the hall to the drawing room. "You are more beautiful than ever," Anna said, then frowned, noticing the faint purple smudges beneath her friend's green eyes. "But you do not sleep, I think. You miss your husband in your bed, no?"

Kassandra flushed at Anna's plain speaking while Ford merely smiled. He was used to Anna by now. In the beginning, like everyone else, he had believed the stories he had heard about her, that she was a scarlet woman, the sort who would flaunt her lover in front of an aging husband. But she had never hurt Edouardo. Anna believed Ford now understood.

"Do not worry about speaking in front of Ford," she said to Kitt. "He knows what has happened between you and Clayton. He has come here to help you." Anna believed if anyone knew a way Kassandra could win back the duke, it was the very perceptive Marquess of Landen.

Ford smiled and Anna's breath caught at how handsome he was, like a golden-haired emperor of Rome.

"Anna has been worried about you," he said. "She thought that perhaps, in some way, I might be able to help with your problem."

"I don't . . . don't know if anyone can help."

Anna merely smiled. "Your Clayton . . . for you, he has the *grand amore*. I have seen it in his eyes when he looks at you. But he no longer trusts you. You have hurt him, *cara*. Now he wishes for you to suffer as he has."

Kitt walked toward the fire, her shoulders not nearly as straight as they usually were. "I want to make it up to him, but I don't know how. I try to talk to him, but he avoids me. I can't even get him to look at me." She turned and tears welled in her eyes. She quickly brushed them away.

Ford's gaze ran over her, assessing Kitt's beauty, her softly feminine curves. "I trust Anna's judgment. If she says Rathmore loves you, then I believe he does. If he loves you, then he wants you." He smiled. "I would suggest, Your Grace, you find a way to make him jealous."

Kitt's eyes widened. "Jealous? Even if that were possible—which I doubt very much it is—wouldn't that just make him more angry?"

Ford shrugged one of his very wide shoulders and

heat slid into Anna's stomach. He was a marvelous lover. She couldn't seem to get enough of him. If that was all she ever had of him, it would be enough.

"Perhaps," he said. "But as long as Clay maintains his careful control, you won't be able to reach him. You need to shake his composure, make him realize how much he still cares."

It was good advice, Anna thought, and exactly the tact that had worked on her. She had ignored Ford Constantine for months, rebuffing his advances when deep inside she wanted more than anything for him to make love to her.

In a last attempt to convince her that she had feelings for him, he'd turned away from her, begun to focus his attentions on Elizabeth Watkins, Lady May. Every time Anna saw them together she wanted to rip off the woman's head.

Forthright as always, Anna had gone to see Ford at Landen Manor. "I do not wish you to see that woman," she had said. "You belong to me, as I belong to you. You know it as well as I do."

Ford had thrown back his head and laughed. Then he had hauled her against him and very soundly kissed her. "Thank God, we finally agree." Scooping her into his arms, he had carried her upstairs and made passionate love to her. He had never cast a glance in Elizabeth Watkins direction again.

"Do you really think it could work?" Kitt asked Ford, drawing Anna back from her wandering thoughts.

He gave Kitt an encouraging smile. "There are no guarantees when it comes to love, Duchess, but it's certainly a place to start."

Kitt grinned, some of her former spirit returning. "I'll do it. Clay is going to the mayor's ball tomorrow night. I can try it there. I'll be terrified, of course. Would you and the marquess go with me?"

Anna laughed, glanced at Ford, who smiled and nodded. "We would not miss it, *cara.*"

Kitt laughed, too. Anna thought, from the look on her face, it had been a very long time since she had done so.

The marquess had told her to make Clay jealous—but how? Lying in her big empty bed, Kitt wrestled with the problem half the night, tossing out one worthless idea after another. As she lay there, staring up at the canopy above her head, she shifted restlessly, missing Clay, telling herself it was useless and in the very next breath convincing herself it would work.

The first yellow rays of dawn slid in through the shutters before the answer finally came. When it did, it struck with crystal clarity.

What she needed was a man Clay respected, a man he saw as his equal. What better man than his good friend, the darkly handsome Earl of Blackwood? With his raven hair, black, slashing brows, high cheekbones, and eyes so blue they looked black, he had an intriguing, dangerous sort of appeal, and a face of uncommon beauty. The fine scar carved along his jaw only added a mysterious air. Women fought to get into his bed, and though he remained aloof, he never failed to take them up on their offers.

Blackwood was intelligent, wealthy, and desirable—the perfect candidate for her plan. And likely, along with Clay, he would be attending the mayor's ball that night.

The day crawled past. Anxiety gnawed at her insides, making her tense and edgy. She wound up in a state of nerves, uncertain how to proceed, determined to go through with her scheme no matter what the cost.

She had ordered a new gown especially for the event, an elegant creation fashioned of rich black silk, the fabric encrusted with gold and jet beads laid out in intricate designs. The narrow skirt slashed up the side, exposing her calf to just below the knee. The bodice was so low it was certain to cause a scandal, but Kitt no longer cared.

She was fighting for her husband, her marriage, and her future. She didn't intend to fail.

She was ready and waiting when Ford and Anna arrived, the marquess in a coat of dark blue trimmed with velvet, Anna in silver-shot silk, both of them excited about the evening ahead and pleased with the gown she had chosen.

The contessa grinned and rolled her pretty blue eyes. "*Cara,* you will drive him mad with desire for you."

Ford chuckled softly. "You won't have to do a thing. He'll be in a blinding, jealous rage at the first man who dances with you. Rest assured it won't be me."

Kitt laughed, her courage bolstered. They set off in the marquess's well-sprung carriage, bowling through the crowded London streets, whipping through the tall iron gates of the Viscount St. Cere's mansion at the edge of the city, a big brick structure set amidst sprawling green lawns. Arriving with the rumble of hooves and the clatter of wheels, they made their way along the red velvet runner leading up to the carved front doors.

The entry was enormous, with a sweeping marble staircase that led to a second-floor ballroom. A maze of elegant salons and drawing rooms, a long gallery, an intimate library, and St. Cere's study, stretched out on the first floor. An orchestra played downstairs as well as in the ballroom, and they wandered in that direction, entering an ivory and gilt drawing room overflowing with guests.

She recognized several familiar faces: Sir Hubert Tinsley; the Earl of Winston and his wife; Lord Percy Richards. She spotted Clay and her stomach knotted. His features closed up the moment he saw her walk in. He took in her black-and-gold gown, noticed the split up the side, the wide expanse of bosom the gown revealed, and his jaw turned to granite. Beside him, the Earl of Blackwood's face looked unusually grim.

There was no way she could do it. She simply could not.

"Steady," Ford said softly.

Kitt steeled herself. She had to do this. She would not run—not ever again. Dragging in a shaky breath of air, she started toward him, Anna and Ford close by her side.

"Clayton—it is so good to see you!" Anna approached him with a smile.

"Good evening, Contessa." Clay bent and kissed her cheek, flicked a cool smile at Kitt. "Kassandra." He greeted Ford, turned to Blackwood. "You know the earl, of course."

"Sì, of course." Anna smiled at Lord Blackwood while Ford, who was also acquainted, made a polite inclination of his head.

"I imagine you're glad to have your wife returned after so many weeks away," Ford said pleasantly, his gaze on Clay's face.

"Of course," he said mildly. "What man wouldn't be?" But his eyes said he wasn't the least bit happy to see her and especially not tonight.

They made small talk for a while, the weather, the latest political scandal, the resumption of the war after a lull that was far too short. Lord Landen excused himself on the pretext of speaking to a friend and the orchestra began to play. Anna smiled and looked expectantly at Clay. With little choice in the matter, he dutifully asked her to dance.

Kitt looked over at the earl, gave him what she hoped was an alluring smile, and waited for his polite invitation. It never came. Silently cursing him, refusing to be thwarted at this early stage of the game, she gave him a long, speaking glance.

"I would very much like to dance with you, my lord." It was a bold move and it tightened a muscle in his cheek. The smile he gave her held not the least trace of warmth.

"Then by all means . . . Your Grace."

They made their way onto the floor and joined in the country dance, all very proper, Clay and Anna partnered down the line not far away. Several times she felt Clay's eyes on her and forced herself to ignore the heat of anger burning in them. Ford said she needed to shake his composure. That was exactly what she intended to do.

As the dance came to an end, she leaned close to the earl. "I need to speak to you, my lord. In private. I promise it will only take a moment."

His mouth went hard. "What game do you play, Your Grace?"

"Please, my lord. It's extremely important."

He eyed her for several long moments, then made a

curt nod of his head. "I'll await you in the library. You know where it is?"

"Yes . . ." She forced herself to smile, but her stomach quivered beneath that steely glare and her legs suddenly felt as if they weighed a thousand pounds.

Blackwood left the room and a few minutes later Kitt followed. She knew Clay had seen them both leave and it gave her a needed shot of courage. She made her way down the hall, opened the library door, and stepped inside. She had no idea what any of this would accomplish but she was determined to go through with it. She had to do something. She was sick unto death of simply being ignored.

Standing in front of the window, long legs slightly splayed, Blackwood turned at the sound of the closing door. He looked cold and remote and not the least bit interested in her as a woman. Feeling those hard, disapproving eyes on her made her insides tighten into an egg-sized knot.

Dear God, why hadn't she chosen someone else?

His gaze remained on her face as he started walking toward her, stopping far too close. He was even taller than she had thought, and far more dangerous.

"Thank you for coming," she said.

"I want to know why I'm here. I asked you before—what game are you playing?"

"No game, my lord . . . I just . . ." She tried for a softly seductive smile. "I just thought that perhaps we should become better acquainted. After all, you're a friend of my husband's. A wife should—"

Blackwood's long fingers clamped around the tops of her arms and he hauled her up on her toes. "That is what you thought?" He felt her start to tremble, must have seen the fear that crept into her eyes. "That we should get better acquainted?" She glanced toward the door, praying someone would save her, praying she could somehow save herself.

Blackwood's fingers tightened like rings of steel. "Why are we here? What do you want?"

She tried to break free but his hold was implacable. She looked into those hard blue eyes and thought that perhaps he was even more angry than Clay. The fight went out of her. Tears sprang into her eyes.

"I-I'm sorry. I just ... I wanted to make him jealous. I thought if I did, that I could ... that I could make him want me again."

He eased her back down, but didn't let her go. "Why? Why would you care?"

Her eyes slid closed. She swallowed a lump of tears. "Because I'm in love with him."

Blackwood released her, took a step away. For a moment, they simply stood there staring, Blackwood pondering her words, Kitt feeling like an utter fool. Turning on shaky legs, she started walking toward the door, doing her best not to run.

Blackwood's voice, deep as thunder, rumbled from behind her. "If you love him, why did you leave?"

She turned, blinked back tears, tried to keep her lips from trembling. The words came out soft, husky. "Because I was afraid."

He said nothing more and neither did she. With a hand that shook, she opened the door and walked out of the library. Hoping no one would see, she brushed tears from her cheeks as she walked down the hall, passed the drawing room without risking a glance at Clay, and made her way toward the stairs leading up to the ladies' retiring room.

She needed time to compose herself, needed to restore her wounded spirit after another dismal failure. Dear God, she would never forget the look of contempt on Blackwood's face.

Or the faint trace of pity.

Clay watched the tall, black-haired earl walk back through the doors of the drawing room. Cold fury made his hands unconsciously fist. His chest rose harshly and his jaw flexed, the muscles so rigid a knot formed in his cheek.

Clay took a long sip of his brandy, felt the liquor burn into his stomach, but the anger remained. Only a few minutes had passed, yet he knew where the man had been, knew Kassandra had followed him. A blond woman stepped into Blackwood's path as he crossed the room. The earl replied to something she said, made a faint nod of his head, and continued walking toward him.

He stopped in front of Clay. Accepting a snifter of brandy a servant offered, he leisurely took a drink.

Clay's fingers tightened around the stem of his glass. "I hope you enjoyed your little interlude with my wife," he said, hanging onto his temper by sheer force of will.

Blackwood's expression remained bland. "Actually, I was acting in your behalf. I thought it best to discover what the lady was about."

"Really. And what did you find out?"

Blackwood swirled his drink. "The little fool was trying to make you jealous." He took a drink, savored the taste as he swallowed. "She doesn't realize you would kill the first man who touched her."

Clay's hard gaze bored into him. "But you do."

The corner of his mouth edged up. "Most assuredly."

Clay's posture relaxed, the tension slowly draining away. Adam was a friend. For a moment, he had forgotten.

"You'll be happy to know that as a seductress your lady is a dismal failure." Blackwood actually smiled. "She is far too honest, I think."

"Honest?" He scoffed. "There is nothing the least bit honest about Kassandra. She is a complete and utter fraud."

"Perhaps. Then again, perhaps she was merely confused."

It was the first time Adam had shown the least bit of sympathy for Kitt. His experience with women had been worse than bad. He saw all of them as conniving and self-indulgent. Clay wondered what his wife could possibly have said in those few short minutes that could have swayed him.

Clay glanced up as she returned to the drawing room. He'd been avoiding her for days, yet he thought of little else. Kassandra was his wife. That wasn't going to change. It was time they settled matters between them. He intended to do so—now, tonight.

He set his brandy glass down on a silver tray. "The hour grows late. If you'll excuse me, I believe it's time I took my wife home."

Adam flicked a glance toward the lady gowned in black. "Past time," he said, and Clay thought he caught another faint ghost of a smile.

24

Clay spotted Kassandra standing next to Glynis Trowbridge, Lady Camberwell, and a small circle of the viscountess's friends. Kitt was smiling at something one of them said and next to her, young Peter Avery couldn't take his eyes off her breasts.

Clay's jaw hardened. Kitt gasped as he caught her arm and spun her to face him. "We're leaving," he said curtly. "My carriage is waiting out in front. I'm taking you home."

She blinked up at him in surprise, then began to glance round the drawing room. "I came with Ford and Anna. I need to tell them—"

"Now." He waited, itching for a fight should she balk. Instead she managed a smile. Perhaps she knew he would carry her out kicking and screaming if he had to.

"As you wish." Taking his arm, she let him lead her through the doors of the drawing room down the hall to the entry, where a servant rushed forward with her black velvet cloak. Clay whirled it around her shoulders, caught her arm, and they started walking again.

"That dress is outrageous," he said as he hauled her down the steps and along the red velvet runner to his coach. "I suppose you got it while you were in Rome."

"Actually, I had it made especially for tonight." She smiled up at him sweetly. "I was hoping you would like it."

Clay paused at the bottom of the carriage stairs, his gaze sweeping over the daringly low-cut neckline. Soft mounds of flesh gleamed in the lamplight and he wanted to press his mouth there, wanted to shove the dress down the scant few inches it would take to expose her nipple, wanted to pebble the end with his tongue. "I loathe the damned thing. I never want to see you in it again."

Kitt cocked her head. "Why not?"

"Because it makes me want to tear the bloody thing off you." He jerked open the door, practically shoved her in, threw himself into the seat across from her. Tension screamed inside the carriage, though neither of them said a word. The moment they reached the town house, he yanked open the door and stepped down, caught her round the waist and swung her to the ground, then hauled her toward the house. With no little haste he led her up the front porch steps, into the entry, and up the sweeping stairs.

He dragged her into the sitting room of the master's suite and viciously slammed the door.

"All right, Kassandra, this has gone on long enough. I want you to tell me why you returned to London. I want to know why you've been following me. I want to know what it is you want."

Her chin inched up, but her bottom lip faintly trembled. She had always been determined and he saw that determination now. "You want to know what I want? I want you, Clay. It's as simple as that. I want to be your wife again. I want you to want me the way you used to." Her voice softened. "The way you want Lillian Wainscott."

Clay ground down on his jaw. For weeks he had ached for her, needed her, waited like a lovesick fool for one of her cold, emotionless letters. Now she was home, wanting the life she'd had before.

There was a time he had desperately yearned to build a future with Kassandra. Now the only thing he wanted from her was her luscious little body.

He flashed her a ruthless half smile. "You want to share my bed again? That is what this is about?"

She swallowed. "Yes."

"You actually believe you're woman enough to play both wife and mistress?"

She nervously moistened her lips, and desire flooded into his groin. She swallowed. "Yes."

His body tightened, went painfully hard. Clay stared at her for several long moments, fighting the lust she could arouse with a single glance, trying to ignore the hope he saw in her eyes.

He wanted to leave, to simply walk away, but it was impossible to do. His gaze held hers, hot brown and beseeching green. He couldn't stop the hands that reached for her, captured her face, tilted her head back for his kiss. Anger mingled with a thread of yearning as his mouth crashed down over hers.

In the past he would have been gentle. He would have held onto his passions, kept them carefully in check. He wasn't gentle now. Instead, he eased her back against the wall and shoved the black beaded gown off her shoulders. He tugged down the top, exposing her nipples, bent and took one into his mouth.

He pebbled the end, sucked it, laved it, then took more.

Soft, warm, full. Incredibly feminine. His loins filled, clenched. God, he wanted her so badly.

He felt her arms sliding up around his neck, her fingers lacing into his hair, and he kissed her again, taking her deeply with his tongue. She kissed him back with an urgency he hadn't expected and his shaft went rock hard. He could feel her trembling as he shoved up her skirt, wedged a knee between her legs, and lifted her a little. She moaned as her softness pressed against the muscles in his thigh and she rode him.

He kissed her again, fiercely, thoroughly, worked the buttons at the front of his breeches to free himself. She wanted him to want her. Couldn't she guess that he had never stopped, that even before they were wed, he had thought of her. As he lay with another woman, he had wanted her even then.

He thought of the empty nights he had spent, blaming himself, wondering what he had done wrong, why she couldn't care for him at least enough to stay. But those days were past and he vowed they would never come again.

She wanted to be his wife, she had said, but this time it would be different. This time she would know the full measure of his passions. If she ran from him, so be it. He was tired of holding back. He wouldn't hold back any longer.

His mouth claimed hers savagely. Kassandra kissed him back with equal fire. She gasped when he slid up her gown, cupped her bottom to lift her up, and wrapped her legs around his waist, leaving her open and exposed to him. But she didn't pull away. He found her softness, began to stroke her, realized that she was wet and hot and every bit as ready as he.

"Say it," he commanded. "Tell me you want me."

She was shaking, her body damp with perspiration, her eyes glazed with desire. "I want you. I've always wanted you."

His eyes closed. It wasn't the truth, couldn't possibly be the truth. Angry again, he drove himself inside her, filling her deeply, sliding out, then thrusting hard inside her again. Kitt clung to his neck, her body arching, tightening around him, her breasts teasing the front of his coat, then pressing more fully into his chest. She moaned his name, began to tremble, and still he drove on, pounding, pounding, holding nothing back, taking what he wanted. She came with violent force, then came again. He gripped her hips as his own climax came, and fierce waves of pleasure washed over him.

For a time he simply held her, their bodies entwined, Kitt still clinging to his neck. He was hard again in seconds, wanting her again as he always did.

Swearing softly, refusing to give in to the urge, he carried her into her bedchamber, set her down in the middle of her bed, turned and started walking away.

"Clay . . . ?"

He looked back, saw her face outlined in the moonlight streaming in through the window, the wild tumble of her fiery red hair, and thought she was the most desirable creature that he had ever seen.

"I can't . . . I don't want to share you with another woman."

His mouth barely curved. "Then let us hope you perform your duties well enough that I won't need one."

He ignored the glitter of tears that sprang into her eyes as he walked out and closed the door.

But he couldn't ignore the tightness in his chest— or the desire for her that still raged like a demon in his blood.

Kitt lay there trembling, her body throbbing with faint little aftershocks of pleasure, thinking of Clay, wanting him still. He had never made love to her as he had tonight, with so much heat, so much fury. And she had never responded with such wild abandon.

He had taken her in anger, not even bothering to remove his clothes. But beneath the anger, she could feel his burning desire for her and it had stirred her own. Always before he'd been gentle, arousing her with tender care, worried that he might frighten her. Now she realized how much of himself he'd held back.

In the past she would have been afraid. But the past was behind her now. Thanks to her husband's patience, her fear of making love had faded to little more than wisps of smoke in a dying fire. And she knew, deep in her soul, that Clay would never hurt her.

As angry and bitter as he was, as wildly, fiercely passionate, he had done nothing more than give her pleasure. He had turned her body into a raging inferno and in doing so, she had discovered a new side of herself, a wild, untamed part of her that craved each brush of his fingers, each wicked, savage kiss. She wanted Clay, wanted to feel that burning heat again and again.

Even that, she knew, wouldn't be enough.

She wanted him to love her. As madly, as desperately as she loved him.

No matter what it took, Kitt vowed, no matter how

long she had to wait, she would find a way to win his heart.

The days passed in a blur. At least they were speaking to each other, though with brief formality and little more. It was better than the cold hostility that had burned between them before. Clay still stayed gone most of the day, returning home to change for the evening, then going out again. Kitt placed herself in his path as often as she dared, and though he seemed a little less remote, he hadn't yet returned to her bed.

On the third day after they made love, restless and moody and wishing she knew what to do to regain his interest, she was standing at the top of the stairs when the brass knocker sounded at the door.

Her father and Judith had sent a message earlier that they intended to pay a call, but with so much on her mind, Kitt had completely forgotten. Wishing she were wearing something more appropriate than her simple morning gown, she pasted on a smile and greeted them in the drawing room.

"Father—it's good to see you." She caught both his long-boned hands, leaned over, and kissed his cheek. "I heard you'd returned from the country this week. I've been meaning to stop by and see you. Time slipped away somehow." She mustered a smile for her stepmother. "Judith—you're looking very well." A little plumper, maybe, but there seemed more of a bloom in her cheeks. Perhaps, now that Kitt was gone, Judith was finally receiving the attention she'd always wanted. It occurred to Kitt that perhaps now they might finally learn to get along.

"High time you got back," her father grumbled. "Stayed gone far too long. You shouldn't have left in the first place, running off from your husband when the two of you were just newly wed. Foolishness— that's what it was."

For once, Kitt agreed with him. "Well, I'm back now and I won't be leaving again anytime soon."

Her father nodded, seemed relieved. "Well, how does it feel, my dear? Married yourself a duke, as it turns out, instead of a bastard son. You've me to thank for that, you know."

Her smile faltered. "I never cared about Clay's parentage. I didn't marry him to acquire a title."

"Never hurts, though. A woman needs security. Rathmore can give you that and more."

Judith surveyed the drawing room with an assessing glance, a little surprised, it seemed, by the tasteful, elegant décor. "When will you be moving into the ducal mansion?" she asked.

"Actually, we haven't discussed it." In fact, it had never even occurred to her. She was content to live in the town house. She didn't need a mansion. Her stomach suddenly rolled. What if Clay moved into Rathmore Hall and left her alone in the town house? Among the aristocracy, husbands and wives often lived apart.

Judith made a little sighing sound. "I should think you would wish to move in right away. Terrance and I attended a ball at the duke's house last year. The place is utterly magnificent."

Her father waved his hand in impatience. "Yes, yes . . . well, I'm certain they'll be moving in soon," he said, obviously pleased with himself for forcing the marriage in the first place.

Henderson knocked just then. He entered carrying a heavy silver tea tray, which he set down on a Hepplewhite table in front of the sofa. As soon as he was gone, Kitt picked up the pot and began pouring the brew into gold-rimmed porcelain cups, trying not to feel guilty for wishing the visit was over.

As she added a chunk of sugar to her father's cup and began to stir, an odd thought drifted up, one she'd had a few times when she was in Italy and even more often since she had returned to London.

"I was wondering, Father ... the night I came home with Clay from Anna's ... how was it you happened to know we were out in the garden? Your bedchamber is in the front of the house. That's a goodly distance away, and we weren't making all that much noise."

He grinned, crinkling the lines at the corners of his eyes. "Wondered how long it would take you to figure it out. Knew you would, sooner or later. You might be a little high-strung like your mother, but you were always a smart little girl."

"Meaning ... ?"

"Meaning that it wasn't mere happenstance. Earlier that afternoon, Clayton came by to see me. He told me what he planned—how he thought you might sneak off to see the Cossack even if I forbid it. If he brought you home, he said—if the two of you were alone together without a chaperon—your reputation would be compromised and the two of you would be forced to marry. He asked for my help and my approval. I heartily agreed."

He grinned again, even wider than before. "You're married to a duke, my girl, and it's all thanks to me."

For an instant, she simply sat there, stunned. A dozen different emotions rose up—anger at Clay for duping her, a feeling of betrayal that her father would go to such extremes to get rid of her, fury that they had all conspired against her. They were washed away an instant later by a single astonishing fact:

If Clay hadn't wed her for her money or because he had been coerced, he must have *wanted* to marry her.

He had never made a secret of his desire for her. But desire for a woman wouldn't be enough for a man like Clay.

Perhaps then, in some way he *had* loved her.

Hope rose in her breast with surprising force. And guilt, and terrible, crushing fear.

If he had loved her, she had hurt him far worse than she had imagined. Dear God, how would she ever convince him to forgive her?

"Kassandra . . . ? Are you all right?" Judith's blue eyes searched her face with concern.

Kitt nodded, working to draw air into her lungs. "I-I'm fine." She took a sip of tea, fought to keep the cup from trembling in her fingers. "It was just a surprise, that's all." She mustered a smile for her father. "You were very clever, Father. You and Clay were both quite resourceful."

He gently squeezed her hand. "I know you don't believe it, but I was thinking of your happiness, my dear." His lips curved up. "Ah, but a duchess—it's more than I ever dared to dream."

So much, and nothing at all, Kitt thought with despair.

Not unless Clay loved her.

Dark wood paneling and heavy velvet draperies surrounded him. The faint scent of tobacco and deep male voices filled the air. Clay had just come from Rathmore Hall. He had finished going over the ledgers on one of the dukedom's distant estates and now sat across from Adam Hawthorne in a small salon at the rear of Adam's club, Brooks, St. James's.

Blackwood eyed him lazily, toyed with his drink. "Rumor has it you're no longer seeing Lily."

Clay set aside the newspaper he had been reading. "Not at present."

"I take it, then, you've worked things out with your pretty little wife."

Clay looked at him, snorted something vulgar. "Hardly. I rarely see her. I make it a point not to."

Blackwood arched a brow. "Why? It's obvious you want her. The way you look at her, it's a wonder the carpet beneath her feet doesn't go up in flames."

Clay lounged back in his chair. "I want her. I always seem to want her. She's like a fire in my blood I can't put out."

"She's your wife. As that is the case, why don't you simply take what you want?"

Clay swirled the brandy he had ordered but didn't really want, inhaled the sweet aroma but didn't take a drink. "Tempting as the notion may be, it isn't quite that simple. In time, undoubtedly, I shall." Kitt had made it clear he was welcome in her bed and yet he hadn't joined her there since the night of the mayor's ball.

He wanted to. He thought about it day and night, imagined making love to her in a hundred ways he never had before. He remembered the passionate way she had responded the last time they were together and went hard as a stone beneath the table.

"If she were my wife," Blackwood said mildly, "I wouldn't be sitting in here thinking about it. I'd be home, hauling her into—"

Clay slammed his brandy glass down on the table.

"I know exactly what you would do." He shoved back his chair, the wooden legs grating on the marble floor. "Your point is well made. The lady belongs to me. I may as well have my fill." Why he hadn't done so already, he wasn't quite sure, but now, at Blackwood's prodding, he intended to do just that.

Adam's mouth edged up as Clay took a fortifying drink of his brandy, set the glass back down, and started for the door. "Enjoy your afternoon, my friend," Adam said softly.

Clay made no reply, just kept on walking. Halfway to the front door, he noticed the shadowy shapes of three men leaving the room from the opposite side of the club. One of them walked with an unsteady, pronounced limp, making his way with the use of a cane. Clay caught the sheen of his golden blond hair, took in his height and slender build, and knew exactly who it was.

"Westerly," he said blandly as the men drew near. "I heard about your . . . accident. My condolences. But I see you are finally up and about."

The earl's smile could have frozen water. "Yes . . . those things happen." The story of the duel had never surfaced. Stephen had explained his injured knee as a hunting accident. For everyone's sake, Clay was happy to leave it at that.

"Hunting can be dangerous," Clay said dryly. "In the future, you might wish to be more careful the sort of game you pursue." With a last brief nod, he continued on his way. Behind him, he could feel Westerly's eyes on him, burning with hatred.

It didn't matter. Not anymore. The man had been dealt with, his punishment severe. At present, it wasn't Westerly, it was Kassandra who concerned him . . . or at least her delectable little body.

Now that Blackwood had pointed out his folly in staying away, he meant to take her, slake his ridiculous, never-ending lust for her. Sooner or later, he was bound to get his fill. Just thinking about her and what he meant to do made him hard again, throbbing with desire like a callow schoolboy by the time he walked out the front door.

Clay cursed himself. But he didn't pause, just climbed into his carriage and ordered the driver to take him home.

Leaning back against the rough brick wall in a dimly lit corner of the Pig & Fiddle Tavern in the Strand, Simon Peel absently toyed with the heavy pouch of coins sitting in front of him on the table. He was tall and gaunt, hardened from the years he had spent in the army. Too many years. At least that's what he'd told himself the day he'd deserted.

He glanced toward the front of the tavern, spotted his friend, Bram Starkie, shoving through the heavy oak plank door. Bram swaggered toward him, a short, squat man, barrel-chested and thick-muscled. Thick-headed as far as Simon was concerned. But he needed help with this job and he could depend on Bram. The man was too stupid not to do what Simon told him.

"Got word ye was lookin' fer me." Bram pulled out the scarred wooden bench across from him and sat down.

"And so I was. I got a job for us, Bram." Simon shoved the bag of coins across the table. Of course, he'd already taken out a goodly sum. "Pay's real good."

Bram hefted the bag and vigorously nodded. "Wot we gotta do, Simon?"

"Not much. There's a gentleman wants to see a debt repaid. Doesn't care how we do it, long as the job gets done and no one knows who paid for it." Simon went on to explain what their employer wished to accomplish and by the time he was finished, Bram was nodding again.

"Ye got a plan yet?" he asked.

"I will have ... soon."

"Might take a bit o' time, seein' as 'ow the bloke wants it kept quiet and all."

"A little, perhaps. You leave the planning to me. Soon as I've worked things out, I'll get word to you."

Bram grinned. "Right ye are, mate. Just tell me wot ye want me to do."

25

Seated in the drawing room, her sketch pad cradled in her lap, Kitt heard Clay's heavy footfalls in the entry. He said something to the butler, waited for his reply, then started down the hall in her direction.

Her heartbeat kicked up. He hadn't been home in the middle of the day since she had returned to London. She sat forward on the sofa as he strode in and closed the door, his jacket off and folded over his forearm, his stock untied and hanging round his neck.

"I wondered if I would find you home," he said. He glanced down at her sketch pad and his eyes darkened as he realized she had been drawing a picture of him. She squeaked as he reached over and yanked it out of her hand, tossed it down on the end of the settee.

He hauled her to her feet and straight into his arms.

"What . . . what are you doing?"

His smile was hard. "You wanted to play the role of mistress. I expect you to please me as she would."

Any reply she might have made went flying out of

her head as he bent his dark head and kissed her. Her hands came up, flattened out on his chest, steadying her against the swift jolt of heat that tore through her. She tasted the faint, warm flavor of brandy, caught a whiff of his cologne, and desire curled around her like smoke.

Clay deepened the kiss, bending her over his arm, his tongue sliding like silk along her bottom lip. He teased the corners, then swept deeply inside. Her hands trembled where they lay open on his chest and his muscles contracted. She could feel the heat of his thighs pressing against her, feel the heavy weight of his arousal, and her stomach turned to butter.

His white shirt rubbed against her breasts, making her nipples bead and begin to throb. His tongue stroked into her mouth, deeply, erotically, making her knees go weak.

One of his big hands slid inside the neckline of her gown, down beneath her chemise, and cradled a breast. She realized he had unfastened some of the buttons at the back. He massaged the heavy fullness, lifted it, squeezed it, lightly pinched the end, and a soft moan of pleasure bubbled up in her throat.

Slow, languid kisses. Hot, hungry kisses. Deep, penetrating kisses left her numb and dizzy and aching for more.

"Turn around," Clay said softly, kissing the side of her neck.

She didn't know what he wanted, but the hot look in his eyes commanded that she obey. He kissed her again, then slowly turned her back to him. The arm of the sofa pressed into her stomach as he bent her over and began to slide up her skirt. She heard the faint pop of buttons being opened at the front of his breeches and for an instant she tensed.

"Trust me," he said softly. "I'm not going to hurt you." The gently coaxing voice belonged to the man she had married, the man she loved without reserve. She relaxed, felt his hands smoothing over her bottom, felt his fingers sliding between her legs.

"I'll make this good for you," he promised, his voice deep and rough. "Good for both of us."

She moaned as he continued to stroke her, lightly at first, knowing exactly how to please her. Heat and need collected inside her, building with incredible force. She could feel his hardness throbbing against her, then gliding slowly inside. Her stomach contracted as he filled her, and a hot rush of pleasure slid into her core. She arched her back to take more of him, felt her softness pulsing around him, heard him groan.

Gripping her hips, he drove himself more fully inside and Kitt moaned at the incredible pleasure. He thrust again, even more deeply, and her insides tightened into a red-hot coil. Long, powerful strokes had her trembling. Deep, penetrating strokes had her whimpering his name. In seconds she reached her peak, shattering into a climax so sweet it tasted like honey on her tongue.

Clay didn't stop, just pounded relentlessly on. She came again, even more fiercely this time, and he followed her to release, his muscles straining, his hard body shaking with the force of it.

He eased her back against his chest, cradling her against him as the pleasure began to ebb. She loved the feel of his arms around her, the solidity of his body surrounding her. She closed her eyes, absorbing the wonder, the joy of simply being held by him.

She had missed him so terribly much.

Finally, he eased away. Dragging her skirt down

over her hips, he let it fall to the floor and fastened the buttons at the front of his breeches. "I didn't hurt you?"

She shook her head, her legs still wobbly, unable to find her voice.

"You're different since your return. You aren't afraid anymore."

"No . . ."

His eyes went dark. "Were there other men in—"

"No! For God's sake, Clay, do you really believe I would let any other man touch me as you have, do the intimate things that we have done?"

He stared at her, remembering how much patience it had taken for him to win her trust. "No. I don't suppose you would." The tension lessened across his shoulders.

He turned, started to walk away, caught sight of the sketch pad lying on the sofa, and went over and picked it up. He studied the charcoal drawing she had made of him, turned the page, found another picture of himself. Kitt flushed as he continued to flip through the pages, finding the endless sketches of him she had made.

He looked up at her, his eyes more golden than she had seen them since her return. "Why?" he asked.

Because I love you. She wanted to say the words, ached to say them, but she knew he wouldn't believe her, and even if he did, he wouldn't trust her not to hurt him again.

"I missed you. I still do. I need you, Clay. I want to make our marriage work."

He stared at her as if he didn't quite believe her, but there was something in his eyes that she had seen before . . . a faint, almost invisible yearning. It was gone in an instant. He folded the sketchbook closed and handed it back to her.

"If that is the truth, then perhaps we'll find a way." Turning, he strode out of the drawing room, leaving her alone once more.

That night he came to her bedchamber and they made love. Afterward, she clung to him, hoping he wouldn't notice the tears in her eyes, praying that he would stay with her. Instead he left and returned to his own room.

Every night after that he came to her bed. He made love to her in a dozen different ways, showing her the passionate side of himself that in the beginning he had concealed. It made her love him more than ever, made her ache for his love in return. But each night, as soon as they were finished, he left and returned to his own bedchamber.

Watching him walk away, one thing was crystal clear. If indeed he had ever really loved her, it was obvious he never intended to do so again.

Fall set in full force, bringing chill winds and frost on the stoop in the mornings. Mr. Pittman at the *Times* sent word through Clay that the paper would like a drawing of Admiral Nelson's ship, the *Victory*, which had just returned to London. True to his promise, Clay escorted her, though they didn't try to board. Kitt had wept as she thought of the great man's remains being carried ashore in a cask of brandy, preserved during the voyage so the crew could return their beloved admiral home.

The days seemed to drag. Clay was gone much of the time, working in the ducal mansion, though he seemed to have no plans to move in by himself, to Kitt's great relief.

"There are a number of estates that belong to the Rathmore dukedom," he told her. "I'll need to visit them in the spring, make certain they remain in good repair."

"Perhaps I could go with you."

His mouth tightened. He glanced off toward the window. "Perhaps. We'll have to wait and see."

It wasn't the answer she wanted. She hoped he would be pleased to have her with him, not simply tolerant of her presence. She continued to sleep alone, praying every night that in time the rift between them would heal, but Clay was determined not to let her past his defenses.

It was nearly week's end when Anna stopped by to see her.

"I have news, *cara.*" The contessa smiled, radiant and beautiful as ever. "The marquess has asked me to marry him."

"Oh, Anna! I'm so happy for you. Ford couldn't ask for a finer wife. He's a very lucky man."

"Perhaps he will be . . . if I decide to say yes."

"But you're in love with him!"

"*Sì*, but marriage is a very big step and I am not yet certain of the marquess's feelings for me. He has never said that he loves me and until he does, I will not marry him." Her blue eyes sparkled. "Besides, Ford is a little too sure of himself. I do not wish him to take me for granted."

Kitt grinned. She should have known Anna wouldn't make it easy.

Settling themselves in the drawing room, Anna accepted the cup of tea Kitt poured for her. "So what about you? How are things with you and Clayton? I have not seen him out so much lately."

Kitt carefully stirred her tea without looking up. "I wish I could say things were better. I don't think he has been seeing any other women. I suppose that is something."

"I do not believe he was ever really interested in other women. He was hurt and he was lonely."

Kitt glanced away. "We live together like strangers. He makes love to me, but he always holds himself back. He wants me, but it's as though he wishes he didn't."

"He fights his feelings for you, *cara*. He is afraid you will hurt him again."

"Clay lost his mother when he was a boy. His father provided him with money, but money isn't the same as love. He was lonely and probably a little afraid. He taught himself not to need anyone."

"*Sì*, that is so. Until he met you, he was afraid to love, afraid he would be hurt again."

Kitt swallowed past the lump in her throat. "I was such a fool, Anna. I should have given our marriage a chance. I'd give anything if I could make him believe I've changed."

"It isn't easy to win back the trust of a man like your Clayton. But he is worth it. The duke is like my Ford—a very special man."

A very special man. Kitt remembered Anna's words all of that day and into the evening. Just before midnight, Clay came to her room as he did each night, and they made passionate love. This time he lingered, lying there beside her, holding her in his arms. Kitt closed her eyes, praying he would stay.

Instead, he rolled away from her and climbed out of bed, reached for his robe and shrugged it across his shoulders. Her heart clenched at the sound of his heavy footfalls padding over the carpet toward the door to his bedchamber.

"Please don't leave. . . ." she called softly. "Stay with me tonight."

In the light of the candle beside the bed, she watched his fingers tighten around the doorknob. For a moment, he seemed uncertain and Kitt's heart clutched with hope. Then the knob slowly turned. Clay walked out of the room and closed the door.

Kitt buried her face in the pillow and began to weep.

Damp fall winds blew red and gold leaves from the trees and sent papers flying along the muddy streets. Sitting in the study at Rathmore Hall, Clay felt restless and out of sorts, though he didn't quite know why. His businesses were running smoothly. He was beginning to get a handle on the vast Rathmore holdings. And his home life was going exactly as he planned.

He was keeping his wife at arm's length while he satisfied himself in her bed.

Well, *satisfied* wasn't quite the word.

He was rarely sated. He wanted more than their single nightly encounters, no matter how incredible they were. He wanted to sleep with her, to wake up with her in the morning. He'd fallen in love with the innocent young woman he had married, but the wildly passionate creature he had released from the once-frightened girl was even more appealing.

One welcoming glance, one soft, seductive smile and he was hers to command.

It infuriated him.

And it terrified him.

He didn't want to love her—not again. His failure where she was concerned still haunted him, the wound as fresh and raw as an open sore.

He stayed away from the house as much as he could, though today he was forced to return home late in the afternoon for some paperwork he needed for a meeting with his solicitor.

He climbed the porch steps with a mixture of dread and anticipation, hoping to see her, yet not wanting to tempt himself. Perhaps he could be in and out without Kitt knowing he was there.

Walking quietly down the hall toward his study, he had just reached the drawing room when voices inside caught his attention, Ariel's high-pitched with worry, Kitt's calmer, more soothing.

"I'm all right, I tell you. Bruised a little, is all. I hardly need a physician."

Clay shoved open the drawing room doors. "What the devil is going on?" Stepping into the room, he froze at the sight of Kassandra, seated on the sofa, her clothes torn and dirty, the side of her face scraped raw.

Staring back at him like a guilty child, she gave him a wobbly smile. "I had a bit of an accident."

He strode toward her, caught her chin and turned it to study her face. "So it would seem." Her hair had come down and hung in limp coils around her cheeks, the heavy red strands covered with mud and leaves. The flowers sewn across the bodice of her muslin gown were ripped and hanging down, her skirt torn up one side, exposing the hem of her chemise and a portion of her leg.

A cold knot tightened in the pit of his stomach. "Ariel is right. You need to see a doctor." So saying, he turned toward the door just as Henderson appeared in the opening.

"The physician has been summoned, Your Grace."

He nodded "Thank you" and turned back to Kitt. "Now—tell me what happened."

She smiled, tried for a light note but failed. "Ariel and I went shopping and . . . and there was this dray, you see, loaded quite heavily with kegs of ale. Apparently, the driver didn't see me crossing the street."

"He saw you," Ariel argued, her blue eyes fierce. "He drove that wagon toward you on purpose! The man belongs in prison."

The worry churning in his stomach cranked up another notch. Still, he forced a calmness into his voice as he reached down and captured her hand. "How badly are you injured? You didn't break anything?"

She shook her head. "I tried to jump out of the way. I must have tripped or stumbled. I hit the ground like a great felled oak. I must have been quite a sight."

"Besides the obvious contusions," Ariel said, "her leg is badly scraped." She lifted away the torn portion of Kitt's soiled skirt to expose the raw flesh beneath. "And there is a shallow cut on her arm. They need to be washed and bandaged."

Clay clenched his jaw, trying to control the anger boiling through him at the man who had done this. Bending down, he slid an arm beneath her knees, ignored her soft gasp of protest, and lifted her against his chest.

"I'm fine, Clay, really. I just need a bath and—"

"And I shall see that you get one. After the physician has had a look at you." Turning, he strode toward the door. "Thank you for taking care of her," he called to Ariel over his shoulder as he continued down the hall, Kitt's arms around his neck to steady herself.

"Send the doctor up when he gets here," he said to the butler on his way up the stairs.

"Certainly, Your Grace."

As soon as they reached the sitting room, he stripped away her ruined clothes, his touch carefully impersonal, for once more worried than aroused. He surveyed her cuts and scrapes, then carried her into her bedchamber and settled her on the bed.

"Doesn't look too serious, just bloody painful." He sat down in the chair beside the bed, reached out and took hold of her hand. "Now, tell me about this dray. Ariel thinks the man tried to run you down on purpose. What do you think?"

Kitt bit her lip. "I don't know. I was simply too busy trying to get out of his way."

Clay didn't press her further. Surely it was an accident. What reason would anyone have to hurt her? But just to make sure, he would alert his footman to keep a closer eye on her.

"Were there any sort of markings on the wagon? The name of the freight company, perhaps?"

"I don't think so. If there was, neither of us noticed."

"We'll have a deuce of a time trying to discover who it was, but it's worth a try. I'll have someone check on it first thing in the morning."

Kitt lay back on the bed. "I'm sure it was an accident. It had to be."

Of course it did, but it made him uneasy nonetheless. The physician arrived, pronounced the wounds superficial, prescribed a bath and a dose of laudanum and a good night's rest.

Clay stayed away from her bed that evening, but he didn't want to. He wanted to be there in case she needed him. As he tossed and turned in his own lonely bed, he dreamed that Kassandra lay hurt and bleeding. She was going to die and there was nothing he could do. His father's coffin rested at the side of her bed and soon he would be alone again, as he had been for so many years.

He awakened bathed in perspiration, unable to return to sleep.

Adam Hawthorne, Earl of Blackwood, refastened the buttons at the front of his breeches and reached for the waistcoat he'd draped over the back of a chair.

"Are you sure you have to leave?" Lavinia purred, her small pale breasts naked above the white silk gown he had unbuttoned to the waist. "It isn't that late. Surely you can stay a little while longer."

Adam shook his head. "Get dressed, Lavinia. Sooner or later we'll be missed if we don't return downstairs."

"Posh! Who cares? I certainly don't. It's my sister-in-law's affair, not mine." She stood up from the bed, shoved her dress the rest of the way down her hips, allowing it to pool on the floor. "Come to bed, darling. Think of how good I can make you feel."

Adam said nothing, just drew on his coat and started for the bedchamber door. He'd had what he wanted from Lavinia Dandridge. It had turned out to be less than he'd thought. But then that was usually the case, he'd discovered.

"Have a pleasant evening, Lavinia." He cast her a last cursory glance, ignored her tight-lipped smile, and kept on walking, closing the door behind him. All he wanted now was to avoid the crush of people in the drawing room, to rid his nostrils of Lavinia's cloying perfume, and down enough liquor to drown the painful memories he carried of the war so that he could fall asleep.

With that goal in mind, he made his way outside the narrow brick house and started walking. It wasn't far to his club nor from there to the house he lived in, now that he was an earl. He enjoyed walking this time of night, when the air was damp and cold and a heavy gray mist crept along the empty streets.

He had always liked being out in the open, away from the confines of the city. Since his resignation from the cavalry, he'd missed the hours he'd spent in the saddle, the nights in the cool crisp air. Tonight he walked the streets as he often did, enjoying the chance to stretch his legs, the chilly dampness against his skin.

Two blocks from the soiree he'd been attending, a carriage rolled past. He noticed the Rathmore crest and recognized the matched pair of bays pulling the duchess's expensive black rig. She had been at the soiree, he recalled, attending the affair with her friend, Glynis Trowbridge, Lady Camberwell. Clay had not been with them.

Adam knew his friend was doing his best to maintain a distance between his wife and himself. Adam wasn't sure it was working.

He paused on the street. Odd, the carriage was turning, pulling into an alley, stopping out of sight in the darkness. Adam stepped back into the shadows as a short, barrel-chested man appeared out of nowhere and jerked open the carriage door. In the fine thread of moonlight that appeared for an instant between two thin fingers of fog, he caught the flash of a pistol barrel, heard one of the women scream.

Adam moved forward in the darkness, working to get closer. On top of the carriage, the coachman pointed a gun at the footman who stood at the rear. Inside the coach, he heard a scuffle, then the stout man dragged one of the women outside. When the hood of her black velvet cloak fell back, Adam caught a glimpse of Kassandra Barclay's fiery red hair.

Swearing a silent curse, he quietly moved through the darkness. Flattening himself against the brick wall, he eased toward the coachman, who dropped down to the ground on the opposite side of the carriage, the footman still solidly in his pistol sights.

"If you want the duchess to live," the coachman said, "I'd advise you to take the other woman and make yourselves scarce."

The footman frantically nodded, jumped down from his perch, opened the carriage door, and Lady Camberwell scrambled out.

"Come on," the young man said softly, tugging her toward the entrance to the alley.

"Are you mad? We can't just leave her!"

"You'd best be doing what he tells you, milady. Or I'll be pullin' this trigger and you won't have to worry about it anymore."

The footman tugged sharply, gave her a pleading look, and the two of them bolted out of the alley, racing toward the soiree for help. It would be too late by the time they returned.

Adam inched forward. He heard a scuffling noise as the men dragged Kassandra along the side of the alley, one of them muffling her attempts to cry for help. The alley formed a dark, narrow tunnel that disappeared into the fog. In minutes, the men would be out of sight.

He moved forward in the darkness on the opposite side of the alley, heard Kassandra's rapid breathing, the shuffling of her feet as the stout man dragged her along.

"If ye know what's good for ye, Duchess," the other man warned in a thick cockney accent, "ye'll stop fightin' me and go along nice and quiet-like."

She didn't, of course, as Adam could have guessed. Inwardly, he smiled at the sound of her small foot colliding with her abductor's shin and the man's muttered curse.

"Ye lit'le 'ellion—I'm warnin' ye—" He never got to finish his sentence.

Adam stepped out of the darkness in front of him, swung a punch that knocked the man sideways, and he lost his hold on Kitt. She jerked free and started to run, her feet slapping puddles of water along the way. Adam hit him again, knocking him down, his thick head cracking hard on the cobbles. Adam whirled as the second man charged, head down, ramming into him like a bull. The impact knocked the air out of his lungs and sent him flying backward against the rough brick wall.

Pain shot into his head. Dark swirling circles appeared at the edge of his vision. He heard Kassandra's unladylike oath, could hardly believe she was running again—back down the alley in his direction.

She had stumbled upon a piece of broken wagon tongue, picked it up, and rushed toward the men, swinging it like a bludgeon across the stout man's back. He stumbled, grunted in pain, whirled to face her. Adam came away from the wall, threw a hard punch into the coachman's middle that buckled his knees, but he stayed on his feet, turned, and started to run, streaking past the stout man closing on the duchess.

Adam started toward him, and the stocky man cursed, realizing he was about to be left on his own. Spinning away from Kassandra, he raced after his friend down the alley. The clatter of running feet and the sound of a barking dog echoed eerily, and a few seconds later, they disappeared into the creeping fog.

Adam swayed a little, still a little dizzy. He shook his head to clear it and strode toward the woman standing in the middle of the alley, small feet splayed, still gripping the length of broken wood.

She blinked when she realized who it was. "Lord Blackwood . . ."

One of his rare smiles appeared. He simply couldn't resist. "At your service, Duchess."

"Those two men . . . they were . . . they were trying to *abduct* me."

"So it would seem." He reached over, took the wood from her hand and tossed it away, hearing it clatter against the wall. He straightened her cloak, which hung off one small shoulder, and drew the hood up over her head. When he felt her trembling, he slid an arm around her waist and urged her toward the carriage.

"It's all right, Your Grace. The men are long gone and I'm going to see you home."

She stopped, looked up at him. "My regular coachman was sick. That man took his place."

That made sense. "This appeared to have been well-planned."

"What . . . what did they want with me?"

"Money, most likely. They risk the gallows for ransom, but to some the risk is worth it."

She dragged in a shaky breath of air. "Thank you. If you hadn't come along when you did—"

"I'm glad I happened past. I'm sure your husband will be grateful."

Her pretty green eyes grew troubled. "Perhaps."

Adam stopped at the door to the carriage. "It took courage to do what you did tonight. I might not have fared so well myself if you hadn't returned to help."

The duchess shook her head. "You're an extremely capable man, my lord. I don't believe you were ever in any real danger."

His mouth faintly curved. "One never knows for certain. At any rate, you're a very courageous woman. Your husband is a man who admires bravery. So am I."

Her eyes welled with tears. She hurriedly glanced away. "Glynis has gone back to the soiree to get help. They'll be frantic if we're not here when they return."

"We'll stop by and let them know you're safe."

She nodded, ducked her head, and disappeared inside the carriage. Adam closed the door and climbed up on the driver's seat. He backed the horses out of the alley and turned them toward the Dandridge soiree they had both just left.

He wondered where Clay was tonight—and exactly what he would do when he discovered someone had tried to abduct his wife.

26

A dozen lamps burned in the windows when Clay stormed into his town house. Just minutes ago, a footman had arrived at his club with a note from Adam Hawthorne saying he was urgently needed at home. With a stomach balled hard as a fist, Clay had barked orders to his coachman, who whipped the horses into a frenzy. They barreled through the fog-enshrouded streets and roared to a halt in front of the town house. Clay jumped down and pounded up the front porch stairs.

He blew past Henderson, tossing the man his hat and coat as he passed, and strode into the drawing room. Perched on a sofa, her slippers off and her stockinged feet curled beneath her, a slightly pale-faced Kitt sat sipping tea with the Earl of Blackwood.

"What's happened?" Clay halted in the middle of the room, his gaze flying from Kitt to the earl and back again.

Blackwood's long fingers curled around a snifter of brandy. "Simply put, after the Dandridge soiree your wife attended with her friend, Lady Camberwell, two men tried to abduct her. I happened to be passing by at the time. Fortunately, I was able to stop them."

The fist in Clay's stomach clenched harder. He sat down on an ottoman in front of Kassandra, reached out, and caught hold of her hand. "Are you all right?"

She smiled, far more composed than she should have been. "Poor Glynis went for help. She was nearly catatonic by the time the earl and I arrived safely back at the soiree, but I am perfectly fine—thanks to his lordship."

His eyes swung to Blackwood. "Tell me what happened."

As concisely as possible, Adam described the events as they had unfolded, as well as Kitt's part in the affair. Kassandra added what little she knew and Blackwood finished the tale, casting an approving glance in her direction.

"Your lady was extremely courageous. I might not be here if she hadn't put herself in danger by returning to the fray."

Clay didn't know whether to throttle her for being so careless with her safety or drag her into his arms and kiss her. He knew he was proud of her—and damnably worried.

"Well, it's over now," Kitt said a little too brightly. "Neither Glynis nor I were harmed."

Clay gently squeezed her hand. "Unfortunately, I'm afraid it isn't that simple." Rising from the ottoman, he plucked the empty snifter from Adam's hand and made his way to the sideboard to refill it, pouring himself a brandy as well. He fixed his attention on the earl. "This is the second time in the past two weeks that a threat has been made against my wife."

Blackwood's casual posture faded. Kitt set her teacup back in its saucer with a clatter. "You aren't talking about the wagon accident?"

"What wagon accident?" Adam leaned forward in his chair.

Returning the refilled snifter of brandy, Clay explained about the runaway dray and how close Kitt had come to being killed.

"I find it difficult to believe what happened tonight is merely coincidence," Clay said. "From what you've told me, the men in the alley weren't interested in Lady Camberwell. They wanted Kassandra. If my theory is correct, they were paid to abduct her, which means it's very likely the same person is behind the two attempts. I want to know who it is."

"Lord Blackwood believes the men meant to hold me for ransom," Kitt said.

Adam took a drink of his brandy. "At the time I did. That was before I learned someone tried to run you down with a freight wagon."

"We don't know for certain that is what happened," Kitt argued. "It may have simply been an accident."

"It may have been," Clay said. "Unfortunately, that's an assumption we can't afford to make." So far his inquiries into the matter of the dray had turned up no answers, and the few witnesses who had seen the accident believed it simply that—a wagon gone out of control.

"Why would anyone want to harm the duchess?" Blackwood asked.

Clay raked a hand through his hair, dislodging several dark strands. "I haven't the faintest idea."

Blackwood spoke to Kitt. "What about you, Your Grace? Can you think of anyone? An enemy you might have made? Someone you might have angered enough to do you harm?"

Kitt shook her head. "No, I . . ." Her turbulent gaze swung to Clay. "Perhaps Lady Simington might have a grievance . . . assuming my husband is no longer spending time in her bed."

Clay's eyes remained steady on her face. "I've never spent time in the lady's bed. Even if I had, Lily isn't the sort to be jealous. To her, an affair is simply a way to pass time. From what I hear, she has currently set her sights on Lord Collingwood."

"You're telling me you never—"

"No. Not the countess or anyone else."

Ignoring the stunned look on Kassandra's face, Blackwood spoke up. "Perhaps it isn't your wife they're after," he said. "Not ultimately, at least. Perhaps, indirectly, the target is you, Clay."

The words snagged his attention. "What are you talking about?"

"I realize you and your wife have been somewhat estranged, but anyone with eyes can see how much the lady means to you. Her loss would grieve you sorely."

Kitt's eyes locked on his face. The longing he read in them made his heart squeeze painfully. Dammit, he had already admitted the truth about Lily. He couldn't afford to let her know how much she meant to him. He refused to give her that sort of hold over him again.

"Kassandra is my wife," he said blandly. "Of course I would care if something happened to her."

The light went out of her eyes and she glanced away. He wanted to call back the words, tell her that if she left him again, if she were injured or killed, it would tear him to pieces. Instead he returned his attention to the earl.

"You're suggesting that the man we're after might be an enemy of mine instead of Kitt's."

"I'm saying it's possible. By harming Kassandra, he'd be getting revenge against you both."

Stephen's tall blond image jolted into Clay's head. "Westerly." He nearly spat the word. "With every painful step the man takes, he has reason to want revenge." Aside from Justin, Blackwood was the only man he had told about the duel, though he'd said nothing about the true reason behind it. "Stephen is just the sort to do something like this."

Clay walked over to the low fire crackling in the hearth. *Westerly.* Dammit, he should have killed the sonofabitch when he had the chance.

"Of course there is also Richard Barclay," Blackwood said mildly, swinging Clay around to face him. "Losing a dukedom is certainly reason enough to want revenge."

It was true. After his father's death and the loss of his inheritance, Richard had made no secret of his loathing for Clay. And now that Adam had pointed it out, it wouldn't take a genius to realize Clay had strong feelings for his wife. The only one who seemed not to know was Kassandra—which was exactly the way Clay intended to keep it.

Did Richard want retribution for the terrible blow his father had dealt him? The scandal alone would have been enough to spur the man's hatred. Would he harm Kassandra merely to get even with Clay?

He had to admit it was a distinct possibility.

"Surely Richard wouldn't go that far," Kitt said, voicing some of his own thoughts, but she twisted the small linen tea napkin she held in her hand and looked no more certain than he.

"Perhaps not. I assure you I intend to find out." Clay left the warmth of the fire and walked back to the sofa. "Until we know more, we have to take precautions. Anna is returning to Blair House on the morrow. Ford will undoubtedly accompany her. I intend that you should go with them."

Kitt jerked upright. "But that's ridiculous. I can't possibly—"

"I want you out of the city, somewhere you'll be safe. At Blair House, you will be. We'll keep the matter quiet. No one need know why you're leaving or where you've gone. Once you're out of London, I'll have a chance to find out who's behind these attacks."

Kitt uncurled from the sofa and came to her feet in front of him. "If it's Westerly, you might be no safer than I. Stephen could be seeking revenge against both of us."

He thought of the earl and anger made his jaw tighten. "Let him come, then. I should like nothing better than to finish what we started that morning in the park."

Kitt hiked up her chin, her small stockinged feet peeking out from beneath her silk skirt. "If you're staying, so am I."

Clay shook his head. "Not a chance, sweeting. You're going to Blair House with your friends and that is the end of it."

"But you just agreed you might also be in danger. If I stay, I can help you search for—"

"You're going."

"What if I refuse?"

"Then I shall tie you up and see that you stay that

way until you are safely arrived in the country. Unless you wish to suffer a very uncomfortable ride, I suggest you do as I say."

Her mouth set stubbornly. "You're the most arrogant, insufferable—"

He grinned, cutting off her tirade before she could gather steam. "True. But I'm also your husband and I intend to keep you safe."

Kitt gave him a vapid smile. "Very well, *Your Grace.* Pardon me for caring that something might happen to you." She turned a kinder look on the earl. "If you'll excuse me, your lordship, I'm sure you and His Eminence have a great deal to discuss, once you rid yourselves of the cumbersome presence of a mere, helpless woman." Her features softened. "Thank you again for what you did tonight."

Blackwood actually smiled. "My pleasure, Your Grace."

With a last haughty glare at Clay, Kassandra swept from the room.

Watching her depart, Blackwood's deep blue eyes flickered with amusement. "She's quite something, your wife." The amusement slowly faded. "It would be a shame if something happened to her."

"Nothing's going to happen—I won't let it."

"What are you going to do?"

"Hire a couple of Bow Street runners to start. The coachman who drove Kassandra's carriage tonight worked for me, at least he did for the last several days. My head groom must know something about him. As for Richard, I'll speak to him myself, see which way the wind blows. Perhaps he'll give something away."

"And Westerly . . . ?"

Clay shook his head. "I'm not exactly sure."

"You might put a couple of men on his house. Have them report anyone who goes in and out. Could be interesting to see what turns up."

"Good idea. I'll see to it first thing." Clay walked the earl to the door. "I haven't thanked you yet for what you did tonight. I'm in your debt, Adam. If anything had happened to Kitt . . ." He shook his head, glanced away.

Blackwood clamped a hand on his shoulder. "I'm glad I could help." They walked down the hall to the entry. "In the meantime, I'll do a little digging myself, see what I can find out."

"I'd appreciate that."

Henderson opened the heavy carved front door and the earl stepped out onto the porch. "One more thing," he said.

"Yes?"

"You might tell your wife how happy you are that she is unharmed. I don't think she realizes how much you care."

Clay made no reply. Blackwood's attitude where Kitt was concerned had shifted one hundred and eighty degrees. He often defended her and it was obvious he admired her for the bravery she had shown tonight, but Clay had never doubted her courage.

He sighed as he climbed the stairs and went into the master's suite, worry weighing heavily on his shoulders. It was the crash of drawers slamming closed in Kitt's bedchamber that made his lips twitch with amusement. Through the door leading in from the sitting room, he could hear her mumbling, muttering curses, her temper hot and barely contained.

His own body grew warm but it wasn't with anger. Pulling open the door without knocking, he walked in.

If she wanted to vent her temper, he would let her. Clay knew exactly the way.

Dressed in a long cotton night rail she had worn just to spite him, her long hair brushed and braided as she knew he disliked, Kassandra tossed another chemise into her trunk, slammed the drawer closed, and opened another. Damn his arrogant hide! High-handed and domineering, that's what he was.

She's my wife. Of course I would care if something happened to her. As he would also be concerned should his butler be injured, or his favorite bloody horse!

He probably just wanted to get rid of her for a while, begin his heretofore unconsummated affair with Lily Wainscott, or perhaps find someone else to warm his bed. Anger kept her from being more appreciative of his fidelity—if indeed it was the truth.

She yanked open the bottom drawer, pulled out her sketch pad and charcoal, and tossed them into the trunk. She almost didn't hear him walk in, jumped a little at the sound of the closing door.

He crossed his arms over his chest and propped his wide shoulders against it, an irritating smile on his lips. "It might be easier if you simply asked your maid to pack for you in the morning."

Kitt tossed her braid back over her shoulder, hanging onto her temper by a thread. "It would be simpler if I stayed in London."

"Not for me." He walked to where she stood with her shoulders thrown back and her eyes snapping with fire. "I want you safe. I can't make that happen as long as you're in London."

"What do you care? You're a duke. If something

happened to me, another wife would be easy enough for you to come by."

The amusement left his features. "I don't want another wife. I've grown fond of the one I have."

Some of the fight went out of her. When he looked at her that way, his eyes full of heat and need and something soft and indescribably sweet that she hadn't seen in weeks, her legs felt suddenly shaky. "You have?"

"Yes, I have. And I'm extremely grateful she wasn't injured tonight."

Her eyes filled. Dammit to hell, she wouldn't cry simply because the man had uttered a few kind words. Clay came away from the door, crossed to where she stood in front of the dresser, and slowly eased her into his arms.

"I want you safe, love," he said softly. "If Adam hadn't arrived when he did, God only knows what might have happened."

She leaned toward him, she couldn't help it, and her arms refused to go anywhere except around his neck. She felt his lips against her hair as he lifted her up and carried her toward the bed. She knew he wanted her. Desire glittered like gold in his eyes.

She thought he would take her swiftly, fan the fire that always leapt between them. Instead, as he set her on her feet beside the bed, he kissed her slowly, gently coaxing her lips apart, teasing her with his tongue.

The kiss deepened, grew more intense, and her body turned boneless with wanting. He reached for her braid, slid the ribbon off the end, combed his fingers through her heavy mass of hair, and spread it around her shoulders. He leaned toward her. Another deep, unhurried kiss. He unfastened the ties on her night rail and slid it off her shoulders, letting it pool in a heap at her feet.

Warm, moist lips moved over her cheek, along her throat, nibbled there, moved lower. He kissed her breasts, took the fullness into his mouth and she arched toward him. She sensed his restlessness, his hunger, yet there was an odd restraint, a gentleness that hadn't been there since her return.

Her heart swelled. She loved him so much. And there had been no other women.

When he lifted her up and set her on the edge of the bed, she made no protest, just waited while he turned down the lamp on the nightstand and started to remove his clothes.

Clay unfastened the cuffs on his shirt and shrugged it off his shoulders. He pulled off his boots, tossed his breeches over a chair, and turned toward the woman on the bed.

He loved her hair, the color of shiny dark copper, loved the way the wild silky curls clung to his hands when he touched it. He loved her body, all soft curves and smooth, feminine flesh. He loved the way she looked at him, with bold appreciation disguised beneath a layer of shyness.

He loved her laughter and the way she wasn't afraid to stand up to him, as she had done tonight. She worried that he might be in danger. Perhaps after his mother had died when he was a boy, his father had worried about him. But that was a long time ago. He was a man now. No one had worried about him in years.

He reached for her, slid his hand into her hair. His thumb moved along her jaw and she leaned her cheek into his palm. He tilted her face up for his kiss, settled his mouth very gently over hers. He could feel her pulse beating beneath his fingers, faster as he deepened the kiss. His own heartbeat quickened. What if he had lost her?

He kissed the side of her neck, kissed her earlobe, heard her soft little sigh of pleasure. He intended to give her more of that tonight, much more. He wanted her to forget what had nearly happened and though he wouldn't bare his feelings any more than he already had, he wanted to show her how much she meant to him.

He kissed her shoulders, lowered his head, and took one of her full breasts into his mouth. The tip pebbled quickly, a rough little bead that tasted so sweet against his tongue his body went rock hard. He licked the crest and a faint shudder went through her. Her fingers slid into his hair and her head fell back.

Outside the window, a dense fog enveloped the house, creating a private world where nothing existed but the two of them. He kissed his way from her breasts to her belly, moved lower, across the flat spot below her navel. She trembled as he parted her legs, began to taste the sensitive skin on the inside of her thighs.

His hand found the soft nest of reddish curls. He kissed her there, felt the tension creep into her body.

"Clay . . . ?"

"Let me love you," he said softly, looking up into her face, his hand moving lower, parting her soft, slick flesh, beginning to stroke her. She made a little whimpering sound as he kissed her again and eased her backward on the bed.

He had wanted to love her this way from the start,

wanted to give her this deep, selfless pleasure, wanted to imprint himself on her in this intimate way and make her completely his.

He did so now, settling his mouth over her warm, female flesh and taking her with his tongue.

"Oh, dear God . . ."

He felt her hands in his hair, uncertain at first, hesitant, then tightening, holding him there, caught up in the pleasure, urging him to continue. The mist outside seemed to find its way into the room, to wrap around them, cocooning them both in sensation. The scent of her hardened his body to the point of pain. The taste of her set him on fire.

He used his mouth and tongue with relentless skill, determined to give her all that he could. Her body quivered, tightened. She sobbed his name and still he did not stop. Not until she cried out in pleasure, her release swift and hard, jolting her with the force of it.

He cupped her bottom, bringing her closer, holding her captive while his mouth moved over her again. Another climax shook her, even more fierce than the first.

He raised himself above her, his heart beating even faster than hers, his body slick with sweat and glistening in the faint yellow glow of the lamp. His eyes held hers as he filled her, slid himself deeply inside, and neither of them looked away. Renewed heat flared between them. His arousal throbbed with every breath, every surge of blood through his veins. He drove into her slowly, heightening the pleasure, holding himself back when he wanted to lose himself inside her, take what he wanted.

Instead, he paced himself, gauging every penetration, every sweet response until he had her moaning beneath him, digging her nails into his shoulders, his name like a litany on her lips.

"Come with me," he softly commanded and felt her body tighten.

"Clay—" Her voice broke as she whispered his name and then she came apart. He drove into her one last time and gave in to the all-consuming heat that seemed to burn him from the inside out. His body tightened and a shudder tore through him. Pleasure welled up, more intense than he had ever felt before.

Little by little, Kitt's breathing slowed. Easing himself down beside her, he listened to the beat of her heart, or perhaps it was his own. He wanted to stay with her, hold her through the night. Make love to her again.

But as the clock chimed on the mantel, the mist of passion began to clear and reality set in. He couldn't let himself weaken, refused to risk himself that way again.

He eased himself to the side of the bed, swung his legs to the carpet, reached down and gathered up his clothes.

"Clay . . . ?" There was a quiver in her voice. It made his chest ache. She came up on her knees at the edge of the bed, bunching the sheet in front of her. "Remember the night I told you I wanted to be your wife again?"

He remembered. Even then he hadn't trusted her to mean it. Kitt was a runner. She always had been. At the first sign of trouble, she would run from him again.

"I remember." In the darkness, he could see the outline of her small, feminine body, but her eyes remained in shadow.

"That was only part of what I wanted."

He stiffened, afraid to hear the rest.

"I want you to love me, Clay—I don't feel whole without you." Her small hand tightened on the sheet. "I want you to love me . . . the way that I love you."

His breathing ceased. There wasn't the least rise or fall of his chest. He stood there for moments that seemed to stretch forever. In a faint ray of moonlight slanting through the fog outside the window, he could see her face, see that there were tears on her cheeks.

He clamped down hard on his emotions, buried them beneath an indifferent façade. In the past he might have believed her. There was a time he had wanted nothing so much as for her to love him. He'd been a fool back then. He wasn't a fool any longer.

He stared at her and told himself to start walking, that it was time he returned to the safety of his room, but his legs refused to move. Knowing he shouldn't, that it was the very worst thing he could do, he walked to the edge of the bed, gathered her into his arms, and kissed her very softly on the lips.

Easing her over a little on the bed, he took his place beside her, drawing her close against him and pulling up the covers.

Neither of them spoke. It took a long time for him to fall asleep. In the morning, long before she awakened, he left and returned to his room.

The thick fog of the night before faded beneath a heavy rain. Anna sat next to Kassandra in the carriage on the way to Blair House while Ford lounged across from them like a tall golden lion. His mood was as dark as the clouds outside the window and Anna knew why.

He was pressing her to say yes to his marriage proposal, but so far she had not answered. Her parents had demanded she wed Edouardo Falacci, a man years her senior. This time the decision was hers and she wanted to make the right one.

Anna leaned back against the seat, studying the handsome man across from her. Ford was everything she wanted in a husband, a marvelous lover and a kind and generous companion. But he had yet to say he loved her, and she wasn't going to marry him until she knew for certain that he did.

Kitt was busy with her sketch pad. Anna closed her eyes and slept for a while. With the roads so muddy, it took an extra hour to reach Hampstead Heath, but at last they arrived at Blair House.

Ford's country estate, Landen Manor in Golder's Green, was only a short ride away, but Clayton had asked him to watch after Kassandra so Ford was staying in one of Anna's guest rooms.

He was up there now, leaving Anna and Kitt alone in a small salon at the rear of the house. Seated in front of the fire, Anna studied her friend's troubled face, certain it was thoughts of the duke, not the abduction attempt, that made her look so forlorn.

Kitt looked up as if she read her mind. "He doesn't love me, Anna. I don't know if he ever will."

Anna reached over and caught her hand. "Do not say something so foolish. You saw him the night you danced with Lord Blackwood. *Santa Maria*—the man was insane with jealousy. He would not care so much if he did not love you."

"Clay isn't the sort to share his wife with another man. That doesn't mean he loves me." Kitt stared off toward the fire. "Last night I . . . I told him that I loved him." She glanced down, swallowed. "He didn't say a word, Anna. He just stood there, his face dark as thunder. I don't think he believed me, I don't know. Whatever he was thinking, it wasn't good. It was obvious he doesn't love me in return and all I managed to do was make a fool of myself."

"That is not true."

"It's completely true. How many women do you think have told Clay they loved him? Two, four, a dozen? I'm no different than the rest and now he knows it." She made a sound of misery in her throat. "For all I know, that may have made him even more eager to send me away."

"He sent you away because he believed you were in danger. He wanted you in a place of safety and that is where you are."

"And what will Clay be doing while I'm gone? Looking for someone new to warm his bed?"

"You are not being fair and you know it. I do not believe your husband is interested in any woman but you. Do you honestly believe that he is?"

Kitt stared into her lap, plucked at a fold of her skirt. "No. He told me he didn't sleep with Lillian Wainscott or anyone else. I must be completely insane but I believe him. I don't think he wants another woman."

Anna smiled. "Good, because it is the truth. Now you will stop worrying about Clayton and enjoy yourself while you are here. In time, your husband will admit his feelings for you."

At least Anna hoped he would. She was certain the duke loved his wife, but she wasn't sure he would ever completely let his guard down with Kassandra again.

For Kitt's sake, she hoped that in time Clayton would realize that his wife had learned her lesson. That she would never run from him again.

"Come," Anna said, taking hold of Kitt's hand. "The children are eager to see you." Leaving the small salon, they made their way to the staircase in the entry, heading for the nursery. "You will also be pleased to know that our Gypsy friends have returned. Perhaps in the morning we will go for a visit to the camp."

For the first time, Kassandra actually smiled. "Oh, Anna, I'd love to. I'd have a chance to see Yotsi again."

"*Sì, cara.*" She grinned. "And perhaps this time we will both join in the dancing."

27

By late afternoon, the rain had slowed to a damp, uncomfortable drizzle. Pulling up the collar of his greatcoat, Clay climbed the steps to his half-brother's town house and lifted the heavy brass knocker.

"The Duke of Rathmore to see Richard Barclay," he said when the door swung open. The reminder of his title alone, Clay knew, would be enough to set Richard's teeth on edge.

"If you will please come in," the butler said, "I shall discover whether his lordship is receiving." As the son of a duke, Richard still enjoyed the courtesy of a title. That, the town house he lived in, and the comfortable yearly stipend he had been granted in his father's will were all that he had left.

"Tell my brother I want to see him *now*."

The butler's thin black eyebrows lifted a little. Making no further reply, he turned and hurried off down the hall.

He came back a few minutes later. "Lord Richard will receive you in his study. If you will please follow me."

Halfway down the passage, the butler opened a polished mahogany door and Clay walked into a book-lined study. Richard rose from behind his desk and started walking toward him. There wasn't the least hint of welcome in his face.

"I won't mince words," Richard said. "Cheswick made it clear that your visit was somewhat urgent. Since this is obviously not a social call, what exactly do you want?"

Clay strolled past him into the study and casually examined a row of paintings on the walls. He paused at a portrait of Joanne Barclay, Richard's mother, a dour-faced woman with cool blue eyes and iron-gray hair.

"I never knew your mother. I've seen her, of course, at various social functions, but we never spoke. Rather a hard-edged woman, I always thought, but Father said he respected her. Quite a compliment, coming from him."

"I asked what it is that you want."

Clay turned a hard look on his brother. "I want to know exactly how much you hate me."

Richard's nostrils flared. "Why would you think I hate you? Oh, yes—because Father took everything away from me and gave it all to you."

"I suppose I might find that sufficient motivation for hating someone."

"Even if it is, why do you want to know?"

"Because someone is trying to kill my wife. Since Kassandra hasn't any enemies of her own, there's a very good chance whoever wishes her harm is actually trying to punish me."

"Interesting."

"Is it?"

"That you think I pose some sort of threat to the duchess? Yes, I believe it is."

"But you don't deny it's a possibility."

He shrugged, but a slight tension vibrated across his shoulders. "It might be—if the man in question were someone other than me."

"What is that supposed to mean?"

Richard didn't answer. "From the rumors I've heard, you and your wife are barely speaking. What would I have to gain by killing her?"

Clay studied his brother's face. "You've never been a fool, Richard. I think you know very well how much Kassandra means to me. Perhaps watching me grieve for my wife would give you some sort of sick satisfaction."

Richard laughed, the high-pitched sound sending a chill down Clay's spine. "Oh, I'm sick, all right—at least according to our late, beloved father. Surely he told you all about it? My disease, as he called it." His mouth curved bitterly. "My preference for young boys."

Clay's hand paused midway to the small teakwood horse he was about to pick up. He worked to keep the shock from his face. The day he had seen Richard with the little Gypsy boy, he had wondered. A rumor had surfaced several years ago, but at the time he hadn't believed it. And since Richard had been heir to a dukedom, the gossip had quickly disappeared.

The day he'd found Richard with the child, Clay had remembered the rumor. There was something in Richard's eyes that day, something wild and unleashed, like a fire burning out of control.

"What's the matter, brother? For once you have nothing to say?"

Clay cleared his throat. "That's the reason, then, that Father changed his will. He found out about your ... preferences."

"Perhaps you should be insulted. Father didn't choose you—he simply disqualified me."

Clay stared down at the small, beautifully carved Oriental horse on the table, but his thoughts remained on his brother. "Are you saying you don't blame me for what Father did?"

"Perhaps I did ... at first. The truth is, I don't blame anyone but myself, and since I seem to have very little control over my ... preferences ... as you call them, it is difficult even to lay blame there. It is simply the way things are. The luck of the draw, you might say, being a man who likes to gamble."

Clay tried to understand what his brother was telling him, but it was difficult to grasp something so foreign to his nature. "If you don't blame me, then it would appear that my wife is in no danger from you."

Richard smiled thinly. "Not in the least."

Clay studied his half-brother's face. If Richard was lying, he was doing a very good job of it. "I don't know if you'll believe it, but I never wanted the dukedom. I wanted Father to accept me as his son. That was all I ever wanted from him."

Richard stared at him with pain-filled eyes. "Funny. That was all I wanted from him, too."

Clay made no reply. He shouldn't feel pity for Richard, but he did. And he was inclined to believe him.

Which meant the man most likely responsible for the attacks on his wife was Stephen Marlow.

It was Westerly. It had to be.

As he left the town house, his hands unconsciously

fisted. Stephen was a powerful man and Clay had no proof.

Somehow he had to find a way to stop him.

Kitt had been at Blair House three days when unexpected visitors arrived: William Plimpton, Sir Hubert Tinsley, Miles Cavendish, and Cedrick Claxton—all of them accompanying Stephen Marlow, who was on his way to Rivenwood, Westerly's country estate.

Kitt's stomach knotted the moment he limped through the door into the entry, his long pale fingers wrapped around a silver-headed cane. Dear God, it had never occurred to her the man might appear at Blair House!

But Anna and Ford knew nothing of Stephen and what he had done to her that long-ago night. They knew nothing of the duel or Clay's suspicions. And unless she was willing to have her past unveiled to her friends, she couldn't say a word.

"The roads are so muddy and Stephen got a late start out of the city." Anna sailed past with a smile. "He decided to detour a bit out of his way and stop by here. Of course I have asked him to stay."

Kitt forced a smile. "Of . . . course. You could hardly turn them away."

"And it is good to have friends in the house. We can play cards after supper." She grinned. "We will give them a lesson, eh, *cara?*" She winked as she whisked herself off to order guest rooms readied and a lavish meal prepared.

Dreading the evening ahead, Kitt quietly excused herself and climbed the stairs to her room. She would plead the headache, stay in her bedchamber until the group left on the morrow. Even if Clay was right and Stephen was the man behind the attacks on her, he had hired men to do it. It was highly unlikely he would try to murder her himself and especially not while they were together at Blair House.

With that thought in mind, several hours later, she made her excuses, declining supper and an evening of gaming—to Anna's disappointment—and curled up in her bed for the night. It took her a while to fall asleep. She could hear faint laughter and the sound of Mozart being played on the pianoforte. Eventually, she fell asleep.

It was well past midnight when her eyes blinked open in the darkness. A sound had disturbed her. Something heavy moving about or perhaps . . .

A thick hand clamped over her mouth, stifling a gasp of fear, and an arm wrapped around her waist, dragging her roughly out of bed. She caught a glimpse of the man's face, saw the scar that slashed through his upper lip, and recognized the coachman who had tried to abduct her after the Dandridge soiree. Then he slammed her back against his chest.

Kitt clawed at the hairy hand muffling her cries for help, but he only tightened his hold, his voice hard-edged and gruff.

"You'd better hold still, if you know what's good for you. You've caused enough trouble already. Any more and I'll have to hurt you." To prove his point, the arm clamped around her squeezed until she could barely breathe.

Wheezing in a gulp of air, Kitt eased her struggles and tried to control the trembling that had started in her limbs. *For God's sake, don't panic!* she told herself. *Just bide your time and wait for your chance to escape.*

Ignoring the fear creeping through her, she glanced toward the window and saw the curtains flutter, realized the man had climbed up the trellis in the garden. Dear God, how had he known which room she was in?

But Stephen could have known. It wouldn't have been difficult to discover. And it was certain now that he was the man behind the attacks.

She turned her head a little as the coachman dragged her toward the bedchamber door, cranked the skeleton key to unlock it, and stepped away. A moment later, the silver handle turned. Kitt stiffened as Stephen Marlow stepped into the room.

"You should learn to take the key out before you go to bed," he said with a mirthless smile. "Bring her over here, Mr. Peel."

She tried to jerk free but the man named Peel merely lifted her off her feet, pinning her arms uselessly at her sides, and started walking. She kicked futilely as he carried her over to where Stephen stood beside the writing desk in the corner and set her on her feet. Peel lifted his hand from her mouth, but before she could scream, Stephen stuffed a handkerchief between her teeth. He jerked a strip of cloth from his pocket and tied it over her mouth, holding the gag in place and cutting off any sound she might have made.

"Now that we're all settled down and comfortable, you're going to write a little farewell message to your husband."

Fear curled inside her. She firmly shook her head.

"Oh, but you are, my dear. If you don't, I'm going to give you to my friend here to enjoy before he wraps his hands around your lovely white throat and squeezes the life out of your body."

Kitt fought down her panic. She had known Stephen

wasn't the man he appeared, but even she hadn't known how utterly ruthless he was.

Opening the desk, he took out a sheet of foolscap, lifted the white plumed pen from its crystal holder, and dipped it into the inkwell. Freeing one of her hands from the coachman's implacable hold, he shoved the pen between her trembling fingers.

"If you want to live, you'll write exactly what I tell you."

She hesitated, glanced frantically around, hoping to find some avenue of escape. Anna and her guests were all downstairs. The music and laughter rang loudly, the house so big they couldn't possibly hear any noise she might make, and most of the servants were in their rooms upstairs. Steeling herself, she slowly nodded.

Stephen shoved the paper in front of her. "Dearest Clay," he started, waiting for her to pen the words. Her hand shook, trailing ink spots across the page. Stephen cursed. He grabbed the paper, wadded it up, and tossed it onto the floor, then laid a clean sheet in front of her.

"Do it properly this time or I'll let him have you right here."

Her stomach rolled with nausea. She couldn't bear it, she simply could not. She sucked in as much of a breath as she could with the miserable gag in her mouth, worked to still her shaking hand, and began again, this time neatly scrolling the words.

"I've decided to return to Italy," Stephen went on, creating his masterpiece with an almost gleeful expression. "Knowing you would surely disapprove, I leave tonight. Please thank Anna and the marquess for their hospitality. I shall write you upon my arrival."

Stalling for time, praying she would think of a way

to stop this, Kitt penned the last sentence with a leaden heart. Clay would believe the letter. In the past, it was just the sort of reckless behavior she had been known for, and far too similar to what she had done before. Clay would believe she had gone without the least regard for his feelings. He would be hurt and angry—he wouldn't even bother to try to find her.

Clay wouldn't realize what had happened to her for weeks, perhaps longer.

"Sign it," Stephen demanded. " 'Your wife, Kassandra'—write it down."

Her hand shook. She took a breath and steadied herself. She started penning the words, wishing there was something she could add, some small clue she could leave that would make Clay understand. She finished the letter and Stephen jerked it away from her, fanning it back and forth in the air to dry the ink.

He read it over carefully, seemed satisfied, and set it back on the desk where the maid would find it.

When he looked at her again, his too-pale eyes held a triumphant gleam. "You thought you were so damn smart, didn't you? I told you to keep your mouth shut, but no—you wouldn't listen. You're just like the rest, nothing but a conniving bitch." He ran a thin finger along her jaw, making her skin crawl. "I put you in your place before—the only way you women understand. Now I'm going to teach you both a lesson—one neither of you will ever forget."

Kitt started to struggle, silently cursing him to hell, hating him more than ever.

"Get her out of here," Stephen calmly commanded, and the coachman began to drag her away.

No! Kitt fought wildly, trying to jerk free, trying to kick him. He held her while Stephen pulled a length of

rope from his pocket and bound her wrists, used another to tie her feet, then the coachman hoisted her
over his shoulder, carried her to the window, and
ducked through the opening into the darkness outside.
Step by careful step, he made his way down the trellis,
his big feet crunching on the dried leaves and
branches wrapped around the painted wood.

With every step, Kitt's heart thundered with fear.
What had Stephen ordered him to do? Rape her? Kill
her?

Peel waited in the shadows till he was certain he
hadn't been seen, then he started to run, keeping his
body low and out of sight, carting her off into the
darkness.

Rain was falling again, thick gray sheets that
drenched the muddy earth. In minutes her nightgown
was soaked clear through, her skin shivering with
gooseflesh. Bobbing against the man's shoulder, she
winced as her stomach slammed painfully up and
down with each of his long, running strides. The ribbon
flew off her braid and her hair floated out around her
shoulders. Wet tendrils stuck to her neck and plastered
themselves to her cheeks.

Raising her head as best she could, she watched the
house receding into the darkness behind them and a
fresh wash of fear flooded into her stomach. Dear
God, where was he taking her? They passed through a
field and into a copse of trees, and a second man
joined them, the stocky man who had appeared that
night in the alley. He said something to Peel and both
of them laughed.

Kitt closed her eyes, fighting a wave of nausea.
They were going to kill her. Stephen wanted revenge
and he was going to get it.

At the edge of the meadow on the opposite side of the trees, a third man appeared in the darkness. Kitt raised her head, squinting to see who it was. Her eyes widened at the sight of the big dark Gypsy named Demetro she had seen at the camp and again in the city. He smiled as his big hand closed around a pouch of coins the stocky man handed him. He tucked it into the waistband of his breeches and opened the door of his brightly painted *vardo,* which was parked at the edge of the woods.

The coachman carried her up the rickety wooden stairs, ducked his head, and carried her into the low-ceilinged wagon. He tossed her onto the narrow bed and bound her hands to the headboard. With a satisfied smile, he turned and ducked back out the door.

Trussed like a bundle of wheat, shivering with cold and fear, she fought to hold back tears. She'd heard stories of women being kidnapped and sold into slavery by the Gypsies, though until this moment she had never believed them.

Icy dread welled up inside her. She'd been certain the men would kill her. Perhaps death would be a welcome alternative to what Demetro had planned. The wagon shifted as his heavy weight settled onto the wagon seat. The horse began to plod through the rain and she struggled against the ropes that held her, but they didn't budge. If only she had stayed in London, stayed with Clay.

I love you, she said silently, and for the first time she was glad that she had told him. She closed her eyes and fought against the tears that leaked beneath her lashes.

She only wished that he had believed her.

*   *   *

Clay left the office on Bow Street that housed the runners he had hired. The report he had received said that Richard frequented a place called Isolde's House of Pleasure. It was a sordid establishment located in the Strand, a brothel that catered to every sort of perverse taste. Knowing there was no shortage of available young men in the house, it confirmed what Clay had already discovered about Richard.

Still, until he found the man responsible for the attacks against Kassandra, he couldn't completely clear him of suspicion.

Clay climbed into his carriage, opened the report, and began to read. As well as investigating Richard, the runners had spoken at length to Clay's head groom, a man named Harry Mullen. The coachman Harry had hired had used false references to obtain the job as Kassandra's driver. No one had ever heard of a man named Edgar Mackey. Undoubtedly no such man existed.

As for Stephen, the only interesting thing the runners turned up was the small matter of Sarah Michaels, a gently bred young girl of fifteen who found herself in a family way. Speculation was that Stephen had fathered the babe, but the girl refused to say and no one knew for certain.

The runners who kept watch on his house reported a number of visitors, most of them recognizable as members of the *ton*. Yesterday, he and a group of friends had departed the city, bound, according to Westerly's butler, for Rivenwood, the earl's country estate.

The notion made Clay uneasy. Kitt was gone and just a few days later, so was Stephen.

Still, Westerly had no idea that Kitt had left the city

or where she might have been headed. She was out of harm's way at Blair House. She would stay there until it was safe for her return.

Clay was sitting in his study, relaying this latest information to Adam Hawthorne, when Henderson knocked on the door.

"I'm sorry to disturb you, Your Grace, but Lord Landen is here to see you. He says the matter is urgent."

Clay's stomach muscles knotted. He was on his feet in an instant, heading for the door.

"I thought the marquess was looking after your wife at Blair House." Blackwood followed Clay into the hall.

"So did I."

The Marquess of Landen stood in the entry still wearing his greatcoat, damp with rain and splashed with mud, his thick blond hair mussed by the wind. His features looked as grim as Clay had ever seen them and the knot in his stomach twisted even tighter.

"What's happened? Is Kassandra all right?"

"As far as I know, she is fine. Unfortunately, she is no longer at Blair House, so I can't say for certain."

His heart seemed to freeze inside his chest. "What do you mean she is no longer at Blair House? Where the hell is she?"

"I'm afraid I don't know." The marquess went on to explain that they had first noticed her absence when Kassandra hadn't made her usual appearance that morning for breakfast. "She'd complained of a headache the night before. Anna was worried, so she went up to check on her. Kassandra's room was empty, but she had left a note."

Ford handed it over. "No one saw her leave the

house. We think she must have climbed down the trellis outside her window."

Clay barely registered the marquess's words. Instead, his eyes were trained on the cold, emotionless letter Kassandra had left him.

Dearest Clay,
I've decided to return to Italy. Knowing you would surely disapprove, I leave tonight. Please thank Anna and the marquess for their hospitality. I shall write you upon my arrival.

It was signed simply, *Your wife, Kasandra.*

He recognized the writing, knew for certain the letter was from her. Clay turned away from the two men standing in front of him and made his way unsteadily down the hall. The night before she'd left for Blair House, she had told him that she loved him. He hadn't believed her, of course. Or perhaps he had wanted to but had simply been afraid to. He hadn't mentioned his feelings for her. And now, she'd run again.

Clay wadded up the note, crushing it in his fist as he continued down the hall into his study. He had told himself he didn't care—not the way he had before. That he wouldn't let himself fall into her trap again. Now his mouth felt dry and a heavy rock formed in the pit of his stomach. He tried to fan his anger, told himself he'd been right about her all along, but the fire of his temper merely sputtered and died.

Instead, his heart was aching, crumbling into tiny little pieces inside his chest. He had tried so hard not to love her, had convinced himself that he had succeeded. Now he realized how miserably he had failed.

He thought of the years he'd lived alone, years he

had succeeded in needing no one. Then he had married Kassandra. For the first time in his life, the loneliness that had always been a part of him was gone. With Kassandra beside him, he felt different, complete.

Now he felt lost again, half a person, the other half floating somewhere just out of reach.

I want you to love me, Clay . . . the way that I love you.

Perhaps if he had said the words she had wanted to hear— But then, how could he? He hadn't quite admitted it to himself. Hadn't dared to admit it. He closed his eyes. The note seemed to burn a hole through the palm of his hand. Slowly, he opened his fingers and read the letter again.

> *Dearest Clay,*
>
> *I've decided to return to Italy. Knowing you would surely disapprove, I leave tonight. Please thank Anna and the marquess for their hospitality. I shall write you upon my arrival.*
>
> *Your wife,*
> *Kasandra*

The words made his eyes burn. He rubbed a hand over his face, hating himself for his weakness where Kitt was concerned, trying not to worry if her journey had ended safely, if she had already boarded the ship that would carry her away.

He glanced once more at the letter, reading the words one final time. As his gaze came to rest on her name, he found himself frowning at the letters.

Your wife, Kasandra.

Odd. That wasn't the way she spelled her name. One of the *s*'s was missing.

He tapped the letter, reading the signature over and over again. No matter how hard he studied the writing, the second *s* would not appear. Why had she misspelled her name? Why hadn't she written the whole word out?

I want you to love me, Clay—I don't feel whole without you.

The memory hit him like a blow, nearly staggering him. The name wasn't complete because *she* wasn't complete. Not without him. He knew the way she felt because it was exactly the same for him.

And she hadn't left him.

Someone had taken her from him.

The study door slammed against the wall as Clay stormed out of the room. He was only a little surprised to see Blackwood and Landen still standing in the entry.

"She didn't leave," Clay said darkly. "Someone's taken her." He turned to the butler. "Tell the groom to saddle my horse—and tell him he'd better hurry."

Henderson nodded and raced away, long arms fluttering all the way down the hall.

Clay turned to the marquess. "Did you happen to check for footprints at the base of the trellis?"

"Too muddy. It rained all night. There wasn't a trace of her anywhere to be found. We presumed she made her way to the village and hired a carriage to take her from there. Anna went there to ask after her while I rode straight here."

"You're sure about this?" Blackwood pressed Clay. "She hasn't merely run from you again?"

Clay felt the strangest sort of calm settle over him. And a certainty he had never felt before. "I'm sure," was all he said.

"Then I'm going with you." Adam started toward the door. "I'll get my horse and meet you in front of the Cock and Crow on your way out of town. I'll be there by the time you arrive."

Ten minutes later, Clay was dressed in breeches and boots. He stuffed a pistol into his belt and shrugged into a heavy woolen coat. Along with the marquess, he rode hard through the rainy London streets, stopping only long enough for Blackwood to fall in beside them, then thundering out of the city on his way to Hampstead Heath. Clay wasn't sure what he would discover when he got there.

He prayed that Kitt was alive and unhurt.

He prayed that God would let him find her.

And this time, damn the consequences, he would tell her exactly how much he loved her.

With every rut in the road that the wagon dropped into, Kitt's arms, high above her head, ached and throbbed. Her wrists were raw and bleeding from her efforts to loosen the rope. Behind the gag, her mouth was so dry, her tongue so thick and swollen, she couldn't swallow.

Endless tears burned her eyes. She tried to stop them, but they slid down her cheeks, dampening the rag tied over her mouth. Where was Demetro taking her? More importantly, what would he do with her once he arrived at his destination?

Her mind conjured a dozen horrible images, all of them centered around her greatest fear: Demetro raping her, Demetro selling her to other men for their sordid use. She knew the humiliation, knew the pain. She didn't think she could bear it again.

Kitt closed her eyes and thought of Clay and how

much she loved him. She thought of his gentle patience, his slow, careful seduction. She remembered the wild, fiery passion they had shared after her return from Italy, more beautiful in some ways than his more tender loving.

She tried to tell herself that Clay would understand the message she had disguised in her note, but she couldn't make herself believe it.

Clay wouldn't notice the error in her name and even if he did, he wouldn't understand it. He would believe every word of the brief, cool letter she had left him. The same sort of letter that she had written to him before.

Had Stephen somehow known? Perhaps, in a way. The gossip had been vicious. Everyone in the *ton* knew she had left her husband just a month after the wedding. She had created another scandal—and this time left Clay to suffer the gossipmongers' malicious tongues. Kitt shuddered, recalling his childhood, the bastardy that had made him the brunt of a thousand jokes. In running away, she had singled him out for mockery again.

She had hurt him.

And everyone knew Clay had yet to forgive her.

The wagon rolled through the long hours of the night and all the next day. Aside from the few stops Demetro had made to allow her to use the chamber pot, she had remained tied up in the *vardo*.

At least her nightgown was beginning to dry, though the inside of the wagon was only a little warmer than the damp, chilly air outside. Once, during a stop among a stand of trees some distance off the road, the Gypsy had removed her gag and given her some dried bread and moldy cheese to eat, but when

she had started pleading with him to let her go, offering him money—more than he could ever spend—he
had grown angry and stuffed the rag back into her
mouth.

Now she lay there, tied once more to the bed inside
the *vardo,* every muscle aching, her body shaking with
fatigue, and still they pressed on. She prayed Demetro
would stop, give her respite from the exhaustion and
pain of lying in such an awkward position for so long.

Then she thought of what he might do to her once
the wagon rolled to a halt, and prayed the endless
journey would continue.

28

Wet and muddy, the men arrived at Blair House late that afternoon. A worried Anna waited in the entry, her short blond hair slightly disheveled, as if she had been running her fingers through it. She led them into one of the drawing rooms and over to where a hot fire roared in the hearth.

"I know you must be worried," she said to Clay, resting a comforting hand on his shoulder. "But this is not the first time Kassandra has gone off on her own."

"I take it you found no sign of her in the village."

"No one saw her, but of course it could have been very late when she left the house."

Ford turned away from where he'd been warming his hands in front of the flames. "Clay doesn't believe Kassandra simply left, Anna. He thinks someone broke into the house and abducted her, as they tried to do the night of the Dandridge soiree."

Anna's gaze flew to Clay. "Surely that is not possible. The house is full of servants. Someone would have seen them."

"Not if the man climbed up the trellis and went in through the window, the way you believe Kitt went out. I want you to tell me exactly what happened last night and don't leave anything out."

Her face a little pale, Anna began with the hours she and Kassandra had spent that day with the children. "She was fine at the time. It was later that she told me she wasn't feeling well. She said it was nothing to worry about, just a small headache, but she wasn't up to joining us for supper. I was disappointed. I wanted her to play cards with our guests, but she said that she didn't—"

"Guests? What guests?"

"I am sorry," Anna said fretfully. "I thought I mentioned that. Sir Hubert Tinsley arrived late yesterday afternoon with some of his friends, the Earl of Westerly and—"

"Westerly was here last night?" Clay nearly shouted the words. "For God's sake, why didn't you say so?"

"What does Westerly have to do with this?" Ford asked, stepping protectively in front of Anna.

Clay reined his temper under control. It was hardly Anna's fault. He should have voiced his suspicions, should have trusted his friends with at least a portion of the truth. "I'm sorry. This is not your fault, it's mine."

Ford's look sharpened. "Surely you don't think the earl would do anything to harm Kassandra."

"It's a very long story. Suffice it to say the limp he carries wasn't caused by a hunting accident. It's the result of a duel. I'm the man who shot him."

"*Santa Maria.*" Anna made the sign of the cross. Her lips trembled and Ford eased her back against him, sliding an arm around her waist.

"I thought no one knew your wife was here," the marquess said.

"I didn't think they did."

Blackwood spoke up for the first time since their arrival. "You had people watching Westerly. If the earl is responsible, there is every chance he had men of his own watching Kassandra, perhaps the same ones who tried to abduct her before. They could have followed her here, sent word back to him. She was in residence several days before his arrival. That would have given him plenty of time to formulate some sort of plan."

Clay ignored the squeezing in his chest. "Very true and a likely possibility. What I need to know now is where he is."

"Lord Westerly was on his way to Rivenwood," Anna told him.

"If that was his destination," Clay said, "why did he stop here? Rivenwood is north. Blair House is a good bit out of his way."

"*Sì,* but he said he was in no hurry. The roads were muddy. He decided to alter his route a little and pay us a visit."

"With the weather the way it was, Anna invited them all to stay," Ford said. "But they left first thing this morning."

"*Sì,* they were gone by the time I went up to check on Kassandra. They have probably arrived at Rivenwood by now."

"I'm going after him," Clay said, starting for the door. "One way or another, he's going to tell me what he's done with my wife."

"He couldn't have taken her with him," Blackwood pointed out, stopping him before he got to the door. "Not with the others along. Stephen isn't a fool. He isn't about to involve himself personally. If he is the man responsible, he had help in this. Odds are your wife is with the same men who tried to abduct her before."

Clay straightened, struggling to think more clearly. "That makes sense, but dammit, how do we find them?"

"You go after the earl," Blackwood said, "as you meant to do before. Find out as much as you can—without killing him. In the meantime, the marquess and I will try to figure out which direction the men headed after they took her. As muddy as it is, it won't be easy, but if we spread out, we might pick up some tracks. If not, we'll split up, take different roads. We'll stop at every inn, find out if anyone has seen a woman with—"

A knock sounded, interrupting Adam's words. A footman entered at the contessa's command. "Excuse me, your ladyship. I'm sorry to bother you, but there is a man outside . . . a Gypsy from the camp." The young, sandy-haired footman shifted from one foot to the other, uneasy with having caused the interruption. "He wishes to speak to you, my lady. He says it's about the red-haired woman who is your friend."

The muscles went rigid across Clay's shoulders. "Where is he?"

"In the kitchen. He appeared at the back door and Cook invited him to come in where it was warm."

"Thank you, Barton." Anna began to walk in that direction. Clay allowed her to pass, then followed, along with Adam and Ford. They arrived en masse in the steamy kitchen where the lean, hawk-faced Gypsy Clay recognized as Janos, the leader of the band, stood in front of the fire.

He glanced at Anna, then saw Clay. In typical Gypsy fashion, he ignored the contessa—a mere female—and walked toward the men.

"You know something about my wife?" Clay asked, meeting him halfway across the room.

Janos nodded. "The boy . . . Yotsi . . . he saw your woman last night. After the camp was asleep, he heard Demetro's wagon pulling out. It was late, but Demetro has always been one to go off on his own, so it was not so unusual."

"What happened then?" Clay pressed.

"The boy was curious. He saw the *vardo* rolling toward the house and he followed. Yotsi saw two men coming out of the darkness. One of them carried your woman slung over his shoulder. He recognized the fire of her hair."

Clay bit back a curse.

"The boy says they loaded her into Demetro's wagon and he took her away with him. Yotsi would have spoken sooner, but he was afraid."

"Of Demetro?" Clay asked.

He nodded. "The man has whipped him for less. But Yotsi is a good boy. He couldn't stay silent any longer."

"Thank him for me. Tell him I wish to reward him for his courage."

Janos seemed pleased.

"Did he say which way the wagon was headed?" Blackwood asked.

The Gypsy turned dark eyes in the earl's direction. "There is only one place Demetro would go. To some, a pale-skinned woman of such fire is worth a very high price. Demetro will be traveling south to Folkestone. From there he can cross the Channel to Calais. There is a ship that sails to Tangier. The captain is a man who will pay him well for such a cargo."

Clay started to turn away, but Janos caught his arm. "Do not judge the rest of us by the deeds of only a few."

Clay inhaled sharply, working to bring his fury under control. "There are good and bad among us all. Thank you for your help, Janos. Tell Yotsi what I said. It applies to you as well. I shall see it done upon my return."

The Gypsy made a slight bow of his head. *"Ja Develesa,"* he said. "Go with God, my friend."

Striding past him out of the kitchen, Clay headed for the door in the entry, with Landen, Blackwood, and Anna right behind him.

"We'll need fresh horses," Ford said to Anna, motioning for the butler to return their heavy coats.

"Sì—I will tell the footman to order it done."

It was only a few minutes later that a groom appeared in front of the house with four saddled mounts.

"What's the fourth horse for?" Clay asked. "We only need three." He looked up to see Anna descending the staircase. She was wearing heavy dark blue riding clothes, a woolen cloak floating around her slim shoulders.

"I am coming with you."

Ford caught her arms. "Like hell you are."

"It will do no good to argue. I ride as well as any man, and Kassandra may need the help of a woman."

Clay's stomach knotted at the implication. Rape was Kitt's worst fear. By selling her into bondage, Stephen had devised the cruelest punishment he could have imagined.

"Demetro will skirt the city," Clay said. "He'll stick to

the less traveled roads. I'll take the back lane that goes through Harlesdon then turns southwest to Croydon."

"Anna and I will take the south road, through St. John's Wood toward Swanley." Ford took Anna's arm as the four of them descended the front porch stairs.

"I'll cover the mail route." Blackwood swung up on his fresh mount. "If one of us finds her, he can leave word at the Bull and Bear in Maidstone—that's about the halfway point. If not, we'll meet in Folkestone."

Clay nodded and wheeled his horse, a tall, quick, dapple-gray gelding. Setting his spurs lightly against the animal's ribs, he set off down the muddy back road.

The wagon rolled forward all that day and late into the evening. Kitt's wrists were scraped raw, her ankles swollen and hurting. Still, she struggled to free herself. Her nightgown was soaked with perspiration, though it was icy cold in the wagon.

At least I'm still alive, she thought, wondering as she had a thousand times what Demetro intended to do with her. So far he had left her alone and that single fact gave her hope.

The wagon rattled into a pothole and a sharp, jarring pain shot up the back of her neck. Her stomach gnawed with hunger. She hadn't eaten anything since he had given her the bread and cheese. It was obvious the Gypsy was in a hurry to reach his destination. She wished she knew where it was.

The *vardo* plodded along, Demetro pressing his little sorrel mare, yet careful not to overtax the animal's strength. She wondered how he could keep going on so little sleep. One of the wheels dropped into a long, narrow rut, shifting her sideways. She stifled a moan and closed her eyes, willing herself to ignore the discomfort and try to get some sleep.

She must have managed, at least for a while. When she awakened, the endless rumble of the wheels had ceased.

Kitt roused herself, jolting wide awake as the door swung open and Demetro climbed in, carrying a white tallow candle. He set it on a narrow ledge that ran the length of the *vardo* and reached for her. Kitt tried to shrink away from him, terrified of what he meant to do, but he only laughed.

"Do not fear, my beauty. I have women enough of my own, women who like what Demetro can give them." He eyed her breasts, saw the nipples pressing upward, stiff with cold. "There will be others who will have such a use for you, but not for a while yet, no?"

The fear she had been fighting curled like a snake in her belly.

"Do not think to scream," he said, reaching behind her head to untie the gag. "There is no one for miles to hear you and it will displease me greatly. I will leave off the gag if you will promise to be silent."

Kitt slowly nodded. When Demetro removed the soggy rag, allowing her to swallow without pain, only a pitiful little mew escaped. Her mouth was brutally dry, her tongue thick and swollen. Respite from the torturous gag would be worth any price. And she believed he was telling the truth. No one would be near enough to hear her. She had learned the powerful Gypsy was not a careless man.

"I will untie one of your hands so you can eat." He did so and blood rushed into her partially numb fingers, making them throb painfully. Still, even that bit of freedom made her want to weep.

She accepted the dry bread he offered, stuffing it in a little too fast, sipping heavy red wine from the metal cup he handed her. Kitt closed her eyes at the sheer pleasure of the simple meal.

"I need to sleep," Demetro said. "If you are smart you will do the same." Gripping her wrist, he retied her free hand to the bedpost.

Kitt glanced around the inside of the wagon, noting only dimly the scuffed black boots in the corner, the worn linen shirt and black breeches hanging from a peg on the wall, the wooden flute resting on the narrow ledge that ran the length of the *vardo*. Then Demetro snuffed out the candle and closed the door.

Exhaustion swamped her and her head fell back on the mattress. She tried not to cry but a tear spilled down her cheek. She tried not to think of Clay, tried not to miss him. She tried not to wonder where she would be, weeks from now, when he finally began to suspect the truth of what had happened to her.

She wondered if she would still be alive.

Or if she would even care.

Clay rode hard for the balance of the day and into the evening. Even more exhausted than the horse, he drove himself on, stopping only to rest the gray, allowing the animal to regain its strength. Riding as he was, he could travel more than twice as fast as the wagon, but the Gypsy had at least a twelve-hour head start.

Still, Clay had covered a lot of distance since he had left Blair House. If Demetro was in front of him, he would catch up with him tonight or no later than early on the morrow.

The back road Clay had chosen was a better bet than the rest, far more likely than the routes the others had taken. The road was in bad repair and a good deal less traveled. There were fewer towns and more forested lands where Demetro could pull the wagon off the road and out of sight.

At several places in the deep, rutted lane, Clay had been able to make out the tracks of a small wagon pulled by a single horse. It could have been a cart or a gig owned by a farmer on his way home from market, but it renewed his hope and gave him the strength he needed to push on. He rode for another two hours, till the thin sliver of moon that appeared off and on through the clouds was completely obscured and darkness settled like a damp weight around his shoulders.

Cursing the cold and the unforgiving night, he drew the horse to a halt beneath a yew tree and pulled out his watch fob to check the time. A little past midnight. The gray's nostrils flared and its sides expanded as the horse worked to catch its breath. Both he and the gelding needed rest, though he knew he would never be able to sleep. Clay nudged the animal forward at a slow walk, looking for a likely place to stop for at least a couple of hours. Then, moon or not, he would continue to search for his wife.

Kitt stirred on the cornhusk mattress. She had tried in vain to sleep and now lay limp with exhaustion, staring up at the rounded ceiling. Earlier, she had heard Demetro's soft snores on the ground beneath the wagon, then a few minutes ago, the sound of him relieving himself in the woods. She heard him now, walking out of the trees back to the wagon and stiffened as his boots thumped up the narrow wooden stairs. The door swung open and Demetro walked in.

Kitt moistened her dry lips. "I thought you wanted to sleep."

Striking flint to steel, he lit the candle on the ledge beside the bed and his eyes ran over her. She wondered what he saw when he looked at the disheveled mess she had become.

"I have been thinking. . . . Perhaps Demetro has not been fair. Is it possible the little *gadjo* woman would enjoy a taste of Gypsy passion?" He reached out and cupped a breast, began to massage it through the barrier of her dirty cotton nightgown.

"No," Kitt whispered, the copper taste of fear rising on her tongue. "Stop it! I don't want anything to do with you."

"You are certain?" Bold dark eyes raked her from head to foot, assessing eyes in a face just short of handsome. "Demetro has pleasured many women. You have never had a Gypsy lover, no?" The arrogance was there, the belief that he could make her want him. He rubbed her nipple, yet he seemed disinclined to go on unless she wished him to.

A thought struggled into her consciousness. If he really wanted to make love to her he would have to untie her. She had been praying for a chance to escape—this might be it. But what if she tried and failed? Demetro would be furious. God only knew what he would do.

Still, the thought of success was enticing. Did she have the courage to try?

Her mouth felt even drier than it had before but she forced her lips to curve and managed a look of interest. "I've heard stories . . . rumors that Gypsy men are skillful lovers. But I never really believed they were true."

His eyes went darker, more sultry. "You wish me to show you, then?"

"You would have to untie me. I don't have any interest in simply lying here while you rut like an animal on top of me."

He stiffened. "Do not insult me."

She gave him a look ripe with sensual challenge. "All right, then—show me what a Gypsy man can do."

His confident smile flashed, showing a row of brilliant white teeth. Reaching down, he pulled a thin-bladed knife from his boot and sliced through the rope that bound her ankles. Blood rushed into her freezing bare feet and it took sheer force of will to stifle a groan.

"You must not try to escape," Demetro warned. "You will only get hurt if you do."

She summoned a smile. "I would rather enjoy myself . . . if you are certain that I will."

He stroked the bulge at the front of his breeches. "I will give you more than you can handle, beauty." She could see he was aroused and, had she been a woman who wanted him, more than well equipped to keep his word. He sliced through the bonds that held her wrists and the pain was so intense she whimpered.

"Soon you will forget the pain," he promised, sliding the knife back into his boot. "You will think only of Demetro and how he can make your body sing."

Praying she could gain enough feeling in her limbs to react, she took a deep breath and collected her strength. Demetro reached for the cord that held up his breeches and the minute he looked down to free himself, Kitt sprang off the bed like a tiger, landing in the middle of his chest. She caught him completely off guard, and he flew backward, knocking open the door, crashing down the narrow wooden stairs, and landing in the dirt at the bottom.

"*Rebuta!*" he swore, shouting something in Romany as she bolted after him down the steps. She feigned right, then dodged left, hoping to avoid him, but his blunt fingers snagged her nightgown, and he jerked her backward, hauling her down on top of him.

"Let me go!" She flailed at his face, landing several solid blows, but Demetro caught her wrists, twisting one of her arms up behind her back. Fighting for breath, her breasts pressed into his chest, her legs neatly trapped by his, she heard him laugh and felt the stiffness of his arousal.

Terror descended, darker than the night around her. Another jolt of fear at what he meant to do, and Kitt started fighting even harder than before.

It was too damned dark to see. He should have stopped hours ago, but Clay couldn't make himself quit. Kitt was out there somewhere, frightened, at the mercy of the man who held her captive. Still, it was dangerous to press on. If his horse stepped into a hole and came up lame, he might not ever have the chance to catch up with them.

Cursing, weary to the bone, he was about to dismount when the night air crackled with the sound of a woman's high-pitched scream. His pulse surged. Tension coiled into his limbs as he caught sight of a shadowy shape through the trees, the faint, dome-shaped outline of a small, enclosed wagon.

Swinging down from his horse, Clay jerked the pistol from the satchel behind his saddle and started forward, the blood pumping hard through his veins. Careful to stay hidden, he slipped into the cover of the trees. The soft luffing of a horse, grazing not far from the wagon, drifted toward him on the cold night breeze. Clay heard the muted thud of his own boots on the soft, marshy earth, then voices, one of them clearly a woman's.

Icy purpose settled in his chest. Tightening his hold on the pistol, he moved stealthily, not stopping till he reached the clearing where the wagon was parked.

Then he saw her—lying at the bottom of the narrow wooden stairs, sprawled on top of the big dark Gypsy, Demetro.

His heart pumped. His hold tightened on the pistol. *Stay calm,* he told himself, unable to shoot, terrified Kitt would be injured in his effort to free her. *Just take your time.* But it was almost impossible to do.

"Let me go!" She struggled frantically, lashed out with her feet as the Gypsy rolled her over and came up on top, trapping her neatly beneath him.

"Such a woman," he said. "You are worth every gold coin I will get for you."

The sound of a pistol being cocked echoed across the clearing in the darkness. "The lady is worth a thousand times more than gold." Clay's voice rang with deadly calm. It was all he could do not to pull the trigger. He saw her raw and bleeding wrists, her small bare feet and muddy cotton nightgown, and his knuckles whitened around the handle of the gun. "Let her go."

The Gypsy made a hissing sound beneath his breath. Keeping his eyes on Clay, he eased himself off her, and slowly came to his feet.

For an instant, Clay's gaze swung to Kitt, who made a tiny whimpering sound and staggered upright. In the same moment, the Gypsy surged forward, ramming headlong into Clay, knocking the pistol from his hand, sending him flying into the dirt. Demetro tried to bolt past him, but Clay caught the heel of his boot, twisted and brought the man crashing down on top of him. They rolled in the dirt, then the Gypsy broke free and both of them shot to their feet.

Circling warily, predators waiting to step in for the kill, they closed the distance between them. From the corner of his eye, Clay could see Kassandra, swaying drunkenly, her fist pressed fearfully against her mouth. Demetro stepped in, swung the first punch with the strength of a mule. Clay ducked easily, hit him hard in the face, and he went down.

Anticipation curled through him. He was glad the man had tried to run. He wanted to hammer the arrogance from his handsome Gypsy face, wanted to beat him into the dirt at the back of the wagon. Demetro rolled to his feet and came up swinging. He was muscular and strong, but Clay had boxed for years and experience often made the difference between winning or losing.

He sidestepped a hard left jab, slammed a fierce right into Demetro's stomach, finished with a solid punch to the chin. The Gypsy went down as if his legs had been chopped off beneath him. Clay grabbed a handful of coarse black hair, hauled him to his feet, and hit him again. Two more heavy blows had him bleeding from the nose and mouth. Another blow sent him spinning, landing unconscious in the dirt.

Still, Clay reached for him, ready to hit him again, his rage so fierce it nearly blinded him.

"Clay! Stop it, Clay—please!" Kitt's shaking voice barely reached through his anger. "Demetro didn't ... nothing happened. I tricked him into untying me. I thought I might ... might be able to escape."

Standing with his legs splayed, his hands still balled into fists, Clay fought to bring his fury under control. Little by little his heart slowed and his attention swung to Kassandra. Her face was the color of her once-white nightgown, her fiery hair hanging in tangles around her shoulders.

His heart clenched hard inside him. Love for her washed over him in nearly staggering waves. How could he have denied it for so long?

Stepping over Demetro's unconscious form, he reached her in two long strides and hauled her into his arms. He could feel her trembling, realized he was shaking nearly as badly as she. She felt so small, so soft. She belonged to him and he had almost lost her. He kissed the top of her head, closed his eyes against the burning mist that threatened to embarrass him.

"It's all right, my love, it's all right. I'm here and you're safe. Everything's going to be fine."

Kitt looked up at him and her eyes filled with tears. "Hold me," she whispered, pressing her face into his chest. "Don't let me go."

His throat closed up. "I won't," he said. "I won't let you go. Not now. Not ever again."

She started crying then, deep pain-filled sobs that tore straight into his heart. His fingers slid into her hair and he cradled her head against his chest.

"I can't believe you're here," she whispered, little more than a sob. "I didn't think you'd come."

She didn't think he would come? He would have followed her all the way to Tangier, all the way to hell and back if he'd had to. He tightened his hold around her, wishing he could have saved her from this, feeling as if he had somehow failed her.

She sniffed, looked up at him. "How . . . how did you know?"

He kissed the top of her head. Tried to muster a smile. "You left me a clue, didn't you?"

Big green eyes, glittering with wetness, stared up at him. "I didn't think you would understand."

He swallowed past the lump in his throat. "I didn't . . . not at first. I thought I'd lost you for good. I felt hollow inside. I felt as if half of myself were missing and that's when I remembered the words you had said. That's when I understood what you had been trying to tell me. And I knew you wouldn't run from me again."

She buried her face in the hollow of his neck and clung to him. "I was a coward. I left because I was afraid you'd grow tired of me. I couldn't bear the thought of sharing you with another woman."

His heart hurt. It was nearly impossible to speak. "There's no one else—not for me. Only you, my love, now and always. I love you, Kassandra. I tried not to, but God knows, I do."

"Clay . . ." She started to cry again and he held her close against him, warming her with his body, aching with love for her.

"In a way, I was a coward, too," he said. "When you came back, I was determined not to care, but no matter how hard I fought, I couldn't stop. I simply loved you too much."

Kitt clung to him even tighter. They might have stood there for hours or minutes, it was hard to tell. He simply felt grateful to be holding her again.

Then Demetro stirred and reality crept in. Clay gently eased himself away.

"Stay here." He walked over and picked up the

pistol, returned and pressed the weapon into her hand. "If he twitches so much as a muscle, pull the trigger."

Kitt gave Demetro a weary, triumphant smile. "That would be my pleasure." Demetro stared sullenly, wiping at the blood beneath his nose, which looked to be broken.

He swore foully as Clay returned from the wagon with pieces of the same rope Demetro had used to tie Kitt to the bed. In minutes the arrogant Gypsy was trussed and hoisted into the *vardo,* cursing all the way. Clay tied him to the bedpost and closed the door, sealing him inside.

Returning to Kassandra, he eased the pistol from her hand. "We'll contact the sheriff at the first town we come to, let him know what happened and where to find the wagon."

Kitt just nodded. Exhaustion slowed her movements. Clay silently cursed, swept her up in his arms, and carried her over to his horse.

"This'll all be over soon, love. Just hold on a little while longer."

"I'm all right . . . now that you're here."

"I passed an inn not far down the road. We can spend the night there. I'll need to send word to the Bull and Bear in Maidstone. The rest of your friends—"

"My friends?"

"Anna, Ford, and Adam. They're on their way to Folkestone in search of you."

"That's where he was taking me?"

"From there to Calais, then on to Tangier."

Kitt shivered. Clay untied the blanket behind his saddle and draped it around her shoulders. Lifting her up, he settled her sideways in front of him, tucking the blanket over her icy feet, then swung himself up behind her.

He eased her back against his chest, curled an arm around his waist, and she relaxed into his warmth. He kissed the side of her neck. "It's nearly over. Tomorrow we'll be home."

Kitt turned and looked up at him and there was so much love in her eyes, the lump returned to his throat. "I am home, Clay. As long as I'm with you, I'm home."

Clay softly kissed her and knew it was the truth.

29

❧⟶

Anna and Ford left the Bull and Bear in Maidstone the following morning. They had received Clay's note that he had found Kassandra, that she was all right, and the two of them were on their way back to London.

The same message was left for Lord Blackwood, who had not yet arrived.

"I hope nothing has happened to him," Anna worried as they rode their horses back along the road to Blair House.

Ford tossed her an unreadable glance. "Adam Hawthorne is one of the most capable men I've ever known. I'm sure he's fine."

Anna tried to read Ford's mood but it was no use. Last night at the inn, tired as they had been, he had made love to her. Afterward they had slept in each other's arms. Since they had received the message that morning that Kassandra was safe, he had been moody and out of sorts.

She glanced at him from beneath her lashes, studying the hard set of his jaw. *Men,* she thought, wondering if she would ever understand them, wishing she knew what was wrong. But his dark mood warned her not to ask him.

They rode for another full hour, till the sun shone directly overhead, penetrating their heavy woolen clothes, and still he had barely said a word. Then those fierce blue eyes settled on her face and Anna sucked in a breath. Riding off the road beneath a plane tree, he drew rein on his horse, caught her bridle to bring hers to a halt, then swung himself down from the saddle.

He came over and lifted her down. "I've had enough of this, Anna."

"What are you talking about?"

"I'm talking about you and me. Clay very nearly lost Kassandra. Surely you can see how short life can be. We're wasting what little time we have and I'm tired of it. I want you to marry me."

She wanted to. More than anything in the world. But she wanted him to love her and she still wasn't sure that he did.

"You know that is what I want, too . . . when the time is right."

"When the time is right?" he repeated, dragging her into his arms. "The time seemed right enough last night. That was you, wasn't it, crying out my name when I was inside you, begging me for more?"

Warmth flared in her cheeks. She wasn't certain whether it was embarrassment or a fresh shot of desire. "There has never been a doubt that we are good together in that way. It is simply that . . . that . . ."

"That what? That you can't forget Antonio? That you can't love me as I love you? Well, it's past time that you—"

"What did you say?"

"I'm not a fool, Anna. I know you still have feelings for Antonio, but—"

"Antonio has nothing to do with this, you foolish man. He is gone from my life and I have accepted that. I want to hear what you said before."

His eyes looked bluer than she had ever seen them. "I said I love you, dammit. Surely you know that by now. I wouldn't have asked you to marry me if I didn't."

"How would I know? You never told me. I have waited . . . hoped that you loved me as I love you, but you never said, and I didn't think—"

Ford crushed his mouth over hers, kissing her until she could barely stay on her feet.

"I love you. I adore you. I need you. Marry me and let me show you how much."

Anna laughed, a sound of pure joy. "Of course, I will marry you, my darling man. Today. This minute— if that is your wish."

Ford grinned so broadly a dimple appeared in his cheek. "Thank the good sweet Lord, the lady has finally come to her senses." Lifting her into his arms, he whirled her around, then kissed her deeply again. "Let's go home, sweetheart. It's time our children learned we're going to be one big family."

Anna grinned. "*Sì*, and perhaps our family will grow even larger. You would like that, no?"

Ford returned the grin. "I would like that, yes."

Anna laughed and kissed him again.

Adam Hawthorne, followed by three of the city's night watchmen, shoved the two bound, disheveled men through the front door of the Duke of Rathmore's town house. Clay strode toward them down the hall.

"What the devil . . . ?"

"I brought you a little present." Blackwood's hard mouth edged up. "As I was riding the mail route in search of your bride, I ran into my old friends here, at Mackelroy's Tavern. They were drunker than seven lords and boasting about the windfall they'd recently earned. I recognized them as the same men I tangled with in the alley after the Dandridge soiree."

Clay gripped the taller of the two men by the shirt-front and dragged him up on his toes. Aside from several days' growth of beard, he sported a bloody lip, a cut across his forehead, an ugly purple eye, and his clothes hung in tatters. Both the squat man's eyes were swollen nearly closed.

"I think my wife might enjoy this present even more than I. Why don't we go and see?" Clay dragged the taller man down the hall while Adam hauled the shorter, barrel-chested man along in his wake. Both of them looked like they'd been through a war.

Clay dragged them into the drawing room and Kitt shot out of her seat. "That's them—the men who abducted me from Blair House!"

"It wasn't my idea," the tall man sputtered. "It was Westerly. He was the one who wanted it done. Paid us in good English coin for it, too."

Clay's jaw hardened. None of the watchmen seemed surprised at the news. "Apparently Lord Blackwood has told you what happened."

"Yes, Your Grace."

"Then I shall leave these men to you. Get them out of my sight."

Wordlessly, he waited while the watchmen dragged

the culprits away, then turned and walked over to the mantel and drew down the polished mahogany box that held a pair of silver-etched dueling pistols.

Kitt walked toward him. "What are you doing? Lord Blackwood has apprehended the men Stephen hired. They'll be eager to lay the blame on the earl and soon he'll be arrested."

"Perhaps." He tilted the gun and poured black powder down the barrel. "And perhaps he'll have fled the country by the time they have enough evidence to go after him." He dropped in a lead ball and rammed it home. "Stephen is a powerful man. The magistrates won't want to make a mistake." Clay slid the pistol into a heavy leather satchel, closed the flap, and slung the bag over his shoulder.

"He's probably still at Rivenwood," Kitt said frantically as she followed him across the room. "Surely you don't intend to go after him clear out there?"

Clay turned to face her. "Stephen returned to the city this morning."

"You hired someone to watch his house?"

"Actually, I did that some time back. At the time, I didn't realize how handy it might become."

Blackwood walked toward him. "You want me to go with you?"

Clay shook his head. "Not this time."

Kitt gripped his arm. "I thought we agreed to let the authorities handle this."

"You agreed to that, my love, not I."

"Please, Clay—you can't just kill him. They'll hang you for sure!"

He turned, gently took hold of her arms. "Try to understand. Even if the man were in prison, neither of us would ever be truly safe." He looked over her head to

Adam. "See that she stays here, will you? I won't be gone long."

Adam made a faint nod of his head. As soon as Clay walked past, he stepped in front of the door. Clay could hear Kitt arguing with him, her voice growing louder, beginning to call him names.

Clay ignored them. He had failed to protect her before. It wouldn't happen again. He wouldn't rest until Stephen Marlow was dead.

Furious and terrified, Kitt stormed back and forth in front of the door to the drawing room, her long braid bobbing with every turn. Blackwood lounged casually against the ornate panels, blocking her escape.

"How can you just stand there? Do you want to get him killed?"

"He did this your way before and you nearly wound up in Tangier. Westerly has to be dealt with. Clay knows that. There is nothing else your husband can do."

"Of course you'd think that—you're just like him! Both of you are insane!" She sniffed, and hiked her nose into the air. "If you wish to stand here, guarding the door like an idiot, that is your business. As for me, I'm retiring upstairs to my room."

Blackwood smiled thinly. "Fine. I'll walk you up."

Kitt made a growling sound in her throat. Back stiff, she climbed the stairs, the earl right beside her. When they reached the master's suite, she went in and slammed the door, not doubting for a moment Lord Blackwood intended to stand guard out front till Clay's return.

Assuming he lived to get back.

Her heart constricted. Dear God, they had been

through so much already. He didn't deserve this burden, too.

Setting her jaw, Kitt stormed into the bedchamber she no longer slept in, crossed to her armoire, and jerked open the drawer at the bottom. Rummaging through an assortment of bonnets, sending half a dozen of them flying, she dragged out the box that held her cousin Charlie's clothes.

In minutes, she had struggled out of her day dress and pulled on breeches and boots. A big oak tree grew just outside the sitting room window. Kitt hurried in that direction. Shoving open the window, she swung a leg up over the sill.

The tree grew a little bit farther away than she remembered, but it wasn't as far to the ground as it had been from the room in her parents' house. Wiping damp palms on her breeches, she tossed her braid back over her shoulder, said a quick prayer, and leapt for the branch.

She made it without a hitch and gave a small sigh of relief. In minutes she had reached the ground and was running behind the mews, along the alley to the street behind the house. She hailed a hack with less effort than she expected and paid the coachy extra to drive as fast as the old horse would go to the Earl of Westerly's town house in Hanover Square.

Clinging to the strap above the door, she braced her feet as the conveyance tilted and swayed through the crowded West End streets. *Let him be all right,* she prayed, repeating the litany over and over. *Let him be all right.*

It didn't take long to reach her destination, though her heart hammered madly all the way. It did a savage leap as the hack wheeled around a corner and she saw the front door of Stephen's town house standing wide open, a group of watchmen streaming into the street.

Oh, dear God! Flinging open the door, Kitt jumped to the ground and began to run. She had just started across the lane when a man stepped out from between two carriages parked opposite the town house. An arm snaked around her waist and she was jerked back against a man's chest.

"I thought I told you to wait for me at home."

Relief spilled through her at the sound of Clay's voice, rough with irritation though it was. Her gaze flew from her husband to Stephen's town house.

"Oh, God, you didn't ... you didn't ... ?"

"No. Stephen is dead, but I didn't kill him. He was already dead when I got here."

"How ... how can that be?"

He stared at the open town house door. "According to one of the watchmen, his lordship met with an untimely accident. Apparently, his bad leg gave out at an inopportune moment. Stephen fell down the stairs and broke his neck."

Kitt blinked up at him. "You don't believe that?"

He shrugged those wide shoulders. "It's possible, I suppose. Extremely convenient, but possible. It's also possible someone pushed him. God only knows how many young women he has ruined. Perhaps one of them did something about it."

"Or perhaps someone who cared about one of them found out what he'd done."

"At any rate, it's over." He reached down, looped a flyaway strand of red hair over her ear. "But I appreciate your coming to help."

"You're not angry?"

His mouth quirked up. Such a beautiful mouth, she thought, and it belongs only to me.

"It's hard to stay angry at someone who has come to rescue you." His eyes roamed over her bottom, outlined in the tight men's breeches. "Did I ever tell you how much I favor you in breeches?"

"You do?"

"More than you'll ever know." He brushed a light kiss over her mouth. "I love you, Kitt Barclay. No matter what you're wearing."

Kitt threw her arms around his neck and kissed him with all the love in her heart.

Clay chuckled softly. "I hope no one sees us. Dressed the way you are, God knows the sort of scandal it will cause."

Kitt laughed as she stepped away. She had caused more than enough scandals already.

Climbing into Clay's carriage, she felt his hand on her bottom, helping her up the stairs. He gave her a wicked, unrepentant grin and followed her in, dragging her onto his lap for the short ride home.

His mouth curved faintly. "I wonder what Blackwood's going to say when he sees you walk in."

Kitt grinned, imagining the dark scowl on his face. "I'm just glad I'm married to you and not him."

Clay caught her chin and very gently kissed her. "So am I, my love. So am I."

**POCKET BOOKS
PROUDLY PRESENTS**

FANNING THE FLAME

KAT MARTIN

**Available August 2002
from
Pocket Books**

**Turn the page for a preview of
Fanning the Flame. . . .**

The battle raged inside his head, the crack of musket fire, the thunder of cannonade, hot lead tearing into flesh and bone, men weeping in fear and despair.

It's a dream, he cried inside his mind, trying to convince himself, to awaken from another of the nightmares that plagued his sleep. Inch by inch, clawing his way back to consciousness, Adam Hawthorne, Fourth Earl of Blackwood, sat upright in his huge four-poster bed. His heart was pounding. Sweat ran in rivulets down his naked chest and dampened his hair, urging it into heavy black waves that stuck to the cords at the back of his neck.

Though a chill pervaded the room, Adam shoved the feather comforter down past his waist and a shiver swept over him, pebbling his skin above the crisp linen sheet. He was used to nights like this one. He had suffered the terrible images for more than six years. Penance, he believed, for the part he had played in the war.

Running a hand over his face to erase the last vestiges of slumber, he swung his long legs to the side of the bed and stood up. Through a slit in the heavy gold velvet draperies, the first gray light of dawn filtered into the bedchamber. As he did most mornings, he poured water into the porcelain basin on his dresser, performed the necessary ablutions, then pulled on buckskin breeches and a white, full-sleeved shirt. Shoving his feet into a pair of high-topped Spanish riding boots, he grabbed his coat off the hook beside the door and made his way downstairs, heading for the stable at the rear of his town house.

His groom, Angus McFarland, a big ruddy Scotsman, formerly a sergeant in the Gordon Highlanders, stood waiting, a beefy hand gripping the reins of Adam's prize stallion, Ramses.

" 'Ave a care, Major. The lad's a bit full o' himself this mornin'."

Adam nodded. "We'll give him a run, then." He patted the stallion's sleek neck. "You'd like a good run, wouldn't you, boy?" The horse was black, as shiny as polished jet, with perfect conformation and a surprisingly gentle disposition. Once Adam had spotted him at Tattersall's, he had spared no expense to have him. It was his single real indulgence since he had unexpectedly come into the Blackwood title and fortune.

He patted the soft dark muzzle, then reached into his pocket and held his hand out, palm up, offering the animal a lump of sugar. "A little fresh air always makes the world seem better."

"Aye, and so it does," the Scotsman agreed.

Adam swung up in the saddle and settled himself on the flat leather seat. After eight years in the cavalry, he felt more at home on a horse than he did with his feet on the ground. He bid farewell to Angus, more friend than employee, and headed for his daily outing in the park, Ram in high spirits, dancing and snorting with untapped energy.

At this early hour, the park was empty. Adam set the horse into a gallop that turned into a flat-out run and pounded around the carriageway. The sun had crested the horizon by the time horse and rider drew to a halt beneath a plane tree on a rise near the duck pond. Adam let the big horse blow, the stallion's sides heaving in and out with spent effort, both of them feeling the benefits of wind and early morning sun.

Giving Ram an absent pat, he turned his attention in another, more interesting direction, scanning the grassy field below in search of his quarry, spotting her on the same wrought-iron bench she had been perched on each morning since he had come upon her three days ago.

The expensive clothes she wore, today a pale green muslin sprinkled with small embroidered rosebuds, marked her as a member of the upper classes. She was slightly shorter than average, with a slender frame and fair, unblemished skin. Beneath the rim of her lace-trimmed bonnet, he could just make out her face, the refined lines and straight nose, the nicely shaped dark copper eyebrows. He imagined her eyes were blue, but at this distance, he couldn't be sure.

What amazed him was how badly he wanted to find out.

Seated on the bench, the woman smiled at the growing cluster of ducks that swam or waddled toward her, fanning out to surround her feet. To each in turn, she passed out bits of bread, watching with delight as several of them plucked a morsel from her hand. She laughed as a mother duck clumsily waded ashore, six tiny ducklings lined up in a row behind her.

He thought she might have glanced his way, spotting him on the knoll, but perhaps he only imagined it, because her gaze fixed once more on the ducks. He wondered who she was and why she came by herself to the pond so early in the morning. He wondered if, as he did, she sought solace from turbulent thoughts.

He wondered if she would be there again when he came to the pond on the morrow.

Departing the carriage from her morning journey to the park, Jillian Alistair Whitney whisked through the big double doors of the Earl of Fenwick's town mansion, a brisk spring breeze having driven her early from her daily morning endeavor. She grabbed the rim of her bonnet to keep the wind from blowing it off as the butler, Nigel Atwater, firmly closed the heavy portal behind her, enclosing her in the entry.

"A bit chilly, is it, to be out gallivanting about?" He glared down his long beak of a nose with disapproval, mirroring the sentiment of a number of the servants, though Atwater was the only one secure enough in his position to blatantly let it show.

"The wind came up rather suddenly," she said matter-of-factly, refusing to let him know how much his censure hurt. "Perhaps we're in for a bit of a storm." It wasn't important what the servants thought, she told herself, and even if it were, there was little she could do to change things.

From the start, Lord Fenwick had scoffed at the

gossip her presence in a bachelor household had caused. He was, he had said, old enough to be her grandfather and was, in fact, a close friend of her father's, who had already seen more than forty years when he had finally sired an offspring.

Jillian thought of the proud man who had died sixteen months past, a man who had doted on her, loved her to distraction, but left her without a farthing to see to her needs. If it hadn't been for Lord Fenwick ... ah, but the earl *had* come to her rescue, and gossip was a small price to pay for all that he had done.

Jillian tugged off her kidskin gloves and started up the stairs to her bedchamber, a cheery room done in pale blue and gold, her mind on her situation and the solitude she found each morning in the park. She always went early, before the fashionable set arrived with their knowing smiles and speculative glances. At that early hour, she had the park all to herself; that is, until three days ago, when she discovered she wasn't alone.

"Beg pardon, Miss Whitney."

She had almost reached the top of the stairs when she heard the butler's footfalls returning to the entry, then his haughty voice coming from below. "If you please, Miss, his lordship would like a word with you in his study."

Jillian paused in the process of untying her bonnet. "Certainly. Thank you, Atwater."

Returning downstairs, bonnet in hand, she walked along the hall to the suite of rooms in the west wing of the mansion that included the earl's private study, her mind still on the tall, dark-haired rider and magnificent black horse she had spotted on the knoll. At first she had been frightened, alone as she was in the park. But there was something in his bearing, something of confidence and self-possession that eased her fear, turning it instead to curiosity.

In truth, if he was half as attractive as he appeared astride his horse, he wouldn't need to press himself on an unwilling woman. He could have whatever lady he chose.

A noise in the study drew her attention in that direction. Jillian knocked on the ivory gilt door, then, at the sound of the earl's gruff voice, turned the ornate gold knob and went in.

"Ah, here you are, my dear. I thought I heard your voice in the entry. You are certainly one for getting an early start."

She walked to where he sat behind his rosewood desk, bent over, and kissed his wrinkled cheek. "Morning is the best time of day, my lord. Everything is so bright and cheerful, and it is quiet enough yet to hear the singing of the birds."

He chuckled, then rose from behind the desk. Oswald Telford, Earl of Fenwick, was a man well into his sixties, with patchy gray hair and a paunch beneath his white piqué waistcoat. He had never been a handsome man, with his sugar-bowl ears and slightly bulbous nose, but he was dear to her and she to him.

"Tonight is the Marquess of Landen's soiree," he said. "I thought you might like to attend."

She shook her head a little too quickly and steadied herself enough to smile. "Your gout is still acting up, and in truth I should rather remain at home. I thought perhaps we might spend the evening playing chess."

For an instant, a twinkle appeared in eyes a cloudy shade of blue much paler than the bright hue of her own. Then he shook his head. "I should like nothing more than to stay here and trounce you soundly, my girl, but I am not getting any younger, and I need to see you settled. It is beyond time I found you a husband, and the only way I can accomplish the feat is—"

"You are not that old! And at any rate, I am already on the shelf."

"At one and twenty? I hardly think so."

"We've had this conversation before, my lord. I hoped you understood my feelings on the subject." Those being that she didn't want a husband. At least not the sort the earl would have to buy for her. She wanted a man she could love, one who would love her in return. She wanted the kind of happiness her father had found with her mother.

Jillian had never known Maryann Whitney. Her mother had died giving birth to her only child, but her father had never remarried. He had loved her that much. And Jillian refused to settle for anything less than that same kind of love.

"Every woman needs a husband," Lord Fenwick grumbled, but he didn't press her further and Jillian was grateful.

"There are endless soirees," she said, "as evidenced by the stack of invitations on your desk." But the stack continued to dwindle as the gossip about her and Lord Fenwick mounted.

As usual the earl ignored it. He was set in his ways and taking her in was as far as he was willing to go in her regard.

"I refuse to have that old battle ax of a cousin of mine in the house just to still the wagging tongues," he had said. But sooner or later, without a proper chaperone, they would be ostracized completely.

Jillian summoned a smile she suddenly didn't feel. "Perhaps by the end of the week you'll feel better."

The earl fought not to show his relief. "Yes, I'm certain I shall."

But Jillian was worried about him. He'd been looking a little more peaked every day. She would have to make certain he got plenty of rest and brew him some rose hip tea.

He had come to her aid when she had no one else to turn to. He had lost his only son, she knew, and perhaps he was lonely. Whatever the reason, he had taken her into his home, become the father she had lost, and she meant to take care of him.

And she didn't give a damn what the gossip-mongers said.

Adam sat astride his black horse at the top of the knoll. The day was fair, the breeze no more than a whisper. Ramses pawed the ground and snorted, lifting his magnificent head to study the lean bay gelding standing placidly beside him. Today Adam wasn't alone.

"Nice view." Clayton Barclay, Duke of Rathmore, stared down at the woman seated on the wrought-iron bench near the duck pond.

"So I discovered several days past." Adam had known Clay since Oxford, where they had been close friends. Since Adam's exit from the cavalry and subsequent return to London, they had become good friends again. "Do you have any idea who she is?"

Clay flashed a roguish grin. He was a handsome man, tall and broad-shouldered with thick, dark brown hair, the sort who could charm the garters off a lady with little more than a smile, which he had done with considerable regularity until he met the woman he had married.

"Actually, I believe I do know who she is." Clay had recently wed the Viscount Stockton's rebellious little redheaded daughter. Though the two had their problems in the beginning, they had worked them out, and Adam had rarely seen a happier man. "The lady's name is Jillian Whitney. We met several months back at one of Stockton's dinner parties. Lately there've been rumors about her. They say she's the Earl of Fenwick's mistress."

Adam felt as if he had just been hit in the stomach. "Fenwick? I can scarcely credit that. The man is thrice her years and then some."

"True, but he's still a man, and Miss Whitney is a very attractive young woman."

Adam silently agreed, wishing he could get a closer look at her.

"As the story goes, her father was a friend of the earl's. When he died, Miss Whitney was left near penniless. She went to Fenwick for help and he took her in. He claims she is merely his ward, though there is speculation she is far more than that."

Adam swallowed the bitter taste in his mouth. Little surprised him anymore, jaded as he was, yet it was difficult to imagine the smiling young woman who sat there placidly feeding the ducks would later be spreading her thighs for the ancient Lord Fenwick.

"Fenwick has never been known for his charity," Adam said. "I'd say he got a nice bit of muslin in return for his generosity."

"I suppose so . . . if the gossip is true."

Adam's attention swung away from the woman and fixed on his friend. "You're saying it isn't?"

Clay shrugged a set of powerful shoulders. "It wouldn't be the first time the gossipmongers have been wrong."

Adam pondered that. He had felt the vicious bite of slander himself, on more than one occasion. And yet in his experience—which was quite extensive where women were concerned—most of those he had known would sell their souls for a few expensive baubles.

Clay lifted a knowing, dark brown eyebrow. "Since it is highly unlikely that mere coincidence brought us here this morning, I assume you would like an introduction."

Adam's mouth only faintly curved. It wasn't exactly the reason he had led Clay in this direction. Or maybe it was.

"Why not?" he said and nudged his boot heels into the sides of his horse.

Jillian straightened as she saw the two men riding off the knoll in her direction. It took her a moment to recognize the Duke of Rathmore as the man on the right; she had met him and his wife a couple of months ago, and he wasn't a man a woman was likely to forget.

She stood up as they slowed their horses and both men swung down from their saddles. Rathmore went through the formalities, making polite morning greetings, then introduced her to the tall, black-haired man beside him, Adam Hawthorne, Earl of Blackwood, the man who had watched her from the knoll.

"I've seen you here before," Blackwood said to her, more candidly than she would have expected.

"Yes, I'm quite an early riser." He was lean and his skin dark, as if he often spent time in the sun. His features were strong, even harsh: black slashing brows and lean cheekbones, a mouth that looked hard, but was perfectly curved, except for a faintly cynical lift at one corner. A thin scar ran from his temple along his jaw, giving him a dangerous air, and yet it was a face of uncommon beauty, the sort a woman would notice the moment he walked into a room. Combined with the powerful presence he exuded, the earl was a potent force.

"For me, morning is the best time of day," Jillian went on, groping for something to say that wouldn't sound inane, forcing herself not to look away from the midnight blue eyes that assessed her with such speculation.

Blackwood barely nodded. "Yes . . . the sunlight has a way of sweeping the demons away."

It was an odd thing to say. She studied him with renewed curiosity and thought she saw something shift behind his eyes, as if the door he had accidentally opened had once again slammed closed.

"Lord Blackwood was in the cavalry for a number of years," the duke said. "I don't think he'll ever get used to spending much time indoors."

"I can understand that. I prefer the country myself." Jillian smiled a bit wistfully, thinking of the small, ivy-covered cottage where she and her father had lived in Buckland Vale, a little village near Aylesbury.

"Is that where you got your interest in birds?" the earl asked.

"The ducks, you mean?" She glanced down at the creatures once again wobbling toward her from the pond. "I've grown quite attached to them, I'm afraid. That's Harold, there; and this little brown hen with the spots on her face, that's Esmerelda. If I don't bring them a bit of bread in the mornings, I worry they won't get enough to eat. Silly, isn't it?"

The duke cast her a glance. "You sound like my wife, Kassandra. She adopts every stray animal that comes her way. Just yesterday she ran across a litter of abandoned kittens in the mews. She was up half the night feeding them with a rag dipped in milk."

But he didn't look disturbed about it. In fact, he looked rather proud of her efforts.

The earl—Blackwood—however, continued to watch her as if he played a game of cat and mouse. There was no doubt about which one of them was the prey. Jillian shivered beneath that intense regard and returned her attention to the duke.

"I hope your wife is well."

"Quite well, thank you. I'll be certain to give her your regards."

She nodded, hoping they would leave, but Blackwood seemed in no hurry. Since that was the case, she made ready to depart herself. "It's been a pleasure to see you again, Your Grace, but I'm afraid you'll have to excuse me. It's past time I returned to the house."

"Yes . . ." Blackwood cut in, assessing her in that unsettling way of his. "Should you be overly late, I'm certain Lord Fenwick would become quite concerned."

Was that mockery she heard in his voice? Had he heard the gossip about her? It had always seemed ridiculous to her, considering the earl's age and health. She couldn't imagine how it had ever gotten started, but it most certainly had. The duke didn't seem the sort to be amused by such things, but Black-wood . . . he was difficult—no, impossible—to read. Her stomach clenched to imagine what the men might be thinking about her.

"It was a pleasure to meet you, my lord," she said to him in farewell.

His dark eyes swept over her. "The pleasure was mine, Miss Whitney, I assure you."

Still uncertain what she heard in his voice, Jillian turned and started walking away. She expected the shuffle of boots as the men remounted their horses and rode off the way they had come. Instead, only one of them departed. Without looking back, Jillian knew which one remained. She could feel the dark earl's gaze on her back until she disappeared out of sight on the path leading off into the trees.